SUMMER OF SCANDAL

Also by Syrie James

Historical Romance
Runaway Heiress

Historical Fiction
Jane Austen's First Love
The Missing Manuscript of Jane Austen
The Secret Diaries of Charlotte Brontë
Dracula, My Love
The Lost Memoirs of Jane Austen

Contemporary Romance
Songbird
Nocturne
Propositions

Young Adult Romance
Forbidden
Embolden

SUMMER OF SCANDAL

A Dare to Defy Novel

SYRIE JAMES

AVONIMPULSE

An Imprint of HarperCollinsPublishers

SUMMER OF SCANDAL. Copyright © 2018 by Syrie James. All rights reserved. Printed in the United States of America. No part of this book may be used or reproduced in any manner whatsoever without written permission except in the case of brief quotations embodied in critical articles and reviews. For information, address HarperCollins Publishers, 195 Broadway, New York, NY 10007.

Print Edition ISBN: 978-0-06-284969-4
Digital Edition ISBN: 978-0-06-284968-7

Cover photographs © Jenn Le Blanc/Illustrated Romance (couple) © Deejpilot/iStock/Getty Images (cliffs); © Helen Hotson/Shutterstock (foreground)

Avon Impulse and the Avon Impulse logo are registered trademarks of HarperCollins Publishers in the United States of America.
Avon and HarperCollins are registered trademarks of HarperCollins Publishers in the United States of America and other countries.

FIRST EDITION

18 19 20 21 22   HDC   10 9 8 7 6 5 4 3 2 1

*With all my heart to my husband Bill, my rock,
my strength, my joy, my love, and the inspiration
for all the heroes I've ever written*

CHAPTER ONE

Bolton, Cornwall, England
June 21, 1889

The brisk wind bit Madeleine Atherton's cheeks as she stepped down from the train. Cornwall might be known for its temperate climate, but it felt more like November than June. At least the rain had stopped—for the moment.

The rural station at Bolton was much smaller than Madeleine had remembered. Just a redbrick building that resembled a cottage, with a single wooden bench facing the tracks. The platform was empty. Beyond the station stretched a single street lined with small houses and shops. Beyond that, wide green meadows were bisected by a narrow road as far as the eye could see. There was no sign of an approaching carriage.

Where was Alexandra?

Madeleine had spent the entire seven-hour train ride from London thinking about this moment, how wonderful it would be to see her sister again, and how happy Alexandra would be that Madeleine had dared to come. But no one was here to meet her.

Madeline pulled her velvet cloak more closely about her, worried. She had sent a wire yesterday to inform her sister of her plans. *I'm stealing away,* she had written, *just like you did last year.* Well, *stealing* wasn't exactly the right word. She had simply left a note, packed a trunk, donned her best green traveling suit, and slipped out of Brown's Hotel early that morning while her mother was sleeping.

As the second of three daughters of one of the richest men in the United States, Madeleine understood that she was expected to make an exceptional match. The quest for a titled husband might be her mother's ambition, to further the family's standing in New York society, but Madeleine had agreed to give it a try. It had worked out so well for her sister, after all. Alexandra had fallen madly in love with Thomas Carlyle, the seventh Earl of Longford, and was now happily married and a countess.

Madeleine wasn't actually opposed to the man her mother was urging her to marry. In fact, she rather liked him. The problem was, unlike most of the girls unleashed on the London Season, Madeleine wasn't a wide-eyed, immature debutante. She was twenty-four years old. She was a college graduate. This was her second Season in London, taking into account last year's half Season, when she'd hastily crossed the Atlantic to take part after Alexandra's impromptu exit.

And Madeleine had specific goals in mind.

Like her sister, Madeleine wanted love to figure into the equation in any match she made. And not just *any* love.

Madeleine wanted a man who adored and respected her, but who also understood her and would be supportive of her dreams.

Was Lord Oakley that man? She wasn't certain.

Her abrupt departure from town would no doubt enrage her mother, but Madeleine desperately needed a few weeks away to clear her head. She had a life-altering decision to make. And she needed her sister's advice.

"Is this everything, then?" The query from a mustachioed porter broke into her thoughts. He and another man had deposited Madeleine's trunk and two bags onto the platform.

"Yes, thank you so much." Madeleine tipped both men, who touched their caps in thanks.

She was trying to decide what to do, when she caught sight of an approaching carriage on the horizon. *Thank goodness. Alexandra was coming at last!*

Just then, from another car further along the train, a tall, well-dressed gentleman descended, carrying a leather satchel. Madeleine's breath caught in her throat.

It was Charles Grayson, the Earl of Saunders. The best friend of her sister's husband.

A man she had no desire to see, much less speak to.

But he had already spotted her. His eyes widened in surprise as he closed the distance between them, then greeted her with a bow. "Miss Atherton!"

Madeleine gave him a terse smile and a dutiful curtsy. "Lord Saunders."

"I had no idea you were on this train." His voice was just as deep as she'd remembered, just as cultured and refined. He regarded her with calm detachment and a hint of something like curiosity, as if unsure where he stood with her or what to make of her. "I spotted you last month at the Fitzhughs' ball," he added, "and another time at the races. But each time I sought you out, you seemed to disappear."

"Did I? I'm sorry," Madeleine replied noncommittally. There was a good reason he hadn't connected with her on either of those occasions. She'd gone out of her way to avoid him.

Looking around, he asked, "Did you travel alone?"

"Yes." She knew it wasn't the "done thing" for a woman to travel by train unaccompanied, but she'd had little choice in the matter. She and her mother were sharing the same lady's maid while in England, and Madeleine couldn't very well have robbed her mother of her only servant. She silently dared Lord Saunders to reprove her. But he only said:

"So did I. My man Evans came up yesterday with most of my things. But why have you left the Season? I pray you are in good health?"

"I'm fine, thank you."

A cloud of steam emanated from beneath the great locomotive, and the smokestack belched a dark, filthy blast.

"I hope you are not here to see your sister?" he further prodded.

His expression and tone sparked another dash of worry within her. "Why do you say that?"

"Because I received a wire from Longford yesterday morning. He and his wife and sisters are away at Bath."

"Oh!" Madeleine's spirits sank. "Then Alexandra never

received my telegram." What a fool she'd been to leave London on such short notice, without waiting for a reply! But it had never occurred to her that her sister wouldn't be home. Alexandra was seven months pregnant, and had said she intended to remain at home until her child was born.

A new thought worried her. "People go to Bath for their health, don't they? Do you know if my sister's all right?"

"I haven't heard otherwise. Bath is also a popular holiday destination."

Madeleine wished she felt more reassured. The train whistle blew, a bell clanged, and the huge wheels began to turn. With a rhythmic *chug-chug-chug*, the locomotive moved out of the station. Leaving Madeleine alone on the platform with Lord Saunders.

"Do you know how long my sister and Lord Longford intend to be away?" she asked.

"A fortnight, I believe."

Two weeks! Madeleine's mind worked on the problem. If she could learn where Alexandra was staying in Bath and contact her, maybe her sister would return earlier. Assuming—praying—that she was all right. If not, Madeleine would go to Bath. In the meantime, she could wait at the Longfords' estate, Polperran House. The carriage she'd noticed earlier was making its approach.

"Well," Madeleine observed, "it looks as though the staff at Polperran House opened my telegram, and have sent a coach for me."

"I am afraid that is my coach, Miss Atherton," Saunders pointed out.

Indeed, as the coach—a smart equipage, painted red and black, with large glass windows—drew up, Madeleine recognized the Trevelyan coat of arms and the coronet of a British marquess emblazoned on the side.

"I see."

"Please, do not distress yourself." Saunders's smile was polite. "It would be my honor to escort you to Trevelyan Manor. You will be most welcome to stay there until Longford and his family return from Bath."

"Thank you, but no," Madeleine replied quickly. She had no desire to spend time with this man, nor to stay at his family's estate. "I would not wish to impose."

"It would be no imposition, I assure you."

"I appreciate the offer, my lord. But I would rather find a way to get myself to Polperran House and remain there, while I send word to my sister."

He nodded. "In that case, pray allow me to offer you a ride thither."

Madeleine considered. It was a two-hour drive from the Bolton station to Polperran House. She could try to find a cab, but she knew it would not greatly inconvenience Lord Saunders to do her this favor. Although she'd never been to Trevelyan Manor, Alexandra had told her that it was situated near the coast some five miles beyond Polperran House, which was more or less on the way.

Still. Did she want to be cooped up in a carriage with this man for such a long period of time? It was bad enough that she'd traveled unaccompanied all the way from London. But to ride in a closed carriage with a man to whom she wasn't related or engaged? An Atherton girl, her mother would insist, did not behave that way.

Noticing her hesitation, Saunders added: "There are no more trains today. Your only alternative is to take shelter at the Inn at Bolton—and I would not wish my worst enemy to stay at that establishment, nor even have a meal there. Unless you are absolutely famished?"

"I had something to eat on the train," Madeleine admitted.

"Well, then?" He quirked an eyebrow. His eyes, she noticed, were an arresting shade of hazel. As he looked at her, it seemed as though he was working hard to take the measure of her, as if she were a problem that needed to be solved. Despite herself, she felt a ripple of sudden interest run the entire length of her body from her head to her toes.

Don't let him charm you, Madeleine.

She'd spent the past two months at endless balls and parties, subjected to the calculating scrutiny of every fortune-hunting bachelor in London. She'd learned to grin and bear it, and after meeting Lord Oakley, to actually enjoy it. But Lord Saunders's gaze made her feel self-conscious somehow. And . . . rattled.

A low rumble of thunder rent the air, recalling her attention to her predicament. Raindrops began to patter against the pavement. It was quite apparent that no one was coming for her. It seemed she had little alternative but to accept his offer.

Madeleine swallowed a sigh. "Thank you. I'd very much appreciate a ride to Polperran House."

"Excellent."

Lord Saunders directed two porters to load Madeleine's

luggage onto the back of the carriage. As the men struggled under the weight of her trunk, Saunders asked her, "What have you got in here? Bricks?"

"Books."

He eyed her with amusement as the coachman secured the trunks and covered them with a tarpaulin. "Did you bring an entire library?"

"Not quite." She'd only packed two dozen or so of her favorites novels in with her clothes. All the other books she'd brought from New York, she'd been obliged to leave at Brown's Hotel. In truth, she felt a bit bereft without them. But, she reminded herself, this was a short trip. She'd be back in London in a few weeks.

"May I assist with your satchel?" Saunders gestured toward the tapestry bag Madeleine carried.

Instinctively, she clasped the carryall to her chest, feeling the weight of the precious cargo within. "No thank you."

He smiled agreeably, then offered his gloved hand to help her board. She took it. His grip was strong and firm, and once again, she felt a sizzle of sparks dance up her arm. *Drat the man for being so charming.*

She climbed inside, withdrawing her hand and settling on the forward-facing upholstered seat. Saunders took the seat opposite. As the carriage pulled out of the station, rain began pouring down in earnest. Saunders removed his top hat and set it down beside him. Madeleine dared a glance at him across the carriage.

She had to admit, he was very good-looking. His nose wasn't perfect, but its slight bend gave it character. His cheekbones were, well, high. His curly hair looked soft and was a lovely shade of dark caramel brown. His three-piece suit was perfectly tailored to his broad shoulders, trim waist, and long legs. It was too much, really. No wonder the debutantes had called him "swoon-worthy."

Madeleine had no intention of swooning before any man, however. Especially this one. No matter what the other ladies had said about him, as they tittered and gossiped behind their fans.

"It is a shame that he makes such infrequent appearances during the Season, and is so skittish about settling down," one of her acquaintances had intoned breathlessly at a dinner party. "He is still young, just a year shy of thirty, and he will one day inherit the title of Marquess of Trevelyan. The way he flirts! Why, he almost married an American heiress a few years ago! Thank goodness *that* did not come to pass."

Madeleine knew all about *that* scandalous affair. It was the reason she disliked him.

"So," Saunders quipped, breaking into her reverie as his eyes lifted to hers, "have you run away from town as your sister did?"

His voice held a teasing lilt to it. Madeleine realized she'd been caught staring and in embarrassment looked away, the question setting her on the defensive. "No! I haven't run away. I have merely taken . . . a small break."

"In the middle of the Season? How unusual. What prompted your departure? Other than a sudden impulse to visit your sister?"

"What prompted yours?" she challenged.

His smile fled. After a pause, he replied: "My father is unwell."

"Oh!" Madeleine had only met Lord Trevelyan briefly, the summer before, but had the impression that he was well-liked and respected in the community. "I'm so sorry."

"He has been ill on and off for years, but never this seriously. It is why my parents remained in the country this Season. The physician and my mother are very concerned."

"I'm very sorry," Madeleine said again. "I do hope he recovers fully and quickly."

"Thank you."

Saunders sat in worried silence as the carriage rumbled along, rain beating against the windows. Madeleine felt bad that she'd deflected his question with one of her own. Hoping to fix her mistake and lighten the mood, she said, "You asked my purpose in coming to Cornwall."

He replaced his frown with a look of genuine interest. "I did."

"I've come because I've had an offer of marriage."

"Congratulations! Who is the lucky gentleman?"

"The Marquess of Oakley, eldest son of the Duke of Courtenay."

"Ah! I know him well."

"Do you?"

"We roomed together for a year at Oxford. Philip is an excellent fellow."

Madeleine hesitated. "Yes, he is."

"You sound uncertain."

"I don't mean to. I'm honored by his proposal." Lord

Oakley was handsome, upright, intelligent, thoughtful. Everything Madeleine wanted in a husband. Her mother was thrilled with the match, and Madeleine knew that where titles were concerned, she couldn't do better than the eldest son of a duke. "But it's a big decision," she added.

"Indeed it is."

"He's gone off on a tour of the Continent, so I have time to consider the matter. I didn't want to accept until I'd discussed it with my sister."

"I understand why. The Countess of Longford is a paragon among women. I should very much like to consult with her myself before making a decision, were I a woman."

The comment made Madeleine's hackles rise again. "Were you a *woman*?"

Her tone seemed to take him aback. "Er . . . Yes."

Madeleine reminded herself to see the humor in the situation. He was, after all, a man. Most men viewed the world as though it were their exclusive dominion, convinced that women were a weaker, less worthy, less intelligent gender. "Are you saying that a man can only turn to another *man* for advice? That you would never seek a woman's counsel on any matter?"

"I . . . did not say that."

"Yet you implied it."

"Forgive me, Miss Atherton. That was not my intention."

"If you think about it carefully, you will see that what you said was condescension, thinly veiled."

He nodded solemnly as he considered her remark. "Perhaps it was. Again, forgive me. I see that I shall have to mind my *p*'s and *q*'s with you."

"*P*'s and *q*'s. That is such an interesting expression."

"It is, isn't it? Now that I said it, I realize I have no idea what it actually means."

"It's thought to be a schoolroom phrase," Madeleine told him. "When pupils were taught to write the alphabet, they were reminded to place the letters in the proper order. *P* comes before *Q*."

"That makes sense."

"There are two other theories, though, that I recall."

"Please enlighten me."

"One is that it's short for 'mind your *pleases* and *thank-yous*'—the latter of which sounds a bit like the letter *Q*. My favorite insists that the phrase derives from English pubs of the seventeenth century, when bartenders were obliged to keep an eye on the *pints* and *quarts* their patrons consumed."

Saunders chuckled. "How on earth did you come to know all that, Miss Atherton?"

"I had a rather remarkable English professor in my second year at Vassar."

He paused. "Ah, yes. Your sister mentioned that you just graduated from college. May I congratulate you on your accomplishment?"

"Thank you."

He cocked his head slightly, regarding her with what appeared to be a mixture of esteem and curiosity. "I find you most unusual, Miss Atherton."

"Do you? Why?"

"Your father is one of the wealthiest men in America. You have no need to work. Yet you chose to attend university."

"Every member of the peerage goes to college," she pointed out, "and you don't engage in a profession."

His brows furrowed at that and he seemed perturbed. After a moment, he commented, "Yes, but that's different."

"Why is it different? Why shouldn't I educate myself? Because I'm a woman?"

An awkward laugh escaped him now and he seemed incapable of a reply.

Madeleine leaned forward in her seat, passion fueling her words. "Women are just as smart as men, my lord, and sometimes smarter. We are equally as capable. We can do anything men can do."

He studied her. "Is that so? Anything?"

"Anything. Women are doctors and surgeons now—highly skilled ones. And we have women lawyers now in America."

"So I have heard," he admitted. "But you must admit, there are *some* limits as to what women can do."

"Name one."

"Well, for example, a woman could not dig ditches."

"Give me a shovel, and I will prove you wrong."

His eyes twinkled. "Something tells me you would. All right, then. A woman could not be a police officer."

"Why not?"

"She does not have the physical prowess the job requires."

"I beg to differ. You'd be surprised how strong a woman can be, my lord, when the circumstances demand it."

He took that in, seemingly considering it, but shook his head. "I do not see it. In the same vein, a woman could never serve in the military or go to war."

"Untrue!" Madeleine protested. "Absolutely untrue."

"How so?" He pointed a finger at her. "And pray do not use Joan of Arc as an example. She was an anomaly."

"Joan of Arc was not an anomaly. Women have served in combat since the dawn of history!"

"Have they? Who?"

"Chinese General Fu Hao, for instance, a woman, led thousands of people into battle in the thirteenth century BCE, and defeated the Shang. In the eleventh century CE, Matilda of Tuscany, an accomplished archer, commanded armies to defend the pope and made kings kneel before her. In our American Civil War, hundreds of women concealed their gender so they could fight alongside their Union and Confederate counterparts. And that's barely scratching the surface of the—"

"Truce! Truce!" Lord Saunders laughed again and raised his hands in defeat. "I stand corrected. This is clearly a subject which you have studied and I have not."

"Given the opportunity, women can accomplish great things, Lord Saunders. And one day—I hope to see it in my lifetime—we *will* have that opportunity. When we have the vote, men like you will be obliged to accept us as your equals." She paused, conscious that she'd put a somewhat negative emphasis on the words *men like you*, and worried that she'd gone a bit too far. After all, she *was* a guest in his carriage, and beyond expressing doubts about women's physical capabilities, he hadn't said anything too terribly chauvinistic.

He went quiet for a moment as he stared at her. "Miss

Atherton, since the first time we met, I have had the sense that you do not like me very much."

"Oh, my dislike for you began long before we met, Lord Saunders." The words tumbled from Madeleine's mouth before she had a chance to stop them. She stifled a gasp at their brazenness, instantly regretting them. "Forgive me, I should not have said that."

"No, I appreciate honesty, Miss Atherton," was his astonished reply. "But pray tell me, what did I ever do to give you offense, before we had even met?"

Chapter Two

Madeleine paused. Every nerve in her body itched to tell him exactly what she thought of him. To say:

I know what happened four years ago. That you stole your best friend's fiancée a week before the wedding and ran off with her to America.

The fact that the best friend in question was Thomas Carlyle, her sister's husband, made the whole thing cut even more deeply. Although Saunders didn't end up marrying the heiress involved, and the woman had been more than a little at fault herself, the circumstances still marked a flaw in his character. He *could* have said no. How Thomas could have brought himself to forgive this man was beyond Madeleine's comprehension. To be betrayed by a dear friend, in such a callous manner! After something like that, a person could never be trusted again.

But did she dare to mention it?

The finishing governess her mother had hired to prepare her and her sisters for their London debuts had impressed upon them the importance of reticence in English society.

"Never say anything," Madame Dubois had insisted, "unless it is unfailingly prudent and polite."

The thoughts coursing through her brain at the moment were neither prudent nor polite.

So, she merely said, "You have a reputation, Lord Saunders."

"Do I? What kind of reputation?"

"I think you know exactly what I mean, my lord."

His lips twitched slightly. "What have you heard? Rumors about myself and . . . *the ladies?*"

It annoyed her that he seemed to find this amusing. "Yes."

Lord Saunders leaned forward, hands clasped together, elbows resting on his knees as he studied her. "I am unmarried, Miss Atherton. Don't you think a single man ought to sow his wild oats while he can, before he settles down for life?"

"I have no problem with that. Unless the woman with whom he's sowing those wild oats is promised to another."

He flinched. Madeleine felt a heat rise to her face. She hadn't meant to be so blunt.

"I presume," he said quietly, "you are referring to my relationship with Miss Elise Townsend?"

It had not been her intention to force the issue into the open or to goad him. And yet she had. Swallowing her misgivings, she answered, "I am."

He let go a deep sigh. "I suppose your sister told you all about that?"

"Yes, but it's common knowledge."

"Is it?"

"How could you do it?" she blurted. "How could you betray your best friend like that?" She knew full well what it was like to be on the receiving end of such a blatant betrayal, knew how much it hurt.

He didn't immediately respond. "What can I say, Miss Atherton? It happened a long time ago." Bitterness took over his face. "And it was a mistake. The biggest mistake I have ever made."

Once again, Madeleine was sorry for bringing up a subject that appeared to cause him distress. Her feelings on the matter remained unchanged, but at least he had the decency to feel bad about the affair. That counted for something.

He turned to gaze moodily out the window at the rainy landscape as the carriage rattled along. Silence stretched between them. Well, they had a long ride ahead of them. She might as well read.

Madeleine slowly withdrew the novel she'd brought from her tapestry bag, being extra careful not to allow a glimpse of the other, more precious cargo the carryall contained. Glancing up, she noticed Lord Saunders watching her. A flush rose to her cheeks as she shut the clasp, then opened her book, and lost herself within its pages.

Charles studied Miss Atherton as the carriage lurched on.

Conversation had ceased long ago. He did not appreciate the topic she'd just brought up—it was something he preferred to never think or talk about again. Despite that, he found himself drawn to her.

Her eyes were focused on the book she had retrieved from her tapestry bag. She certainly seemed possessive about that bag. He wondered what was in it. Gold bullion? Diamonds and rubies? She was an heiress, after all. He wouldn't put it past her to carry her weight in jewels whenever she traveled.

Today, her jewelry was relatively modest, though. Just a pair of pearl drop earrings. They looked well on her.

Everything looked well on her.

Madeleine Atherton was, unequivocally, an attractive woman. Her complexion was fair. Her reddish-brown hair was woven up in a becoming style beneath her fashionable hat. Her velvet cloak masked her figure, but he remembered the lines and curves of her body. He had seen it before.

Charles would never forget the moment he'd first set eyes on Madeleine Atherton. It was at a party at Polperran House the previous autumn, a week before Longford's wedding. Charles had been speaking with the vicar when he happened to look up and catch sight of Longford's bride-to-be descending the grand staircase with two other young ladies. The resemblance between them was striking; they were clearly sisters, each as lovely as the next. But it was the woman in the middle who had captured his attention.

Madeleine Atherton's gown had been of lilac satin, embellished by spectacular beading that glimmered beneath the chandeliers. Her figure, he remembered, was lithe yet curvaceous in all the right places. As she'd regarded the festivities below, her smile had been incandescent, as though she were lit by a flame from within.

Charles had lost sight of her as she'd made the round of introductions. Suddenly Longford was at his elbow, he turned, and there she was. Beauty incarnate, standing before him.

Except that instead of the radiant smile he had formerly observed, her face had held a frown, and her eyes had flashed with something like disgust. He'd had no idea what was behind that expression, had certainly never dreamt that it had anything to do with *him*—that it was a reflection of her disapproval over something he had done years before.

He had bowed and said hello, she'd murmured something in response, and Longford had hurried her away to greet someone else.

All evening long, Charles had looked in vain for an opportunity to speak to her again. They had barely exchanged three words at the wedding. Soon after that, she and her parents and younger sister had sailed back to New York.

When he'd spotted her last month in town, she always seemed to be frustratingly just out of reach. He now suspected that she had been dodging him deliberately.

And why? Because of the *Miss Townsend affair*?

He'd thought the subject long since dead and buried. No one else had mentioned it in years. Her brother-in-law had been affected, yes, but it hadn't affected *her*. And no one regretted that episode more than he did. He wondered if Miss Atherton knew the whole story. If she did not, it bothered him that she was judging him based on an incomplete picture. That of all things, *that* was the reason she disliked him.

Not that he required her to like or approve of him.

It wasn't as if his attraction to her could ever go anywhere. A relationship with her was out of the question—not just because of Sophie, or because of the offer Miss Atherton had just received from Osborne—but because she was an heiress in search of a title, and therefore in his eyes, *persona non grata*.

He had been down that road before. He had vowed to never venture there again.

He drummed his fingers on the seat, recalling the other things she'd mentioned about him. That thing about his reputation was interesting. Even though she had it all wrong.

It was true that he'd had a number of relationships over the years. Never with a debutante or a virgin, though—he knew better than to entangle himself in something like that. He restricted his affairs to experienced women. Even *those* liaisons had been few and far between, and nowhere nearly as plentiful as people believed. It had been months since he'd ended the last one.

The hints which he deliberately dropped, to let it be presumed that he was with some unnamed actress or widow, suited his purpose. They explained his absences from many events in town, allowing him the time to pursue his secret passion. A preoccupation of which his father—and society—would surely not approve, and was therefore best kept under wraps.

In the meantime, did he enjoy flirting during the Season? Of course he did. What was the harm in it? Time was fleeting. One day soon, he would be tied down for life. His mother and father had nearly lost their minds when he had defied them and run off to America with Elise, a lapse in judgment that had nearly destroyed his friendship with Thomas. When it all blew up in his face and, to his great relief, he found himself still single, his parents had made him solemnly promise that he would never do anything so harebrained again.

That he would marry an English girl. A woman who suited their notion of a proper marchioness.

His cousin Sophie.

The daughter of his mother's favorite brother.

It was a hope of long standing, that had been born in his mother's breast on the day of Sophie's birth. No one had asked *his* opinion on the matter, of course. But then, he was only seven years old at the time. If his mother had had her way, Charles would have married Sophie years ago and be living in Parmoor House now, raising five children.

As the eldest son, Charles knew he was obliged to follow a particular path. Oxford was supposed to have been a minor step on the road, a suitable education followed by a lifetime of socializing, hunting, drinking, and card-playing, interrupted by the occasional duties required in overseeing the estate.

But he didn't fit the mold. Never had. Never would. Not without giving up a piece of his soul.

He was to be the next marquess, no way of getting out of it. When the time came, he would grit his teeth and do his duty. But until that day, he'd be damned if he wasn't going to spend every spare second doing what *he* wanted. Following *his* inclinations and dreams.

It was those inclinations and dreams that kept his mind engaged. That made life worth living.

If only he could make his parents understand that. His entire life, his father had looked down on everything Charles aspired to, insisting that it was a waste of time. His mother had been more interested and appreciative, but refused to stand up for him. His father's word was law.

And *she* wanted grandchildren.

"Sophie will make you the ideal wife, Charles," his mother had been insisting over far too many breakfasts and dinners to count, ever since he could remember. "You are approaching thirty," she had reminded him only last month. "What are you waiting for? It is high time you asked Sophie to marry you and settled down."

He hadn't seen Sophie in a couple of years. During her last visit, he had caught her staring at him meaningfully several times from under her pale lashes. He'd heard that she had turned down two offers of marriage because she was waiting for him. He felt a bit guilty about that. He hadn't promised her anything, not yet.

Unless you counted the talk they'd had all those years ago when she was what, sixteen? The one and only time he had kissed her. He hadn't felt any particular excitement in the event. But Sophie had practically swooned. Every day since, he had been keenly aware of her and his parents' expectations.

Charles closed his eyes, trying to imagine what his life would be like if he married Sophie. She was the daughter of an earl, and a true English rose. Pale. Quiet. Pretty. What society called *accomplished*. She had impeccable manners, was adept at small talk, played the piano, sang a little, excelled at dancing, spoke some French, had been taught (so he had been told) how to manage a household and throw a dinner party, and did prodigious amounts of needlework. All the skills which were required of the wife of a peer.

Why, then, did he feel that something was lacking? Why, then, was he dragging his feet?

His mother was probably right, he told himself now. When he decided to settle down, Sophie would make him the ideal wife. If he should wish to go off for days at a time to pursue his other interests, Sophie would look the other way. She was not the kind of woman who would openly question his activities, or his *reputation*.

He would certainly never marry someone like—

The carriage came to a sudden, jarring halt, casting his thoughts to the wind.

Rain was pouring down in sheets and battering against the windows. Why had they stopped? Charles heard Ned jump down from the box. Seconds later, the carriage door was yanked open.

Ned, looking more like a drowned rat than a human being, said in his strong Cornish accent: "Beggin' yer pardon, milord. A tree be fallen 'cross the road. It so be we can't pass this way."

Charles wiped condensation from the inside of a window with his coat sleeve and glanced out. He could perceive the large tree trunk that impeded them. "I suppose we shall have to backtrack then, and take the longer way around to Polperran House."

Ned shook his head. "Nary can do that, milord. I seen that road when we passed it by. It be flooded and so deep in mud, no coach could pass through this day. We best ways go back to the main road and on to Trevelyan Manor, right quick."

Miss Atherton looked up from her book. "I beg your pardon. What did your man say?"

Charles frowned. "He says we are unable to reach Polperran House after all. I have no alternative but to take you home."

CHAPTER THREE

Madeleine gazed out the window in frustration as the carriage rumbled along, pelted by the interminable downpour.

Under normal circumstances, Madeleine adored the rain. Growing up in their old house in Poughkeepsie, she'd loved snuggling in her bedroom under the eaves, listening to the raindrops batter the roof during a storm. In the gilded mansion her parents had built on Fifth Avenue in New York City, she'd enjoyed cozying up with a book by her favorite window, watching the rain dance against the pavement as horses and carriages passed by in the street below.

Today, however, the rain was just a cold, wet inconvenience. It was freezing inside the carriage. The windows were too fogged up to see out. How she longed for a hot bath and a seat by a warm fire.

She was grateful to Lord Saunders for extending the invitation to stay at Trevelyan Manor, and giving her a ride. But she had imagined such a different outcome to this day. By now, she should have been sitting around the dinner table at Polperran House, laughing and exchanging stories with Alexandra, Thomas, and his sisters Julia and Lillie.

Instead, she was going to spend who knew how long at a strange house where she was not expected, barely knew anyone, and would surely feel in the way. And every day spent there she would, no doubt, be obliged to see Lord Saunders.

Although she'd sensed an initial warmth from him, after their conversation, he'd been moody and distant, exchanging only the briefest of comments. An unspoken tension filled the confined space that they shared. She knew that she'd upset him with her comments about the infamous Miss Townsend, and felt bad about that. But she'd spoken only the truth. It wasn't *her* fault that he'd betrayed his best friend.

The coach rumbled on for what seemed like an eternity. Madeleine was just starting to nod off when at last, she heard the crunch of gravel beneath the wheels.

"Here we are," Saunders said matter-of-factly.

Madeleine wiped at a window with her handkerchief and peered out. The carriage was making its way down a long drive past tall, dripping trees and masses of shrubbery. Ahead stood an immense two-story Palladian building of granite and gray slate, featuring a triangular central pediment and a rooftop teeming with chimneys and dormers.

"What a lovely house," Madeleine murmured. It occurred to her that Lord Saunders had been born and raised here, and would inherit this place one day.

"Thank you," was Saunders's curt reply.

The coach stopped beneath the stone portico covering the front entrance. The driver pulled down the steps from the vehicle and they descended. Saunders dutifully offered his gloved hand to help her alight. This time, she felt no romantic stirrings when his hand gripped hers, and she was glad of it.

As her feet touched the gravel, Madeleine felt a chill through the thin soles of her low boots. The cry of a distant gull pierced the air, an accompaniment to the steady beat of the rain. She inhaled deeply, detecting the scent of the sea in the air as she studied the immense house before them.

"How close is the coast?" she inquired.

"Less than a quarter mile," Saunders answered. "Shall we?" He gestured toward the massive mahogany front door, which had just swung open.

An imposing man in a black tailcoat appeared. His jet-black hair was threaded with hints of gray. "Good evening, my lord," he said to Saunders, his keen blue eyes registering surprise as he stepped back to admit them entry.

Saunders returned the greeting, then said, "Miss Atherton, may I present Woodson, our butler. Woodson, this is Miss Madeleine Atherton, Lord Longford's sister-in-law. She will be staying with us for a while."

"How do you do," Madeleine told the butler.

Woodson bowed. "It is a pleasure to meet you, Miss Atherton."

Saunders handed his gloves and hat to Woodson, who also took Madeleine's cloak. She glanced about. The entrance hall was spacious and beautiful, featuring several tall windows beneath a ceiling at least fifteen feet high. A fire burned in a marble fireplace, imbuing the room with warmth.

"How is my father?" Saunders asked the butler.

"He is sleeping, my lord. Dr. Hancock was just here and gave strict instructions that he not be disturbed until morning."

"What did the doctor say? Is Father . . . ?"

"He said His Lordship is doing as well as can be expected."

"Whatever that means." Saunders sighed, obviously distressed. "And my mother?"

"She is awaiting your arrival in the saloon."

"Thank you. We shall make our way there."

"Shall I speak to Mrs. Dean about preparing a room in the guest wing, my lord? The green room, perhaps? And set another place for dinner?"

"Yes, exactly so. Thank you, Woodson."

The butler bowed and vanished. Saunders silently beckoned Madeleine to follow him. Tension radiated off of him in waves. She wondered at the cause of it. Was it because he was worried about his father? Or was it her fault—because she was an unwelcome visitor who had called him on his bad reputation and mentioned a former, unhealthy alliance? Or all of the above?

She moved after him with a sigh, searching for something to say. "Woodson seems to be a capable fellow."

"He is," was Saunders's brief reply. He led her through an arched entryway into a central hall, where a huge mahogany staircase swept up to the next level, its walls hung with seemingly endless numbers of ancestral portraits in gilded frames.

As they passed through, Madeleine tried again. "Has Woodson been here long?"

"Since I was a boy. Woodson knows precisely what a person needs before he or she even realizes they require it."

"What a handy person to have around."

"Indeed."

And there the conversation ended. They continued down a long hall. Madeleine knew she had an uncomfortable few days ahead of her unless she could figure out how to mitigate the discord between them. She might not approve of this man, but she felt now that some of the comments she'd made in the carriage *might* have been a bit insensitive. Perhaps she owed him an apology.

"Lord Saunders," she began.

But her voice broke off as they entered a large, refined chamber, the beauty of which captured all her attention. Carved dark paneling gleamed on walls hung with so many works of art, it resembled a museum. The furnishings were elegant and of the finest quality. Brocade curtains framed a row of tall windows topped by fanlights, overlooking a green lawn. Everything beyond was shrouded in low-lying mist and the steady rain which poured from the early evening sky. "Oh," Madeleine breathed in appreciation.

Two women were seated in wingback chairs facing an immense white marble fireplace. Madeleine could see their long skirts, but not their faces. One of them set aside her needlework and stood.

It was Lady Trevelyan. An attractive woman in her midfifties, she was attired in a perfectly tailored dove-gray gown. Her hair, styled in the newest fashion, was the same shade of dark brown as her son's, and laced with a few silvery streaks. "Charles!" she called out in a throaty voice, holding out her hands as she crossed the room to greet him. "How was your journey?" Catching sight of Madeleine, her brows lifted with curiosity.

"Uneventful," Saunders replied. "I am so sorry to hear that Father is ill."

"Thank you, dear," Lady Trevelyan responded with worried eyes. "I have been beside myself these past few days, but I trust Dr. Hancock is doing all he can."

Lady Trevelyan and Lord Saunders clasped hands and he leaned down to kiss her on the cheek. At this display of affection, Madeleine felt a twinge of envy. Her own mother was anything but affectionate. Their relationship was often fraught with difficulty, a tug of war between what her mother wanted for her and what Madeleine wished for herself.

"Mother, do you remember Miss Madeleine Atherton, from New York?" Lord Saunders gestured to her. "You met at Longford's wedding. She is his sister-in-law."

"Of course." Lady Trevelyan smiled. "How delightful to see you again, Miss Atherton."

"And you, Lady Trevelyan. Please forgive me for dropping in so unexpectedly. My plans for today have gone awry."

"I found her at the train station in Bolton," Saunders explained, "hoping to go to Polperran House."

"Is not the family away at Bath?" Lady Trevelyan inquired.

"Apparently, everyone seemed to know that but me. Lady Trevelyan, do you know why they went to Bath?" Madeleine added urgently. "Is my sister unwell?"

"I do not believe so," Lady Trevelyan replied. "I recall Dr. Hancock mentioning something the other day about the countess being in fine health, but even so, Lord Longford wished her to take the waters at Bath."

"I see. Thank you, that is a relief to hear."

"Miss Atherton arrived at Bolton unexpected, with no means of transportation," Saunders said matter-of-factly. "We found the road to Polperran House flooded, so I insisted that she stay with us."

"I'm only here until the roads are clear," Madeleine put in hastily. "Which I hope won't be more than a day or two."

Lady Trevelyan let go a short laugh. "You are clearly unfamiliar with the roads of Cornwall, Miss Atherton. With these rains, the road to Polperran House may be impassable for a week entire. And what would you do there in any case, with no one in residence except the servants? No, my son is right. You must stay with us until your sister returns." She glanced at Saunders. "Have you spoken to Woodson?"

"He said something about preparing a room in the guest wing, and setting a place at dinner."

"Perfect." She gave Madeleine another smile. "You see, it is all arranged."

"You are too kind. Thank you so much. But I feel terrible, imposing like this." She looked to both Lady Trevelyan and Lord Saunders as she spoke from the heart. "Especially with Lord Trevelyan being ill. And Your Ladyship, I know you have children—"

"It is no imposition at all," Lady Trevelyan assured her with a wave of her hand. "My son James is in Ireland with friends for the entire summer. Helen and Anna are cared for by the governess. Your being here actually comes at a good time. We have another guest who I believe will appreciate your company." Lady Trevelyan turned to the unseen lady in the other wingback chair and called out, "My dear, do come and be introduced to Miss Atherton."

A young lady stood and, calmly smoothing out her skirts, strode over to join them. Her clothing proclaimed her to be a member of the upper class. She looked to be in her early twenties, and her pale blond hair was swept up in curls above a pretty face.

"Sophie, may I present Miss Atherton from America. Miss Atherton, this is my niece, Lady Sophie Caswell."

"It's a pleasure to meet you, Lady Sophie." They exchanged a curtsy.

"And you, Miss Atherton," the young lady responded in a gentle voice.

In her rose-colored gown, Lady Sophie reminded Madeline of a spoonful of sherbet. Cool and sweet. Yet her expression was open and sincere, without a trace of haughtiness. Madeleine decided at once that she liked her.

Lady Sophie turned to Lord Saunders and added with undisguised affection, "Hello, Charles."

"Sophie," he said.

It was only then that Madeleine noticed Lord Saunders's expression.

He was frozen in surprise. And he didn't look particularly happy.

Charles recovered his wits, took his cousin's hand, and kissed it. "To what do we owe the honor of this visit?"

"It all came about rather suddenly, Charles," his mother said, before Sophie could reply. "You know that Sophie and her mother have been cast adrift these past three years, ever since my brother Dermot passed away?"

"Of course I do." To Sophie, Charles added, "I admired your father. Again, I am so very sorry for your loss."

"Thank you. It was a very hard blow indeed, losing Papa." To Lady Trevelyan, she continued, "But we were not truly cast adrift, Aunt Charlotte. Indeed, we did lose our home—"

"Which is such a shame," his mother interrupted with a frown. "I do not agree with this entail business being reserved for sons, but not daughters." For Miss Atherton's benefit, she added, "As Sophie is my brother's only child, his estate and earldom went to a distant male relation. His poor wife and daughter were left homeless and nearly penniless."

"It was not so bad as that," Sophie insisted softly. "We have a small income and many friends and relations who were so kind as to put us up. Your mother invited us ever so many times, Charles. But then . . . Mama married again."

"Clarissa has just wed Baron Kedleston of Derbyshire," Lady Trevelyan explained, "and they have gone off to Cairo on the first leg of a world tour. I would not hear of Sophie going with them, so I invited her to stay."

"Just for the summer," Sophie put in, casting a quick look at Charles. "I mean to join them in Greece at the end of September."

Charles registered this information, aware of what had been left unsaid: that his mother had brought Sophie to

Trevelyan Manor in the hopes that he would finally propose, making Sophie's departure for Greece unnecessary.

The doe-eyed look on Sophie's face signaled that she was desirous of the same thing.

His chest suddenly seemed to be constricted by a rigid band of steel.

He sensed Miss Atherton's eyes on him as well. Her look of silent, amused comprehension implied that she, too, suspected what was going on. Which made him want to hit something. Hard. It wasn't so much the idea of being wed to Sophie that bothered him. It was the setup. The hope in her eyes. The look on his mother's face. The apparent urgency of it, when there seemed to be no good reason to hurry.

Charles gritted his teeth and forced a smile. "I wish your mother and her new husband all the best," he told Sophie. "And how wonderful to have you here, cousin," he added. "I only hope you will not find it too dull to pass the entire summer in our company."

"You know I have always loved Trevelyan Manor," Sophie replied. "It will be even more pleasant now that you are home."

Thankfully, at that exact moment, Woodson appeared in the doorway with a maid and announced, "I have sent up Miss Atherton's trunk to the green room, my lady. I thought you might wish Martin to assist her to change for dinner."

"Right you are, Woodson," his mother responded. "I was just about to ring for you."

As his valet helped him change into his tailcoat and tie for dinner, Charles reflected with annoyance on the situation at hand. He had come home specifically to see his father, but was banned from doing so until tomorrow. In the meantime, he was stuck at the manor house with two women he had never thought to find here, with whom he would be obliged to dine and make small talk. *Bollocks.*

Sophie was a lovely person. He ought not to object to her company. But . . . Sophie had expectations. Justifiable expectations, to be sure. But those expectations felt like a weight around his neck every moment he was in her presence.

As for Miss Atherton—she was just too damned appealing for his own good. Even knowing that she was on the cash-for-coronets treadmill, a path he abhorred, he had been attracted to her from the moment of their first meeting. An attraction that had only increased when he'd encountered her at the train station today. He admired her spirit, and had greatly enjoyed their banter in the carriage—at least the first part of it.

The accusation she'd made (*How could you do it? How could you betray your best friend like that?*) still rang uncomfortably in his ears, making him testy and irritable. He could hardly believe she'd had the temerity to ask the question. At the time, he had not attempted to defend himself. It had felt wrong to discuss such an intimate piece of personal history with someone he did not know very well. He wished there were a way to apprise her of the truth. But how did one even broach a subject like that?

If only he could shake off this unwelcome interest in her. The interest was clearly one-sided. Which was just as well, since for a great many reasons, he needed to nip *his* in the bud straightaway.

Damn it all to hell, she was going to be at Trevelyan Manor for days, possibly a week entire. How was he going to get through it, running into her in the halls, seeing her every day at breakfast, tea, and dinner? There was only one solution: he had to get his arse out of here. See his father in the morning and quit the house, the sooner the better.

Charles had just settled on this plan of action and was striding down the hall on his way to dinner, when he ran into Miss Atherton at the head of the stairs, coming from the guest wing.

He caught his breath at the sight of her. Her slender arms, tiny waist, and well-proportioned bosom were displayed to perfection in her low-cut evening gown of teal silk, which complemented her creamy complexion and made her blue eyes look even bluer.

"My lord," she said, tugging her long white gloves into place.

A familiar, inconvenient tug of attraction coursed through him. He struggled to ignore it, reminding himself that she disliked him, and he was annoyed with her. "I hope you found your room comfortable, Miss Atherton?" he said politely.

"It's lovely. Thank you again for your hospitality."

"It is not my doing, but my mother's, and the efforts of the staff."

"Even so. If not for you, I might still be standing on the platform in Bolton, drenched to the bone."

"I doubt that. You seem to me a very capable person. Had I not been present, I feel certain you would have found someone else to help you."

"I suppose I would have." She looked at him. "Lord Saunders," she added boldly and without sentiment, "I wanted to apologize for what I said in the carriage earlier. I regret bringing up . . . a certain incident four years ago."

Charles started. He hadn't expected *that*. "I appreciate the apology, Miss Atherton," he replied quietly. "Please, trouble yourself no further. I know I am not a perfect man."

"Well, I feel bad. I think we got off to a rocky start. I was hoping we could go back and start over?"

He hesitated. Even though he didn't perceive any lessening of the indictment in her eyes, her apology and wish to make amends appeared to be sincere, which took some of the sting out of the situation. If only he could tell her what had really happened, right now, this very moment. But they were standing at the top of the stairs, in earshot of passing servants, and there wasn't time in any case—the dinner bell had already rung. "I would like that as well."

"Good."

They started down the staircase together.

"So, am I reading the situation correctly?" she asked suddenly. "Is it your mother's hope that you will marry your cousin Sophie?"

The boldness of the question took Charles aback. This woman did not pull any punches, did she? She just said straight out whatever was on her mind. It was so un-English of her. "It is more than a hope," he admitted. "It is more like a mandate."

"Is that what you want?"

His jaw tightened. "I want to do my duty." Charles glanced sideways at her as they descended. "What about you? You have a marriage proposal on the table. When does Oakley expect your reply?"

"When he returns from his European tour, at the end of the summer."

"Well then, it looks as though we both have our futures laid out for us."

"Does it? I am not entirely sure about mine."

Charles took that in. He had long owed a debt to Oakley. Here, he realized, was his chance to repay it.

"I know you are waiting to speak to your sister, Miss Atherton, and I applaud that. But in my opinion, you would be mad not to marry Oakley. He is the best of the best. And what woman in her right mind would refuse the chance to be a duchess?"

Chapter Four

Madeleine awoke to the sound of drapes being pulled open. Rolling over in bed, she opened her eyes and squinted against the bright morning light.

"Good mornin', miss," announced Martin. A stout, cheerful woman in a prim black dress and white apron, she had helped Madeleine to dress and undress the evening before.

How kind of Lady Trevelyan to share her lady's maid. Madeleine returned the greeting, sat up, and stretched. She'd been so tired after her long day of traveling, she could barely remember anything that had been said at dinner last night. She'd gone straight to bed afterward and now, after a sound sleep, felt wide-awake and refreshed.

Her room was delightful. The four-poster feather bed was sumptuous and comfortable. The wallpaper was lime green with a pretty pattern of multicolored flowers and birds, and the bed linens and upholstery were tastefully matched. Sunshine poured in through the tall windows. Madeleine bounded out of bed to take in the view. The sky was a bright,

cloudless blue, the complete reverse of the gloomy grayness
that had pervaded everything the day before.

The room, which faced the back of the house, overlooked
a wide, verdant lawn and manicured gardens blooming with
flowers in a variety of hues. Beyond the gardens stretched
green woods, and then the world seemed to drop off, replaced
by the vast blueness of the sea. In the distance, the coastline
curved away, high cliffs towering above blackened rocks and
golden sand beaches, where seagulls swooped and cawed
shrilly above the crashing waves.

"What a glorious morning!" Madeleine relished the
estate's proximity to the sea. She looked forward to exploring both outside and in. The house, Madeleine had been
pleased to discover, boasted modern plumbing and gas
lighting, improvements which were new and rare in English
country houses.

She was going to be at Trevelyan Manor for several days
at least, maybe even a week. The notion that she had all that
time ahead of her with nothing planned filled Madeleine
with excitement. She didn't have to remain idle while she was
here. Hopefully, she could put the time to good use.

First, she had to let her mother know where she was staying. Then she had to contact Alexandra in Bath, and write to
Kathryn in New York. After that. . . .

Madeleine's gaze touched on her tapestry bag lying atop
the bureau. At last, she could get back to her manuscript.
The book that had been her dream and her passion for as
long as she could remember. Every moment spent on the
novel brought her immense creative satisfaction, a kind of

joy and fulfillment she found in no other endeavor. But after three years of hard work, she still wasn't even finished with the first draft.

There had been so many other things pulling at her. Her determination to receive highest marks in every class at Vassar and graduate early had required an intense study regime. Immediately afterward, she'd been obliged to sail to France for last-minute adjustments to her new Worth gowns. Onboard ship, her mother had drilled her in preparation for the Season. The moment they'd reached London, she'd been thrust into a whirlwind of events from dawn until dusk, seven days a week. All under her mother's dictatorial eye.

She had been subjected to Mother's criticisms about posture, facial expressions, the way she held her fan, her performance on the dance floor, her tendency to talk too much or too little. Her mother's incessant reproaches hadn't eased up when Madeleine met Philip Heyer, the Marquess of Oakley. That illustrious young man's attentions had only prompted Mrs. Atherton to even more claustrophobic oversight, insisting that this was the match to end all matches, and on no account must Madeleine make a mistake.

"Such a man doesn't *ask* a woman to marry *him*," her mother had told her excitedly, "he *offers* to marry *her*." As though his title and all he possessed was a gift he was bestowing.

As though Madeleine's fortune, which was very much required to save his family's impoverished estate, was of only minor value in the equation.

Madeleine's courtship with Lord Oakley had been another whirlwind. She had sensed that he was a man to whom she could be happily attached. But when the day came and Oakley actually proposed, Madeleine had frozen up, finding it impossible to give him the reply he wanted.

Now here she was in Cornwall, her mind in a muddle, with no idea why she was so confused or what she ought to do about it.

Maybe, she told herself, she ought to stop thinking and face the music, as her father liked to say. Oakley had already left on his European tour. But if she contacted his mother, she might be able to learn where he was staying, write to him, and be done with it. As an engaged woman, she wouldn't have to attend any more events of the Season. If she and Oakley were betrothed, they could correspond. She could return to London and start planning their wedding.

Their wedding.

The idea sent a shiver down Madeleine's spine and she let go an anxious laugh. *It's just nerves. Every prospective bride feels the same way.* Aloud, she heard herself say: "No. *No.*"

"I beg yer pardon, miss?" Martin said.

Madeleine gave the maid a smile. "Don't mind me, Martin. I was just talking to myself."

"Would ye like a fire, miss? I can send in the chambermaid to light one."

"No thank you," Madeleine replied. "Who needs a fire on a day like this?" After unlatching the window, she pushed it open and inhaled deeply of the salt-tinged air, reveling in the sounds of birdsong. How could she have even considered going back to London? She would not make a decision in haste. She had all summer to make up her mind. The interval away from the Season would be good for her. And a talk with Alexandra, whenever it came about, would surely help clear her head.

She turned to the maid. "Thank you, Martin, for unpacking my clothes last night." It had all magically happened while Madeleine was at dinner. All the underthings and accessories she'd brought were ensconced in the bureau, and her dresses and riding habit hung in the wardrobe.

"Ye're most welcome, miss," said Martin. "They be right lovely gowns. More beautiful than any I've yet seen."

You haven't seen the half of it. Madeleine wondered what Martin would think of the three dozen other gowns still hanging in her suite at Brown's Hotel. Some were so elaborate and encrusted with beading, they seemed to weigh a hundred pounds. Although they were beautiful, Madeleine had been a bit embarrassed to wear them.

She'd only brought the most modest of her day dresses to Cornwall, along with a few evening gowns, but even they were quite elegant. "Between you and me," Madeleine confided, "I prefer simpler frocks and suits. But my mother insisted that I have only the best for the Season."

"I will take extra special care of 'em," Martin promised. "You have my word."

After helping Madeleine dress in a raspberry-colored summer frock with white lace trimmings, Martin told her that breakfast was served on the buffet in the morning room, and she could come downstairs at her convenience.

"Martin," Madeleine asked as the maid opened the bedroom door to leave, "before you go. I need to write to my mother and sisters. Do you know where I might get—"

"I beg your pardon, Miss Atherton?"

The interruption came from Woodson, who appeared in the doorway with several envelopes and sheets of paper in his gloved hand.

Martin gave him a nod before promptly and silently departing.

Woodson entered in her wake. "Forgive me for intruding," he told Madeleine, "but I thought you might require telegram forms and letter-writing materials this morning."

Madeleine smiled. "Woodson, how kind and perceptive you are."

"You will find pens and ink in the desk drawer," he noted.

"Thank you." She accepted the items he'd brought. "There is one more thing. My sister Alexandra and her husband, Lord Longford, are in Bath, but I have no idea where they are staying. I was wondering if you might be able to find that out for me."

"I took the liberty of sending a groom to Polperran House early this morning, miss, to secure that information from the staff." Woodson removed a note from his coat pocket and handed it to her.

Madeleine gaped at him. "How did you do that so fast? I thought the roads would be impassable for days."

"Impassable to carriages, miss. But a good horseman can navigate even the worst of roads."

Madeleine shook her head in amazement. "You are a wizard, Woodson. I am truly grateful."

"It is my pleasure to be of assistance," Woodson replied with a departing bow.

Madeleine filled out a telegram form with a brief message to her mother, apprising her of her changed circumstances. She could write to Kathryn later, she decided, but should contact Alexandra as soon as possible. She considered which means of communication to use.

A wire would be faster. But Alexandra disliked telegrams, felt they were impersonal and should only be used in cases of emergency. And this was not an emergency. According to Lord Saunders, Alexandra had only left for Bath a day or two before. Madeleine didn't want her sister to feel that she must rush home on her account.

Besides which, Madeleine thought, glancing out the window again with a smile, it was so beautiful here. She wouldn't mind staying at Trevelyan Manor by the sea for a few days longer.

She picked up a pen and began a letter to Alexandra:

Trevelyan Manor, Cornwall
June 22, 1889

Dear Lexie,

You will be surprised when you read the location above, and realize where I am. I have no doubt that you wrote to tell me of your trip to Bath, just as I wired you to say that

I was coming to Cornwall to see you! Our communications must have just missed each other.

Lord Saunders rescued me at Bolton yesterday and I have been kindly invited to stay at his home until you return. I have news, which you have probably already heard from Mother, even though I asked her not to write or say anything!

If you suspect my news has to do with Lord Oakley, whom I've mentioned innumerable times over the past four weeks, you will be right on the mark. He has asked me to marry him. I have not given him an answer yet. I have time to consider, for he has embarked on a three-month tour of the Continent.

Oh, Alexandra! My head is spinning. I had no idea matters of the heart could be so perplexing. Before I decide anything, I must speak to you. Lord Saunders mentioned that you are to be away for two weeks. Please don't cut your trip short on my account—I can wait here until you get home. But I need your advice more than ever, and count the days until I can see you again and be in your arms.

With deepest love, your sister,
Maddie

Madeleine brought the letter and completed telegram form downstairs. Woodson was waiting by the bottom step to receive them on a silver tray.

"I will see to it that they are delivered to the post office immediately," he promised.

"Thank you, Woodson."

He escorted Madeleine to the breakfast room, where the tantalizing aromas of eggs and bacon emanated from beneath silver-domed serving trays. Lady Trevelyan and Lady Sophie were already at breakfast, seated across from each other at the table. Madeleine filled a plate at the sideboard and joined them.

"Good morning," Madeleine said cheerfully as she sat down beside Lady Sophie, who returned the sentiment. A footman poured coffee.

"I hope you slept well?" Lady Trevelyan asked.

"I did, thank you." The empty seat at the head of the table was a painful reminder that the head of the family was absent. "How is Lord Trevelyan?"

"Not well, I am afraid," was Her Ladyship's somber reply.

"I'm so sorry. Lord Saunders said he has been ill before, though, and always recovered," Madeleine commented hopefully. "I hope that will again prove true."

"I hope so, as well," Lady Trevelyan answered with a sigh. "But this time it is worse than ever. He has always had good days and bad days, but the bad days seem to have taken over rather permanently."

"Does the doctor know what is wrong?"

Lady Trevelyan shook her head. Tears welled in her eyes and she dabbed at them with a handkerchief. "Thank you for asking, Miss Atherton. But it is not really something to discuss at the breakfast table."

"Forgive me." Madeleine's heart went out to Lady Trevelyan and His Lordship. She wished there was something she could do. "I would so like to see him while I'm here, to pay my respects and to wish him well."

"I will try to arrange that. He rarely comes downstairs anymore. But if Lord Trevelyan feels up to it, perhaps he can join us briefly for tea this afternoon."

"That would be wonderful. I'd love to see Lady Helen and Lady Anna, too, if that's possible?" Madeleine had only met Lady Trevelyan's daughters once, at Alexandra's wedding, but remembered them as sweet, well-behaved young ladies in their early teens.

"They come down for an hour at tea, after their lessons," Lady Trevelyan replied.

An hour a day seemed a painfully short time to spend with one's children, Madeleine thought. But then, it wasn't really so different from the way she and her sisters had been raised. They'd been at school all day. Their mother had been involved in society affairs, and their father had worked long hours. The only time they'd really spent together as a family was an hour each night at the dinner table.

"How have you been enjoying the Season, Miss Atherton?" commented Lady Sophie as she sipped her coffee.

"To be honest, it's been pretty exhausting," Madeleine answered.

"I thought the same at my London debut," Lady Sophie admitted. "I only had one Season. After Papa died, Mama could not afford to take me again."

"Never you mind, my dear," Lady Trevelyan remarked with a twinkle in her eyes. "Society's loss is our gain." The two women exchanged a quiet look of understanding that made Lady Sophie lower her gaze, her cheeks reddening slightly.

Madeleine hid a smile, aware of the meaning beneath that statement. She wondered if their hope—that Sophie would be Lord Saunders's bride—was a recent development. Madeleine recalled what Lord Saunders had said the night before: *I want to do my duty.* Surely Lord Saunders would never have run off to America with Miss Townsend four years ago, if he had felt duty-bound to marry his cousin.

"Now you must tell us more about your proposal from Lord Oakley." Lady Trevelyan's voice broke into her thoughts. Madeleine had mentioned the proposal at dinner the night before as the reason she'd come to Cornwall, seeking her sister's advice.

"There's not much to tell. We met at a dance and saw each other on various occasions after that. Last week, my mother and I were invited to Hatfield Park to meet Lord Oakley's parents." Madeleine paused. "That's where he popped the question."

"How thrilling that you have had such a fine offer," Lady Sophie enthused. "If you accept him, you will be a duchess."

Madeleine wished people would stop pointing that out, as if it were reason enough on its own to marry a man.

"Lord Oakley comes from a very good and old family," Lady Trevelyan commented. "I have met the Duke and Duchess of Courtenay and seen their estate in East Sussex. The house is magnificent and they have truly lovely woods."

"She will not be marrying Oakley for his woods," a masculine voice intoned.

All heads turned as Lord Saunders strode into the room.

"I know that, darling," Lady Trevelyan replied. "I was just making an observation."

Despite herself, Madeleine's heartbeat began to increase in tempo. She recalled that, the few times she'd observed Lord Saunders enter a room in town, he had always made heads turn. Just by walking in, he seemed to transform a space and become its focal point.

He was certainly the focal point for Lady Sophie, whose attention was captivated by his every move.

Maybe it was his handsome face, which made it hard to look at anyone else. Or maybe it was the way he carried himself. He exuded an unstudied air of intelligence, a trait she hadn't found in many men. He also had a habit of arriving late, as if he'd rushed there from some other pressing engagement, which couldn't help but make one wonder where he'd been. But despite his tardiness, he was always well-dressed and perfectly tailored.

This morning, he wore a gray suit with a cravat that matched his hazel eyes. Eyes that met hers briefly, before giving a smile to the room at large.

Madeleine tore her glance away, struggling to remind herself that Lord Saunders didn't deserve such warm thoughts. Although she'd apologized to him the night before at the top of the stairs, and they'd shared a few pleasant moments in the carriage, this man had once betrayed his dearest friend and her brother-in-law. He seemed to be proud of his "reputation with the ladies." He was a man she could not admire, a man who could not be trusted.

"Have you seen your father?" Lady Trevelyan was saying.

Madeleine refocused her attention on the conversation. Saunders, helping himself at the sideboard, answered his mother, "I am going straight up after breakfast."

"Good. He is expecting you."

As Saunders took his seat across the table from Madeleine, Lady Trevelyan finished her last bite of toast. "Charles, didn't you room with Lord Oakley at Oxford?"

"I did." Saunders swallowed a forkful of eggs. "Good old Philip. Very fond of architecture, as I recall."

"Yes, he is," Madeleine agreed. "He gave me an in-depth tour of the house at Hatfield Park."

"You will never find a more straightforward, honorable, trustworthy fellow than Philip. I will never forget one night at school when I was out late drinking with friends. First-year antics, you understand. Philip had refused to go, because it was against the rules—"

"Charles!" Lady Trevelyan interrupted. "*Must* you share that awful story again?"

"It is nothing to be ashamed of," Saunders responded.

"I'd *love* to hear it," Madeleine insisted.

Saunders grinned and went on: "I got in late after curfew, and was attempting to crawl in through the window. This was a second-floor room, mind you. I had barely managed to reach its heights by scaling the attached shrubbery. In my drunken state, I would have surely fallen to my death, had not Oakley bravely reached out and heaved me inside, putting his own life in danger in the process."

"Thank goodness you did not fall," observed Lady Sophie, aghast, and gazing warmly at Lord Saunders.

"You make Lord Oakley sound like quite the hero," noted Madeleine, amused by the tale.

"He was, indisputably," Saunders agreed. "Particularly since he did not report me. I owe my life *and* reputation to him. I promised to one day repay the debt, although it is my shame to admit, I never did."

Madeleine laughed. "I am glad to hear such a good account of Lord Oakley. And that you survived the incident unharmed. My own college experience seems rather dull in comparison."

Lady Sophie looked at her in surprise. "You went to college?"

"She just graduated," Saunders replied with a wave of his fork.

"I have never met a woman who went to college." Lady Sophie's expression was both amazed and fascinated. "What was it like?"

"It was wonderful. There wasn't enough time to pursue everything that piqued my interest."

"What was your primary course of study?" Saunders asked.

"English Literature."

Before he could reply, Lady Trevelyan said, "I admire your courage and pluck, Miss Atherton. I imagine college must have been very difficult. But may I ask *why* you pursued higher education?"

"Why? I might ask, why should men learn all there is to know, while women sit home in ignorance and simply run the household?"

"There is nothing simple about running a household, my dear," Lady Trevelyan pointed out. "If you marry Lord Oakley, and I presume you will, your husband, home, family, and obligations to society will quite naturally become your entire province."

Madeleine paused before answering. She never ceased to be amazed at the number of well-bred women who espoused this point of view. Who were satisfied with the smallness of their lives. She glanced up and caught Lord Saunders's eye. He shot her a teasing look as if to say, *You see? It's not just me.*

"I hope that isn't entirely true," Madeleine said finally. "I'd like to think that even well-bred women can accomplish other things as well—creative things that open their minds and stir their hearts."

Lord Saunders's eyebrows lifted. "Creative things? What kind of creative things?"

A rush of blood rose to Madeleine's cheeks. She wished she hadn't brought up the subject. "I don't know," she replied evasively. "Whatever catches their fancy, I suppose."

"Needlework is creative," Lady Sophie suggested.

"Needlework is a fine pursuit," Lady Trevelyan agreed. "As are music, drawing, and painting in watercolors. These are the accepted creative outlets for a lady. And they do not require a college education."

Madeleine could see that she would get nowhere with this line of dialogue. "Well, I hope my Vassar education will, at the very least, make my conversation at garden parties and the dinner table a little more interesting," she said lightly.

Saunders laughed. "I am sure it will."

To Madeleine's relief, the conversation turned to a more banal topic: the weather and the state of the roads. After some discussion about the horrid rain the day before, Lady Sophie observed, "I am so pleased that the sun is out again. I was thinking of going for a walk along the beach."

"A fine day for it." Lady Trevelyan gave her son a meaningful look. "Charles, why do not you accompany Sophie?" As an afterthought, she added, "Of course, Miss Atherton must go as well. I am sure she would like to see our beautiful coastline."

Lord Saunders wiped his mouth and put down his napkin. "A splendid notion, Mother. Wish I could, but I must see Father straightaway. Following that I have a great deal to do, as it is my first day home. Forgive me, Sophie. Perhaps another time?"

With that he stood, bid them all a good morning, and quit the room.

Lady Sophie watched him go, disappointment in her gray eyes. After a moment, she let out a small sigh. "He is always so busy. But I understand, his duties must come first." Turning to Madeleine, she added with a smile, "I should be most delighted if you would care to accompany me on my walk this morning, Miss Atherton."

"Thank you," Madeleine replied. "That would be delightful."

CHAPTER FIVE

The old man looked very ill indeed.

Wrong. He is not so very old, Charles corrected himself as he sat at his father's bedside, worry serving to tamp down the irritation he usually felt in the man's presence. *He is only fifty-eight years of age.*

It was his father's pale complexion, his overall appearance of fatigue, and the way his facial features were contorted in apparent pain, that made him seem a good twenty years older.

"So damn sick of lying in bed all day, Charles. Cheer me up, boy. I want news."

"News? Well. We have a visitor."

Lord Trevelyan's bushy gray eyebrows lifted. "So your mother said. American girl, is she not? Sister to what's her name, from over at Polperran House?"

"Yes, Miss Madeleine Atherton." As Charles gave his father an overview of Miss Atherton's circumstances, his attention was drawn to the window, where he noticed the young lady in question, accompanied by Sophie, strolling across the back lawn in the direction of the coast. The two women made a pretty picture, chatting in the morning sunshine.

There was something about Miss Atherton's posture and gait as she walked that captured his interest. What was it? Ah, yes, he knew what it was. She didn't mince along demurely and delicately like Sophie and all the other women he knew. Miss Atherton took bold, deliberate strides, marching along with purpose. Almost like a man. It was refreshingly different and, to his surprise, rather charming.

He caught himself. He had no business studying Miss Atherton's gait, much less finding it *charming*. Despite himself, though, his eyes continued to focus on her alluring backside as she walked away.

The comments Miss Atherton had made at breakfast came back to him. She appeared to be very proud of her university education; and why shouldn't she be? The only other woman he had ever met who held a college degree was the young lady's sister, Alexandra. Charles still did not understand the point of higher education for women of their stature, any more than his mother did; but if it made the Atherton sisters happy, then so be it.

He was intrigued by what Miss Atherton had said about her interest in creative endeavors. She had seemed uncomfortable after bringing it up, though, and unwilling to elaborate. He wondered what lay behind it. Did she—

"Strange creatures, do not you agree?"

His father's voice broke into his thoughts. Charles realized he had missed part of the conversation. "I beg your pardon?"

"I said, these American girls are such strange creatures. So wild. One never knows what they are going to say or do next."

Charles had to admit, many of the American women he had met in town did tend to speak with less reticence than their English counterparts. If his few conversations with Miss Atherton were any indication, she also had a tendency to blurt out whatever was on her mind. "Well," he said with a shrug, "I agree that some Americans can be outspoken, but I do not know that I would call them strange."

"They are! Nothing even remotely British about them! They come from such an untamed country. Thank God you did not marry that Townsend girl, Charles. You got a lucky escape there."

Miss Townsend, again. It was the second time in as many days that someone had brought her up. Was he to spend the rest of his life being reminded of that unfortunate affair? On the night in question, he'd been thinking with his cock, not his brain. Charles had vowed that he would never again find himself in a similar situation—that he would never again allow a woman to take advantage of him in a moment of weakness. "I did indeed," he solemnly agreed.

His father heaved a sigh, rubbing his cheek with his hand. "Does not look as though *I* am going to be so lucky. No escape for me."

"Do not say that, Father." Charles's other worries vanished from his mind, replaced by this more pressing anxiety. "You *will* get well." He might not get along with the old man at times, but he didn't want him to die.

"Why pretend? My belly aches something fierce, all the time. Now my teeth hurt. I have cramps in my legs. Tingling in my hands and feet. And I am so damned tired."

"You have had these complaints many times over the years. You always came back from it. Surely this is no different?"

"This is worse than ever before." Lord Trevelyan looked him in the eye. "Dr. Hancock thinks it is cancer."

Charles's pulse skittered with alarm. "There must be something he can do."

"The man has tried everything. Nothing brings me any relief. I thought I should have . . . I *hoped* for another good twenty years at least. But I fear this will be the end of me."

"It will not." The threat of tears burned behind Charles's eyes and he blinked rapidly, refusing to let his father see any sign of weakness. "You will rally."

"I cannot fight my own body, son." His father readjusted the covers around himself, as if wishing to hide his ailing form from view. "I *can*, however, take advantage of whatever time I have left to tell you what I expect to take place when I am gone."

Charles swallowed hard over the lump in his throat. "Yes, sir?"

"Item one: I have done my best to maintain the house and estate, but you will be caretaker now. Do well by it. Keep the mine going, Charles. Do right by our tenants. Preserve the Trevelyan legacy for future generations. It is your duty."

"I understand, sir." Charles's voice now sounded so strangled to his own ears, he scarcely recognized it.

"Item two: Take care of your mother and sisters. Provide

the girls with dowries. Be good to your brother. He is still young and will need your guidance."

"Yes, sir."

His father gave him another direct look and intoned sternly, "Item three: Promise me you have *given up* that silly hobby of yours."

"Father—" Charles began, frustration now curling in his gut.

"I permitted it when you were a child. But an earl cannot engage in such useless activity. And for the Marquess of Trevelyan? It is quite out of the question."

Charles wanted to defend himself. His work—the inventions he created—gave his life meaning. His mind never stopped working even when he was away from it, and he was always itching to get back to it. In his youth, he'd tried so hard to get his father to appreciate his interests and passions, seeking the man's approval, all in vain. Finally, he'd given up trying. For years now, he'd had to work in secret.

If only he could show his father what he was doing. If only he could make him see its value. But he realized it was of no use. The Marquess of Trevelyan would never understand, would never change his opinion—and he might be dying.

Lowering his eyes, Charles gave what he hoped would pass for a nod.

"Item four," his father went on.

"There is more?"

A determined gleam lit his father's eyes as he said: "Promise me that you will make your mother happy, and marry Sophie."

Madeleine inhaled the brisk, salty sea air of the sheltered cove with a smile. Craggy black cliffs towered above them, beneath a bright blue sky dotted with puffy clouds.

As she and Lady Sophie walked along, their low boots made indentations in the wide stretch of beach that spread out around them like a golden fan. Nearby, waves crested in furls of white foam, dashing against dark rocks that were scattered across the sea. Other waves rushed up just a few yards from them, wetting the sand and receding, in nature's continuous cycle.

"This is breathtaking," Madeleine enthused.

"Isn't it?" Lady Sophie agreed. "Walking on the beach is one of my favorite things to do here. Where I grew up in Hampshire, we were nowhere near the sea."

"The same for me. Before we moved to New York City, my hometown was upstate on the Hudson River, but miles from the ocean."

"I have never been to America. What is it like?"

"It's a big country full of people with big ideas. Every day, it seems, someone comes up with a new invention or a new way to change and improve things."

"There must be a great many clever people in America."

"There are. Ambitious people, too."

"Well, you are my first American friend, ever." Lady Sophie smiled. "I am so glad you have come, even if it is only for a short while. It is splendid to have a companion close to my own age."

"I feel the same," Madeleine admitted.

"Trevelyan Manor is one of my favorite places in the world. I adore Aunt Charlotte and Uncle George. And my cousins Helen and Anna."

Madeleine gave her a sideways glance. "I suspect there is someone else you adore, as well?"

A rosy hue crept over Lady Sophie's cheeks. "Is it that obvious?"

"Perhaps only to me," Madeleine replied kindly.

Lady Sophie sighed gently. "I think I have loved Charles all my life."

"*All* your life?"

She nodded. "My parents and I used to spend a month here every summer. Aunt Charlotte was my father's only sister, and she and Mother and Father were very close. It has been their stated wish, I think from the day of my birth, that Charles and I would marry when I became of age. My earliest memories are of digging in the sand with Charles here on this beach. He is so handsome and clever. I have never thought of him in any other terms than as my future husband."

Madeleine pondered this information, surprised. She had supposed that the idea of a union between Lord Saunders and Lady Sophie had come about rather recently. At the very least, *after* his failed elopement with Miss Townsend. And yet, it seemed the families had wished for this for over two decades, which made his misdeed seem even worse. She wondered, too, if Lady Sophie even knew about the Miss Townsend affair. And about Lord Saunders's other rumored affairs in town. It would be dreadful, Madeleine thought, to be in love with and waiting for a man who dallied with everyone in a skirt.

"What a wonderful history you two have shared," Madeleine noted carefully.

"Yes. It was not always perfect. I am seven years younger, and for the longest time Charles just seemed annoyed with me. I was the little girl cousin with whom he was obliged to play. Then on my sixteenth birthday, he gave me a gift." She pulled back the sleeve of her blouse to reveal a delicate bracelet made of interwoven strands of bright copper.

"How lovely," Madeleine said. It truly was.

"I treasure it and wear it always. The day he gave it to me, he kissed me." Her cheeks bloomed pink again. "I have never looked at another boy since. Never. During my one Season in town, I felt guilty, as though Papa's money was being wasted, because he and Mama wished for me to wed Charles, and so did I. None of the gentlemen I met could hold a candle to him. But a debut was absolutely necessary in the eyes of society. We all expected Charles to offer for me that summer, but he did not. Instead, he . . . that was the summer that—" Darting Madeleine an embarrassed glance, she went on: "That summer, he took up with someone else. An American woman."

"I heard about that," Madeleine said softly. "That must have been painful for you to endure."

"It was."

Madeleine's heart went out to her. "I experienced that kind of pain myself," she admitted, "at the same age."

"Did you?"

"It happened at my debut ball in New York." Madeleine

concentrated on the acrobatic feats of two seagulls circling overhead, trying not to think about the heartache she had endured on that occasion.

"What happened to the young man?"

"He married someone else."

"Oh. I am so sorry." Lady Sophie bit her lip, then said, "I hope it will turn out differently for me."

Madeleine touched the young lady's arm gently. "Perhaps it will. He did not marry that other woman, after all."

Lady Sophie nodded. "And I do not blame him for what he did."

"Don't you?"

"No. By all accounts, she was beautiful and wealthy, whereas I have no fortune, nothing to recommend me but our family ties. In the end, all I really want is for Charles to be happy. I like to *think* he will be happy with me. But he must come to that decision himself."

Well. Lady Sophie is a far more forgiving person than I.

"I believe that episode was an aberration," Lady Sophie went on. "Charles is such a good and generous man. He would never hurt me or anyone else deliberately. Shall I give you an example of his goodness?"

"By all means."

"When Papa died, I cried for months. I missed him so, and our future was so uncertain." A faraway sadness came over Lady Sophie's face. "Lord Trevelyan and one of my other uncles gave us financial assistance, but it was not enough, and we did not wish to ask for more. Then money began arriving from an anonymous source, which made our lives ever so much more comfortable. We later learned that Charles had been providing the funds from his own allowance."

Hmm. Here was a side to Lord Saunders that Madeleine had never imagined. And, she thought begrudgingly, it spoke well of him. "That was kind and generous of him. He must think very highly of you."

"That is what Mama said. The last time I was here, two years ago, Mama was so bold as to ask his intentions. She went up to him and said, 'Charles, what are your plans for the future? Do you intend to marry my daughter?'"

Madeleine gasped. It sounded like something her own mother would do. "What did he say?"

"Mama said he went red in the face and told her that he greatly esteemed me, and did indeed have intentions in that direction, but he was not yet ready to settle down."

"Well! That sounds as close to a promise as I've ever heard." Madeleine remembered what Lord Saunders had told her the night before: *I want to do my duty*. Rake that he was, he might have dozens of affairs with other women before he got around to doing that duty, but hopefully he would eventually make good on his *intentions* to *settle down*. Madeleine gave Lady Sophie a smile. "I suppose you must just be patient."

"I know. I am trying. But yesterday, he did not seem particularly happy to find me here." Lady Sophie sighed. "Oh, Miss Atherton! Sometimes I feel as though I am caught in the middle of the sea, forever treading water. My life will not begin until Charles and I are wed."

"That is not true." Madeleine shook her head as they walked, the sand soft beneath her feet.

"A single woman of twenty-two has no real status," Lady Sophie countered, "and so little to do."

"Surely you have interests and pursuits that you enjoy?"

Lady Sophie nodded. "I do. Every morning, I play the piano for an hour before breakfast. If the weather is fine I take a long walk or I ride. Every day, I write letters to my mother or my friends back home. After lunch I take a nap. Late afternoons and evenings I devote to needlework, or play cards. Sometimes I read." She looked at Madeleine. "I suppose that sounds rather dull to you, being a college graduate."

"Not at all. I enjoy all those things, too—except for needlework," Madeleine admitted with a laugh. "Although I admire the finished product, I don't have the patience or the attention span to stitch anything decorative myself. But! I love nothing better than a good gallop on a fine horse, and a long walk in a beautiful spot like this is paradise to me." She lifted her face to the warmth of the sun, delighting in the sounds of the crashing waves and squawking gulls.

Lady Sophie linked one arm through Madeleine's affectionately. "Someday, when we are both married, you and Lord Oakley must come to visit us, and we can walk here together every day."

An image presented itself to Madeleine's mind: Lady Sophie strolling arm-in-arm with Lord Saunders, and herself similarly positioned with Lord Oakley. For some reason, the idea brought a twinge of discomfort. "I would like that, Lady

Sophie," Madeleine said with a determined smile, as they turned and headed back toward the path leading up to the bluffs.

Lord Saunders was absent for lunch. Following the meal, while Lady Sophie went upstairs to nap, Madeleine returned to her own room, thinking it would be the ideal time to write.

Removing her manuscript from the tapestry bag, she grabbed a handful of blank paper from the stash she'd brought and sat down at the escritoire, excited at the prospect of working on her book again. But as she picked up a pen and prepared to dip it into the inkwell, she discovered that her mind was a blank. So much time had passed since she'd last written, she couldn't remember what had been happening in her story at the point she'd left off.

She read through a portion of her outline and the last chapter of her manuscript, trying to recapture its essence and flow. But she felt no connection to it. It wasn't the first time this had happened. She knew what she needed to do—a solution that always worked when there had been too long a gap between writing sessions. She needed to find a quiet place, free of distraction, where she could think, dream, and plan. And take notes. Lots and lots of notes.

Her gaze drifted to the window, where the blue sky and green gardens beckoned. It was too beautiful a day to spend inside, in any case. What better place to dream and take notes, than in the garden?

By the basin and ewer, Madeleine found a wicker basket filled with soaps, lotions, and small towels. She emptied it and replaced its contents with a book, several pencils, and a stack of writing paper. Then she pinned on her hat and ventured out into the gardens, where she wandered for a while, looking for a good spot to work. In time, she found it: a stone bench on the edge of a wooded area in the shade of a giant tree, overlooking a stone fountain.

The fountain was large, a good twenty feet across, embellished by stone dolphins and a statue of Neptune spouting water from its center.

Madeleine sat on the bench, balanced a fresh piece of paper on a book on her lap, and took out a pencil. The rustle of the breeze in the nearby trees and the sounds of the splashing fountain were a soothing backdrop as she focused on her novel-in-progress. It was slow going at first, but the ideas soon began to come so fast and furiously that she could barely keep up. Her pencil flew, filling page after page with thoughts, notes, imagined scenes, and dialogue, until her pencil grew dull and she had to replace it with another.

She'd worn down the second pencil, and was reaching into the basket to retrieve yet another, when a sudden gust of wind blew up, flinging her stack of papers up into the air.

"No!" Madeleine leapt to her feet, watching in distress as all her notes danced and whirled on the breeze, and then plunged into the fountain. "No!" she cried again.

Bending over the edge of the fountain, Madeleine tried to grab one of the pages, but they were all too far away. She was tempted to take off her shoes and wade into the fountain, but realized that was impossible. The water looked to be at least four feet deep. She'd get soaked completely and ruin her clothes.

A voice broke the stillness. "Miss Atherton!"

She turned to find Lord Saunders appearing from around a bend, carrying his folded coat as he busily rolled down his shirt-sleeves. He hurried forth, surprised to see her, taking in the dozens of pages floating in the fountain. "What on earth? Has it been raining paper?"

"It has," Madeleine replied with a sigh, "and strangely only in this small hemisphere."

"What are they?"

"My notes."

"Notes? For what?"

"Something I'm . . . planning," she said, unwilling to go into more detail.

"That is a *lot* of notes. What are you planning? Your schedule of appointments for the next five years?"

Madeleine felt a smile tugging at her lips. "I couldn't plan that far ahead if I tried."

"Your itinerary for a trip around the world?"

Now she laughed. "Sorry, nothing quite so exciting or glamorous."

He looked at her. "I take it these notes are important to you?"

"Yes. I've been working on them for hours."

"Did you write in ink?"

"Pencil."

"Then they might be salvageable." Setting his coat on the bench, he glanced around, as if seeking inspiration. His gaze landed on the basket she'd brought. "Empty that basket for me, will you?" He picked up a stone about the size of a baseball and handed it to her. "You might use this to weigh down the rest of those pages. I will be back in a moment."

"What do you mean to do?" she asked.

"I mean to construct a device," he answered, "to rescue drowning notes which have floated out of reach."

Chapter Six

From the nearby woods, Charles secured a long, slender branch from which he snapped off extraneous twigs and leaves. After removing one of his shoelaces, he used it to snugly tie the handle of the basket Miss Atherton had brought to the far end of the branch.

She watched with apparent fascination as Charles extended his newly fashioned apparatus over the surface of the water in the fountain and then, with careful aim, scooped up one of the half-drowned notes.

"How clever," Miss Atherton said.

"One down. Twenty or thirty to go," Saunders replied.

"Thank you for doing this."

"I am glad to be of service."

They said nothing more for some minutes as Charles dipped the makeshift scoop in and out of the water, rescuing the pages. He had no idea what the notes were about, but they mattered to *her* and were therefore worthy of retrieval.

His focus, as he worked, kept shifting from his activity

to Miss Atherton herself. Was it chance or fate that had brought them both to this spot at the exact same moment? From his first glimpse of her, leaning over the edge of the fountain, the raspberry hue of her gown reflected in the sparkling water like some exotic flower, he'd felt another frisson of attraction. He felt it still.

She was entrancing. He reminded himself yet again that he had no business being entranced. She was the opposite of what his parents wanted for him, the opposite of what he wanted for himself. She was very nearly promised to a friend of his. And more importantly, Charles had given *his* promise to his father that he would ask Sophie to marry him before the summer was over. What choice did he have? After a lifetime of trying and failing to please his father, this was the one thing Charles could do to make him happy, and he must do it before it was too late. Before the old man died.

Which meant he had only a few short months in which to immerse himself in his work and try to make some real progress, unencumbered by the expectations and demands of a fiancée or wife.

As he retrieved the notes from the fountain, he glanced again at Miss Atherton, who was trailing her hand in the water. Although she was off limits in any romantic sense, that didn't mean he couldn't befriend her. She had never been far from his mind since the previous afternoon, when he had brought her home from the train station.

The accusation she had thrown at him in the carriage haunted him.

How could you betray your best friend?

Despite her apology the evening before, Charles sensed that Miss Atherton still thought less of him due to that episode. He had never expected to have an opportunity to discuss it with her again. Yet here they were, alone together. She seemed to be a modern woman, who wouldn't be squeamish about such things. It was the perfect moment to set the record straight.

Charles cleared his throat. "Miss Atherton. I am pleased that I ran into you."

"As am I. I so appreciate your help with this."

"Yes, well. Apart from the satisfaction I derive from demonstrating my paper-rescuing skills . . . in fact, I have been hoping for an opportunity to speak to you."

"Have you?"

"I have been thinking about our conversation yesterday in the coach. A topic was brought up. Do you recall it?"

Miss Atherton sat down on the rim of the fountain and looked at him. "We discussed a great many things."

"We did. But it troubles me to think that your opinion of me has been tainted by a . . . particular matter."

From her expression, he deduced that she had guessed what this was about. "Do you really care so much about my opinion, my lord?"

"I do. You asked me how I could have ever stooped so low as to betray my best friend."

She flushed slightly. "I don't believe I used those precise words—"

"The implication was there. Perhaps aptly so. But I cannot help but wonder if you have heard the whole story. I wish to rectify that, if I may."

"All right. I'm listening."

"I am not sure what Longford or the countess may have told you on the subject?"

"It only came up once, to be honest. Thomas refused to talk about it, except to say that he'd forgiven you. My sister wouldn't say much, either. But I got the gist of it. Alexandra said that Miss Townsend, although affianced to Thomas, apparently set her sights higher. She was determined to be a marchioness. So she . . . she . . ." Her cheeks grew almost as pink as her dress, and she seemed reluctant to say more.

"Forgive me. Perhaps I should not have brought up the subject. I realize it is a delicate one."

"No," she said, recovering her composure. "It is I who originally asked the question. I'd really like to hear what you have to say." With more confidence, she went on, "I am aware of the facts, Lord Saunders. About what happened between you and Miss Townsend during a party at the manor house. But that is no excuse. You could, and should, have refused her advances."

"You are absolutely right. I should have. I know what I did was wrong. Admittedly, alcohol had compromised my judgment that evening, but I fully shoulder the blame and do not wish to make excuses for myself." He scooped more notes from the fountain, then turned to her. "It is what happened afterward that I wish to explain."

"Afterward?"

"After . . . what happened, I felt my obligation to Miss Townsend overruled any loyalty I had to Thomas. That is why I offered to marry her."

"So you're saying you sailed to America with her, basically, to protect her reputation?"

"Yes. To make the situation more . . . palatable, I suppose, I convinced myself that I felt something for her. But it soon became clear to both of us that our regard was unfounded, and we were unsuited. Thankfully, there were no . . . lasting repercussions from our one evening together. Even so, I waited until that had been definitively proven, before breaking things off amicably and returning home."

"I see." Miss Atherton seemed to be processing that. "And what about your cousin?"

"Do you mean Sophie?"

She nodded.

"I had made no promise to Sophie yet, nor have I since."

"But you have an *understanding*, don't you? She and your parents have hoped, expected you to wed her for many years."

He nodded. "True." Letting go a sigh, he added, "I regret any pain which I may have caused my cousin over that affair. I have beaten myself up over it more times than I can count, Miss Atherton. If I could take it all back, I would."

Madeleine fell silent, thinking about what Lord Saunders had told her. It was the first time she'd ever held such a frank discussion with a man, on a topic so intimate. On *any* topic, for that matter. She felt special that he'd chosen to confide in her.

"Thank you for sharing that, Lord Saunders. It doesn't

forgive everything you did. But it does put a somewhat different light on things."

"I am relieved to hear you say so."

Madeleine didn't know why her opinion mattered to him, but was flattered that it did. She felt, now, as though she'd rushed to a judgment about him without knowing all the facts. "I guess I can understand now why Thomas forgave you."

Saunders scooped up the last of the notes from the fountain. She was impressed by the device he'd created. It was simple, yet ingenious. As he untied the dripping basket from the branch, she found herself admiring his hands. They were strong, manly hands, dusted with brown hair. An idle thought crossed her mind. What would it feel like to touch those hands, or to have them touch her? She suddenly grew hot under her collar. *What am I doing thinking about his hands?*

"Longford refused to speak to me for three years," he was saying. "It was only at your sister's insistence that he listened to my side of the story. So you see, I am in your family's debt."

"And I am in *your* debt, my lord." She cleared her throat and accepted the basket from him. "Thank you again for rescuing these."

"It was my pleasure." Sitting down on the nearby bench, he began rethreading his shoelace into his shoe. "I hope it was worth it."

"Oh, it was." Madeleine examined a few of the sodden pages. "Thank goodness, they're still readable." Even so, it was going to take great effort to dry them all out.

"What are the notes for, if I may ask?"

Madeleine considered making something up. She rarely discussed this with anyone. But after what he'd done for her, and the personal revelation he'd just made, she felt he deserved to know the truth. "If I tell you, will you promise not to say anything to anyone?"

"You have my solemn vow of secrecy."

"They're for a book I'm writing." She braced herself for the remark that would surely follow. *Why on earth would you, a woman and an heiress, waste your time writing a book?* It's what everyone always said.

"A book?" He looked at her, astonished. "You are writing a book?"

"I am. A novel."

"Indeed? But that is remarkable." He finished tying his shoe and stood. Then he slid his arms into his coat and buttoned it up, eyeing her with undisguised amazement. "I have never met anyone who has written a novel. Have you always been fond of writing?"

"Yes, ever since I was a child."

"I wish you much luck with it."

"Thank you." The fact that he hadn't made a negative comment about her endeavor—in fact, seemed to see it as a positive undertaking—came as a pleasant surprise.

"What is your book about?"

Again, Madeleine wanted to evade the question. The story was far too personal, and she dreaded being ridiculed. But he had just bared *his* soul to her, after all. "It's about two American women whose father becomes obscenely rich overnight. This thrusts them into a level of social prominence that they must learn to navigate, while still trying to stay true to themselves." Saying it aloud, Madeleine felt embarrassed, and wished she'd kept the information to herself.

"Interesting. I imagine it would be a very popular book."

"Do you?"

"I think most people imagine that wealth and social prominence guarantees a life of ease. They have no conception that these same privileges can be challenges as well. To some, rather than bringing one happiness, they can be a burden." His observation seemed to be deeply felt, a subject about which he held a keen and personal connection.

"My sentiments exactly." Madeleine was intrigued to hear him say this. She had never imagined a man like him could understand how she felt, not to mention share a similar conviction. "My mother thinks the idea is completely awful and the entire enterprise a waste of time. Worse yet, it embarrasses her, because society looks down on women authors."

"Society can be brutal. Its rules are often limiting and shortsighted. And parents do not always understand the wants and needs of their children."

Again, she suspected a deeper meaning behind his words. She was trying to phrase a proper reply, but lost her chance when he pulled out his pocket watch and gestured in the direction of the house.

"We had best get on. I was on my way to the house for tea. Mother is a stickler for teatime, and we are already ten minutes late."

"Are we? Oh dear." They began walking together down the path. "Where were you coming from?"

He hesitated, then said, "The stables. I was visiting a tenant."

Something about the way he said it made her think he was being less than candid. There was something else about their circumstances—the way he'd looked when she first caught sight of him—that suddenly didn't feel right. But she couldn't put her finger on it.

Nodding toward the basket she carried, he went on, "I suggest you give that to Woodson when we get back."

"Isn't that rather out of his job description?"

"Woodson considers everything to be in his job description. If anyone can save those wet pages for you, he can."

"But I wouldn't want anyone to know about this. Or to read my notes."

"Woodson is the soul of discretion."

She nodded. "All right then."

The path that led through the manicured flower gardens was just wide enough for two. As they walked along, Madeleine was suddenly, disconcertingly, aware of Saunders's proximity. Aware of his pleasant, masculine scent. She had a strong urge to inhale deeply, to see if she could identify the name of the woodsy cologne he wore.

Stop it, Madeleine.

Yesterday, she had struggled at the very idea of sharing a carriage with this man. Today, she'd been staring at his hands like a schoolgirl, and wondering how his skin smelled. It was ridiculous. It wasn't right or proper. The man was going to marry Lady Sophie.

And she wasn't supposed to be thinking about him at all. She was supposed to be thinking about Lord Oakley.

"There you are, at last," Lady Trevelyan called out, as Madeleine and Lord Saunders crossed the saloon to where she and Lady Sophie were seated.

Woodson had been only too happy to take over the project of drying out Madeleine's notes, promising to return them intact and freshly pressed the next morning. Madeleine and Saunders had then hurried in to tea, apologizing for their tardiness.

"I ran into Miss Atherton in the garden," Saunders explained, "and we became so engaged in a conversation about literature, we forgot the time. You are looking well, Mother. Is Father coming down?"

"I believe so," was Lady Trevelyan's cheerful reply.

Madeleine greeted her hostess and Lady Sophie, then sat down. Saunders bowed and kissed Lady Sophie's hand. "I trust you had a pleasant day, Sophie?"

"I did, thank you." Sophie smiled, her eyes fixed on his.

"Woodson, you may pour now," Lady Trevelyan directed.

As Lord Saunders took a seat nearby, Woodson poured tea and a footman served poppy-seed cake and scones. Madeleine couldn't help but murmur her delight as she bit into a scone, which was light, fluffy, and delicious, complemented to perfection by its toppings of sweet butter, cream, and strawberry jam.

Saunders glanced her way in amusement. "I see you enjoy our Cornish tea, Miss Atherton?"

"Oh yes," Madeleine admitted, "I *adore* it."

A few minutes later, to Madeleine's further delight, Lady

Trevelyan's daughters entered the room. They were accompanied by a plump, fortyish woman, whom Madeleine presumed to be their governess. The woman silently curtsied to Lady Trevelyan and Lord Saunders before leaving.

The Grayson girls were both brunettes, like their mother and brother, and wore frocks that were the height of fashion. In other respects, they were a study in contrasts. Helen stood silently to one side with clasped hands and hooded eyes, darting only the merest glimpse at the occupants of the room, as if she were determined to appear grown-up, even though she was just fifteen.

Anna, who Madeleine recalled was eleven years old, bubbled over with enthusiasm. She rushed straight up to Lord Saunders, who leapt to his feet as they embraced. "Charles! I am so glad you are home! Why were you away so long? We missed you terribly!"

"I missed you as well, Anna," Lord Saunders said, chuckling, then added, "Hello, Helen. How are you?"

Helen remained where she stood and uttered a brief "Hello."

"How is my favorite youngest sister?" Saunders asked, eyeing Anna warmly.

"I am fine! Have you heard? Mama is talking about holding a birthday ball!" To her mother, she went on effusively, "You *are* going to have the ball, aren't you Mama? And it *will* be a fancy dress ball, the way you have always wanted?"

"We shall see," Lady Trevelyan replied. "It all depends on how your father is feeling."

"Well then he *must* get better *very soon!*" Anna noticed Madeleine now, and crossed to her with a friendly smile. "Hello. Miss Berry said we had a visitor. I think we have met before, but I have forgotten when. Who are you again?"

Madeleine laughed and reintroduced herself.

"Oh yes! I remember now. You were at the wedding at Polperran House last autumn. You are from America."

"I am," Madeleine concurred. "It is lovely to see you again, Lady Anna. And you, Lady Helen."

Helen said nothing.

"I would love to go to America." Anna sighed.

"Maybe you will one day." Madeleine gave her a smile.

Anna skipped back to her brother and cried: "So, Charles! What have you brought us from London?"

"Ah. So you are only happy to see me if I brought you a gift?"

"No," Anna replied sweetly, "but you did promise us a gift from town upon your return."

"So I did. And I never break my word." Saunders reached into his coat pocket and withdrew two small packages, each about the size of a playing card, which were wrapped in brown paper and tied with string, and inscribed with his sisters' names. He handed one to each.

Anna caught her breath in excitement. "May we open them now?"

Even Helen had a hint of eagerness in her eyes.

"Wait a moment. I have two more to distribute." From his other pocket, he withdrew two similar packages, and gave one to his mother.

"Charles! What is the occasion?" Lady Trevelyan asked.

"No occasion. I simply hoped to make you smile." Giving the last package to Lady Sophie, he added, "I thought to give this to you the next time I saw you. It appears to be that time."

"Thank you, Charles."

To Madeleine, he added: "Forgive me for leaving you out, Miss Atherton. I had no idea you would be here."

Madeleine waved off his apology with a laugh. "Don't give it another thought."

"*Now?*" Anna asked, nearly bursting with anticipation.

"Yes, now," Saunders replied.

All four ladies simultaneously ripped off the paper and string from their gifts, to reveal decorative hairpins fashioned out of shiny copper wire, and embellished with tiny stones.

"Oh," Lady Sophie murmured. "How lovely."

"They're all different," Helen noted with delight.

"Mine is a bird!" Anna cried. "Charles, did you make—" She stopped herself, glancing at Lady Sophie and Madeleine before turning her gaze on her brother, as if unsure whether to finish her sentence.

"How thoughtful, Charles," Lady Trevelyan intervened quickly. "Where ever did you find these?" There was something odd about her expression and tone as she said it.

"From an artisan at a street market," he replied smoothly.

Helen and Anna were staring at the floor. Something felt off—but what? Lady Sophie was the only one who was acting normal.

"Thank you, dear," Her Ladyship announced cheerfully, studying the hairpins. "You know us so well. A robin for Anna, a flower for Helen, and a tree branch for me. What does yours have, Sophie?"

"A butterfly," Lady Sophie answered with pleasure.

"Thank you!" his sisters said in unison, giving him a hug, which he returned with warmth. Lady Trevelyan and Lady Sophie expressed their thanks with grateful smiles and pecks on his cheek.

"You are most welcome." Saunders's face glowed under their praise as he reseated himself.

"Isn't it lovely?" Anna said, bringing her hairpin over to Madeleine to admire.

"It's truly exquisite," Madeleine observed. The copper hairpin was clearly handmade, by someone who was highly skilled at working with metal wire.

She considered the strange mood in the room, when Anna had asked her aborted question. It was almost as if Lord Saunders had made these lovely hairpins himself, and everyone but Lady Sophie knew it—but the others were determined to hide it. Why?

Before she could wonder about this further, a deep male voice called out, "Here I am! What have I missed?"

Lord Trevelyan, seated in a wheelchair with a blanket over his legs, was being pushed into the room by a nurse. He looked pale and gaunt, but nevertheless was smiling.

Lady Sophie instantly rose and glided over to him. "Hello, Uncle George. How are you feeling?"

"Been better, thank you, lambkin." Catching sight of Madeleine, Lord Trevelyan motioned for the nurse to wheel him in that direction. "Who is this, now?"

"I told you, dear," Lady Trevelyan replied, "it is Lord Longford's sister-in-law, Miss Madeleine Atherton. She has come to stay for a few days."

"Ah, yes. The American, come over for the Season." The wheelchair stopped before her. Lord Trevelyan eyed Madeleine up and down beneath bushy gray eyebrows.

"Your Lordship. It is a pleasure to see you again."

Lord Trevelyan returned Madeleine's firm handshake. "What is this I hear? You have snagged the Marquess of Oakley?"

Madeleine laughed lightly. "He has made me an offer. I have not yet accepted."

"What are you waiting for? I know his father, the Duke of Courtenay. Capital fellow. Their estate in Sussex has lovely woods."

Why, Madeleine wondered, was everyone always talking about their woods? She was searching for a reply, when Lord Trevelyan noticed Anna struggling to hide something in the folds of her skirts.

"What have you got there, Anna?" he asked.

Anna blushed scarlet and held up the hairpin. "It is . . . a gift from Charles."

"Really. Let me see it." Lord Trevelyan gestured for the girl to bring it over. Anna hesitantly gave him the hairpin. As he studied it, his eyes darkened. He turned to Lord Saunders. "Where did this come from, Charles?"

Lord Saunders looked his father directly in the eye. "London."

"Is that so? Why, then, does it have such an uncanny resemblance to the kind of thing you used to make yourself?" Lord Trevelyan's voice dripped with disdain.

Aha, Madeleine thought.

"George," Lady Trevelyan admonished, "you know Charles has not made anything for years."

"I would wager he made *this*. How many others are there? Did he make one for all of you?"

Lady Trevelyan frowned. Helen held her hairpin behind her back. Lady Sophie looked confused and uncomfortable.

"Do not spoil a nice moment, George," Lady Trevelyan insisted softly. "The hairpins were a lovely gesture on Charles's part. I am certain he bought them, just as he says. Where on earth would he make such things, anyway?"

"He could *find* a way." To his son, Lord Trevelyan added, his ire rising, "Do you *swear* you did not make these?"

"How could I?" Saunders replied calmly, but his eyes were like flint. "You destroyed my workshop years ago."

"And I would do so again in a heartbeat! We are Graysons! We do not *make* things! That is an occupation for tradesmen!"

"So you have said, on occasions too numerous to count. Sir."

Madeleine felt bad for the ladies, who now seemed to feel guilty about the treasures they held. She felt even worse for Lord Saunders, whose body looked to be coiled with tension. If he really *had* made the hairpins, his reason for wishing it to remain a secret was now obvious. And his earlier comment was made even more clear:

Parents do not always understand the wants and needs of their children.

"Five generations in this house!" Lord Trevelyan was shouting, his face growing redder by the second. "I will not abide useless tinkering! Far beneath your station! Never again do I wish to see—"

Suddenly, Lord Trevelyan's facial features seemed to freeze. At the same time, the rest of his body began to twitch violently.

Madeleine gasped in shock as His Lordship fell sideways from his chair and tumbled heavily to the floor.

CHAPTER SEVEN

The clock ticked in the silent room. Every nerve in Charles's body felt as if it were on edge.

Dr. Hancock had been upstairs with his father for more than half an hour. The girls had been sent back up to the nursery. His mother and Sophie were focused on their embroidery, while Miss Atherton sat quietly, appearing to be lost in thought.

Was his father alive or dead? Charles hoped and prayed that it was the former.

And not just because, if his father passed away, all the responsibility for the estate would fall on Charles's shoulders. He could handle it if he had to—all the endless meetings, papers to sign, issues at the mine and outlying farms—even if it meant little or no time for the work he craved.

He didn't want the bastard to die because the bastard wasn't ready to go. *I hoped for another good twenty years at least*, his father had said. The man had a great zest for life. He might never understand his eldest son, but he made a damn fine marquess. The rest of the family adored him, and the tenants practically worshipped him. No man should be taken before his time.

Thank God they had a good medical man.

Although Dr. William Hancock was new to the parish, and young—he could not be a day over thirty—Charles liked and trusted him. So did his mother, which was all that mattered, really. With his dark hair and piercing eyes, Hancock exuded an air of calm capability and intelligence that Charles admired. He was a gentleman, the eldest son of a well-to-do landowner. He had trained in Edinburgh with the world's best and liked to keep abreast of everything new in medicine. If anyone could help his father, Charles believed it was Dr. Hancock.

Footsteps resounded in the corridor and Charles leapt to his feet. The ladies all looked up anxiously as Dr. Hancock strode into the room.

"Doctor?" Charles's mother cried. "Is he—?"

"I believe His Lordship suffered a seizure," Dr. Hancock announced. "I examined him thoroughly, and from what I can tell, it does not seem to have done any serious damage. I gave him a sedative, and he is resting comfortably."

Charles's mother let out a sigh of relief and sank back down onto the sofa. "Thank God it is no worse."

"What caused the seizure?" Charles inquired.

"It is hard to say," Dr. Hancock replied.

"Could it have been something he ate?" Lady Trevelyan asked. "It is so often after eating that Lord Trevelyan feels particularly ill."

"That is a concern," Dr. Hancock agreed, "but indigestion does not cause seizures. It could be any number of other things. I understand he was quite agitated at the time?"

With a flicker of guilt, Charles nodded. "He was."

"Well, then," Dr. Hancock responded.

"My uncle *will* be all right, won't he?" Sophie said, worried.

Hancock's eyes met Sophie's and he hesitated, his brow furrowing. "I do not wish to give anyone false hope, Lady Sophie. In truth, Lord Trevelyan has had a wide array of symptoms that do not fit any one known disease. However, rest assured: I am doing everything in my power to help him."

"Is there anything we can do, Doctor, to make him more comfortable?" Miss Atherton asked.

Dr. Hancock turned to her and held out his hand. "I do not believe I have had the pleasure. I am Dr. William Hancock."

"Forgive me," Charles said, quickly making the requisite introductions.

As the two shook hands, the doctor remarked, "Atherton? Are you perchance related to the Countess of Longford?"

"She is my sister," Miss Atherton answered with a smile.

"I thought I noted a resemblance. How nice to meet you. I am caring for Lady Longford during her confinement."

"How is she?" Miss Atherton asked. "I understand she's in Bath at the moment. It seems rather late in her pregnancy to make such a journey. I hope she's all right?"

"She is perfectly well, in my opinion," the physician assured her. "The earl, however, insisted on her taking the waters and seeking the advice of a colleague of mine at Bath. There is a direct train to Bath so the trip is only a matter of hours. I would not worry. In answer to your question about His Lordship, he just requires rest at present."

"Thank you, Doctor," Miss Atherton said.

Charles accompanied the physician to the front of the house, pausing in his study to take a guinea from the box in his desk drawer. After wrapping the money in paper, Charles discreetly set it down on a table in the foyer near the physician's hand, as per the custom.

Dr. Hancock scooped it up without comment, put it in his pocket, and replaced his hat on his head. They shook hands.

"Thank you for coming so quickly."

"I instructed the nurse in the specifics of your father's care," Hancock replied. "I will return tomorrow."

After the doctor left, Charles returned to the saloon and sat down. The women were embroiled in a discussion about the marquess, expressing their shared concerns for his welfare. His mother kept questioning what might have caused his father's illness. Miss Atherton suggested remedies that she had heard of being successful in similar cases.

Charles found himself tuning them all out. What was the point of all this endless debate? His father was ill. Hancock was in charge. Only time would tell if Father would recover or not. In the meantime, it was best to think about something else. Take one's mind off the worry.

Unfortunately, the *something else* that came to mind was that awful scene at tea.

Charles had thought today would be the perfect time to deliver the hairpins he had made. They were just a side project, a lark, something to give pleasure to the ladies in his life. The making of them had given *him* pleasure, as well. He'd had the excuse that he had just been to London, figured he could pass them off as purchased there.

No such luck. He had been obliged to lie, bald-faced, to his father. Again. So had his mother and sisters. They knew, of course. And knew better than to let on. This time, though, Father hadn't seemed to believe it.

Sophie knew about his "tinkering" when they were children. But she was so close to his father, and so practical and principled, Charles hadn't dared to confide in her about his latest activities. He had let her believe he'd given it all up years ago. She hadn't seemed to catch on earlier. He wasn't so sure about Miss Atherton, though, and wondered what she had read into the whole thing.

Miss Atherton.

He closed his eyes, recalling the moment he had come upon Miss Atherton that afternoon, by the fountain. The distress on her face had caught at his heart. He was pleased that he had been able to assist with her dilemma, and glad he'd had a chance to tell her the facts about Miss Townsend. She seemed to have rethought her opinion of him, which felt like a good thing. Their walk and talk as they returned to the house had been one of the highlights of his day.

It intrigued him to discover that she was fond of writing. His own projects took a certain amount of imagination and industry, but he couldn't begin to envision undertaking a task as complex as writing a novel. It proved she had both a creative mind and a drive to achieve, traits which he found appealing.

His gaze took her in where she sat a few yards away, chatting away with his mother. A beam of late afternoon sunshine filtered through the window, burnishing the highlights in her hair an even deeper shade of red. Her eyes were a lovely indigo blue, he noticed, like the sky on the verge between dusk and dark. And her skin—

Don't think about her skin.

The woman was all but engaged to Oakley, he reminded himself. Charles had already made the mistake of getting involved with the fiancée of a friend, an episode he would forever regret, and vowed he would never repeat. Not to mention his own obligations. With a dash of guilt, he glanced at Sophie, and caught her looking at him. She quickly refocused her attention on her needlework.

Best to stop thinking about Miss Atherton. Best to stay away from her entirely.

In truth, there was no point in sticking around here the next few days. The old man was upstairs, sedated. There was nothing Charles could do for him.

Work was waiting for him just a few miles away. Work he was itching to get back to.

The next morning, just as Madeleine was preparing to come downstairs, there came a discreet knock on her bedroom door. It was Woodson returning all her notes, which were now dry and looked to be freshly pressed. To her relief, her pencil scribblings were perfectly legible.

"Thank you so much, Woodson. I am in your debt."

"Think nothing of it, miss."

She asked after Lord Trevelyan's health.

"Thankfully he did not suffer any more seizures last night," Woodson told her, "but otherwise he appears to be much the same. He is keeping to his rooms today."

Lord Saunders didn't appear at breakfast. When Madeleine asked where he was, Lady Trevelyan replied indifferently, "I believe he has gone to Truro."

"Truro?" Madeleine repeated, as she buttered her toast. "Where is that?"

"It is a town some miles south of us."

"What does Charles do in Truro?" Lady Sophie asked as she cut into her kippered herring.

"His friend Leonard lives there," Her Ladyship responded. "He often visits Leonard for days at a time. What they do, I can only suppose. Drink? Ride? Play at billiards and cards? The kinds of things men do."

"Well," Lady Sophie commented with a smile, "he *is* a man. And men do require such outlets."

Madeleine studied the ladies seated across from her. Lady Sophie didn't appear to suspect that anything unusual was going on with Lord Saunders. Madeleine had the distinct impression, however, that Lady Trevelyan *did*, and was lying. This *Truro* story seemed to be a cover-up for wherever Lord Saunders had gone, and whatever he was really doing.

Madeleine had a suspicion what that might be. *Useless tinkering,* Lord Trevelyan had called it.

She would bet good money that Saunders had made those copper hairpins with his own hands. He was certainly clever enough. She couldn't forget how quickly he'd created a device to rescue her notes from the fountain. Her attention was drawn to the copper bracelet Lady Sophie was wearing, a gift she said he'd given her many years ago. Had Saunders made that, too? Was he a jewelry artisan?

How could I? You destroyed my workshop years ago.

The statement Saunders had made proved that, at one time, he *did* have a workshop and *did* make such things. He must have another workshop now, Madeleine decided. A secret workshop. But where? For obvious reasons, it couldn't be in the house.

She recalled his sudden appearance the day before at the fountain. She now realized what had seemed out of place about that moment. Saunders's coat had been folded over his arm, and he'd been in the act of rolling down his shirt-sleeves. He'd said he'd come from the stables, that he'd been visiting a tenant. But if that were true, would he have been so casually dressed? She doubted it.

They had walked straight from the fountain to the house for tea, where he had presented the hairpins as gifts. They'd been stowed in his coat pockets, ready to deliver. If he'd bought the hairpins in London, why would he have taken them on an errand to visit a tenant? No, Madeleine decided. He must have been returning from his workshop at the time.

She was curious about where said workshop was. Lady Trevelyan had mentioned a town called Truro. But if Truro was miles away, it seemed unlikely that he would have had time to ride there and back again and return in time for tea. Something told her that *if* he had a workshop, it was closer than that, perhaps somewhere on the property.

That afternoon, while Lady Sophie took her customary nap, Madeleine headed outside to investigate. She began by returning to the fountain and heading off in the direction from which he'd come. This, however, only led to the stables.

There was nothing suspicious about the stables. All the rooms were used for the care and maintenance of horses.

Madeleine struck out on a long walk around the estate, visiting parts she hadn't yet seen. It was a large property with many outbuildings, ancient barns, and sheds. To her disappointment, although she explored every structure she came upon, everything was either in use for some legitimate purpose or abandoned. On the outer rim of the estate she found a quaint, cozy-looking redbrick house and wondered if it might be the place she sought. But when she peered in the unshuttered windows, she saw the place was empty and uninhabited.

After three hours at her quest, with no sign whatsoever of an artisan's workshop, Madeleine gave up in defeat. On her way back to the house, though, she passed the stables again, and had an idea.

One of the grooms was brushing down a handsome stallion. Stopping to affectionately stroke the beast's velvety nose, Madeleine said hello to the stable boy, who tipped his hat in response. "Can you show me which horse belongs to Lord Saunders?" she asked.

"His horse not be here, miss," the lad replied.

"Oh? Where is it?"

"Lord Saunders rode off early this morning, miss."

"Do you know where he went?"

"Dunno, miss. I 'spect he went off to Truro, like always."

Truro, again. Madeleine thanked him and returned to the house, mulling over what she'd learned. If Saunders *had* a workshop, she was pretty sure it wasn't on the Trevelyan estate. He'd ridden off that morning. Maybe, Madeleine thought, she was just imagining things. Maybe he really *had* gone to Truro to see a friend.

Or maybe his workshop *was* in Truro. In which case, she was never going to find it.

Madeleine rose early the next morning, took out her manuscript, and sat down at her desk to write, grateful to have her notes in her possession. The thoughts and ideas she'd jotted down proved to be incredibly helpful. Next thing she knew, two hours had sped by and Martin was entering the room, surprised to find her awake.

Lord Saunders was still away. At breakfast, Woodson gave Madeleine a newly arrived telegram. She tore open the envelope, hoping it was from Alexandra. But it was from her mother.

TO: MISS MADELEINE ATHERTON
TREVELYAN MANOR, CORNWALL

OUTRAGED BY YOUR DEPARTURE. HAVE YOU
LOST YOUR SENSES? WRITE TO LORD OAKLEY
AT HATFIELD PARK AND ACCEPT HIM. THE
DUCHESS CAN FORWARD YOUR LETTER TO
HIM IN ITALY. RETURN TO LONDON AT ONCE.
   MOTHER

Madeleine sighed and shoved the message back into its
envelope.

"Is it bad news?" Lady Sophie asked with concern.

"It's exactly what I expected. My mother is upset. She wants
me to write and accept Lord Oakley and return to town."

"I understand her completely," Lady Trevelyan commented. "She is your mother. She wishes to see you happily
settled."

"I don't know if happiness has anything to do with Mother's
wishes," Madeleine replied. "But it's certainly paramount in
mine."

Would marriage to Lord Oakley make her happy? Could
she make *him* happy? Madeleine still wasn't sure. Her need to
speak to her sister was growing more urgent by the day. But
all she could do was wait.

After breakfast, Madeleine filled out a telegram form in
reply to her mother, which Woodson promised to have sent
from the local post office.

**TO: MRS. JOSEPHINE ATHERTON
BROWN'S HOTEL, LONDON**

CORNWALL IS LOVELY. STAYING HERE. WILL
GIVE OAKLEY MY ANSWER WHEN HE RETURNS
END OF SUMMER.
    MADELEINE

Having completed this task, Madeleine found herself anxious to get outdoors again. "Lady Sophie, what would you say to a ride this morning?"

"I should like nothing better," the young lady admitted.

They borrowed horses from the Trevelyan stables and rode along the beach. Madeleine had spent summers riding in her youth, and in preparation for their London debuts, her mother had insisted she and her sisters receive additional riding instruction. Lady Sophie was an equally experienced horsewoman. They enjoyed the refreshing sea air, exchanging memories about their youth, how different it had been for Lady Sophie growing up as an only child, taught by a governess, whereas Madeleine and her sisters had gone to school, and only (briefly) had a finishing governess many years later.

When they returned to the stables and dismounted, Madeleine said, "I really enjoyed that."

"So did I." Lady Sophie brushed back an errant lock of blond hair from her forehead. "Miss Atherton," she added, as they headed for the house, "I must tell you, even though we have only been acquainted a few days, I feel as if I have known you for years. You have become very dear to me."

"I feel the same way, Lady Sophie," Madeleine admitted with feeling.

"In the spirit of friendship, then—I hope you will not think this too bold—would you be open to the idea of dispensing with the formality of *my lady* and addressing each other by our given names?"

"I would like that."

Lady Sophie stopped and, smiling, held out a hand. "Please call me Sophie henceforth."

Madeleine took her hand and clasped it. "I will. And you must call me Maddie, as my sisters do."

After dinner that evening, after Sophie played the piano, Lady Trevelyan announced that she wished to play cards. In order to make up a foursome, Helen was invited to stay up past her usual bedtime and join them. Anna insisted that she must be among the party as well.

The small parlor rocked with laughter as Madeleine, Sophie, Helen, and Lady Trevelyan battled it out in a game of Hearts, while Anna sat nearby, looking at pictures on her stereoscope. The jolly gathering reminded Madeleine of similar, delightful evenings she'd spent with her mother and sisters in her youth. Even Helen got caught up in the competitive spirit of the game, at which she so excelled that she maintained the winning score all evening long.

Madeleine noticed that Lady Trevelyan and Sophie were both wearing the hairpins Lord Saunders had given them. Still wondering about their origin, she decided to fish for a little information.

After one particularly boisterous hand, Madeleine complimented them on the ornaments, and said, "It was sweet of Lord Saunders to present you with such lovely gifts."

"He is so thoughtful," Sophie agreed.

"I am only sorry that His Lordship disapproves," Madeleine observed.

Lady Trevelyan paused and glanced at her, as if carefully considering her reply. At length, she said discreetly, "Lord Trevelyan has high expectations for Charles, and he expects things to be done his way."

Madeleine decided to try a more direct approach. "I got the impression the other day," she said conversationally, as she shuffled the cards, "that Lord Saunders used to make things like those hairpins when he was younger."

Helen darted her mother a look, then lowered her eyes. Anna glanced up from her stereoscope, but said nothing.

"Charles has always been a clever boy," Lady Trevelyan answered. "He *used* to make all sorts of things."

"He fixed things, as well," Sophie remarked. "I remember once, when I was a girl, he repaired his own pocket watch."

"Of course, being a grown man and an earl," Lady Trevelyan pointed out quickly, "he can no longer indulge in such activities."

"Of course," Madeleine said, believing nothing of the kind.

"He does love to browse through street fairs and antique

shops, though." Lady Trevelyan touched the pin which orna-
mented her upswept hair, then gestured to a nearby chiffonier,
upon which rested a small metal sculpture of a tree. "He got
that for me for Christmas a few years ago."

Madeleine had spotted the sculpture upon entering the
room, and thought it beautiful. Now, knowing that it had been
a gift—or perhaps more than a gift—from Lord Saunders, her
curiosity was piqued. "May I take a look?"

"By all means."

Madeleine rose and crossed to the sideboard. The tree
sculpture stood about eight inches high. Made of copper
wire, it was both elegant and delicate, with branches that
appeared to be moving in the wind, and tiny seashells and
gemstones in the place of leaves. "What a lovely work of art,"
Madeleine enthused.

"It is not *half* as nice as my clockwork raven," Anna
commented.

"Clockwork raven?" Madeleine was intrigued.

Anna nodded vigorously. "Charles . . . gave it to me on my
tenth birthday."

"He gave *me* a clockwork giraffe," Helen announced
proudly.

"May we show them to her, Mother?" Anna asked, hope
in her eyes.

"I am certain Miss Atherton has no interest in your toys,"
Lady Trevelyan objected.

"I am most interested, I assure you," Madeleine insisted.
"I have never seen a clockwork raven or giraffe."

Lady Trevelyan hesitated. "Well then. Go on, girls."

Helen and Anna raced out of the room. Several minutes later, they breathlessly returned, each carrying a small sculpture about the size of her hand. The girls allowed Madeleine to hold and study their treasures in turn.

"My giraffe is called Frederick," Helen explained.

"Mine is just Raven," Anna stated happily.

"What fine names." Madeleine had been impressed by the hairpins and the sculpture of the tree, but these were even more intricate works of art. They had been fashioned from tiny pieces of metal of different sizes, shapes, and colors, as well as what looked like the parts of a watch or clock. Anna's raven had tiny wheels for feet and wing and tail feathers created from fragments of old metal rulers. Helen's giraffe was particularly clever, with articulating legs and neck.

"See how it moves?" Helen demonstrated the giraffe's working parts. "You can bend its head so it looks like it's drinking from a stream."

"Raven and Frederick are truly marvelous," Madeleine exclaimed. To think that Lord Saunders might have made these! And yet, if that were true, how sad it was that his family couldn't openly admit to his accomplishments. "How lucky you are to have such a thoughtful and generous brother."

And such a clever brother.

But Madeleine didn't say that aloud.

Chapter Eight

The following afternoon, Lady Trevelyan took Sophie to a dressmaker in the village to be measured for a new gown, and Madeleine walked out again on her own.

It was a cloudy day, but the sun peeked out at intervals. Madeleine was in a sunny mood herself. By her mother's decree, she *must* have fancy dresses, and this was one of her favorites: a pale yellow cotton lawn creation featuring numerous tucks and lace embellishments and a full twelve inches of pleated hem. Her shoes had been dyed to match, and her hat was fashionably small, adorned with ribbons and silk daisies.

Madeleine struck out from the house with anticipation, intending to keep to the gravel paths in the garden and revisit some of the favorite places she'd encountered on her earlier walks. But the cries of the seagulls and the salt tang in the air beckoned, and she soon found herself at the point where the property met the cliff overlooking the coastline.

She had been down to the beach several times, but had never ventured along the dirt path extending in both directions atop the bluffs. Madeleine knew she was wearing the wrong shoes for such an outing. But the expansive deep blue sea framed by the curve of the rugged cliffs made such an enthralling picture, she couldn't resist the opportunity to further explore the view.

Heading off to the south, Madeleine inhaled deeply. The sea air was invigorating. Wind rustled through the grass and nodded the heads of tiny pink flowers that bloomed like a carpet on either side of the path. Madeleine found it hard to believe that less than a week ago, she'd been in smoky, traffic-ridden London. She felt so free here. Part of her wished she could stay forever.

As she strolled, Madeleine's thoughts drifted to her sisters. Madeleine graduated from Vassar in early April, and her mother had whisked her away to New York City that same morning to prepare for their voyage abroad. That was the last time she'd seen Kathryn. She hadn't seen Alexandra since her wedding the autumn before. She missed them both dearly.

Growing up, they had talked about everything and rarely made a decision without consulting the others. A letter could never take the place of a personal conversation. Madeleine could hardly wait until she saw Alexandra again, to hash out the question that was hanging over her head: Should she, or should she not, marry Lord Oakley?

She recalled the night she and Oakley met, at the ball at Wellington House. She had noticed him immediately upon his arrival, a tall, good-looking man with ginger hair and an athletic build, who stood elegantly in his white tie and tails, as if unaware that the eyes of the entire female population of the room were upon him. As the eldest son of a duke, he was naturally the subject of much conversation and speculation. It was said that he was looking for a wife, and all the young ladies longed to dance with him.

Just before the first set began, Oakley arranged an introduction and asked her to dance. Madeleine's dance card had already been full except for one waltz toward the end of the evening, which she had given to him.

In the exhausting rush of dancing and making small talk with one partner after another, Madeleine had entirely forgotten about Lord Oakley, until he'd appeared before the designated set and held out his hand. He proved to be an excellent dancer, and his conversation was both gentlemanly and discreet.

She danced with Oakley at two more balls after that, sat beside him at two dinners, and he escorted her and her mother to the theater and the races. On each occasion, Madeleine had enjoyed his company. The four days that she and her mother had spent at his family estate had passed pleasantly. Although it was clear that Hatfield Park would benefit from an infusion of funds, Oakley had only mentioned Madeleine's fortune once, and seemed to admire her for who she was.

Madeleine knew she should be over the moon about the match. To live at Hatfield Park would really be something. And to be a duchess! She had sensed that he would make her an offer. But when the moment came, Madeleine had unexpectedly frozen. She hadn't been able to say the words. When she'd told Oakley she needed time to consider his proposal, he'd been as gracious as could be. She could give him her answer when he returned to England in three months, he agreed, after his European tour.

It felt strange to be in this state of limbo, to have her future so unsettled. If only Alexandra would reply, and say when she'd be coming home. It would be a relief to go to Polperran House, to discuss the situation with her sister.

These musings were interrupted by a gust of wind that tugged at her hat. Madeleine reinforced the pins holding the hat in place and refocused her attention on her surroundings.

She was in an area with wide-open vistas that looked very wild. Waves crashed against the black rocks below, sending up plumes of foamy spray. It occurred to her that she'd walked further than she'd intended, and might be quite a long way from the house. The clouds had grown darker now, completely obscuring the sun. She suddenly worried that it might rain.

It had been a mistake to wear one of her best day dresses and hats on this outing, and her new yellow shoes. At the very least, she should have worn her cape and brought an umbrella.

Madeleine was about to turn back for the house, when she caught sight of a tall, roofless stone building in the distance with an attached tower, that was situated close to the edge of the cliff. Pausing, she noted several workers milling about the structure, and wondered what it was.

At the same time, she noticed a man on horseback heading away from the building, in her direction.

The horseman was Lord Saunders.

Madeleine's heart skittered. She'd thought he was still in Truro. Or wherever he'd gone. Even from this distance, she saw that he had recognized her as well. He smiled and waved.

As he rode toward her on his dark horse, she couldn't help but notice how well he looked in the saddle. He sat tall and straight, his riding breeches hugging his muscular legs, his gray suit coat seemingly molded to his lean frame.

She realized she was glad to see him. Her earlier reservations about Lord Saunders had mostly been mitigated. There was still that thing about his reputation where women were concerned, but it didn't bother her much anymore—she'd discovered so many things about him that she admired. He was generous and thoughtful. He was beloved by his family. And, if her theory was correct, he was a highly talented artisan as well.

"Good afternoon," he said, trotting up. He brought his horse to a halt with a nudge of his knees, gently patting the beast as it waited and snorted. He wore no hat, and the brisk afternoon air whipped through his curly brown hair. "On a solo jaunt, are you?"

"I am."

"I have had no news of my father for several days. Do you know . . . can you tell me how he is faring?"

"From what I heard, there has been no change. Thankfully, he has had no more seizures."

"Thank God for that."

Madeleine decided to satisfy her curiosity with a bold question. "Your mother said you were in Truro?"

He nodded, his expression unreadable. "On my way home now. Stopped at the mine on the way."

"The mine?"

He gestured at the stone edifice in the distance. "Wheal Jenny, the Trevelyan mine."

"I had no idea your family owned a mine." Madeleine was fascinated.

"Are you walking on?" he asked. "Or returning to the house?"

She gazed up at the dark clouds. "I'm heading back. It was so nice when I set out, but I suspect we are in for a shower. I am woefully unprepared."

"As am I." He glanced down at her. "May I walk with you?"

"I have no objection," she admitted readily. "But if it's going to rain, hadn't you better ride? You'll get home faster."

"True, but I wouldn't want to leave you to face the elements alone." In one smooth motion, Saunders dismounted from his steed, still holding on to the stallion's reins. "And I am sure Tesla would enjoy your company."

"Your horse's name is Tesla?" Miss Atherton asked with a grin.

Charles nodded as they walked side by side along the path atop the bluffs. "It is."

He had been surprised to come upon her like this, but it hadn't been an unwelcome surprise. That morning, several days ago by the fountain, he'd sensed that Miss Atherton's attitude toward him had changed and softened, which pleased him. He liked her—liked her a great deal—and preferred her as his friend, rather than his enemy.

Over the past few days, although he had dived into his work with relish, his thoughts had often drifted, despite himself, to the lovely Miss Atherton.

He knew he couldn't have her. And shouldn't want her.

But a man could look, could he not? And in her yellow summer frock, she looked as fresh and pretty as the daisies adorning the hat perched atop her reddish-brown curls.

He found himself wondering what she would look like *without* that summer frock. Stripped down to her corset and knickers. Her luscious hair down and long and cascading around her shoulders.

His mind took one step further. *Imagine her naked in bed. Writhing beneath you. Or on top of you.*

No, don't. Do not imagine that.

Three words: Title. Hunting. Heiress. Just like Elise Townsend.

Although in truth, she was nothing like Miss Townsend.

"In honor of Nikola Tesla, I presume?" she was saying.

He blinked and stared at her. "You have heard of Nikola Tesla?"

"Last year, I believe his alternating current induction motor was licensed by Westinghouse Electric?"

Charles laughed. "I don't know why I should be astonished that you know that. But yes. Tesla is one of my heroes."

"There has been quite a furor, hasn't there, of competition between the electric companies?"

"Yes." Saunders laughed again, both impressed and delighted to have someone with whom to discuss a subject which was of such great interest to him. "Edison Electric has been trying to claim that their direct current system is better and safer than alternating current."

"Which system do you think is safest?"

"Tesla's, no question."

They launched into a lively discussion about what had been dubbed the "war of the currents." Charles gave her a sidelong look as they talked and strode along, Tesla nimbly keeping pace at his side. He had been convinced that Thomas had found and wed the only woman on earth who combined beauty and wit with a bold nature and fiery intelligence. He now saw that these traits ran in the family.

"You know," Charles said at length, "you are the first woman with whom I have ever held such a conversation."

"I hope I am not the last," she said, smiling. Glancing back in the direction from which they had come, she added: "Lord Saunders. About your mine. What did you call it again?"

"Wheal Jenny."

"Has it been in your family long?"

"Over a hundred and fifty years. It is nearly played out now. Most of our tenants are farmers—oats and barley. But Wheal Jenny brings in a small income and more importantly, keeps a few of the locals employed."

"Why is it called Wheal Jenny?"

"Most Cornish mines are prefixed with *Wheal*. In Cornish it means a place of work. Jenny was the name of my great-great-grandmother. It was named after her."

"What a wonderful legacy. What minerals do you extract?"

"Tin and copper."

"Copper?" Her eyes lit up, as if that fact was of some great significance. After a pause, she said carefully: "That's one of the materials used in those beautiful hairpins you gave the ladies, isn't it?"

Her tone and expression made it clear that she suspected something. He didn't want to open that door, however. "I suppose," he answered with a shrug. "I didn't ask the artisan what they were made of."

"The artisan?" She gave him a look. "Lord Saunders. You don't have to play coy with me. Your mother and sisters informed me of your . . . shall we say, *creative talents* . . . in your youth. I understand why your father disapproves of such activities, and why you feel you must hide them. But I don't agree with him. And I don't believe for a minute that you've given them up."

"Miss Atherton." Charles searched for a proper reply, but she went on:

"I know about Raven and Frederick."

That caught him off guard. Why on earth had his sisters shown her Raven and Frederick? "What do you mean?"

"I mean that, no matter what you say, I am *certain* you made them. And that you made the lovely copper tree for your mother, as well. They are magnificent sculptures, Lord Saunders, so imaginative and intricate. If you will take me into your confidence, I promise I will say nothing to your father."

Charles opened his mouth to deny it, then shut it again. He didn't like lying to her or anyone else about this. But she was so complimentary. Could he trust her to be discreet? He sensed he could. He could tell, in any case, that she was never going to take no for an answer. With a small chuckle of resignation, he said, "You win, Miss Atherton. I did make the hairpins. And Raven and Frederick."

"And the copper tree?" Her blue eyes sparkled with triumph.

"And the copper tree."

"I knew it! What an incredible talent you have. I am quite in awe." The wind whisked a strand of hair loose from beneath her hat and made her skirts billow. "Where did you learn to make such things?"

"I taught myself. When I was about seven or eight, I found an old broken clock in the attic and took it apart, trying to fix it. I failed miserably. But I had an idea for a way to reassemble the wheels and gears and other parts to make myself a tiny toy wagon. I asked my father for some metalworking materials, and he provided them, although begrudgingly."

"It's a shame your father is so firmly against the endeavor, just because you are a peer. Alexandra's husband faced a similar issue with his art. Although Lord Longford desperately needed the income, he wasn't allowed to sell his paintings."

"There is a difference, though," Charles pointed out. "I have no need to sell anything. I pursue my *art*, if you will, because it is my passion. I am happy to give it away. Yet still Father disapproves, because he sees it as rather grubby work. Because it involves working with my hands."

"I wish it were otherwise." She gave him a bittersweet smile. "It is painful to be obliged to hide something which means so much to us."

He glanced at her, catching her drift. "You have to hide your writing?"

"I do. My mother has no idea that I cart my manuscript around with me."

"Also a shame." He thought it interesting that they had this problem in common.

"What would you call yourself, then? A sculptor? A metalworking artist?"

Charles paused before answering. She seemed to think his activities were limited to the kind of ornamental objects he had made for his mother and sisters and Sophie. He decided it was best not to correct her misconception. "Something like that."

"Is Truro just where you *say* you're going, when you're actually going away to work somewhere?"

His lips twitched with the effort to hold back a smile. "Perhaps."

"Where do you work?"

"Ah. *That* is a state secret. I could tell you, but then I would have to kill you."

She laughed. "I think I read a phrase like that in a novel by Dumas."

"Did you? And here I thought I was being so original."

"You may not be original, but you are being coy again. I know you must *have* a workshop. The day you rescued my notes from the fountain, you had those hairpins in your pockets. You were only gone for half a day. So your workshop cannot have been *too* far away."

Charles grinned. It didn't surprise him that she had

figured that out, clever as she was. "I have said all I am willing to say on the subject, Miss Atherton."

"Really?" She didn't try to hide her disappointment. "After all that, you're going to leave me in the dark?"

"I am." Just then, a fat drop of rain smacked Charles in the eye. He blinked it away, aware that the sky had grown black and angry. "Do you ride?" he asked her.

"Yes. Why?"

"Because I think we are in for a shower. Tesla is a spirited beast. Do you think you could handle him?"

CHAPTER NINE

"Thank you for the offer," Madeleine told him as they walked along. "I'm sure I could handle Tesla. But I only ride sidesaddle."

Saunders blew out a disapproving breath. "Do you know *why* women ride sidesaddle?"

Madeleine had never given the matter much thought. "I believe it's partly for modesty's sake, and partly because we wear long skirts."

"A commonly held yet mistaken impression."

"Is it?" Scattered raindrops began to dance lightly on the ground.

"The practice dates back to 1382, when Princess Anne of Bohemia rode a specially constructed sidesaddle across Europe on her way to marry King Richard II. It was seen not just as a way to protect her modesty, but also her . . . virtue."

Madeleine felt her cheeks warm at the implication. "I didn't know that. But even so, the practice has been accepted for hundreds of years. It is the done thing to do."

"I would never have expected *you* to hold such a conservative view."

Madeleine flinched at that. "Even if I wished to fly in the face of convention, my lord, I couldn't ride astride today. I'm not wearing my riding habit. Anyway, a little rain never killed anyone."

"Perhaps not. But if you keep walking, the hem of that beautiful dress will get muddy, and you will ruin your shoes. Whereas I can happily walk beside you in my boots."

Madeleine hesitated. She *did* hate the idea of ruining her gown and shoes. But . . . "How would I manage it?" she asked uncertainly. Her riding habit had trousers beneath the skirts and a long drape on the left side to cover her legs. But in *this* dress, were she to climb up onto the horse, her petticoats and ankles would be on view. And her drawers were open at the crotch!

"I shall keep my eyes averted until your skirts are properly arranged," he promised.

The whole idea was scandalous, and entirely outside of Madeleine's comfort zone. But the gentle pattering of the rain was picking up in tempo. Now that he'd brought it up, the whole sidesaddle business *did* seem a bit absurd, as did so many other rules she had followed all her life without question.

Until a few days ago, when she'd left the London Season to come to Cornwall.

A rush of rebelliousness shot through her. "Okay. I'll do it. I will ride."

Saunders stopped and the horse stopped with him. "Excellent. Do you require assistance?"

"No thank you. Close your eyes. And don't peek."

"I won't peek." His deep voice was tinged with amusement.

Carefully raising her skirts, Madeleine placed her left foot into the stirrup and grabbed hold of the horn. In one swift movement, she swung her right leg up and over the steed, and seated herself on the saddle in gentlemanly fashion.

"Are you decent?" Saunders asked.

"Yes," she answered after a flurry of adjustments. Her skirts were partially rucked up, and a portion of her petticoats and ankles were on display, but otherwise she felt reasonably respectable. "You may open your eyes now."

Saunders smiled as he gave her the reins. "Sit up straight. Keep your legs directly under your hips and in gentle contact with the horse's body." He gave her a few other brief instructions as to how to manage and direct the beast. Following his advice, Madeleine urged the horse forward at a walking pace. Tesla easily responded.

"That's it. I hope you are comfortable?"

"As comfortable as can be expected." The position felt strange at first, but Madeleine soon grew accustomed to it, discovering a greater sense of security and power than she ever had experienced riding sidesaddle.

"I see you know your way around a horse," Lord Saunders commented approvingly as he walked beside her, wiping rain from his brow with the back of his hand.

"A child could ride at this pace," Madeleine countered mischievously.

"Oh?"

"Just last week, I was galloping across the fields at Hatfield

Park." She didn't know why she'd said that. In fact, when she'd ridden with Oakley, he'd insisted that they move at no greater pace than a tedious trot for safety's sake.

Saunders looked at her. "You galloped with Oakley?"

She could hardly take it back now. "You sound surprised."

"He does not seem the galloping type to me. He was always a rather conservative fellow." He seemed to be about to say something else when there was a crack of thunder, and suddenly the skies opened up with a pelting downpour.

"Good God! Free the stirrup!" Saunders exclaimed urgently.

She wasn't sure what he intended by this, but did as ordered. No sooner had she removed her left foot from the stirrup than Saunders used it to boost himself up and onto the back of the horse, settling behind the saddle, with only the cantle between them.

Madeleine had barely a second to be shocked.

She had ridden double numerous times with Kathryn when they were children. But this was different. Completely different. Riding astride was improper enough. But *riding double* with a gentleman? What if anyone were to see?

"Go!" he cried.

There was no time to think. Rain was coming down in torrents now. Madeleine re-gripped the stirrup and nudged the horse forward into a canter.

Lord Saunders's arms slipped around her waist.

The contact was so intimate and unexpected that Madeleine gasped. Riding was a matter of balance and she suspected that he, an experienced horseman, had no need to hold on to her at all. Or instead, and far more properly, he could have taken hold of the saddle. But the weight of his arms about her—and now, the press of his chest against her back—was so exhilarating, she had no wish for him to alter his position.

"Do you like it?" His voice was a low rumble just behind her ear. His breath, warm and sweet against her neck, made her skin tingle.

Madeleine's heartbeat drummed in time with the horse's hoofbeats. Strange new sensations flowed through her. She felt as if every vein and muscle in her body were quivering beneath her skin. "Do I like . . . what?" she asked breathlessly.

"Riding astride."

Oh, that. "Yes." The single whispered syllable was more a sigh than a word.

"I thought you would." She both felt and heard his answering chuckle. Then he said, "Faster."

Madeleine's pulse raced in alarm. "That wouldn't be safe."

"I trust you and Tesla." His deep voice resonated though her. "You said you like to gallop, didn't you?"

It was true. She loved to gallop. But he had no saddle. Going any faster could put him at risk, and possibly the horse as well. She felt, however, as if a gauntlet had been thrown. They were being drowned by rain. When was the last time she had taken a real risk? Without further thought, she urged Tesla into a gallop.

Charles tightened his grip around her trim waist, his heart seeming to pound as fast as the thundering hooves beneath them. They flew down the path in a volley of splattering water and mud, the deluge continuing with pummeling force.

Suddenly, the wind snatched Miss Atherton's hat, whipping it off of her head. Charles heard her gasp, saw the brief, regretful look in her eyes as she turned to watch it tumble to the beach far below, where it melded with the surging white waters that crashed upon the rocks.

He could not regret the loss of the hat. It had exposed the nape of her neck. The delectable-looking skin below her hairline, which glistened with sparkling raindrops, now lay just inches from his mouth. So close that he could almost taste it. It was all he could do not to press his lips against that creamy, wet whiteness.

Everything was so slippery wet. As they galloped along, his chest pressed firmly against her back, his legs nudged up against her own, their bodies were so closely entwined that, with the rocking motion of the horse beneath them, it was akin to making love.

Desire spiraled through him. Charles felt himself grow hard. If he were to raise his hands just a few inches, he would be cupping her breasts. *Oh how he yearned to cup her breasts.* But no. That was unthinkable. He thrust the thought from his mind, trying not to think about another kind of thrusting he wished he was doing at that very moment.

Being this close to her, holding her against him without being allowed to explore further, was a torment, but a kind of torment from which he wanted no reprieve. When they reached the path leading toward the Trevelyan grounds, Miss Atherton turned the horse inland.

"Shall I go to the stables?" she asked breathlessly.

"No," he directed, "go straight to the house."

A few minutes more brought them to the back entrance to the manor house, under shelter of the rear portico. Charles was relieved to be out of the rain at last, yet at the same time, sorry that the ride was over—sorry to have no further excuse to hold her in his arms.

Reluctantly, he released her and leapt down nimbly from the horse. Wiping his sodden brow with the back of one arm, he raised his hands to help her down.

"I can manage," she insisted. "Please look away."

Charles bit back a smile. After that ride in the rain, she was still so damned concerned about propriety? He dutifully averted his eyes, but hovered close in case she needed assistance.

His heart still hammered in his chest. His breath was coming quick, and blood still ran thick and hot in his veins. He didn't want to say good-bye, not yet. Not yet.

He heard a rustling of skirts and petticoats as she lowered herself from the mount. When he heard her feet touch the ground, he turned and leaned in, pressing his hands against the saddle on either side of her, sandwiching her in between himself and the horse.

She went still. Their eyes met. For a long moment they stood, unmoving, as close as if they were dancing a waltz. Although soaked to the bone, Charles felt strangely warm.

"You see?" he intoned softly.

"Do I see . . . what?" The tremor in her voice mirrored the riot of sensations coursing through him.

Charles swallowed hard, struggling to keep his own voice even. "We were safe. Not a scratch on us."

She nodded silently.

Rain pounded against the portico overhead and spattered against the nearby pavement. Her gaze seemed to be reluctant to leave his face, and he felt a similar reluctance. The glint in her blue eyes told him that she'd found their adventure as exciting as he had.

His glance lowered to her lips and paused there. He realized that he wanted to kiss her. Wanted it more than anything he'd wanted in . . . forever.

Their mouths were only inches apart. *All you have to do is lean in and press your lips to hers.* He had the distinct impression that *she* wanted him to kiss her as well.

But kissing her would be wrong for so many reasons.

Don't do it, a stern voice in his head commanded. The women he sometimes saw in London welcomed such caresses. Kissing *them* did not come with any promises or expectations. It was a means of experiencing mutual pleasure, a way to satisfy an itch, and nothing more.

But one did not just go about kissing American heiresses. Not without the intention of a lifelong commitment, which under no circumstances was he willing or able to make. In any case, he reminded himself, Miss Atherton would never be interested in such an offer from him. She had her future set with Oakley, after all, who would make her a duchess.

No matter how willing she appeared, at the moment, to indulge in a kiss with *him* in the rain.

Madeleine waited with bated breath. Did he intend to kiss her? She had only kissed one man in her life. The kiss had been brief and chaste, a mere meeting of lips on a terrace at a ball in New York, and only memorable for being the first and only of its kind. She couldn't even remember the man's name.

Lord Oakley had never even *tried* to kiss her. He was far too proper for that.

Everyone knew that well-bred women didn't kiss men until they were engaged.

Even so, all her life, Madeleine had hungered to know what it felt like to be kissed. *Really* kissed.

With sudden clarity, she realized she *wanted* Lord Saunders to kiss her. Their ride together had been . . . well, practically indecent. It was also the most exciting thing she'd ever experienced in her entire life. She suspected that a kiss from him would be equally as memorable. Even though, in a corner of her mind, she knew it would be wrong.

To her disappointment, he inhaled sharply, lowered his arms, and took a step back. Was that disappointment she read on his face, as well?

He seemed to be struggling to regain his composure, and at the same time searching for something to say. "You handled Tesla expertly," he told her finally. "Thank you."

"Thank *you*." Madeleine hoped he couldn't detect her chagrin, or the fact that her hands were trembling slightly. She clasped them firmly together, adding, "He's a wonderful animal. It was exciting to ride him. And chivalrous of you to let me."

"It seems to be my fate, Miss Atherton, to rescue you or your possessions from circumstances involving bodies of water or inclement weather."

She laughed at that, a laugh that mingled strangely with the rapid cadence of her own heart.

"I regret, however," he continued, "that I did not save you and your clothing from harm on this occasion, after all."

Madeleine had been so overwhelmed by the feelings enveloping her during that ride in the rain, she hadn't given a thought to the extent of damage to her person. That damage didn't become fully apparent until she caught sight of her ravaged reflection in a window of the house, which the dark afternoon had turned into a mirror.

She looked like she'd fallen into a lake. Her dress and shoes were completely soaked, her hat was gone, and her hair was disheveled and halfway down. "Oh dear." She laughed again.

He ran his hands through his own sopping wet hair. For a brief interval they were overcome by merriment, the sound of their laughter echoing beneath the portico.

At length, Madeleine caught her breath and said, "Thank you again, Lord Saunders, for bringing me home." *Even though the way you did it was positively scandalous.*

A quirk of his eyebrow, and the look in his eyes, suggested that he'd read what she'd left unsaid. "It was my pleasure, Miss Atherton. Now, if you will excuse me, I must return Tesla to the stables." Leaping into the saddle, he trotted off without a backward glance.

Madeleine watched him go, her heart still pounding as

she recalled the way it had felt to sit astride the horse, Saunders's arms wrapped around her as they charged through the mud. It was a sensation she would never forget.

Just now, she'd been so ready for his kiss.

As the realization of that settled, a stab of guilt chased through her. *Madeleine! What has come over you? Why was she thinking about Lord Saunders like this, and pining for his kiss?* It was a misplaced infatuation. And it was completely disloyal to Lord Oakley.

Oakley had been a consummate gentleman since the moment they'd met. He would never have leapt up on the back of her horse or urged her to gallop together in such a dangerous, wanton manner. A future duke of the realm did not behave that way. Neither did an Atherton.

Well, Madeleine told herself, it had been a moment of weakness. She had control over herself now.

A movement at the edge of her field of vision caught Madeleine's eye. In one of the rear windows, a curtain was fluttering. Madeleine's breath caught in her throat.

Awash with anxiety, she hurried inside the house. Had someone seen her and Lord Saunders riding up together, or observed them standing in such an intimate posture under the portico? If so, who? She hoped it wasn't Lady Trevelyan. Or worse yet, Sophie. Madeleine shuddered to think of the pain such a thing would cause her new friend.

As she crossed the rear foyer, Woodson suddenly appeared.

"Miss Atherton."

"Woodson! Forgive me for dripping all over the floors. I was out walking and got caught in the rain."

"I suspected as much, when you . . . and Lord Saunders . . . did not return for tea." The tiniest lift of one dark eyebrow, and the hint of a glimmer in his blue eyes, suggested that it was he who had noticed her and Saunders outside.

Madeleine wondered how much Woodson had seen. It didn't seem to matter, though. To her relief, she saw no censure in his gaze.

"I had Bessie light a fire in your room," Woodson went on, "and instructed Martin to lay out a set of clean, dry clothes for you. Shall I send her upstairs to help you dress?"

"Yes, thank you, Woodson. You are a marvel."

"So my wife informs me, every day."

Madeleine glanced at him, surprised. "I didn't realize you were married, Woodson."

"Martin and I have been wed these past five years."

"Martin? Why then doesn't she have the same last name as you?"

"By the time we married, she had been Martin to this family too long for them to learn a new name."

Madeleine laughed. "Well, she is a lucky woman."

"I am the lucky one, miss. By the way, this came for you, while you were out." From a nearby table he retrieved a silver tray containing an envelope.

Madeleine's heart leapt when she saw the sender's name. It was the letter she had been waiting for, from her sister. "Thank you, Woodson."

Madeleine ran upstairs and, after pausing only a moment to towel off her hair and face, sat down to read her newly arrived missive.

Sydney Place, Bath
June 24, 1889

Dearest Maddie,

I am just this minute in receipt of your letter, and have sat down to dash off a reply.

What exciting news! I'm thrilled, but not surprised, to hear that Lord Oakley proposed. I have heard such good things about him from Thomas, who knows him from school. From everything you said in your last few letters, he does seem like the ideal partner for you. I can't wait to hear more about him. I'd be honored to share any thoughts I have, if they'll be of help to you in making this decision. I'm just sorry I wasn't home to greet you! If only I had known, I would never have gone away. This trip to Bath was very last-minute. I did write to tell you, and am sorry my letter didn't reach you in time.

I haven't felt myself the past few months—but what can you expect, I am carrying a child! Despite Dr. Hancock's assurance that I am fine, Thomas insisted that I consult with a physician of note at Bath, a specialist who came highly recommended. Julia and Lillie were excited to go, and as I had never been—and Dr. Hancock promised that taking the train would be no problem even at this stage in my pregnancy—we packed and off we went.

Bath is truly a marvelous, well-planned city. All the buildings were elegantly designed over a hundred and fifty years ago, made of a lovely white stone that is fading over time to a golden hue. The Roman baths are fascinating, and the girls have gone slightly crazed with shopping. You must visit one day!

I met with Dr. Andrews, who said I am in excellent condition, thank goodness. Even so, he recommended a series of treatments which have included daily baths and tonics. My last treatment is tomorrow. Now that I know you're in Cornwall, wild horses couldn't keep me away a minute longer than necessary. Thomas has agreed that we'll leave the following morning, returning home Wednesday night. I'll send a carriage for you on Thursday morning, shall we say 11 o'clock?

No need to wire me a reply. Just send a message to Polperran House if you can, to let me know if that suits. I can hardly wait to see you!

With all my love,
Alexandra

P.S. Don't let Mother bully you. She is a tyrant! I'm on your side.

Madeleine clutched the letter to her chest. Her sister's words brought her such comfort, they were almost like a hug.

She grabbed a piece of paper and dashed off a note to Alexandra, approving her plans for Thursday morning. Woodson would see to it that the note was delivered to Polperran House, waiting for Alexandra when she got home.

As she laid down her pen, Madeleine let go a relieved sigh. The day after tomorrow, she would go to Polperran House. Thank goodness it was all settled. Not only because she was anxious to see her sister.

Because every day she spent at Trevelyan Manor was another day that she might see Lord Saunders.

A man who could set her heart racing with just a look or a smile. A man with whom she had just ridden double on horseback—*astride*, no less—and had wanted to kiss. A man who was very nearly engaged to a sweet young woman, whom Madeleine considered a friend.

Thursday morning couldn't come soon enough.

Madeleine slipped quietly out of the house, grateful that no one else was up except the servants. The previous day, Sophie had kept to her room with a headache. Madeleine had similarly ensconced herself, passing the time in writing her book and another letter to Kathryn, determined to stay out of Lord Saunders's sight.

This was her last morning at Trevelyan Manor, though, and she was dying to walk on the beach one more time. Madeleine recalled that Thomas's sisters, Julia and Lillie, were fond of seashells, and she determined to collect as many shells as she could as a gift for them. She had therefore risen early, breakfasted by herself, and arranged for her luggage to be brought down, in preparation for the carriage that would take her to Polperran House.

Walking on the beach at this hour, she reasoned, also meant she wouldn't have to see or talk to Lord Saunders. To her distress, he had been invading her dreams.

It was the same exact dream, and she'd had it twice now. They'd been riding on horseback together in the rain, just as they had been the other day. Except that in the dream, he'd turned her in his arms on the saddle, gazing down at her with a smoldering look as the beast rocked back and forth beneath them.

Just as Saunders had been about to kiss her, Madeleine had awakened, her pulse racing madly. Afterward, she had lain awake in bed for a long while, wondering what the dream said about her.

Thank goodness, Madeleine thought, as she wended her way down the rocky cliff path to the shore, that a person's dreams were private. She'd be mortified if anyone knew she'd been thinking about Lord Saunders that way.

Taking a deep breath of the pure sea air, Madeleine stared up with pleasure at the sky, which was a bright, cloudless blue. The morning sun sparkled like diamonds on the surface of the sea. Madeleine enjoyed the brisk nip of the wind as, gloveless, she picked up small shells and stones of various sizes, varieties, and hues, and stowed them in the small drawstring bag she'd brought.

She'd been at the activity for about fifteen minutes, when she heard a far-off voice calling her name. She looked up. Her pulse leapt.

It was Lord Saunders.

CHAPTER TEN

When Charles had observed Miss Atherton leaving the house a half hour past, he had told himself to leave her be. She had the right to enjoy the solitude of an early morning walk.

But it was her last morning at Trevelyan Manor. For all he knew, she might slip out the door when he wasn't looking, and he would not have a chance to say good-bye.

At least, that was the reason he had given himself as he strode in the direction she had taken, and began searching the most popular paths in the gardens. It had nothing to do with the fact that, for the past two days and nights, he had been unable to stop thinking about her.

Or dreaming about her.

His mind was invaded by the memory of all the conversations they had shared. She was the most interesting, intelligent woman he had ever met. He wished her visit wasn't so short, that they'd had more opportunities to talk.

And that ride together in the rain! It had been one of the most arousing experiences of his life. When they had reached the house and she had dismounted into his arms, it had been all he could do to step back and ignore the impulse to kiss her.

All day yesterday, he'd had the feeling she was avoiding him. He could guess why. Despite all her feisty talk about women being equal to men, she seemed to worry a great deal about propriety. The idea of riding astride had greatly distressed her. She had probably been chastising herself for that. Not to mention riding double. And that almost-kiss.

She was leaving that very morning. Who knew when or if he would ever see her again? He hadn't wanted things to end between them on such an odd note. A word or two of apology perhaps, a parting handshake and a smile, would hopefully make all the difference.

Charles had reached the edge of the gardens without encountering her, then continued to the bluffs with its open vista of the sea. Looking down, he'd caught sight of a lone figure walking on the beach—Miss Atherton. She was collecting shells. He had watched her for a moment, transfixed, then quickly made his way down the path that descended the rocky cliffs.

His heart began drumming to a different cadence as he made his way toward her across the golden expanse of sand. The ocean setting in all its fresh, morning glory was a fitting backdrop for the woman who, in a peach-colored dress that clung to her perfect figure like a second skin, resembled a goddess newly risen from the sea.

"Miss Atherton!"

Charles wasn't certain if his voice had carried over the crash of the waves and the raucous calls of the gulls. He tried again.

This time, she turned in surprise. Good lord, she was beautiful. The wind brought out the roses in her cheeks and whipped through her skirts and the loose tendrils of her upswept hair.

He ventured closer and tipped his hat. "Good morning."

"Good morning." Her eyes and voice held a note of reluctance, as if undecided as to whether or not she was pleased to see him.

"Collecting seashells?"

"I am." She held up a small cloth bag. "And stones. For Julia and Lillie. They are fond of them."

"What a nice gesture." Standing this close, looking down at her lovely face, he realized he had been wrong about the color of her eyes. Under the bright morning sun, they were more cobalt than indigo.

Stop waxing poetic about her eyes.

He drew a line in the sand with the toe of his boot. "I understand you are leaving us today?" Despite himself, he couldn't disguise the remorse he felt at the prospect.

She hesitated, as if surprised by his tone and what it implied; yet her guard was still visibly in place. "A carriage is coming for me in a little over an hour."

"I am glad, then, that I caught you before you left. I wanted to make sure I had an opportunity to say farewell."

"That was thoughtful of you."

He gestured for them to walk on together. As they strode across the hard-packed sand, he groped for words. "I hope you did not suffer a chill from our little adventure in the rain the other day?"

"Thankfully, no."

He darted a glance at her. Their eyes briefly met and held. He saw her cheeks grow rosy. Was she thinking about the horseback ride? The near-kiss? Or both? She looked away without further comment.

"I know you felt uneasy about riding astride," he commented. "I hope you have not berated yourself for that."

"I haven't. It was the sensible thing to do at the time."

"I hope, as well, that you will forgive me for joining you on Tesla's back. It was not, perhaps, the most gentlemanly thing I have ever done . . ." He broke off.

"It's all right. It was pouring cats and dogs. We had to get back to the house as quickly as possible."

"And so we did."

"And so we did," she repeated.

Her eyes met his again, now visibly and unexpectedly on the edge of mirth. They both let out a laugh, relieving the tension between them. A seagull squawked overhead, then swooped down to collect some unseen tidbit from the wet sand nearby.

"If it helps, I promise to never breathe a word of it to anyone," he told her.

"Well. Just so you know: I saw a curtain fluttering when you rode off. I'm pretty sure Woodson saw us."

"How do you know? Did he say something?"

"Just that he understood why we had both missed tea. And he gave me . . . a look."

"Ah. A look from Woodson can speak volumes."

"He didn't seem to be passing judgment, though."

"As well he shouldn't. We were the bedraggled survivors of a downpour, returning to home and hearth."

"Indeed we were." Miss Atherton laughed again. "He also mentioned that he is married. To Martin! I had no idea."

"They are the heart and soul of our household, and have been these many years. I cannot imagine what we should do without them." The morning sun was growing hotter. Charles lifted his hat, running his fingers through his hair to cool his head, wishing this moment could last forever.

"They are certainly devoted to your family," Miss Atherton agreed. "I have been meaning to ask. Is there any news about your father? He has been indisposed almost the entire time I have been here. I worry about him."

"I worry, too. Dr. Hancock has apparently been here every day. All we can do, I am told, is to pray for my father."

"I have been, and will continue to do so. I wish with all my heart that he will soon be well."

"You and me both, Miss Atherton. We should probably make a wish on that at the wishing pool."

"The wishing pool? What is that?"

"It's a pool of freshwater which, according to legend, is magical. If you drink the water and make a wish, it will come true." He pointed to the nearby cliffs with a smile. "We have our own local wishing pool just around that bend."

"Is that so? I would love to see it."

"Would you?" He paused. "It is in a cave."

"I love caves almost as much as I love legends."

"Well, then. Come with me." Charles led the way down

the beach to the mouth of the cave, which was so hidden
by the enclave of craggy black rocks surrounding it as to be
imperceptible to anyone casually strolling by.

"What a charming spot," Miss Atherton commented. "I
would never have found it on my own."

"All part of its magic." Charles hesitated, uncertain of
her intention. "If you prefer to go in on your own, I would
understand. I can try to tell you how to reach the magic
pool. But it is a bit tricky."

"I see. I suppose it *would* be most improper for us to venture
in at the same time, without a chaperone." As she said it, her lips
curved up mischievously.

He found himself staring at those lips. Imagining what it
would be like to taste them.

It was no wonder she was talking about chaperones. Charles
gave himself a mental shake.

"I was just teasing." She laughed lightly, and in a more
determined tone went on, "Please, lead the way."

He wasn't sure if it was the best idea in the world to go into
such a secluded place with her alone. But any further protest
would only make clear his own secret longings. So he did as
bidden, determined to be a gentleman. Inside the cool interior,
the cave opened up into a space the size of a small bedroom, its
dark granite walls carved by water and time.

"Follow me," Charles told her. The profusion of small
stones which infused the sandy floor crunched beneath their
feet as they advanced, the light growing dimmer with each
step. "Can you see?"

"Not very well," she admitted.

"If you will allow me to take your hand," he offered, "I can better guide you from here."

She paused only the briefest of seconds, then complied. Neither of them were wearing gloves. He felt a spark ignite as his hand clasped hers and sensed, from her small intake of breath, that she felt it as well. His heart began to patter in his chest.

"It gets darker as we go," he said, "but our eyes will adjust. At the pool itself, there is a fissure that lets in a bit of natural light."

She nodded and they moved forward, hand in hand. It was such a casual contact, this hand-holding, yet his pulse was pounding as strongly as if he were brushing his fingers over her naked form.

There you go again. Envisioning her naked.

Stop it stop it stop it.

The sound of dripping echoed in the distance, increasing in volume as they moved deeper into the cave. He guided her through a series of channels in the rock, past columns, stalagmites, and stalactites. After one final turn through a narrow passage, they entered an open chamber at the end of the cave and stopped.

"Oh!" Miss Atherton said in wonder.

They stood in a roundish chamber, enclosed by rock walls that stretched to a high ceiling. The air felt cool and damp. A narrow fracture above connected somehow to the outer cliff, because it let in a shaft of sunlight that illuminated the interior and sparkled on the surface of the small blue-green pool before them.

"Is it really freshwater?" Miss Atherton asked, her voice

echoing slightly inside the chamber. As if suddenly aware that she no longer needed guidance, she let go of his hand.

He regretted the loss of her touch. "Yes, it filters down from the bluffs above." In confirmation, a drop of water could be seen and heard as it plinked into the pool. "There are many caves with freshwater pools all along the Cornwall coast. I am told they all come with legends, some hundreds of years old."

She gazed about in fascination. "It *is* a rather magical place."

Charles turned to gaze at her. She made such a lovely picture standing there, just a foot or two away. The damp air had caused a few of her curls to frizz becomingly into ringlets around her face. Her peach gown fit so snugly that it showed off her every curve. Her rhythmic breathing was doing its own kind of magic, drawing his attention to her bosom, which was rising and falling and making it impossible to look away.

"How does the magic work, again?" she asked.

He blinked twice, yanking his gaze back up where it belonged, on her face. "You drink the water and at the same time, make a wish."

"I see. Shall we?"

He nodded. "You first."

"All right." She set her bag of shells on the damp rocky out-cropping fronting the pool and bent down. After pausing in thought, she scooped up a handful of water. "I wish that Lord Trevelyan will get well soon." She sipped from her palm.

The simple act looked so wanton to his errant brain, he struggled to regain his wits.

"Can I make another wish?" she asked, looking up at him.

"There is no limit on the number of wishes, as far as I know."

"All right." She dipped her hand again, this time closing her eyes and, apparently, making a silent wish before drinking. With a smile, she stood. "The water tastes delicious."

Staring at her, Charles could think of a few other things that would also taste delicious. He cleared his throat. "What was your second wish?"

"I cannot tell you," she answered in a tone of mock-mystery, "or it might not come true."

"Is that an American superstition?"

"I believe it's a commonly held superstition, where wishes are concerned."

"It is the first I have heard of it in Cornwall."

"Well, even an earl can learn new things." She gestured toward the pool with a smile. "Your turn."

Charles removed his hat and rested it on a ledge. He bent down, dipped a cupped hand into the pool, and drank, dashing off the following: "May my father live to a ripe old age."

He stood. Silence stretched between them, slow and catlike. There was no sound other than the intermittent drip of the water and the pounding of Charles's heart, which was so loud in his ears now, he worried that she could hear it.

"I wonder," she said softly, "how many people have come here over the centuries, and what they wished for."

"I suppose some were fishermen and their wives from the village," he suggested. "Wishing for a good catch."

"Some might have been women wishing for their husbands' safe return from sea."

"Or farmers wishing for a good harvest."

"Or men and women wishing for a loved one to return to health."

"Or lovers making a wish for their future." His breath caught. He had not planned to say that. The words seemed to hang in the air like a live thing between them. *Lovers.*

Their eyes met, and for a long moment neither of them moved. Tension coiled within his body and vibrated in the air between them. He was so aware of her nearness, he couldn't speak. From the expression on her face, she was equally aware of him.

In the small, intimate chamber, Charles could hear her every intake of breath, which was coming as fast and unsteady as his own. He felt as if he were suspended in time. They were alone in this quiet spot. In an hour or so, she would be gone. This opportunity would never come again.

Desire came over him, hot and heavy. Charles knew it was wrong. Reckless. Irresponsible. But if he did not kiss her, he would spend the rest of his life replaying this moment in his mind, wishing that he had.

His arms were out before he could stop himself. Sweeping around her waist. Drawing her to him. One hand cradling the back of her neck, angling her head so that her lips were just inches from his.

Through the layers of their clothing, he could feel the thud of her heart against his chest, a rapid pounding that matched his own. He drank in the vivid blueness of her gaze that seemed to say, *Yes. Yes. Yes.*

And then he kissed her.

CHAPTER ELEVEN

Lord Saunders was kissing her.

Even more shocking, Madeleine was loving every second of it.

She had worried a bit, when he brought her here, that something like this *might* happen. The way he'd looked at her, after their horseback ride . . . the way he'd been looking at her just now, on the beach. She knew he was attracted to her.

She could no longer deny her own attraction to him. But it was just an infatuation, she'd told herself. Surely she would be safe in his company for a few short minutes inside a cave.

Then he'd suggested that she take his hand. Her heart had pounded every step of the way. Now she was in his arms. His lips were on hers. Madeleine had so little experience with kissing, she hardly knew what to do. But Saunders didn't seem to mind.

His first kiss had been fervent, an impassioned assault, as if he were giving in to an impulse he had been holding back for a long time. But now, after taking a ragged breath, his kisses softened. With skill and tender slowness, his mouth moved back and forth over hers with a touch as soft as velvet. Lingering a bit longer with each new kiss.

Madeleine was so enthralled by the sensation, she could barely think. A tiny voice from somewhere far off was trying to be heard, telling her this was wrong. But she didn't listen.

All she could do was to hold on tight. Her breasts were pushed so firmly against his chest, she could feel his pulse racing, as if beating in time with her own. He paused briefly so they could both take a breath, and then his mouth was on hers again.

This time it was different. His lips were more driven, insistent. His tongue pressed against the seam of her lips, urging them apart, and then slipped inside her mouth. Madeleine gave a little gasp. She'd heard that kissing involved tongues, but hadn't been prepared for it.

He taught her the way of it and she found herself responding, their tongues intertwining in a sensuous dance. He tasted as clean and fresh as the pool from which they'd just drunk. Madeleine felt enveloped by his scent: woodsy, sun-warmed. His hands ran over the curves of her back, caressing her. Her own hands traced the hard muscles of his shoulders, smoothing down to his waist. As she pressed him more firmly against her, she heard a soft noise, somewhere between a sigh and groan, and wasn't sure if it came from his throat or her own. Or both.

She felt something else, too, pressing hard and insistent against her lower body. She had no experience with such things, but had read enough to recognize it as evidence of his desire, which raised her own excitement to an even higher level.

Time had no meaning. She was shocked by her wantonness. They kissed and kissed some more. Her entire body began to burn in a way she'd never before experienced. A surprising warmth settled in her most feminine spot, between her thighs.

The only sounds that broke the silence were their own labored breathing, their ecstatic murmurs, and the sensuous backdrop of plinking water. The cave was like a safe haven, an intimate space just for the two of them, separate from the rest of the world.

His hand skimmed up the curve of her waist now, lingering at the side of her breast. She wondered, hazily, if he meant to touch her there. No man had ever taken such liberties with her. Nor had she ever wanted them to. Until now. She felt the muscles in his body tense with need, and sensed that he wanted more.

How much more was *she* willing to give him? The thought entered her consciousness despite herself, unanswered. At the same moment, with what appeared to be great effort, he ended the kiss, breathing hard. One of his hands rose to caress her cheek. His gaze met hers with an affectionate smile. Then he pulled her close and simply held her against him, her face buried in the crook of his neck.

For a long while they stood that way, silently entwined in each other's arms. Madeleine trembled with sensation. She was elated about what had just happened. She had wondered what kissing was like. Now she knew. Kissing was wonderful. She *loved* kissing.

She had made two wishes just now. In the second, silent wish, she had asked for a sign, to help her understand whether or not she was supposed to marry Oakley. Then Lord Saunders had kissed her. And oh, what a kiss it had been.

Was that the sign? Madeleine asked herself. *Am I not supposed to marry Lord Oakley after all, but rather, Lord Saunders?*

As these thoughts crossed her mind, Saunders stepped back, letting go of her. He rubbed one hand across his chin, a distracted expression on his face. "*Damn it,*" he said. "Longford was right. I *am* the biggest bastard who ever lived."

Madeleine stared at him, all the pleasure of the encounter they'd just shared vanishing in an instant, taking her recent surmise with it.

Apparently, he deemed their kiss to have been a terrible mistake. Yes, she acknowledged, there were plenty of reasons for him not to have kissed her, and for her not to have kissed him. Still, she wouldn't have minded if he'd admitted, just for a second, to having enjoyed it. Told her that she was so alluring, so beautiful, so . . . something, that he hadn't been able to help himself.

"I swear, I did not plan this," he went on, regret in his eyes. "I was entirely out of line. I have no wish to come between you and Oakley. Forgive me."

Madeleine flinched. Now he was *apologizing* for kissing her. When a man kissed you like *that*, one didn't want an apology. A kiss like that ought to mean something. It had meant something to *her*. But apparently not to him.

She reminded herself of what all the debutantes had said about him during the Season. It was absolutely true: he *was* a flirt and a rake. He'd probably kissed dozens of women. He was the type who kissed women in caves because he felt like it, then discarded them like an unwanted plaything. He'd kissed her, now he was done with her, and apparently he felt bad about it. What bothered her was that he didn't seem to feel bad because he might have hurt her, but more because he was upset with himself for breaking some personal code of honor.

Well, he didn't have the monopoly on *that*, Madeleine thought with sudden shame. Now that time and space were causing reason to return, she realized that she had broken a code of honor, too. Her face grew hot as the voice in the back of her head awoke and said, *Madeleine, that was so, so wrong, and you know it.*

Was it really only a few short days ago that she had considered the betrayal of a friend as one of the worst things a human being could do to another? She had once judged Lord Saunders harshly for that offense. *Yet she had just done that very thing*—and quite willingly. In kissing Saunders, she had been disloyal not only to Lord Oakley, but Sophie as well.

An awkward silence fell. Madeleine couldn't remember when she'd ever felt so uncomfortable. She swallowed hard, sweeping the ill feelings aside, struggling to reassemble what was left of her pride.

Buck up, Madeleine. You are to blame for this as much as he is. Be dignified. Move on.

"We both got carried away," she said finally. Picking up

her bag of shells and stones, she added, "But don't worry, Lord Saunders. I'm leaving shortly. I promise, I will never breathe a word about this. Let's pretend it never happened."

He nodded gravely. Without further comment, he replaced his hat on his head, turned, and led the way out of the cave. When they reached the beach again, both of them squinting against the sunlight, he asked if she would like him to walk her back to the house.

Madeleine shook her head firmly. "No thank you. I think it's best if I return on my own."

He gave her another nod.

Madeleine sprinted away down the beach and climbed the steep path up the cliff as fast as her stays would allow. The trek across the Trevelyan grounds had never felt so long or so exhausting. By the time she reached the rear door of the manor house, she was gasping for breath.

Some fifteen minutes later, she had gathered the last of her things from her room and returned downstairs, where the clock was striking eleven.

"Your carriage has arrived, miss," Woodson told her. "Your luggage is all on board."

"Thank you, Woodson. I'll just be a minute."

Madeleine hurried to the breakfast room, where Lady Trevelyan and Sophie were finishing their coffee.

"Maddie!" Sophie rose and hurried over. "Woodson said you went out walking, but did not know where. I was so afraid I would not see you before you departed."

A blush warmed Madeleine's cheeks and spread to her chest. How could she look her friend in the eye after what had just happened in the cave? But she *had to* look. "I'd never leave without bidding you good-bye, Sophie."

"I'm glad. I have a gift for you." Sophie retrieved something from a nearby chair. "When I said I had a headache yesterday, it was just a ruse. I was actually in my room, making this." She offered the gift to Madeleine with pride. It was a linen handkerchief, embroidered with a spray of violets and monogrammed with the letter *M*. "I wanted to give you something as a symbol of our friendship."

"Oh, Sophie." Madeleine felt another stab of guilt at this sweet offering from a woman who, just moments ago, she had secretly wronged. "It is lovely. But I feel terrible. I have nothing to give you."

"Please! Do not even think of that. It gave me such pleasure to make you this. I do not expect nor require anything in return."

"Thank you, Sophie. I will treasure it always." Madeleine embraced Sophie, tears of shame stinging her eyes.

"I am sorry you are leaving. I shall miss you."

"I'll miss you, too." Swallowing hard, Madeleine turned to Lady Trevelyan. "Your Ladyship. I can never thank you enough for your gracious hospitality this week. You have been so kind."

"I enjoyed having you." She came over, holding out her hand for Madeleine to shake. "I hope you will come and see us again, Miss Atherton."

"I hope so too," Madeleine said, knowing that she never could.

Lady Trevelyan pursed her lips now. "Where is Charles? He ought to be here to say good-bye."

"We said good-bye last night," Madeleine insisted, flushing. "I really must go."

"Promise me you will write," Sophie implored, as she accompanied Madeleine down the hall and outside to where the coach awaited.

"I promise." Madeleine hugged Sophie one last time before climbing aboard the vehicle. As it traveled down the drive, she waved through the window, relieved to be heading for Polperran House at last. Relieved to be putting distance between herself and Trevelyan Manor.

And her unsettling infatuation with Lord Saunders, which had no place in her life. Or his.

From now on, she promised herself, she would think no more about him. She would direct her thoughts along a more proper channel, and think about Lord Oakley.

Who was her reason for coming to Cornwall in the first place.

"**Y**ou must tell us everything."

Alexandra's blue eyes shone as she reached out from her wicker chair and clasped Madeleine's hand. In her seventh month of pregnancy, Alexandra looked more beautiful than ever, her face glowing with a quiet happiness that Madeleine had never witnessed before.

Upon arrival, Madeleine had been so happy to see her sister, she'd fairly thrown herself into her arms. Once she'd established that Alexandra was truly well, Madeleine had hugged Thomas and his sisters with affection, and then enjoyed a tour of the house.

Polperran House had undergone many changes since Madeleine's last visit. The work of the past ten months had produced outstanding results. Necessary repairs had been made to the massive Elizabethan manor home's roof, windows, and masonry; indoor plumbing had been installed in some areas; and many new furnishings had been purchased. A great deal of work had also been done on the grounds, Alexandra had informed her, to restore them to their former glory.

If the gloriously blooming formal gardens, which Madeleine could see from their vantage point on the rear veranda, were any indication of what had been done on the rest of the property, she suspected the estate must be a real showplace now.

"Everything?" Madeleine replied now, smiling at her sister. The whole family was assembled under a sunny sky, enjoying a luncheon of chicken salad sandwiches, iced tea, and fresh fruit. "Where should I start?"

"Start with your proposal," cried Julia, a golden-haired, sixteen-year-old beauty whose interest in fashion was exemplified by the chic ensemble she wore.

"Who *is* he?" prodded Lillie, thirteen, with excitement. Her white dress and long brown curls were both embellished by blue satin ribbons.

"Yes, do tell." Thomas had been the caretaker of his younger sisters since the death of their parents some years before. Relaxing in a comfortable chair with his long, lean legs stretched out in front of him, he looked every bit the lord of the manor as he regarded Madeleine with interest in his brown eyes, his blond hair glinting in the sunlight.

"Alexandra would tell us nothing!" Julia added admonishingly.

"That's because I only know what Mother has told me," Alexandra insisted. "I thought it best to wait for Maddie to share her news with all of us."

Madeleine paused, struggling to hide the turmoil still simmering within her after the events of that morning. She had hoped for a private conversation with her sister to discuss Lord Oakley, but it seemed that it was to be a matter of discussion with the entire family.

"Well . . ." Taking a deep breath, she plunged in. "His name is Lord Philip Heyer. He's the fifth Marquess of Oakley, the eldest son of the Duke of Courtenay."

"The eldest son," exclaimed Lillie. "Then he will be a duke."

"Yes, he will," Madeleine responded.

"Your mother must be over the moon about that," Thomas pointed out dryly.

Alexandra nodded. "Naturally, she is very much in favor of the match."

"I remember him from Oxford," Thomas commented. "A good sort of fellow."

"I believe he is," Alexandra agreed.

Madeleine turned to Alexandra in surprise. "Have *you* met him, too?"

"We danced together once, during my Season last year.

I recall him as being very tall, a distinguished sort of young man."

Madeleine nodded. "He is. The family has a grand, ancient estate in Sussex. Mother and I visited there a few weeks ago. It is a lovely place."

"Hang the house, Maddie. Talk about the man," insisted Thomas.

"Yes. Do you like him?" Alexandra asked.

"I do. I like him very much." Madeleine told them the story of how she and Lord Oakley met. "He makes good conversation," she finished, "is attentive and very thoughtful."

"You did not say if he is handsome," observed Julia.

"He's quite handsome," Madeleine admitted.

"When he proposed, did he go down on one knee?" asked Lillie breathlessly.

"He did."

"Just like in a storybook." Lillie sighed.

Alexandra's eyes were circumspect as she studied Madeleine. "He sounds like an exemplary man," she noted carefully. "But if I understand your letter correctly, you haven't yet accepted his offer?"

Madeleine shook her head. "Not yet."

"Why not?" asked Julia.

"What are you waiting for?" inquired Lillie.

Madeleine recalled Lord Trevelyan asking her the same question, and began to feel uncomfortable. How should she answer?

Alexandra raised a hand and said sternly, "I think that's

enough on *that* subject. This is a private matter for a later discussion, sister to sister."

Lillie groaned with disappointment, and Julia said, "What? That is not fair."

Thomas, with a sympathetic glance at Madeleine, quickly steered the conversation in a new direction. "Lillie, tell Maddie about the books you have been reading. You know how much she loves novels."

This new topic captured Lillie's interest, and to Madeleine's relief, the girl launched into an animated explanation of her new literary favorites, a subject which was also dear to Madeleine's heart.

Recalling Julia's crush the year before on Lord Saunders's younger brother, James Grayson, Madeleine commented that she'd heard the young man was spending the summer in Ireland.

"Oh! I have no interest in him anymore," Julia insisted, tossing her head. "I have far more important things to do." Julia brought out her sketchbook of women's fashions, all pretty and imaginative ensembles she'd designed herself, which had Madeleine and Alexandra oohing and aahing.

"Thomas has also been giving me watercolor lessons," Julia enthused, "and he promised to teach me oils when I am ready."

Over the course of the afternoon, Madeleine was caught up on all the latest news of the family. The girls' governess, who had been hired the previous summer after Alexandra's short stint in that position, had gone home to care for her sick mother, and Thomas had not yet found a replacement. In the interim, Alexandra had taken over their daily lessons again, and also volunteered once a week at the local school.

"I so love teaching," Alexandra explained, "and it is gratifying to see how much the children in the village have improved in their studies over the past year."

Thomas, a highly skilled artist who had been trained in Florence, was now a member of the Academy of British Artists, the first member of the peerage to be so admitted, and he had won an award for one of his paintings.

"I should love to paint the two of you," Thomas announced at dinner, gazing fondly at his wife and Madeleine over a glass of cabernet. "A sisters' portrait. What say you?"

"That would be wonderful, but I doubt I'll be here long enough to sit for a portrait," Madeleine replied with a regretful smile.

That evening, after the girls went to bed, Thomas retreated to his study to give Madeleine and Alexandra what he called "sister time."

"At last," Alexandra said, turning to Madeleine when they were alone in the elegantly furnished upstairs parlor, "we can talk freely."

Madeleine sank down on the sofa beside her. "Now that I'm here, I suddenly feel a bit ridiculous."

"Why?"

"I don't know. I guess because I rushed down to Cornwall to consult with you on a matter that I ought to be able to figure out on my own."

"Dearest, matters of the heart can be confusing. If there's any way I can be of help to you, I will. But I think you'd better start from the beginning."

CHAPTER TWELVE

Grateful for the listening ears of a compassionate sister, Madeleine told Alexandra in detail all about her courtship with Lord Oakley.

"I knew he was going to offer for me, otherwise why did he invite us to Hatfield Park?"

"I presume his family needs your fortune?"

"Yes. But he said he loves me." Madeleine let go a sigh. "It should be an easy decision, shouldn't it? As Mother keeps pointing out, if I marry him, I'll be a duchess."

"Maddie. You know as well as I do that being a duchess means nothing if you're not happy. Let's leave Mother and her aspirations out of the equation entirely. You will be marrying a man, not his title. And, from what Thomas tells me . . . from what *you* tell me . . . he does seem like a nice young man."

"That's the problem. He *is* nice. Very nice." Madeleine closed her eyes, conjuring up a mental image of Lord Oakley on the night they met, when he took her hand and led her out onto the dance floor. To her dismay, when the man in her mind smiled at her, it wasn't Lord Oakley at all. It was Lord Saunders.

Madeleine's eyes blinked open in frustration. This was maddening. She couldn't even *think* about Oakley, without Saunders interfering!

Her thoughts darted to their kiss in the cave. A sudden heat settled over her like a blanket, accompanied by a bundle of emotions and sensations she knew she shouldn't be feeling. "Lexie: How can I know if what I feel for Lord Oakley is not mere *liking*, but is actually *love?*"

"I think love defies explanation," Alexandra replied.

"Please *try*. You're madly in love with Thomas, anyone can see that. What does it feel like?"

"I don't know," Alexandra began slowly. "It's as if Thomas is my kindred spirit. My other half, a part of my soul. Making him happy is more important to me than my own happiness. Because when *he's* happy, it fills me with so much joy." She gave Madeleine a shrug. "But that is after almost a year of marriage, dearest, of being as close as two people can be on a daily basis. What I feel now is much deeper than what I felt when we first met."

"What did you feel at first?"

"I suppose it started with physical attraction. Do you find Lord Oakley attractive?"

"I do," Madeleine assured her.

"Do you admire and respect him? Do you feel joyful in his company?"

"Yes." Madeleine thought of all the pleasant times she

and Lord Oakley had spent together. "He's kind to animals and dotes on his mother."

Alexandra hesitated. "Dotes on her?"

"Not overly so. In a good way."

"All right then, these are all marks in his favor. Do you have interests in common?"

"Yes. We both enjoy music and riding and a good glass of wine. He's an excellent dancer."

"And?"

"Well. He's very interested in architecture. He knows everything there is to know about buttresses, colonnettes, gables, and rose windows." Madeleine paused. "He's also fond of hunting and talks a lot about guns and hounds. But I could get used to that."

Alexandra seemed to choose her next words carefully. "Did you tell him about your aspirations?"

"Yes. He doesn't seem to mind about my writing."

"Doesn't seem to mind? That doesn't sound like a very enthusiastic seal of approval."

"Well, at least he doesn't *disapprove*. He's not much of a reader, but I haven't met many gentlemen this Season who were." As Madeleine said it, her thoughts veered to Lord Saunders again. How complimentary he'd been about the book she was writing. How he'd rescued her notes from the pond.

"Do you think of him frequently when you are apart?"

"*Yes*," Madeleine heard herself say. As the word rushed from her mouth, she realized she was referring to Saunders, not Oakley.

Alexandra smiled, responding to her unintended enthusiasm. "Well then. Now we're getting somewhere. Tell me: When you're with Lord Oakley, does your heart race? Does his touch make your nerves tingle?"

Madeleine faltered, her thoughts still fixed upon the man who had made her feel precisely that way—on a wild horseback ride, and that morning in the cave. She again recalled that illicit kiss. Had her body tingled? *Oh, yes.* Madeleine felt a blush creep up to the roots of her hair. "I—I don't know."

Alexandra studied her. "Why are you blushing?"

"Am I blushing?" Her hands flew to her cheeks.

"Yes. What aren't you telling me?"

"Nothing."

"Have you kissed him?"

"Kissed who?"

"Who do you think? Lord Oakley."

Madeleine's heart pounded. "No. No, I haven't kissed Lord Oakley. But . . . but . . ." Her hands covered her eyes now. "I *have* kissed Lord Saunders."

"What? You kissed *Charles Grayson?*"

Madeleine nodded, mortified, still unable to look at her sister. "In point of fact, he kissed *me*. But I definitely kissed him back."

Alexandra sounded astonished. "When?"

"This morning. Down at the beach. There was this cave . . ."

"What were you and Lord Saunders doing alone together in a cave?"

Madeleine uncovered her face. "He was showing me a wishing pool. And . . . and . . ." She couldn't go on.

"What kind of kiss are we talking about? Surely it was just a brief kiss?"

Madeleine shook her head. "It wasn't brief. It was . . . *oh, Lexie*. It was positively *scandalous*. And it was everything I've ever dreamt a kiss would be."

"I see." Alexandra nodded slowly. "I take it this was your first kiss?"

"My first *real* kiss, of course! What kind of girl do you think I am?"

Alexandra's cheeks reddened at that, and for a moment she seemed lost in memory. "I was just asking," she said quickly. Then: "Are you attracted to Lord Saunders?"

"No! Yes! No! I mean, I know I shouldn't be." Madeleine sighed in confusion. "I thought I disliked him at first. But this week, I've gotten to know him better."

Alexandra studied her. "And?"

"And . . . he's smart and kind and generous. He is very interested in science. He's an artisan as well."

"What kind of artisan?"

"He makes decorative objects. Hairpins and the most intricate sculptures made of clock parts."

"Thomas mentioned that Charles used to make such things when they were children," Alexandra mused. "I didn't know he was still involved in that."

"He has to hide it because his father is adamantly against it. The same way Thomas used to have to hide his work as a portrait artist."

"Oh, that's too bad."

"This rule about peers being too high and mighty to

engage in trade, it's so stupid and limiting. Lord Saunders is a truly gifted artisan."

Alexandra looked at her. "You *do* like him."

"Oh, Lexie. I suppose I do."

"He must like *you* if he kissed you."

"I don't know about that. All Season long, the ladies said he is a great flirt. He made it clear that kissing me was a mistake. He actually *apologized* for it."

"As well he should! He took liberties with you that were most improper." Unaccountably, Alexandra's cheeks reddened again.

Madeleine suddenly understood why. "Lexie! Now *you're* the one who's blushing. Did you and Thomas engage in similar . . . *improprieties* . . . before you were engaged?"

Alexandra looked away in embarrassment, her lips twitching slightly. Finally, a laugh escaped her and she admitted, "I shouldn't really speak of this, but—if it will help you to know it—then yes. Thomas did . . . kiss me . . . several times in fact, before he proposed."

"Several times!" Madeleine was shocked.

"The first time, he also apologized and said it could never happen again. But things changed, Maddie. They could change for you, too."

"Nothing is going to change in this scenario. Nor should it. There can never be anything between Lord Saunders and myself."

"Why not?"

"Because he's *Lady Sophie's* intended."

"Who is Lady Sophie?"

"Lord Saunders's cousin." Madeleine filled her sister in on the relevant details about Lady Sophie.

"From what you say," Alexandra pointed out slowly, "although there may be an expectation that they'll wed, they are not yet engaged."

"They will be. Sophie loves Lord Saunders. And Saunders said he is prepared to 'do his duty.'"

"'Do his duty'? That's hardly a profession of love."

"Even so, I *won't* come between them." Madeleine speared her sister with a look. "Have you forgotten what happened at my coming out ball? What Pearl did to me?"

"I haven't forgotten."

"I would *never* do that to anyone. I like Sophie. I couldn't bear to hurt her."

"I understand." Alexandra paused. "Perhaps Lord Saunders *will* marry his cousin, and if so, I hope they'll be very happy. But perhaps he *won't*. In the meantime, Maddie: this thing that happened between you and Charles—you can't just ignore it. These feelings you have must be explored."

"What do you mean, explored?"

"I mean, you can't marry Oakley if you're attracted to someone—*anyone*—else."

Madeleine shook her head vigorously. "I'm not going to *explore* my attraction to Lord Saunders. I'm going to stay as far away from him as humanly possible."

Alexandra gave a disappointed sigh. She seemed to be lost in thought for a moment. Madeleine thought she detected a brief gleam in her sister's eyes, as if she were planning something, but it disappeared as quickly as it had come. "Okay," she said finally. "But even if you leave Lord Saunders out of this, there remains your responsibility to Lord Oakley. Marriage is forever. If you accept him, you must love him more than any man you have ever met."

"I agree. But how am I supposed to know if Lord Oakley is my forever love, when he's off in Italy or France or somewhere?"

"How long will he be gone?"

"Three months."

"Then use that three months to search your soul. You've spent enough time in his company to form an opinion of him. He asked for your hand, which tells *me* that he has excellent taste."

Madeleine laughed. "*You* are biased."

"They say, after all, that absence makes the heart grow fonder. By the end of summer, if he's the right man for you, you'll *know*." Taking Madeleine's hands in hers, Alexandra added: "Meanwhile, you must stay here with us."

The offer filled Madeleine with delight. "May I? Really? For the entire summer?"

"I can't think of anything I'd like more."

"Oh, Lexie. I'd love that. I've missed you all so much. It would mean everything to me to be here when the baby comes, and to help out afterward. But don't you need to ask Thomas?"

Alexandra smiled. "I already have. He'd love to have you here, and I know the girls would, too."

A thought occurred to Madeleine. "What about Mother?"

"What *about* Mother?"

"She spent so much on my clothes and the hotel in London, and worked so hard to make connections. I'm not *officially* engaged. She won't like me staying down here. And if I don't end up accepting Lord Oakley, she'll never forgive me for missing out on the rest of the Season."

Alexandra's eyes blazed like blue flames. "After what I went through last year, I hope you know better than to let Mother force you into doing anything, especially marrying a man you don't love. You've been a model daughter, Maddie. It's time to think about yourself for a change, to do what's best for *you*."

Madeleine nodded, a quiet excitement building within her at the prospect of spending the summer at Polperran House. "Maybe I will."

After saying good night to Alexandra, Madeleine retreated to her spacious guest room, where she penned a letter to her mother, explaining her plans for the summer.

As she climbed into bed and lay back against the pillow, Madeleine let go a sigh of relief. She felt as if a great weight had been lifted. The past few years had been utterly exhausting. The prospect of a real vacation, here in Cornwall with her beloved family, seemed like a dream come true. Surely, by the end of summer, she would be ready to make a decision about Lord Oakley.

Madeleine closed her eyes, reminding herself of Oakley's many attributes. She drifted off into a lovely dream. A dream in which she was bathing in a blue-green pool in a luminescent cave. A handsome man was immersed in the semidarkness of the water nearby. It was Lord Oakley.

Madeleine boldly swam up to him and wrapped her arms around his body. "Kiss me," she whispered into his ear.

Oakley's mouth took possession of hers. Madeleine returned his kisses with increasing passion. As they kissed, Madeleine was once again aware of a strange, warm sensation building between her thighs. Without quite understanding how she knew it, she recognized this new feeling as sexual desire. Panting, Madeleine pulled back from the kiss to look her lover in the eye.

She awoke with a start, her pulse racing.

The man she'd been kissing wasn't Lord Oakley. It was Lord Saunders.

CHAPTER THIRTEEN

"That will do very well. Thank you." Charles gave a nod, approving the new windows the workman had installed in one of his tenants' cottages. After paying the man and exchanging a few words with the grateful tenant and his wife, Charles took his leave.

As he rode away, Charles mentally ticked off this final duty on his checklist. He had spent all day yesterday at the mine, ensuring that things were moving there like a well-oiled machine. This morning he had visited several farmers in their fields to see how they were getting on with their new equipment, and committed the afternoon to checking up on various repairs such as this one.

At last, he was almost done. Just one more stop at the manor house to see his father. Then, finally, he could get back to his shop and the other work that pulled at him, ever-present in his mind.

His work, however, wasn't the only thing occupying his mind recently.

The past two days and nights, ever since Miss Atherton left, had been a study in frustration.

Try as he might, Charles couldn't stop thinking about her. She was different from any woman he had ever met. And not just because she was so highly educated and well-read—although that did set her apart as someone very special. There was something else about her that stood out. Maybe it was her open curiosity about life, her avid interest in so many subjects. Or maybe it was her intelligence and wit, which shone with every question she asked and every observation she made. He had never felt so alive as he had when they were conversing. He could talk to her for hours on end, he believed, and never run out of things to say.

On top of that, there was a kind of physical attraction which he had never before experienced. He had felt drawn to her at first sight, and the feeling had never wavered.

And that kiss they had shared in the cave! He couldn't get it out of his head.

Charles had kissed many women. But kissing Miss Atherton had been different. He had sensed, by her initial response, that she'd never been kissed before. But oh, how quickly she had learned. Although they'd shared no more than a kiss, it had been so passionate, so infinitely arousing, he almost felt as though he'd stolen her virginity. Just thinking about it made him grow hard.

As Tesla trotted on, the motion of the horse just served to remind him of the time he had ridden on horseback with Miss Atherton. Holding her tightly against his chest. His lips at her nape, drinking in the scent of her wet skin. The memory did nothing to ease the smoldering sexual tension that rose within his body.

He longed, more than anything in the world, to see her again. To hold her in his arms again. To kiss her again. To once more feel that luscious, beautiful body beneath his hands and explore its every inviting curve.

But of course he knew full well that never could, never would happen.

We both got carried away. I will never breathe a word about this. Let's pretend it never happened.

The words Miss Atherton had spoken after the kiss reverberated inside Charles's head, making him frown. She was right: they *had* gotten carried away. Or more to the point, *he* had gotten carried away. He was the one who had initiated the kiss. She had definitely kissed him back, and he sensed that she had enjoyed it every bit as much as he had. But he took full responsibility for his actions.

He should never have kissed her. Yes, he was attracted to her in a manner that almost bordered on obsession. But his attraction wasn't right and never had been. They both had obligations to other people. After that kiss, damn it, he'd been consumed by guilt. And from the look on her face after he'd apologized, so had she.

He had let a moment of passion get out of hand. Thank God things had not progressed any further than they had.

Passion was a dangerous thing. Giving in to a momentary passion had almost ruined his life. *Never again*, he reminded himself. Never again would he let sexual desire overcome reason.

Not that such a thing could ever happen with Miss Atherton. He couldn't imagine Miss Atherton deliberately trying to seduce him, or taking advantage of him after the fact if she did. But then, he had never expected it of Miss Townsend, either. One never knew what other people were capable of.

Arriving at the Trevelyan Manor stables, Charles dismounted, handed Tesla to the groom, and strode off toward the house, heaving a sigh. He had to stop thinking about Miss Atherton.

A safe, sane relationship with a modest, decorous English-woman, that's what he needed.

Sophie was calm and grounded, the proper balance for his sometimes chaotic distractedness. His regard for her, admittedly, was more akin to that which he held for his sisters. But that was not necessarily a bad thing. Better men than he had shared marriage beds with women for whom they held only distant feelings, and sired heirs. He could do it. Of course he could.

Charles entered the house and dashed upstairs to see his father. The marquess was sitting up in bed, eating a Cornish pasty and washing it down with ale. He didn't seem to be enjoying the meal much, though. In fact, he looked more poorly than Charles had ever seen him.

They barely exchanged ten words before his father said he wanted to sleep.

Charles left the room, more worried than ever. How much time did the old man have left? Not much, from the look of things. Could Charles truly wait until the end of summer to make good on his promise to his father, and make his engagement official?

He hoped so. There was so much he wanted to accomplish before he tied himself down.

Checking his watch as he descended the stairs, Charles realized that tea would be served in half an hour. If he stayed, it would give him a chance to say hello to his sisters, which he would very much enjoy. On the other hand, it would mean sitting in the saloon for a good hour conversing with his mother and Sophie. Who would keep sending hopeful glances in his direction, hanging on his every word.

All the while, he knew, his mind would keep drifting back to another woman. A woman who had left Trevelyan Manor, and whom he might never see again. Except in his dreams.

Setting his jaw, Charles turned, hurried out through the rear door of the house, and headed back to the stables. He had promised to join the family that evening for dinner. In the meantime, his work was waiting for him.

Hopefully, a few hours at his shop would be consuming enough to take his mind off the tantalizing Miss Atherton.

"Charles, I need you to take Sophie into the village today," his mother said at breakfast on Monday morning.

Charles washed down his eggs with a swallow of coffee. "Oh? Why is that?"

"Sophie's new gown is ready. The dressmaker had promised to deliver it personally, but sent a note with her apologies.

Her horse has gone lame and she won't be able to get out this way for quite some time."

"If you are otherwise engaged today, I understand, Charles," Sophie said quietly. "The gown can wait."

"Well," Charles began, "I do not know if—"

"Charles." His mother shot him a look, implying that this was an order, not a request.

Charles thought about it. It *had* been a long time since he had paid any real attention to Sophie, and he felt a bit ashamed about that. It would not kill him to take his future wife to the dressmaker's, would it, to try on her gown?

I'd rather see Miss Atherton try on a gown. And then remove it.

A spike of arousal darted from his brain to his groin. Charles tensed and drew a quick mental curtain over the thought. *Damn it all to hell.* The few stolen hours he had spent banging away at projects in his workshop the past two days hadn't been as therapeutic as he had hoped. With every strike of the hammer and every twist of the screwdriver, the image of similar motions he'd like to be experiencing with Miss Atherton had invaded his mind.

He required some new activity to help banish thoughts of her. A trip to the village would be a welcome distraction.

"I am happy to take you, Sophie," Charles told her.

She rewarded him with a grateful smile and rose. "I can be ready in half an hour."

Charles ordered the chariot to be brought around, and within the hour he and Sophie were seated side by side on the rear leather seat, on their way into the village.

He glanced at her, figured he ought to say something kind, something a future husband might say. Perhaps a compliment was in order. "You look nice today, Sophie." She did. Her green dress and hat were very pretty.

"Thank you, Charles. I appreciate you doing this."

"It is my pleasure."

"It has been a long while since we shared a carriage together."

"Yes, it has."

He sensed now that something was bothering her; he had no idea what. "I considered taking the curricle and driving myself. But I did not like the look of those clouds. I thought it might rain."

Rain. Miss Atherton on horseback in the rain. My arms wrapped around her tiny waist. Tesla thundering beneath our thighs.

"Did you enjoy your visit to the tenants' farms yesterday?"

Charles blinked. Hard. Farms? Yesterday? Oh yes. "Um . . . well, it was a productive day. Thank you for asking. Have you been enjoying your time here?"

"I have. I have written to my mother every day. I enjoyed walking and riding with Maddie, and I made her a mono-grammed handkerchief."

"Maddie?"

"Madeleine Atherton. Maddie is what her sisters call her."

Of course. Damn it. Did every comment in every conversation have to come back to her? "You call Miss Atherton by her Christian name?"

"We became close in a very short time," Sophie said simply.

If you only knew how close we became. Another thought he was obliged to censor.

Sophie went quiet for a minute or two. He racked his brain for something else to say, but before he could think of anything, she said, "Charles. Do you still want to marry me?"

The remark caught him completely off guard. His eyes flew up to hers. A frown marred her otherwise perfect features. Could she guess where his mind kept going? "What? Of course I do." He wished his reply sounded more convincing. "Why on earth would you ask that?"

"I have been waiting so long. Sometimes I sense that perhaps you would rather it never happened."

His pulse quickened in dismay. "That is not true."

She stared at her hands in her lap. "I saw you once, looking at Miss Atherton."

"Miss Atherton?" His heart jumped now, with a dash of guilt. "What does she have to do with this?"

"I don't know. I just thought that maybe . . . you cared for her."

"Do not be ridiculous. I barely spoke to Miss Atherton when she was here." That wasn't true, but it was what Sophie needed to hear. Charles took her gloved hand and brought it to his lips. "You are perfect, Sophie. It has been decreed by powers higher than ourselves that we will be wed one day. And so we shall."

Her smile returned, which gratified him. "When?" she asked.

When. He let go of her hand as perspiration gathered on his brow.

Charles thought about the promise he had given his father. His mother had deliberately invited Sophie down for the summer, hoping Charles would make his move. And Sophie had been so patient over the years.

I might as well get on with it. The heirloom ring was sitting in a drawer in his bureau. But he didn't need the ring. He didn't need to drop down on one knee, either. He could simply take her hand in his again and say the words that would bind them together forever.

A painful spasm curled in his gut. *No.* No. Not yet.

What was the rush? He had all summer to make good on his promise. *If only Father lasts that long.* He was aware of Sophie's eyes on him, waiting for a reply. He cleared his throat.

"Soon, my dear," he said. "There are some projects I need to complete first."

"What kind of projects?"

"I doubt you would be interested," he answered evasively. "They have nothing to do with you. Once we are married, I doubt I shall have the time required to devote to them. If you will only be patient."

"I will, Charles." Her voice was heavy with meaning as she added, "Did you know your mother has been talking about holding a ball this summer, in honor of her birthday?"

"Has she?" He had an idea where Sophie was going with this, hoped he was wrong.

"Even if you do not wish the wedding to take place yet, the ball might be the perfect time to make an announcement. I know it would make your mother happy. And I should be happy as well, to know that it is finally settled."

There was such hope and affection in her eyes, he couldn't bear to hurt her. Nor could he give her the reply she wanted. He settled for: "Excellent notion. I will think about it."

"Thank you, Charles." A small smile curved her lips as she turned to the window. She said nothing more.

Charles was in no mood for further talk, either. Crossing his arms over his chest, he stared silently out the window for the rest of the journey.

The tiny fishing village of Trevelyan was known for its whitewashed buildings and steep cobbled main street that led uphill from the harbor, where fishing boats rested on the muddy banks, evidence of the shifting tides. Ned parked outside the dressmaker's shop, and while Sophie went inside for her dress fitting, Charles wandered into the pub next door and ordered a pint.

The pub was filled with fishermen back from their morning runs and elderly locals chatting and smoking pipes. Several ruddy-faced chaps stopped by the bar to tip their hats respectfully and ask Charles how his father was getting on.

When he left the pub sometime later, he was surprised to see Dr. Hancock exiting a house across the street. Charles went up to him and they shook hands.

"What brings you to town?" Hancock asked.

Charles gestured toward the dressmaker's shop. "Sophie is picking up a new dress. What about you? Seeing a patient?"

"Yes, a good, kind woman. Ninety-two years of age, God bless her. I predict she will live to be a hundred and five."

Charles grinned, then added more soberly, "If only my father's health was in such good order."

Hancock frowned. "His case is one of the most puzzling I have ever encountered, Saunders. I believe it's cancer, yet in many ways, it doesn't present as cancer. I wish I could do more for him."

At that moment, Sophie exited the dressmaker's shop, holding a large parcel. Charles was about to offer to take it from her, when Hancock strode up to her and doffed his hat. "Lady Sophie. Pray allow me to carry that for you."

"Thank you, Doctor." She gave him the box.

"A new gown, is it?" Hancock commented. "I hope you are happy with it?"

"I am. I had it especially made in my favorite color."

"Ah. Would that be lavender?"

Sophie stared at Hancock, dumbfounded. "How do you come to know my favorite color, Dr. Hancock?"

"It was just a guess," he admitted with a laugh. "I once saw a letter you had left for posting. Your writing paper was lavender, as was the sealing wax you used."

Sophie smiled. "You are most observant, Doctor."

This dialogue was abruptly interrupted by a sudden commotion in the street, which drew their collective attention. Three rustically dressed men thundered up on horseback and dismounted. Two of them dashed into the pub. From the anxious, determined looks on their faces, Charles guessed that they had some kind of news to share with the patrons, a surmise which seemed to be proven when the sound of shouting soon issued from within. The third man, who Charles recognized as Abner Dowrick, the father of one of his workers at the mine, hurried up to where Charles and Dr. Hancock stood. The man's face was contorted with worry.

"Dowrick? What is going on?" Charles asked.

"There's been an accident at Wheal Jenny, milord," Dowrick said urgently, removing his hat.

"Dear God," Charles exclaimed.

"I was sent to fetch ye, Dr. Hancock. There be a good many injuries, and I fear some 'ave died as well. I just thank the Lord it not be my son."

"I will go at once," Hancock said.

"May I ride with you?" Charles asked.

"Of course."

Charles turned to Sophie, whose face had gone pale. "Sophie, you will have to go home with Ned."

She nodded. Hancock deposited her parcel into the chariot. After seeing her off, Charles and Hancock leapt into his own waiting carriage and high-tailed it out of the village. When they arrived at Wheal Jenny, everything was in chaos with workers milling about and women crying. Half a dozen bloodied men lay on the ground, tended by anxious wives. Two more forms, covered by dirty sheets, could only be dead bodies.

Charles spotted the foreman and raced up to him in anguish. "What happened?"

"An explosion, milord. The men say it were a lamp what ignited."

Charles cursed aloud. Light was essential to a miner's labor. But the open flames of the lamps they used could also be lethal, as had once again been proven here.

"Thanks be to God," the foreman went on, "it happened in a part o' the mine where only a few men were working."

Charles nodded grimly. It could have been so much worse.

Dr. Hancock immediately got to work tending to the wounded. Charles rolled up his sleeves and strode forward to help in any way he could. When he learned the names of the miners who had died, tears of anger and sadness burned behind his eyes. They were both good men with families.

This kind of accident, he thought, should never happen. Not in this modern age of invention. Charles vowed that he would perfect the device he was working on, so that a tragedy like this would never occur again.

On her fifth day at Polperran House, Madeleine received the following telegram:

**TO: MISS MADELEINE ATHERTON
POLPERRAN HOUSE, NEAR LONGFORD, CORN-WALL**

YOU'RE A FOOL. I PRAY THAT OAKLEY DOESN'T CHANGE HIS MIND. CHECKED OUT OF BROWN'S

HOTEL. TRAVELING TO THE CONTINENT WITH
A FRIEND. SENDING YOU 5 TRUNKS OF GOWNS.
  MOTHER

"Well," Alexandra said when Madeleine showed her the
wire, "it looks like you'll have plenty of frocks to choose
from this summer."

They laughed.

The conversation turned more somber, however, when
Thomas told them about the terrible accident at Wheal Jenny.
The mine explosion was, he explained, an unfortunate but
common occurrence. It was lucky so few lives had been taken.

The next morning, Thomas rode off to see Lord Saunders and to offer his assistance. Alexandra, Madeleine, Julia,
and Lillie brought food and medicine to the families of the
wounded men in Trevelyan village, and stayed to comfort the
grieving. They ran into Lady Trevelyan, Sophie, and Helen
on the same errand. Despite all their comings and goings,
Madeleine never encountered Lord Saunders, for which she
was grateful.

The tragedy of the mine explosion cast a pall over everything in the region. Alexandra and Madeleine, seeing how
deeply this had affected Julia and Lillie, and feeling it necessary to lift their spirits, invited Helen and Anna to visit on
July the Fourth. In honor of the American celebration, they
decided to make an event of it with a ladies only picnic on the
Polperran House grounds.

It proved to be a lovely day. They played lawn games and

then relaxed on blankets spread on the grass, enjoying the sandwiches, fruit, biscuits, and cakes that Mrs. Nettle had prepared. When they had finished eating, Madeleine read aloud from one of her favorite books, *Little Women*.

The girls listened in rapt attention, and were particularly enthralled by the part where the March girls performed a play for their friends.

"*We* should put on a play," Lillie suggested, when Madeleine had finished reading the second chapter, "just like the March girls."

Julia's eyes lit up. "What a grand idea."

"A play? I've never acted before," Helen pointed out dubiously.

"That doesn't matter," Julia insisted. "Lillie and I were both shy about performing when Alexandra first came as our governess last year. But in no time at all, she had us reading aloud from books. It would be even more thrilling to put on our own theatrics." She glanced at Alexandra. "Could we?"

Alexandra pondered for only the briefest of seconds, then a smile crossed her face. "Why not? I think it's a splendid idea. A play would be the perfect summer activity for you girls." Glancing at Madeleine, she added, "And it would be fun for us, too."

From Alexandra's expression, Madeleine had a sneaking suspicion that her sister was hatching a plan of some kind. But Alexandra just went on, "When Maddie and I were your age, we used to stage plays at home all the time with our sister, Kathryn."

Madeleine nodded, recalling their childhood antics. "We

roped our parents and the servants into attending, made all our own costumes and props, and drew up playbills and everything."

"May we invite *our* parents?" Helen asked. "And Charles?"

"Absolutely," Alexandra replied. "You must invite your whole family."

Madeleine glanced up, alarmed now, as she guessed what Alexandra might be plotting. Did she hope this would create an opportunity for Madeleine to see Lord Saunders again, and set off more sparks? *That* was the last thing she wanted.

"Of course we must invite your family," Madeleine said quickly, "but I wouldn't get your hopes up that they'll attend. Your father is unwell, and your brother is a busy man. Lord Saunders has had a lot to deal with recently, with his mine." She darted a glare at Alexandra, as if to say, *Get that thought right out of your mind.*

Alexandra responded with an innocent shrug.

"Well," Anna said, "even if they do not come, it will be heaps of fun."

"When you put on your plays," Lillie asked Alexandra, "where did you get your scripts?"

"Every one was original," Alexandra replied proudly. "Maddie always wrote them."

Four pairs of eyes now turned to Madeleine in wonder. "You *wrote* the plays you performed?" Helen asked, astonished. "Just like Jo in *Little Women?*"

Madeleine's face warmed with modest pride. "I did."

"They were wonderful, too," Alexandra said. "Everyone said so."

"Everyone except Mother," Madeleine pointed out dryly. "Mother always called my writing a stupid hobby. We were lucky she allowed us to perform at all."

"Mother disapproved of everything fun. She still does." Alexandra sighed.

"Maddie," Lillie said, "will you write a play for us?"

The question gave Madeleine pause. "I don't know, Lillie." She'd been making steady progress recently on the book she was writing, and would rather not break that momentum.

"Maddie: you absolutely *must* do it," Alexandra insisted. "You could whip one up in a few days, I've seen you do it."

"Please?" Julia said.

"Yes, please!" Anna enthused.

Madeleine hesitated again. It had been a long time since she had written a play. She wasn't certain she could write one so quickly, and more importantly, one worth performing. But the girls had such hope in their eyes, how could she say no? "What kind of play do you want?" Madeleine asked.

"A drama," answered Julia.

"Something filled with action," Helen said.

"A love story," Anna countered.

"A comedy," Lillie insisted.

Madeleine laughed, delighted by their diverse replies as well as their enthusiasm. "I'll tell you what," she replied with a smile. "I'll write you something with all of those elements combined."

CHAPTER FOURTEEN

Madeleine spent every spare minute of the next four days writing a play for the girls. She wrote from the moment she arose until long after dark, only taking breaks to eat and sleep.

The piece she concocted was about two daughters of a duke who were being courted by noblemen who bored them. One of the girls was in love with a young solicitor who broadened her mind, but of whom the duke violently disapproved. Madeleine threw in an aborted elopement, a carriage accident, an escape through a field of sheep, and a resolution in which the duke allowed his daughters to put off marriage in order to attend a women's college.

The girls adored the play from the start. It was decided that Lillie and Anna would play the sisters, while Julia and Helen would take on multiple roles as their dim-witted beaux, their parents, and other minor parts.

Alexandra begged off performing, insisting that she was too pregnant to participate, but would be happy to serve as stage manager. Madeleine was appointed director, and the girls insisted she must also play the dashing solicitor.

The group spent a long day working in the library, each writing out her own copy of the script. After sending out invitations to their families and servants, the real work—and fun—began. Eight days were devoted to rehearsals, gathering props, and drawing up playbills. Costumes were assembled from their own wardrobes and from the Polperran House attic, which was stuffed with ancestral offerings.

Madeleine enjoyed every aspect of the preparation and planning. So many years had passed since she had been similarly occupied, that in a way, it was like reliving the best memories from her own childhood.

Visitors were banned from rehearsals. Although Helen struggled at first to find a comfortable footing onstage, she was a whiz at memorizing lines and soon came into her own. Anna and Lillie threw themselves into their parts with verve. Julia was particularly hilarious as one of the suitors, and gave a heartwarming performance as the father at his daughter's bedside, as she hovered on the brink of death before making a miraculous recovery.

In the beginning, Helen and Anna drove back and forth from Trevelyan Manor to Polperran House for rehearsals. But this was seen to be a great waste of time, so for the last few days leading up to the performance, the girls stayed at Polperran, where it felt like one grand slumber party.

The enterprise was so all-consuming, that during this period Madeleine had no time to give a single thought to Lord Oakley, or to ponder her misbegotten attraction to

Lord Saunders. Well. She *did* dream about Saunders once or twice. Or three times. Dreams in which they exchanged erotic kisses, and from which she awakened hot and heavy, full of self-recrimination.

And which she promptly put out of her mind.

At the moment, she told herself, she wasn't an heiress with a crush on an unavailable earl, and an offer of matrimony from a future duke. She was simply a playwright creating a work for the stage. In *that* role, Madeleine felt as though she were truly in her element.

The performance was held on a Thursday afternoon in mid-July in the gallery, a magnificent hall that made up the entire east wing of Polperran House, with a barrel-shaped plasterwork ceiling and windows framed by red velvet draperies.

They set up rows of chairs facing an area they cleared and designated as the stage. In lieu of a curtain, two folding screens were placed at each side to conceal the actors while they changed costumes or waited for their cues. The primary scenes took place in a drawing room, which was created with assorted furniture from the house. A few more adventurous scenes, such as the runaway carriage, were depicted in pantomime.

At the appointed day and hour, the audience began to arrive. Madeleine's stomach curled in nervous anticipation as she peered out from behind one of the screens, dressed as "Mr. Danvers, solicitor."

Her costume, which had belonged to Thomas's father,

reportedly a man of slight build and short stature, fit surprisingly well. It was the first time since Madeleine was a child that she had dressed up as a man, and the ensemble of wool trousers, shirt, tie, and frock coat, topped off by a high silk hat, felt both foreign and excitingly scandalous. She had completed the look by drawing a mustache in charcoal across her upper lip.

The girls, made up, costumed, and coiffured, giggled beside her.

Madeleine caught sight of Alexandra ushering Thomas to his seat in the front row. He had a smile on his face, as did the dozen or more servants who were taking seats near the back, murmuring amongst themselves. An air of simmering excitement filled the room. Moments later, some bustle was heard from the corridor. Alexandra reappeared, escorting in Lady and Lord Trevelyan.

Madeleine started in surprise. She knew they had been invited, but as expected, Lady Trevelyan had written to express her regrets, citing Lord Trevelyan's precarious health. Yet here they were. His Lordship was seated in a wheelchair, being pushed by a nurse. He looked ashen and weak. Madeleine couldn't begin to imagine the effort it must have taken for him to rise from his bed and come all this way to see Helen and Anna perform. It was a real testament to his affection for his daughters and his strength of will.

If *they* were here, Madeleine wondered suddenly, did it mean . . .

She barely had time to register that thought when Lord Saunders strode into the room, accompanied by Sophie.

Madeleine froze, her heart banging in her chest like a drum. The last time she'd seen Lord Saunders, they had been kissing in a cave. Three weeks had passed since then. During that time, she had tried to persuade herself that she had overestimated the degree of his attractiveness in her mind.

She hadn't.

The twosome paused just inside the doorway. Clad in a dark suit that accentuated his broad shoulders and tall, masculine frame, Saunders radiated a charm that seemed to affect the entire room. Sophie wore a lavender silk frock, her upsweep of luxurious blond hair showing off her pretty face.

Madeleine had never expected *him* to come, had rather hoped he wouldn't. Didn't he have better things to do than to watch his sisters perform in an amateur theatrical? Apparently not. She watched as he and Sophie took their seats.

Madeleine turned away and closed her eyes. She refused to let his presence affect her. She and the girls had worked hard on this play. She was going to give it everything she had.

And try not to think about how perfect Saunders and Sophie looked, sitting there together in the second row, his handsome magnetism complemented by Sophie's fresh-as-a-daisy look.

Whereas Madeleine was standing there dressed like a man. In a frock coat and trousers. And a mustache.

The play ended. The small audience erupted into applause. Many of the women leapt to their feet.

Charles took their cue and rose, clapping for all he was worth.

He had expected the play to be a mere trifle. Just something for his and Longford's sisters to do during the summer. He had only come because his sisters had begged him to. His attendance had nothing to do with the fact that he had known Miss Atherton was at the helm of the whole thing. That it would give him an opportunity to see her again.

It had nothing to do with *that* at all.

He had anticipated an hour of amateur acting and an amateurish script. What he'd just observed had turned out to be something else again. The play itself, although clearly meant to entertain, was also marvelously clever and heartfelt. He'd had no idea a woman could write like that. The plays he'd attended in town had all been written by men. Miss Atherton's message, about the importance of education for women—a theme which didn't surprise him one bit—had been slyly interwoven with an exuberant plot.

The girls' lack of experience had been made up for by the obvious joy they had felt in the performance. And Miss Atherton—he would never have guessed it, as her expressed passion was writing, after all—had a natural ability onstage and an excellent sense of timing. She was damnably funny. And she'd played a man! She'd had the role down pat. He might have actually mistaken her for a man—albeit a very *attractive* man—if not for the feminine curves which that tight-fitting frock coat could not hide.

The young actors came forward now to receive their embraces, jumping with excitement. Charles hugged his sisters and told Julia and Lillie what a great job they had done. His father took the girls' hands from his wheelchair and offered his praise, as did his mother, Thomas, and Alexandra.

While the servants came up to pay their respects, Charles noticed Miss Atherton standing off to one side, watching all this with a grin. He debated whether or not to go up to her. After what had happened in the cave, he would not blame her if she never wanted to speak to him again. But he felt drawn to her like a magnet.

I will never breathe a word about this. Let's pretend it never happened.

He could do that. He *would* do that, difficult as it might be. His heart hammered in his ears as he crossed the room and offered her a bow. "Miss Atherton."

Her blue eyes lifted to his. She appeared guarded. "Lord Saunders," was her polite reply.

"Pray allow me to congratulate you on an excellent performance."

"Thank you."

An awkward silence followed. There was so much he wished he could say to her, but none of it was possible, not with all these people about. "You got some excellent performances out of those girls. But more than that: the script was wonderful, both funny and meaningful. I admired your theme, radical though it was."

"You thought it radical?" Her mouth curved with amusement. That damnable charcoal mustache curved into a smile of its own.

Charles fought a sudden urge to wipe that mustache away

with a fingertip. Or, alternatively, to rub that same fingertip over the pink lips beneath it.

Stop it stop it stop it. "Most radical indeed," he heard himself say. "The daughters of a duke attending college? I doubt that will happen anytime this century."

"Well, the century is nearly over, my lord. Let us hope for more progressive thinking in the next."

He started to reply, but was prevented when Sophie glided up and said, "Maddie. I am in awe. That was absolutely wonderful."

"I'm so pleased you liked it."

"Liked it? I loved it. Everyone did."

"The girls had fun," Miss Atherton said. "That's the most important thing."

"I should never have your courage! To act upon the stage!" Sophie lowered her voice, her eyes teasing. "And how scandalous you are, to dress as a man!"

Miss Atherton laughed at that and seemed to be about to reply, when his mother and father appeared. "Miss Atherton?" his father said, weak and pale, from his wheelchair.

"Your Lordship," Miss Atherton answered, reaching down to take his hand. "I can't tell you what an honor it is to see you here. How are you feeling?"

"Fair to middling," the old man answered. The mere act of talking seemed to wear him out. "But let us not talk of that, young lady. I wish to congratulate you on a job well done. I do not approve of all this girls-going-to-college nonsense, but the play had its moments."

"I *loved* it," his mother interjected. "Helen and Anna have talked of nothing else but this play for weeks. I have never seen Helen so animated. You have quite brought her out of herself, Miss Atherton. I know it was all due to your hard work and genius. Thank you."

Miss Atherton bowed her head at the compliment. "Thank *you* for saying so, Your Ladyship."

"Now I fear we must take our leave," his mother said, casting a worried glance at his father. "Charles? Will you call for the coach?"

Charles nodded, tamping down his frustration. "Of course." He had wanted to talk longer with Miss Atherton. Now all he could do was to give her a parting smile. "Good day, Miss Atherton."

"Good day," she answered to his party at large. "Thank you all so much for coming."

"I would not have missed it," Charles insisted. With that, he was forced to leave the room.

Madeleine and Alexandra spent the rest of the afternoon supervising the girls while the servants cleaned up after the performance. Helen and Anna had been granted permission to stay one more night to help put costumes away.

The talk at dinner consisted of nothing but the play. The girls reveled in their accomplishment, recounting the audience's reactions and laughing over tiny mistakes they'd made which, in retrospect, only made the experience more humorous and exciting.

When it came time to retire for the night, the house still

buzzed with energy. As Madeleine lay in bed, listening to the girls' chatter and laughter from down the hall, she struggled to calm her own brain.

She was proud of the girls. The play itself had been a triumph as well. People had laughed at all the right places and gasped at every twist of the plot. Although playwriting was not her ambition, it was rewarding to have her writing so well received.

She recalled the moment when Lord Saunders had come up to her after the play. It had been disconcerting to speak to him again. Madeleine sensed that he'd also found it rather awkward, which was understandable, with Sophie standing right there. They'd only had two seconds to talk, which was just as well.

Hopefully, Madeleine thought as she finally drifted off to sleep, she would have no reason to encounter him again over the next two months. She could forget about him, move on, and enjoy her summer at Polperran House in peace.

This idea was disabused two mornings later, upon the arrival of a letter from Trevelyan Manor.

"This just came for you, Miss Atherton," intoned Hutchens, the distinguished, white-haired butler, as Madeleine arrived in the breakfast room.

Julia and Lillie had not yet risen. Thomas was taking care of a matter for one of the tenants. Hutchens extended a silver salver with an envelope upon it. Who, Madeleine wondered idly, and not for the first time, had come up with this absurd practice of presenting the mail on a tray? And why was it always silver?

"Thank you, Hutchens." Madeleine took the envelope, fully expecting it to be from Sophie, with whom she had exchanged numerous missives since she'd come to Polperran House. However, she didn't recognize the handwriting on the envelope.

"Another letter from Sophie?" Alexandra brought her plate over from the sideboard and sat down.

"No." Madeleine noticed a distinctive coronet imprinted on the envelope, along with the marchioness's name. "It's from Lady Trevelyan," she said in surprise.

"A servant is waiting downstairs for your reply, miss," Hutchens told her. "It seems to be a matter of some urgency."

Intrigued, Madeleine withdrew the letter and read it through:

Trevelyan Manor
July 20, 1889

My Dear Miss Atherton,

May I begin by reiterating how grateful we are for the effort you put into the marvelous play performance. My daughters are still floating on a cloud of excitement and satisfaction from the experience. I feel certain that it will be the highlight of the summer, if not the entire year.

I now wish to apprise you of another matter entirely, which is of more serious note. I am writing on behalf of my niece.

Yesterday morning, Sophie was out riding with Charles,

*when she was thrown by her horse. I am alarmed to say that
she suffered a mild concussion of the brain, a small broken
bone in her hand, and a twisted ankle—injuries which,
thankfully, Dr. Hancock assures us will cause no permanent
impairment. Indeed, her headache is nearly gone today.*

*However, the doctor said her hand will require about
three weeks to heal, and her ankle, which appears to be a
serious type of sprain, may take equally as long.*

*It is Sophie's right hand, making it impossible for her
to write, which is why she asked me to pen this letter. The
thought of being kept indoors for three weeks entire, being
unable to take the daily walks and rides to which she is
accustomed, or even to write the letters to her mother which
she likes to send on a regular basis, has left her in very low
spirits.*

*Sophie begs me to ask if you would be so kind as to
come to Trevelyan Manor to keep her company during her
convalescence. I believe that having a friend her own age
here would make all the difference in her recovery. I know
you and Sophie are of short acquaintance, but in that time,
she said, you have become very dear to her. She insists that
she would prefer your company to anyone else's.*

*I realize this is asking a great deal of you—that you
may have plans to return to London, or prefer to spend the
coming month with your own family. But if it is at all within
your power to accede to Sophie's request, I know it would
make her extremely happy.*

*Be assured as well that Lord Trevelyan and I would
be pleased to receive you again at our home, where you are*

welcome to stay as long as you like. Should Lord Longford's
coach be available, please feel free to make your way hither
immediately. This afternoon would not be too soon. Or,
should you wish me to send a carriage, I would be happy to
do so.

I eagerly await your reply.

With all best wishes,
Charlotte Grayson

Madeleine, with equal parts astonishment and distress,
handed the letter to her sister. "Poor Sophie," she said, after
Alexandra had read it through.

"You should go to her," Alexandra advised.

Madeleine shook her head. She felt terrible that Sophie
had been so seriously injured. And she was honored—
flattered—that Sophie sought *her* companionship to get
through the difficult weeks ahead. But returning to Trevelyan
Manor meant being, once again, in the presence of Lord
Saunders.

It had been difficult enough to contend with her confusing
attraction to him on her first visit. Before they had kissed.
A kiss which still burned on her lips, and infiltrated her
memory at the most inconvenient moments. Even now, she
felt her cheeks grow warm at the thought of it.

"I don't think so," Madeleine said. "I've been so looking
forward to being here with you all summer. I don't want to
miss the baby's birth."

"The baby isn't due until August twenty-third. That's five

weeks away. She's asking you to come for three weeks only. You'll be back in plenty of time."

"Sophie doesn't need me. There are plenty of servants to help. Lady Trevelyan can write her letters for her."

"Sophie asked *expressly* for you. She's your friend. She's been injured. You could be a real help to her, Maddie. How can you even *think* of not going?" Alexandra looked at her. "What are you *really* worried about? Is it Lord Saunders?"

"Of course it's Lord Saunders! If Sophie had even the slightest inkling that he and I had kissed, she would never have asked me to come. If Lady Trevelyan knew, she would never have written that letter."

"I suppose that's true, but—"

"It was one thing to see him the day of the performance," Madeleine interrupted. "That was brief and in a room full of people. But to live at Trevelyan Manor again for three entire weeks? To see him every day? No. No. That would be too difficult."

"It might be." Alexandra took Madeleine's hand in hers and looked her in the eye. "On the other hand, this could be your chance to see how you really feel about Lord Saunders. And for *him* to discover how he feels about you."

"He feels nothing, believe me," Madeleine insisted. "I'm just another in a long line of women he has kissed."

"I don't believe that. I don't care what other ladies say about him, Maddie. I've known Charles longer than you, and I think him a good, decent man. He kissed you and then profusely apologized, which means it wasn't some meaningless act; his emotions were invested. I think he might have feelings for you that he hasn't allowed himself to examine. If you spend more time together, you might well discover that your attraction to each other is unfounded, and has no future in it. If that's the case, it would help clear your mind to see what Lord Oakley means to you, and allow *him* to move forward with his plans to marry Sophie without qualms."

Madeleine took that in. She swallowed hard. "What if the reverse proves true? What if I discover that I *do* have feelings for him, but they aren't returned?"

"Whatever happens, isn't it better to know the truth than to hide from it?"

"I don't know. Maybe." Madeleine blew out a long sigh, then shook her head again. "It feels wrong for me to go to Trevelyan Manor under such circumstances. It isn't fair to Sophie."

"Sophie is far from home and needs a friend," Alexandra insisted. "If the man she expects to marry doesn't love her, she deserves to know the truth." Alexandra paused, then added resolutely, "Maddie: if you don't go there now and find out where *your* heart lies, you'll spend the rest of your life wondering what might have been."

Chapter Fifteen

By six o'clock that evening, Madeleine was once again ensconced in the same bedroom at Trevelyan Manor which she had formerly occupied, where she was immediately made to feel at home and welcome.

Two vases of cheerful yellow roses adorned the dresser and end table. A stack of writing paper, pens, and a brand-new bottle of ink awaited on the desktop, which she decided could only have come from Woodson. Madeleine wondered if he'd guessed she was writing a book, or if the supplies were just meant for writing letters. Either way, it was a thoughtful and insightful gesture.

Being here still didn't sit well with Madeleine, though. She felt as if she'd returned to the scene of a crime and wished she hadn't let her sister talk her into it. But she was here now, and had to make the best of it.

She would make up for it, Madeleine determined, by being the best friend to Sophie she could possibly be. And, she determined, she wouldn't seek out Lord Saunders's company.

With any luck, based on the amount of time he seemed to spend away from home, she'd see him only rarely. If she happened to run into him, she'd make sure it was a brief encounter, and that only casual conversation ensued between them.

There would definitely be no more kissing.

Madeleine had arrived this time with more baggage than on her first visit, bringing some of her favorite day dresses from the trunks her mother had sent down from London. As she unpacked, a knock came at the door. She opened it to find Sophie seated in a wheelchair pushed by Nancy, a maid.

"Maddie!" Sophie cried as the maid wheeled her into the room. Sophie sported a cast on her right hand that went to the elbow, and her right ankle, peeking out from beneath her summer gown, was encased in an unwieldy-looking bandage. Even so, she looked pretty as a picture and seemed to be in good spirits. "They told me you had come! I could not wait another minute to see you. I am so happy you are here."

She wouldn't be so happy if she knew about the kiss. Madeleine managed a smile. "I'm glad to be here," she answered sincerely, "but so sorry you have injured yourself so grievously."

"It is not nearly so bad as it could have been. My horse lost her footing in rocky terrain. By some miracle my head hit a patch of grass. Had I banged my head on a rock, Dr. Hancock says I would have suffered a far graver concussion, and might have even died."

"Oh!" Madeleine winced. "You were indeed lucky."

"I *was*. And I know I should not complain. But this cast is itchy. The thought that I cannot walk or write for three entire weeks is tormenting. I cried all day yesterday. When your note arrived this morning, I was cheered up immensely."

Lady Trevelyan greeted Madeleine with grace at dinner, murmuring under her breath, "I am so grateful to you for coming. I know it will make all the difference to Sophie. She is herself again already."

Madeleine was sorry to hear that Lord Trevelyan was still unwell and unable to join them at the table. Lord Saunders was away for a couple of days, "visiting his friend Leonard in Truro." Although relieved to discover that she wouldn't have to face him for a while longer, at the same time, Madeleine felt a pang of disappointment at his absence, and found herself wondering, yet again, where his secret workshop *really* was.

The conversation at dinner centered mainly on Sophie's accident and her depiction of her cousin's heroic actions in helping her home to safety.

"I cannot imagine what would have happened had Charles not been with me." Sophie smiled in between sips of soup, which she accomplished slowly and carefully, holding her spoon in her left hand. "Charles was so kind and gentle. He carried me all the way back to the house."

An image flashed into Madeleine's mind of Sophie, her arms wrapped around Lord Saunders's neck, her face nuzzled gratefully against his cheek as he carried her through the woods to safety. Madeleine's stomach prickled with an uncomfortable sensation. Was it envy?

Don't be a ninny. Lord Saunders could carry Sophie in his arms all he liked. No matter what Alexandra might say,

Madeleine was certain that Saunders and Sophie were to be married. *You should reserve such thoughts for Lord Oakley.*

It occurred to Madeleine that she hadn't thought about Lord Oakley in quite some time.

She closed her eyes, trying to envision Lord Oakley sweeping her off her feet and carrying her across the lawn at Hatfield Park. Oakley was so refined and proper, and his mannerisms so cautious and tentative, Madeleine suspected that—were he ever to attempt such a thing—it would be an awkward affair, and he would probably drop her. The idea was so amusing that she couldn't prevent a small laugh.

"Do you find Sophie's accident humorous, Miss Atherton?" Lady Trevelyan was looking at her in puzzlement.

"No, indeed," Madeleine replied quickly. "I feel certain that Lord Saunders's actions prevented Sophie from incurring further injury, which may have proved quite grave." She immediately changed the subject, commenting on Sophie's new frock, a subject which was dear to the hearts of both the young lady and her aunt. The ensuing conversation about the new fashions kept them occupied for the remainder of the meal.

That night, after the rest of the household retired, Madeleine retrieved her manuscript from her trunk and indulged herself in a few hours of solid work. After the distraction of the play, it felt good to get back to her book, which was progressing chapter by chapter.

The next morning found her in the library, scribbling a

letter to Sophie's mother, which Sophie dictated from her reclined position on the sofa. They were several paragraphs into what promised to be a lengthy missive, including the details of Sophie's injury, the heroism of Lord Saunders, and the attentiveness of the doctor, when Dr. Hancock himself strode into the room.

"Good morning," said he, crossing to them with a bow.

Sophie quickly sat up, straightening her skirts as both ladies returned the greeting.

"I have just seen His Lordship, and wanted to inquire after my other patient. How are you feeling, Lady Sophie?" Dr. Hancock's smile was personable and professional at the same time.

"I am well, Doctor," Sophie answered, returning his smile. "My headache is gone."

"Excellent. What a pleasure to see you again at Trevelyan Manor, Miss Atherton."

"And you, Doctor. How is Lord Trevelyan?"

"He is much the same."

"Her Ladyship mentioned that you find his case puzzling," Madeleine commented.

He nodded. "He has an array of symptoms that do not normally go together, or point to any one disease. Unfortunately, these past months, I have seen no improvement."

"I'm so sorry to hear that."

"We are all sorry," he remarked with feeling.

Setting down his black bag, Dr. Hancock set to work unwrapping the bandage from Sophie's ankle. With great care and attention he examined the injured appendage, which was swollen and discolored. He added that under no circumstances must she put any weight on that foot until he felt certain it was healed. After exchanging some further dialogue with the patient, and giving her medication to relieve the pain, the doctor took his leave.

Later that morning, Helen and Anna were allowed to accompany Madeleine as she pushed Sophie around the garden in her wheelchair. After lunch, Sophie was carried upstairs to take a nap, and Madeleine returned outside for a solitary walk.

Rather than return to the coast, Madeleine set out in a new direction, through the woods and across the meadows. She hummed to herself as she ambled along, passing farmhouses and climbing over the stiles that separated one property from another. The landscape was lush and serene, the only sounds the whisper of the wind in the trees and grasses, the buzz of insects, and the bleating of sheep.

After walking for perhaps three quarters of an hour, Madeleine came upon a tidy-looking farm. A man was hard at work in the fields. The farmhouse was well maintained, and the barn and stables appeared to be relatively new. In the yard, a woman hung wet laundry on a line, while two small children played tag among the sheets.

At the far edge of the acreage stood an ancient barn constructed of stone, brick, and timber. Its few windows were all shuttered. The thatched roof gave it a charming appearance. A small adjacent building looked to be an old abandoned stable. Madeleine guessed that the farmer had replaced these older buildings with the new ones.

Just then, a horse stuck its head out through the opening of a Dutch door in the old stables, which she'd thought to be abandoned. Madeleine stopped, recognizing the beast. It was Tesla. As she processed this information, the door to the old barn suddenly opened.

Madeleine's heart gave an involuntary leap of astonishment as Lord Saunders himself stepped out.

He stood about thirty feet away. And he looked . . . in a word . . . disheveled.

He wore no coat or tie, just a white shirt that was open at the neck, with his sleeves rolled up above the elbows. Over this he wore a long, dark gray apron that was badly stained— the kind of apron a blacksmith or carpenter might wear. His brown hair was in disarray, sticking up in several directions, a tousled look that was inexplicably captivating.

She stared at him, wondering if that's the way his hair looked when he got up out of bed in the morning. Blood rushed to Madeleine's cheeks. *What am I doing, thinking about him getting out of bed?*

This perusal took place in the blink of an eye. As she watched, Saunders bent down and placed a tray of dirty dishes and glassware on the stone path by the front door. When he stood up again, his gaze traveled in her direction . . . and he froze.

Shock rendered him speechless.

Madeleine also found herself at a loss for words. She knew perfectly well what she had, inadvertently, come upon. The place where Lord Saunders had made those beautiful hairpins and clockwork sculptures.

His secret workshop.

Who knew what else he was working on in there? She had promised herself that she wouldn't seek him out—and she hadn't. She had further promised that if she did run into him, it would be only a brief encounter. Well, she could be brief. Curiosity overcame her scruples.

Madeleine strode deliberately up the path and stopped a few feet away from him. "Good afternoon, my lord."

Charles stared at her.

Last he knew, Miss Atherton was safely stowed at Polperran House. *Safe*, he had told himself, because she'd been out of reach, out of sight. *But not out of mind.* Since the day, weeks ago, when she left Trevelyan Manor, she had continued to be foremost in his thoughts. He had constantly found himself wondering where she was and what she was doing.

Since he'd retreated to his workshop a couple of days ago, the wondering had escalated and become carnal in nature. He had imagined in graphic detail what he'd like to do with her—*to her*—if only he could be alone with her in his private space. The daydreams had been incredibly arousing, leaving him hard as a rock and aching.

He had been entirely aware that those daydreams would never happen, not in his lifetime. He could wish all he wanted, but she was never going to suddenly, magically appear on his doorstep and jump into bed with him.

Yet here she was. How on earth had she found him?

Part of him rejoiced at this apparition, while another part

of him—the sane, rational part—warned him that she was an excellent, highly intelligent woman who had no idea what was going on in his mind. Under no circumstances should he let her enter his shop. Not just because he wasn't keen to share what he was working on. More because, after all the erotic fantasies he'd had about her, he couldn't be certain he could keep his hands off of her.

Especially the way she looked at the moment—so damned attractive in a wispy white summer dress that hugged her curves and contrasted perfectly with her fair complexion and shiny reddish-brown hair. It suddenly occurred to him that he was wearing his oldest clothes and the world's filthiest apron.

Embarrassed, he shut the door behind him, running his fingers through his unruly hair to tame it. "Miss Atherton. What brings you out this way?"

"I was taking a walk. I've never explored this area." She gave him an innocent smile.

Innocent? He wasn't so sure. For ten years, he had managed to keep his workshop's location a secret. She had been in Cornwall for what, a little more than a month? And she'd managed to find it. He wouldn't put it past her to have come out deliberately looking for the place. He didn't know whether to damn her tenacity or admire her for it.

"Hooo. It's so hot." She removed her hat and fanned herself with it. "Are we still on the Trevelyan estate?"

His glance fell on the moisture that had collected on her brow. Moisture she wiped away with the back of her hand. He wished he could be that hand. *Idiot, answer her question.* "No. Just beyond it."

She glanced at the dirty dishes on the tray at his feet. Then in the direction of the farmhouse. Then back at him. Her silent look inferred that she knew what those dishes signified. "So, this is the place, huh?" she said. "This is where you stay for days at a time, to make your magic?"

Despite himself, a grin tugged at his lips. There was no point in denying it. "It is. I would appreciate it, though, if you would keep that information to yourself."

"No problem, my lord. That's just one more secret I'm keeping where you and I are concerned."

He felt his face flush at that. She was referring to their kiss, of course. Shouldn't she be blushing as well? She didn't even bat an eyelash. "Why are you here? At Trevelyan, I mean? I thought you were at your sister's."

"Your mother asked me to come. To be a companion to Sophie while she convalesces."

"Ah. How kind of you." Poor Sophie had taken an awful spill. It could be weeks before she recovered. Would Miss Atherton stay at the manor house the entire time? If so, how would he cope with all these fantasies and feelings that continued to haunt him every time he thought about her? Which was basically all the time? "Well, you found me out, Miss Atherton. Congratulations." He stepped back, his hand on the doorknob. "I bid you good afternoon."

"Wait! You're not going to turn me away, are you? Without showing me what you're working on?"

"I am doing precisely that."

"But I'd love to see—"

"There is nothing here that you would find of interest."

"I doubt that. Anything you would sculpt or create would be of interest to me, Lord Saunders."

That's right. She thinks I am a sculptor. "Curiosity killed the cat, Miss Atherton."

"I am not a cat."

"My shop is not a fit place to show a lady." This was true.

"I'm not a lady. At least, not according to the British definition of the term." She gave him an impish grin.

"I do not show my workshop to *anyone*."

"Why not?"

"My projects are ongoing, unfinished. They are my own business."

"I feel the same way. Whenever I'm in the process of writing something, I don't like to show it to just *anyone* until it's finished."

"Well then, you understand why I don't—"

"But," she interrupted, "there *are* certain people to whom I *do* show my work. People whose input and opinions I value. Working in solitude is vitally important for a while, but it's lonely, too. At times, having another pair of eyes can be useful."

He paused. There was truth in what she said. It is why he went to London so often. To discuss his work with like-minded people. She was a creative person herself. He recalled the conversation they had shared, that day on the bluffs. How informed she had been regarding scientific matters. Perhaps she *would* be interested in what he was doing. It would not hurt to give her a peek, would it?

No. No. No. It was a bad idea to let her inside his shop—to spend any time alone with her. And it wasn't as if he could spell out the reason why. "Sorry. That might work for you, Miss Atherton, but not for me."

To his dismay, she plunked down on the path at his feet.

"What are you doing? You will mess your white gown."

"I don't care. I have nowhere else I need to be. I am happy to sit here all afternoon long if necessary. And the nights are warm."

"You cannot be serious."

"I have never been more serious in my life."

Charles shook his head in disbelief. "You are never going to leave until you have your way, are you?"

"No." She gave him a determined smile.

Charles heaved a sigh. He could not very well leave her out here, camped on his doorstep. Well, he'd just have to keep his distance from her and be on his best behavior. He opened the door, allowing her access to the building. "Very well, Miss Atherton. But do not say I didn't warn you."

Chapter Sixteen

As Madeleine stepped inside the cavernous space, her senses were immediately struck by the scents of metal and machine oil.

It took a moment for her eyes to grow accustomed to the change in lighting from the bright outdoors. When she was able to see properly again, she couldn't prevent a small gasp.

She'd been expecting an artisan's studio. A table heaped with wire, boxes of clockwork pieces, maybe a few sculptures in progress.

There *were* boxes of wire and clockwork pieces, but no sculptures that she could see. Because this wasn't the studio of an artist.

It was the workshop of an *inventor*.

The barn must have been modernized, because it had a floor of hardwood planks and the walls were finished and whitewashed. Scads of machines and tools, whose purposes she couldn't even begin to imagine, were set up around the room. They looked like the kinds of things she'd seen when she'd visited a machine shop owned by her father. A series of scattered gas lamps shed light on a dozen or more long tables in the large, open space. Everywhere were boxes overflowing with wood pieces and metal parts. The tables held innumerable devices that appeared to be in various stages of construction. Things made of wood. Metal. Wire. Fabric. Cardboard. Tubing. Along with stacks of drawings and endless piles of scribbled notes.

"As I mentioned, it is rather a mess." Saunders had removed his apron and was washing his hands at a nearby basin.

"It's not. It is amazing." Madeleine shook her head in wonderment. "I thought you were a sculptor or an artist. But that's not true, is it? You're an inventor."

He shrugged lightly. "I aspire to be."

"How long have you been coming here?"

"About ten years. I had a small workshop on our own grounds when I was younger. But on my fourteenth birthday, Father demolished it. I tried to give up the practice, but found I could not. So, in time, I found . . . other accommodations."

"You mother and sisters seem to know about it, although they won't admit it."

"They know I *have* a shop. I have never disclosed its location. The only people who know are the farmer who rents me this building and his wife, who keeps me fed."

A potbelly stove stood by a far wall, beside a small table where Madeleine guessed he must take his meals. Glancing up, she noticed that the barn's former hayloft had been remodeled into a pristine living space, reachable by a set of stairs. She spied a bed covered in a heap of quilts. "You sleep here?"

"At times."

An image infiltrated her brain of Lord Saunders, splayed out on the bed, naked except for a narrow bit of sheet draped over his private parts. The mental picture made her cheeks flame. *Stop it, Madeleine.*

"Sleeping here allows me to work without interruption," Saunders was saying, "and reinforces the illusion that I am away."

His glance met hers.

"In Truro," they said in unison. They both laughed.

"So whenever you want to work, you tell your family that you're visiting your friend Leonard?"

He nodded.

"Do you even *have* a friend called Leonard?"

His green eyes twinkled as he gave her sidelong grin. "No. I invented him."

"Your stock in trade." Madeleine smiled. "Did you perchance name your imaginary friend after Leonardo da Vinci?"

He looked surprised. "An astute guess, Miss Atherton."

"It wasn't a wild leap. Da Vinci *was* a brilliant inventor."

"Indeed he was."

Saunders tucked his thumbs into the pockets of his trousers. The movement caught Madeleine's eye, and her gaze lingered on his hands and forearms beneath his rolled-up sleeves. The memory of those hands touching *her* hands, her body, her face, swept through her like a lightning strike, reigniting the feelings he had inspired the one time he had kissed her.

Madeleine averted her gaze. She wanted to smack herself.

That kind of touching should never have happened. And she shouldn't be thinking about it now.

Clearing her throat, she crossed to the nearest table. It was covered with metal boxes about the size of a small loaf of bread. "What are you making here?"

"I am trying to build a better battery."

Madeleine was fascinated. "Didn't Alessandro Volta invent the first battery nearly a hundred years ago?"

"Yes." Saunders seemed impressed that she knew this. "But his had a host of problems, including a very short life. Scientists across the world have been working to improve it ever since. It is a long and laborious process. I need a battery that is not too large or too heavy to carry, and will provide power for a full day if possible."

"For any particular purpose?"

"Yes. To power an electric lamp, to save lives."

"An electric lamp to save lives?" Madeleine considered that, suddenly understanding the motivation behind his project. "Oh! You are thinking of the mine."

"I am."

"Forgive me, I never got a chance to tell you how sorry I was to hear about the accident at Wheal Jenny."

"Thank you. And thank you for the help I hear you and your family gave to many of our workers afterward."

"You're welcome." Madeleine paused. "Tell me, Lord Saunders, if I understand this correctly. If a miner's lamp were powered by a battery instead of an open flame, it wouldn't be prone to explosion. And thus much safer."

"Exactly." He glanced at her with appreciation in his eyes.

She sensed that, despite his reluctance to admit her into his shop, he was pleased to have someone to share this side of himself with.

"What an excellent notion."

"That is only part of my plan. Miners currently wear soft caps." Saunders picked up a metal helmet, one of several prototypes. "I am designing a helmet that will protect the head, while providing direct illumination right where the man requires it." He showed her the parts of the device. "This flexible cable attaches to the head lamp, then runs down to the battery pack on the miner's belt."

"That's ingenious. You must tell your father about this. It will benefit his workers. Surely, he'd be proud if he knew what you've accomplished."

"He would be the *opposite* of proud, Miss Atherton. You heard him. He loathes the very idea of a member of his family working with his hands. And I have accomplished nothing." He plunked the device down onto the table with a sigh. "The infernal thing doesn't work."

"But it *will*. Think of all the lives you'll save when you *do* get it to work."

"Well. That is of course my hope."

She was about to say more on the subject, when she noticed the picture.

Propped up against a box on the table, as if to allow optimum viewing, was a picture postcard. *Dear God, it was a pornographic picture*. Featuring a naked girl on a bicycle.

Madeleine had heard of such pictures, although she'd never actually seen one. The woman in the photograph was a dark-haired beauty, entirely nude, seated atop a bicycle festooned with floral garlands, her right foot resting atop the front wheel.

Heat bloomed in Madeleine's chest and rose to set her cheeks aflame. She was shocked. Yet at the same time, she couldn't take her eyes away. Looking at the picture made her feel warm in other places, as well. Like her belly. And below.

Lord Saunders, apparently noting the direction of her gaze and her reaction, quickly flipped the postcard upside down on the table with an unapologetic shrug. "I told you my shop is not a fit place to show a lady."

Madeleine forced herself to breathe and to look elsewhere. Her eyes, however, fell upon another, similar postcard propped up on the adjoining workbench. She couldn't identify the precise details, but it was evidently of the same family.

What kind of man collected nude pictures of women and decorated his workshop with them?

This kind of man, apparently.

A new awareness seemed to fill the air, as if the elements in the room had shifted. She was suddenly all too aware of being alone here with him. *Maybe this wasn't such a good idea after all.* But no. He was behaving like a perfect gentleman. It was *her* mind that had been in the gutter.

"Would you like to see what else I am working on?" His voice tore her from her thoughts.

"I would."

They wandered from table to table, where Lord Saunders explained two other inventions he had in progress: a rudimentary dictation machine and a battery-powered teakettle.

"I imagine there would be endless uses for that battery of yours, if you could make the power source last," Madeleine noted.

"Yes. Automobiles, for example."

"Automobiles?"

"They are developing an automobile in Germany with an internal combustion engine, but I cannot help but think a battery-powered vehicle would be cleaner, quieter, and cheaper."

Each device he showed her was as intriguing as the last, and his passion for his craft was obvious.

His passion for picture postcards was equally as obvious. Saunders politely turned each one over at their approach, but not before Madeleine had caught a glimpse of it. One card featured a photograph of a woman reclining on a chaise, clad in a transparent negligee and ropes of pearls. In another, a naked woman was draped against a fluted column, a serene expression on her face.

The shock of them gradually wore off. Although Madeleine knew that such pictures were not respectable, from a purely artistic point of view, the manner in which the photographer had captured the naked female form was truly beautiful.

Looking around the shop again, Madeleine said, "You really do all this work entirely on your own?"

"More or less. I travel up to London frequently to attend lectures and meet with and get input from other scientists and inventors."

She stared at him. "Is *that* why you go to London? But . . . I've seen you at social events. And I heard . . ."

"You have heard about my awful *reputation?*" Saunders gave her a teasing smile. "I recall you mentioning that on our drive from the train station. I *have* seen women from time to time in town, but not all that often, and it has never been my primary reason for going. I quite enjoy the rumors, though. They make it easier for me to disappear when I need to, with no questions asked."

Madeleine shook her head in amazement. Here she'd been holding his "reputation" against him, and it had never been true, just a ruse.

She heard Alexandra's words in her mind: *I think him a good, decent man.* It seemed that her sister was right. "It's so unfair that you have to hide what you're doing. All your inventions are worthy, and those mining helmets will save lives. When you do get them to work, how will you market them? I mean, if you're not allowed to sell anything?"

"I don't know. I will cross that bridge when I come to it."

By now they had made their way to the far end of the shop. Madeleine's gaze fell on two more tables, where at least a dozen small machines were displayed. A dash of excitement zinged through her. "Are those typewriters?"

"They are."

Madeleine darted over to study the machines. Some of the typewriters looked to be factory-built. Others, which appeared handmade, were in various stages of development. "My father has a few Remington typewriters at his bank that are used for correspondence, but I've never tried one," she said eagerly. "I have always thought it would be wonderful to have a machine like this for writing books. To better keep pace with my thoughts, and so that my fingers wouldn't get ink-stained and my hands wouldn't ache."

"I had the same idea. I purchased a Remington and a sample of every other machine currently being manufactured, so I could gauge the competition and see if I could improve them. They are still quite rudimentary."

"May I try one?"

"Of course." Saunders withdrew a blank piece of paper from a package and offered it to her.

She crossed to the Remington machine. "How does the paper go in?"

"Like so." He moved in close behind her, reaching around with both arms to insert the page. Madeleine felt a flurry of sparks travel the length of her body as his arms came into contact with hers and his hard frame pressed up against her back. He turned a lever, rolling the paper into place in the machine.

Her breath caught in her throat. "Now what?"

"Now type something."

Saunders didn't alter his position. Instead, his hands came to rest on the edge of the tabletop on either side of her, cocooning her as if in his embrace. Her heart started skittering like raindrops on a roof. Madeleine knew she ought to tell him to step back, that it wasn't proper for him to be standing so close.

Instead, she looked down at the keys, struggling to focus. "What a strange keyboard. Why aren't the letters arranged alphabetically?"

"Early keyboards were alphabetical," he answered, his breath warm against her ear, "but the keys kept jamming.

So manufacturers changed the layout. They call this the QWERTY keyboard. It is deliberately designed to slow typists down, placing letters that are often pressed in a sequence as far away from each other as possible."

"Oh. I see." Madeleine tapped a key with her right index finger. The type bar lifted upward toward the paper, but fell back without making contact.

"Try again," Saunders encouraged. "You have to strike firmly."

Madeleine tried again, this time hitting the key more forcefully. It banged against the black inked ribbon with a satisfying *thwack*.

"Excellent. Keep going."

Madeleine continued, forcing herself to concentrate on the activity at hand, and not on the sensations zigzagging through her as his body pressed intimately against hers. Striking the letter keys firmly, she tapped out the first thing that came to mind:

"The typewriter is a fascinating machine and this is an interesting exercise."

A bell dinged as she neared the end of the page. She glanced up and was about to press on the return lever, when something caught her attention. "I can't see the sentence I just typed."

"Every typewriter is like that. The text, when typed, is covered by the platen. But it becomes visible when you return the carriage." He hit the return lever, causing the paper to scroll up and bring into view the line she had just typed.

"Why is it built that way?"

"It is the only arrangement anyone has been able to come up with for the type bars."

"You ought to change that."

"Ought I?"

"Yes." He was behind her and all around her. Her blood sizzled in her veins. "It is a strange design. Like writing with your eyes closed."

"Hmm. An intriguing suggestion, Miss Atherton." His cheek was nearly touching her own cheek now. "I shall have to take it into consideration."

She held her breath, her heart hammering so loudly in her chest she could barely think. She felt his breath hot against the sensitive skin at the side of her throat. His lips now brushed the hair at the nape of her neck, where he lingered with a gentle touch that was like the promise of a kiss.

Madeleine felt as if she might implode. Through a haze of desire, she was aware that she wanted him to kiss her there. She wanted more than that. So much more. She slowly turned within the circle of his arms until their faces were almost touching.

Their eyes met. His were alight with a kind of fire. His gaze traveled down to her lips and rested there. She longed to feel those lips, once more, against her own. She sensed that he longed for the same. He dipped his head. His mouth was millimeters from making contact with hers, when there came a sudden, sharp, staccato sound.

"Damn it," Lord Saunders exclaimed, releasing her.

The loss of contact was a jarring blow. It took a moment

for the intrusion to sufficiently infiltrate Madeleine's brain to be recognizable as a knock. On the front door.

Lord Saunders answered it. Madeleine remained in the far corner of the shop, out of sight from the doorway. From the conversation that ensued, she understood that it was the farmwife delivering Saunders's dinner. Had she seen Madeleine pass by and enter the shop? Was she aware that Madeleine was still here? A twinge of embarrassment gripped her.

"Thank you, Mrs. Smith." Saunders gratefully accepted a tray of food. The woman left. Setting the tray on a table, he crossed back to Madeleine. "Sorry."

She wasn't sure what he was sorry for—the interruption, or the fact that he'd almost kissed her. Which was *she* sorry for? *Both*, she realized suddenly. "I'd better go."

He nodded but looked regretful. An awkward silence fell as he walked her to the door.

"Thank you for the tour," Madeleine said finally. "I loved seeing what you're working on."

"It was nice to have someone to share it with," he admitted. "I appreciate what you said about the typewriter."

"When do you plan to come home?" she asked, then immediately regretted saying it. It shouldn't matter to her if or when he decided to come home.

"In a day or two." Parting a shutter, he peered out. "The coast is clear."

His statement reinforced her awareness that being here with him hadn't been exactly proper. Nor had they behaved properly. Madeleine said good-bye and rushed off, thankful that Mrs. Smith had arrived when she did. Otherwise, who knew what might have happened?

Her cheeks burned as she headed down the lane and across a field, in the direction of the manor house. She had promised herself so solemnly when she went inside that workshop, that it would be a brief and casual encounter. Yet once again, when alone in his presence, she had found herself wishing for something else entirely.

She had agreed to stay another two-and-a-half weeks at Trevelyan Manor. How in the world was she going to get through them?

CHAPTER SEVENTEEN

"I cannot think of planning a party right now." Lady Trevelyan cast a loving look across the table at her husband.

"My dear, I will not take no for an answer," Lord Trevelyan insisted.

The marquess was making one of his rare appearances at dinner, but Madeleine questioned whether or not he should have come down. He seemed to be very tired and in a lot of pain.

Madeleine poked at her fillet of beef, wishing Lord Trevelyan felt better, and finding it difficult to concentrate on the conversation around her. Since returning from Lord Saunders's workshop that afternoon, she'd had trouble concentrating on *anything*. Her mind was full of all that had transpired.

Inside his own private space, Saunders had come to life in a manner which Madeleine had never seen before, giving her a glimpse of a rare and brilliant mind. She'd been enthralled by his inventions and by the intellectual and creative passions that drove him.

Another kind of passion drove him as well. Madeleine's heart fluttered at the memories of the times she'd spent alone in his company. The kiss in the cave. And that moment in his workshop today, when she had tried out one of his pieces of equipment . . .

Tried out one of his pieces of equipment? The sexual connotations therein made Madeleine's pulse race even faster.

She felt like Hester Prynne in *The Scarlet Letter,* as though a letter *A* had been embroidered in red across her chest. Glancing at Sophie beside her, then across the table at her hosts, Madeleine was grateful that all were engaged in discussion and unaware of her own discomfiture. *They* would consider it unseemly that she'd gone inside his workshop at all, without a friend or chaperone.

Madeleine cringed at the idea of the hurt and betrayal she'd see in Sophie's eyes were she to find out about their almost-kiss that afternoon, and the one that had occurred at the cave. *How could you do this to me?* she would say. Their friendship would come to an abrupt end. Madeleine would be obliged to leave this house in an instant, her reputation in tatters.

They will never know. I'll make sure of that. No one will ever know.

"I am sure Madeleine will be happy to help as well." Sophie's voice interrupted her thoughts. "Isn't that so, Madeleine?"

Madeleine glanced up, startled. What had they been talking about? Some kind of party? "Of course," she answered quickly, unsure what she had just committed herself to.

"Invite as many people as you like," Lord Trevelyan told his wife. "Fancy dress, food, music, dancing. Do it up right."

"Do you mean it?" Her Ladyship still sounded hesitant.

"Absolutely. It is your birthday, my dearest, and I want you to celebrate it in style."

"But George. I don't know. With you being so unwell . . ."

He took her hand. "I insist that the status of my health shan't stop you from having the party you have been dreaming about all year. I promise I shall make an appearance and stay as long as I am able. And in the meantime, you—and everyone else—will have a jolly good time."

Lady Trevelyan considered for a moment, then gave in and beamed at him. "Thank you, George. I will set the date for August eighth. Hopefully, Sophie's injuries will be healed by then, Madeleine will still be staying with us, and it gives us two and a half weeks to plan."

The following morning, Lord Trevelyan kept to his rooms. Lady Trevelyan and Sophie huddled together after breakfast, putting together the invitation list for Her Ladyship's party.

It wasn't an activity in which Madeleine could be of any assistance, which left her feeling out of sorts. She had come to Trevelyan Manor specifically to help Sophie. How, Madeleine, wondered, ought she to occupy her time?

She decided to go upstairs and retrieve her manuscript from her trunk. No one would miss her for a few hours, and she couldn't deny that she was anxious to get back to writing. As she started up the stairs, however, she encountered Woodson coming down, a worried look on his face.

"Woodson? What is it?" Madeleine paused on the step below him. "Is it His Lordship?"

Woodson hesitated, then said in a lowered voice: "Yes, miss. I am sending for the doctor now." Glancing beyond her, as if to be certain no one was listening, he added, "He begs me to say nothing to Her Ladyship. He does not wish to distress her or interrupt her party planning."

"Mum's the word," Madeleine nodded. She was sorry to hear this, hated to think of Lord Trevelyan suffering alone in his room all day. A thought suddenly occurred to her—a way that she might be of service to him. "Woodson. Is Lord Trevelyan well enough to receive a visitor?"

"A visitor, miss? Whom do you mean?"

"I mean *me*."

A quarter of an hour later, Madeleine found herself seated on a chair at Lord Trevelyan's bedside with a book on her lap. An elderly nurse knitted in a corner.

"So, Miss Atherton." Lord Trevelyan lay beneath the quilts, pain and discomfort haunting his eyes. "Woodson said you wished to see me?"

"Yes, please forgive the intrusion," Madeleine replied. "I know you aren't feeling well."

"I am not feeling so ill that I cannot appreciate a visit from a pretty young lady."

Madeleine smiled. "You're quite the charmer, my lord."

"You have got my number, Miss Atherton." He gave her a small smile in return. "The Lord of Charm, that's me. Bothers me, though, to see a beauty like yourself buried here in the country, with the Season still underway. Keeping Oakley on tenterhooks, are you?"

Madeleine was determined not to be offended by his comment. "Lord Oakley is away in Europe for the summer. I thought to take that time to consider my answer. Marriage is a big commitment."

"So it is. End of summer then, I hope to hear good news! I expect another engagement to be announced by then as well—Charles and Sophie. You know they are to marry?"

The remark made Madeleine's stomach tense. "I've heard something about it."

"It has been Charlotte's dream since that girl was born, to see those two united in holy wedlock. Sophie is a sweetheart. She will make Charles a fine wife. Don't you agree?"

"I think Sophie would be very lucky to have him," Madeleine answered softly.

"There is that, too. One day she will be a marchioness, after all." He glanced at her. "So. What is all this about? Woodson said you wanted to read me something?"

"If you're up to it, my lord." Pushing thoughts of Lord Saunders and Sophie from her mind, Madeleine went on: "I used to read to my grandmother when she was sick. She said it cheered her up to no end."

Lord Trevelyan made a scoffing sound. "I have not been read to since I was a child."

"Then you're missing out, Your Lordship. Listening to a book can be very relaxing. It can help you forget how bad you feel. It's like a kind of reader's theater just for you."

"Theater, eh?" He scratched an elbow through the sleeve of his nightshirt. "Well, I enjoyed that bit of theater you did at Polperran House, Miss Atherton. Can you read to me like that?"

"I'll give it my best shot, my lord."

"What do you propose to read?"

She held up the volume she'd brought. "*The Diary of Samuel Pepys*. Have you read it?"

"Cannot say that I have. Where did you find it?"

"In your library." Madeleine had been excited to discover the beautifully bound and gilded four-volume collection on the shelves. "I don't know your taste, but I took a wild guess and hoped you might enjoy a slice of history."

"I am very fond of history."

"Well, this is one of the most fascinating private memoirs ever written. Samuel Pepys began as a clerk and rose to be Chief Secretary to the Admiralty under two kings. He gives a frank, firsthand account of some of the greatest events of the seventeenth century, from the Great Plague and Great Fire of London to the inner workings of the Royal Court and Royal Navy."

"Indeed?" Lord Trevelyan waved a hand at her. "Get on with it, then."

For the next hour, Madeleine read aloud to the marquess, who seemed to enjoy both the material and her performance of it. Twice, she noticed his hands close over his belly through the quilts, as his face contorted with pain. The first time it happened, she paused and asked if he wanted her to stop. He insisted that she continue, so she didn't ask again.

She couldn't help but stop, however, when he suddenly

winced and started massaging his hands. "My lord? Can I help you?"

"No, no. Nothing you can do. It is just this damn tingling in my hands and feet."

"They tingle?" It upset Madeleine to see him in such distress.

"It is nothing to the agony of the leg cramps at night. But I do not wish to bother you with my problems, Miss Atherton. Please go on," he urged. "I am quite enamored of this Mr. Pepys."

There was a sudden tap at the door. The nurse opened it and Dr. Hancock strode in.

"Doctor!" Lord Trevelyan called out cheerfully. "You are not needed. I have found a new medicine: book-reading by an agreeable young woman."

Dr. Hancock chuckled. Greetings were exchanged. Her visit was clearly at an end. Lord Trevelyan thanked Madeleine. She excused herself, and left.

As she returned to her own chamber, though, Madeleine's thoughts remained on Lord Trevelyan. Dr. Hancock's words from the first morning she'd returned to the manor house rang in her ears: *He has an array of symptoms that do not normally go together, or point to any one disease.*

Something about Lord Trevelyan's symptoms struck a familiar chord with her, but she didn't know why. She paced back and forth in her room, struggling to remember. Suddenly, the answer came to her.

Madeleine ran back down the hallway, into the connecting wing, and down yet another corridor. To her relief, when she arrived at Lord Trevelyan's chambers, Dr. Hancock was just exiting.

"Doctor!" Madeleine called out, stopping to catch her breath. "May I speak to you for a moment?"

"Certainly. How may I help you, Miss Atherton?"

She walked with him as he made his way down the hall. "I know I am but a visitor here, and no relation to the family. But I am concerned about Lord Trevelyan. As I understand it, he's had digestive pain for quite a while now."

"True."

"I noticed him scratching. He told me he suffers from leg cramps at night and tingling in the hands and feet?"

Dr. Hancock seemed surprised that she would mention such things. "He does," he replied carefully.

"You said his symptoms do not point to any known disease. This might be nothing. But when I was in town last month, I overheard something that might interest you."

The doctor appeared to be striving for patience. "What is that, Miss Atherton?"

"I was at a party," she began slowly, "that was rather boring, so I hid in the library. I was reading a book in a corner when two gentlemen entered the room. They were clearly unaware of my presence, as they began discussing their health concerns. One of them had been suffering from digestive issues, and had just been cured. He'd had severe stomach pain, he said, accompanied by leg cramps that woke him up, tingling in his extremities, and rashes on his elbows, even tooth pain."

"Indeed?" Dr. Hancock looked intrigued now.

"The man said this had been going on for years, he'd

never been so sick in his life, but he was now fully recovered after being treated at St. Bartholomew's Hospital in town."

"I have heard of it." Dr. Hancock stopped and turned to her. "Did he say what the treatment was?"

"As I recall, it was something about . . . diet."

"Diet? What do you mean?"

"I don't know. But His Lordship's symptoms are so similar, I thought I should mention it."

"I am glad you did." Dr. Hancock gave her a nod and started off again. At the top of the stairs, he paused and glanced back. "Miss Atherton. Did the fellow mention the name of the physician who treated him?"

"I think he said 'Dr. G.' Which I thought strange at the time, as if he were just using the first initial of the doctor's name to hide his identity."

"Dr. G? At St. Bartholomew's Hospital?" Dr. Hancock seemed to be lost in thought for a moment. Then his dark eyebrows lifted and he nodded slowly. "Thank you, Miss Atherton. Good day." With that, he placed his hat on his head and descended the stairs.

Charles glowered at the typewriter in front of him.

His attempt to redesign the type-bar fork was a complete failure. And no matter how many times he adjusted and readjusted the type bars, he could not get them to swing upward with more speed or agility. If he typed any faster than a snail's pace, the bars always crashed into each other and stuck.

"Infernal bloody machine," he spat in disgust. Two days straight, and he'd gotten nowhere.

It hadn't helped that for all that time, his ability to concentrate had been fractured. Try as he might, he could not prevent his thoughts from continually returning to Miss Atherton.

He could not forget the way she had looked when she'd arrived on his doorstep the other day. The way her cheeks had glowed from her long walk. The way the sun had sparkled on her hair. Once she'd finagled her way inside his private sanctum, it had, just as he'd anticipated, been difficult to keep his thoughts in order, when all he wanted to do was to reach out and touch her.

At the same time, though, it had proven incredibly satisfying to show her what he was working on. She understood him and what he was trying to accomplish. He had enjoyed every moment of her visit. If he closed his eyes, he could almost smell her perfume, could almost imagine that she was standing here again in front of him at this very table while he rolled that piece of paper into the Remington.

He recalled the sensation of his body pressed against her back. The curve of her waist and buttocks. The heat that had emanated from the nape of her neck, so close to his lips, and so inviting. When she had turned in his arms—oh, how he had wanted to kiss her. And not just kiss her. He had wanted to strip every article of clothing from her body, bring her upstairs, and make passionate love to her.

Just as he had wanted to do the day they had kissed in the cave.

The memory of that kiss sent blood coursing through his every vein. He could still feel the sparks that had pulsed through him as his hands had traced patterns on her lithe form. She'd made it clear with every touch of her lips and tongue, every moan and hitch of breath, that she'd enjoyed that kiss in the cave every bit as much as he had.

They both knew it had been a mistake.

We got carried away.

Let's pretend it never happened.

He had tried to forget. It had proved impossible.

He had tried to stay away from her. But fate kept throwing them together.

Now, she was back at the manor house again, acting—of all things—as Sophie's companion. The irony was not lost on him. The woman he admired and desperately wanted in his arms was not only almost betrothed to a friend of his, but had become close friends with the woman *he* was expected to marry. It was the most vexing conundrum in the world, with no solution in sight.

With a sigh, Charles tossed the tool he was holding onto the littered workbench, determined to rise above these useless reflections, which did nothing but torment him. He pulled out his pocket watch. It was after midnight. He was tired, but his stomach rumbled.

He realized he was starving. The last thing he had eaten was the Cornish pasty Mrs. Smith had left for him at six o'clock. Before that, it had just been a ham sandwich at noon. And there wasn't a thing to eat in his shop.

He went to the window and glanced out. It was a clear

night with a three-quarter moon, which should provide sufficient light for the ride home.

Madeleine dipped her pen into the ink bottle and returned it to the page.

It was marvelous to be writing again. There were few occupations that filled her with such pleasure or satisfaction. If she continued working every night after everyone else went to bed, she might actually complete a first draft of the book during her stay at this house.

She scribbled on, her story taking a direction she hadn't anticipated. Madeleine paused uncertainly and scratched out a sentence, only to have the split-tip metal nib of the pen catch, splashing ink across the page. She sighed in frustration. Now she'd have to copy out the entire page again.

Just then, the clock in the hall struck one. The single, resonant chime caused her to sit up in surprise. Was it really so late? Where had the time gone? She had better retire or she'd never be able to get up in the morning.

Madeleine got ready for bed, climbed beneath the sheets, and closed her eyes. Her entire being, however, still buzzed with the excitement that came from writing. Thoughts and ideas, plots and dialogue, all clamored for attention in her brain.

Finally, unable to sleep, Madeleine threw back the covers and sat up. A cup of hot milk. That was the ticket. Back home, whenever she was up late writing, hot milk had always helped to calm her.

After slipping into her silk dressing gown, Madeleine lit a candle and quietly made her way down the stairs. Although this was her second visit to Trevelyan Manor, she had never actually seen the kitchen, but knew it was on the basement level.

Instinct led her to the far end of the lower floor, where she entered the vast, silent room, expecting to find it cold and dark. To her surprise, a small fire glowed in the enormous hearth, and several lamps were lit. Madeleine heard rustling from a room next door, which she presumed to be a pantry. She wondered if the cook was up late—or very early—preparing something for the morrow.

Hopefully, Mrs. Green wouldn't object to Madeleine heating up some milk.

Madeleine selected a small copper saucepan from the row of pots hanging above the huge black stove. She was wondering if they kept the milk in the pantry, or had a separate cold cellar, when she heard approaching footsteps. A deep, masculine voice called out in surprise:

"Miss Atherton."

She whirled. Her heart jolted.

Lord Saunders—casually dressed as he had been at his workshop, sans coat or tie—was standing halfway across the room. He held a bottle of wine in one hand and a plate of cold chicken in the other.

"We have to stop meeting like this," he said, his eyes twinkling with amusement.

Chapter Eighteen

Miss Atherton was clearly as surprised to see him as Charles was to see her. "My lord. I had no idea you were home."

"Just got back." Charles set the plate of chicken on the table in the center of the room. "I was hungry." *Hungry to see you.* Had he said that aloud? He hoped not.

She was a vision, clad in a pale blue dressing gown that was tied over a white cotton nightdress, her hair billowing loosely about her shoulders. He ached to cross the room, take her in his arms, and kiss her senseless. Instead he just stood there, drinking her in.

"I was thirsty," she volunteered, waving a saucepan at him. "I thought a glass of hot milk to help me sleep."

"Excellent notion. That is, it would be, if there were any milk. I just checked and the jug is empty."

"Oh. That's too bad." She replaced the saucepan on its hook. "Well, I suppose I should go."

Yes, you should. If she stayed—especially half-dressed like that—only a monk would be able to resist her. And Charles was hardly a monk. But after thinking about her nonstop for far too many days, he couldn't bring himself to send her away.

"Why go? There are plenty of other things on offer, besides milk, to help you sleep." Charles gestured with the bottle of cabernet. "A good wine is always relaxing, and this is a fine vintage. Will you join me in a glass?"

She hesitated, glancing at the floor. "I don't know. I'm not sure it's advisable for us to . . ."

". . . be alone together?" he finished for her.

She nodded.

It was a risk, to be sure—but a risk he was willing to take, if it meant spending a few more minutes in her company. He uncorked the bottle, trying to make light of the matter. "We did nothing the other day to be ashamed of." He gave her a devilish look. "Unless you count typing as a disrespectable activity."

She laughed. "Even so. We *almost* did. And at the cave . . ."

"We agreed to forget about the cave."

"Yes. But . . ." She hesitated further.

"I'll tell you what. Let's set some ground rules. You can sit there." He pointed to a stool that was drawn up to the table. "And I'll sit here." He indicated a second stool standing two feet away. "There will be no physical contact of any kind. Just two people enjoying a glass of wine. Are you up to the challenge?"

Her cheeks flushed. She was adorable when she blushed. "Challenge accepted." She came forward.

"Excellent." After retrieving two wineglasses from a shelf, Charles poured out the cabernet and offered her a glass.

She took it, careful that their hands didn't touch. "To what shall we drink?"

He raised his own glass, far too conscious of the fact that she was standing before him, mere inches away, no doubt wearing nothing beneath that silk dressing gown other than a thin nightdress. "Let us drink to the Queen."

"Everyone toasts the Queen. Can't we be more original?"

"All right." He spouted the first other toast that came to mind, one that reminded him of her. "To beauty without affectation, and virtue without deceit."

Her smile fled, and a pained looked came into her blue eyes. "I've never heard that one."

He immediately recognized his mistake. He should never have said *deceit* to this woman, who clearly felt guilty about . . . well, the kiss they had shared. "It's an old British toast," he explained quickly. "I have others." He went for a safe one. "To the protectors of orphans and widows."

"So old-fashioned," she scoffed. Thinking for a moment, she raised her glass. "How about: May the tax-gatherer be forgiven in another world."

"There is one *I* have never heard."

"It's a good one, right?"

"I prefer not to *toast* the tax man. How about: May an Englishman's house be his castle forever."

"Your house is nothing like a castle."

"It is a turn of phrase."

"How about: To our absent friends on land and sea," she suggested.

"I'd rather drink to friends who are present." He considered, then lifted his glass again. "Champagne to our real friends, and real pain to our sham friends."

She laughed again. "I prefer to think that all my friends are real."

"You are a difficult person to toast with," he pointed out congenially. "At this rate, we will not taste a single drop of wine."

"How about this: May we never want of a friend, nor a bottle to share with him. Or her."

"I'll drink to that," Charles agreed.

"Cheers."

They clinked glasses and each took a sip.

"Mmm. Delicious," she purred.

The wine *was* delicious. So was she. He could not take his eyes off of her. It was killing him to stand a few feet away from her in this dimly lit room, and know that he couldn't touch her. Now. Ever.

After a moment, she said, "Are you going to offer me any of that chicken?"

He choked back a laugh, then swallowed his mouthful of wine. "Be my guest. I did not realize you were hungry."

"I didn't realize it either, until you put cold chicken in front of me."

"Why stop at chicken? There is a larder full of food. I was just getting started raiding the pantry when you appeared."

She grinned. "Let's take a look."

The pantry contained everything one could wish for a late-night snack. They took turns bringing out platter after platter of delicacies, from meats and cheeses to fruits and pies and other sweets. After setting out the feast on the kitchen table, Charles got plates and cutlery.

"So," Miss Atherton said as they sat down beside each other on the stools and dug in, "what have you been working on? The miner's lamp battery or the typewriter?"

"Typewriter."

"Have you made any progress?"

He carved two slices from a smoked ham and flipped one onto her plate. "None whatsoever."

"I'm sorry."

"Don't be. These things take time and patience."

She nodded, swallowing a forkful of leek pie. "'Patience is a conquering virtue.'"

He glanced at her, recognizing the quote. "You have read Chaucer? Wait. Forget I said that. Of course you have."

"*The Canterbury Tales* is a seminal piece of literature." She sipped the wine.

"'People can die of mere imagination,'" he pronounced with a flourish, before devouring a forkful of ham.

"'The Miller's Tale.' That's my favorite Chaucer quote."

"And mine."

She tried the potatoes au gratin. "Mmm. Good. Do you really think one can die from an overabundance of imagination?"

"Yes, at least where inventors are concerned. It has happened to two of your own countrymen, in fact."

"Who?"

"Horace Hunley developed a submarine for the Confederate army, but when he took command, it sank. William Bullock died at the hands of his own web rotary press."

"Oh no. That's horrible."

"Imagine the peril involved were one to attempt to build a flying machine."

"Do you think flying machines are possible?"

"Absolutely. In the meantime, I content myself with safer, more mundane inventions."

"Your battery lamp is hardly mundane. I would call it brilliant. Oh look at that!" She speared a pickle with her fork. "I unintentionally made a pun."

She sucked on the pickle, then bit into it. The movement of her lips on that item sent his mind in a direction it shouldn't have gone. He blinked fast, struggling for a comeback.

"I . . . appreciate the compliment, Miss Atherton, and should like to return it. That play you wrote for the girls was brilliant." *Don't look at her lips. Look anywhere but at her lips.* He refilled their wineglasses. "The same play, were it to be performed by professional actors, would have been perfectly at home onstage in the West End."

"That is high praise indeed."

"And I mean it sincerely. You have quite a gift." He picked up a chicken leg and determinedly bit into it. "How is your novel going?"

"Well, I think. Although I just hit a roadblock of sorts."

"What kind of roadblock?"

"My story took a turn I didn't expect." She sipped more wine. "One of my heroes, an American banker, just discovered that his biggest investor is defrauding the public. If he reports the activity to the authorities, he'll lose millions and his bank will go under. If he says nothing, however, his position at the bank is assured, and he can marry the woman he loves."

"You say this a roadblock . . . why?"

"I feel as though I've given my hero an impossible choice."

"Your hero's course is clear. He must follow his conscience. All a man really has in life is his honor. Without that, he is nothing."

"I suppose you're right." She frowned. "But that will put his romance in jeopardy. How am I to achieve a happy ending?"

"That, I cannot help you with. But I feel certain an answer will come to you in time."

"I hope so." She tackled the apple crumble now. "Mmm. This is absolutely wonderful. You have to try it."

Charles leaned in and took a forkful from her plate. In such proximity, he couldn't help but study her for a moment. His eyes treacherously returned to her lips. The way they moved when she chewed was so ridiculously arousing, it was all he could do to tear his gaze away, and return his thoughts to their discussion. "Writing . . . seems to me an arduous endeavor."

"Nowhere near as difficult as inventing."

"I disagree," he replied. "The ability to create a story out of thin air, and the drive to keep at it when it proves difficult or seems to be going nowhere at all, this is the very definition of the inventor's dilemma."

She nodded slowly. "Do you ever find your work in progress invading your mind, when you are supposed to be thinking about something else?"

"All the time," he acknowledged. "Once, in the middle of Christmas dinner with my family, a notion struck me about a way to create a refillable fountain pen that wouldn't leak. I rode off to my workshop in a snowstorm to test my theory."

"Did it work?"

"No."

"How frustrating! I was at a ball in New York when I suddenly figured out why my heroine was averse to dancing. I fled the ballroom in search of pen and paper, but could find none. The thought vanished from my head." As she spoke, she gestured dramatically, causing the belt of her dressing gown to loosen.

The garment fell open at the waist, revealing her creamy skin above the scooped neckline of her summer nightgown. Charles's gaze moved lower, to where the shape of one breast was outlined beneath the thin fabric and the shadow of her nipple visible. The sight made his mouth go dry.

Charles drained his wineglass, struggling to look somewhere else. "Sometimes I get my best ideas in the middle of the night, and I have to get up and jot them down." *Sitting alone in the kitchen with her in the middle of the night was not one of my best ideas.*

"When I'm writing, six hours can go by in a heartbeat," she admitted eagerly.

"If Mrs. Smith did not leave food on my doorstep, I should probably never stop at all."

"Who would have thought such diverse occupations could prove to be so similar?" She picked up a strawberry. "You have the *best* berries in Cornwall."

He sensed she was a little tipsy. He watched as she savored the strawberry, taking the piece into her mouth and gently biting it off at the stem. His brain went to another place, just as it had with the pickle. Imagining those lips sucking on something else. A rush of blood infused that very organ.

He took an unsteady breath. He ought to call it a night. Leave the room this minute. Before she noticed the evidence of his arousal. Before they did something they would both regret.

Instead, he grabbed another strawberry, dipped it in the bowl of clotted cream, and leaned forward on his stool, offering it to her. "A berry is always better with cream."

A soft laugh. "I never say no to a strawberry with cream." She slanted toward him to accept the berry. Her dressing gown opened even wider now. She didn't seem to notice. He couldn't help but look. Beneath the thin fabric of her nightgown, her breasts were perfect globes, their protruding points mere inches from his hand.

Charles swallowed hard as he placed the berry into her open, waiting mouth. She chewed, a dollop of cream decorating her upper lip.

"You have a bit of cream, just there." His voice sounded rough.

"Here?" She wiped at her mouth, missing it.

"No, there." He tried to resist touching it. He couldn't. His index fingertip traced the top of her lip, then moved to her mouth.

She sucked the foam from his finger. The sensation went straight to his groin like a thunderbolt.

"Did you get it?" she asked softly.

"Not . . . all of it." A slight smudge of froth still clung

to her mouth. He could no longer restrain himself. He had to taste it. In one fluid motion, Charles leapt from his seat, slipped one arm around her, pulled her to her feet, and pressed his lips to hers.

Madeleine knew she should stop him.

But she didn't want to stop.

Her hands moved up to the back of his neck of their own volition, pulling him closer as they kissed. His tongue parted her lips, invading her mouth. He tasted luscious, like strawberries and cream and cabernet sauvignon.

For weeks now she'd been dreaming of this, wanting it, even though she knew it was wrong. Every word they'd exchanged had only made her feel closer to him, wanting it more. Through a dizzy, wine-induced haze, the familiar voice of warning was trying to make itself heard, but she didn't want to listen. They kissed and kissed. Taking a ragged breath, his lips moved from her mouth to dance down the side of her neck, sending ripples of erotic sensation zinging through her body.

"Do you like this?" His voice was husky.

"Yes," she breathed.

He kissed his way further down, to the top of her chest. His hand hovered at the side of her breast, a delicate touch like the brush of a feather. She was suddenly aware that her dressing gown had come open, that nothing stood between his palm and her naked breast but the thin fabric of her nightgown.

This was the moment to stop him. *He's not yours*, that little voice insisted. She swept it away. His eyes met hers, dark and smoky. "Do you want me to touch you . . . here?"

She nodded.

His palm claimed her breast and gently kneaded it. The sensation was wondrous. Then his thumb and fingertips began doing even more wonderful things to her nipple. Uttering a moan, he gripped the fabric of her nightgown, pulling it up, until that same hand slipped beneath it and smoothed its way up her naked body, seeking and finding her breast. Madeline gasped for breath as his ministrations continued on her breast and nipple. A bolt, like an electrical charge, zinged to her belly and lower still.

He brought his mouth back to hers and they met and clung in another impassioned kiss. He continued to manipulate her breast beneath her gown. Madeleine felt the hard length of his arousal pressing against her belly. She knew it meant that he wanted her, that he felt the same aching need that was taking over every part of her own body. A hot and heavy feeling began to build inside her core, as if she were reaching for something vital and primal yet still unimaginable.

Never, never had she felt sensations like these. Never had a man touched her like this. The kiss they'd shared in the cave had been wondrous, but this was far more sensuous, far more carnal. It made her feel powerful, feminine, to know that she could inspire this kind of passion in a man so remarkable, a man she so deeply admired.

He drew her even closer with his free arm as the kiss continued. Her hands ran up and down the expanse of his back. She wanted *his* hands to touch her other places, secret places that now ached to be stroked and molded. His legs tangled in her dressing gown and they bumped with wild abandon against the table.

Then came a sudden loud crash and the sound of breaking glass.

Chapter Nineteen

They stilled in each other's embrace, both of them breathing hard.

"Save the pieces." Saunders let out a low chuckle.

Madeleine gazed up at him, slowly becoming conscious of where she was and what was happening. "What are we doing?" she whispered.

"Enjoying a late-night feast." He kissed her again.

"We have to stop," she murmured against his lips.

"Oh no we don't." His voice was low and throaty.

"Oh yes we do." Madeleine gently but firmly pulled herself out of his arms, drew her dressing gown closed, and tightened the soft belt around her waist.

She glanced at Lord Saunders. He ran one hand through his hair, and seemed to be trying to calm himself. She saw his arousal straining against his trousers, which made all the places in her own body that were still hot grow even hotter. *How could I have let that happen?* The question pummeled her brain as she also struggled to compose herself.

Alexandra had wanted her to "explore her feelings" for Lord Saunders. Well, she'd certainly been exploring them. After that flagrant display, Madeleine could no longer deny that she *did* have feelings for him. Very strong feelings. How could she even consider a relationship with Oakley or any other man when she was obviously, totally, infatuated with this one?

Did he feel the same way about her? Clearly, he had enjoyed that kiss every bit as much as she had. Clearly, he wanted her. But what were his intentions? Had anything changed? She had to know.

She swallowed hard. "What should we do about this?"

"Do?" He looked at her. "What do you mean?"

"Um. I mean . . . about *this*. About us."

He started to reply, then seemed to rethink it. His eyes, as he glanced at her, were filled with desire and undisguised yearning, followed by a dash of self-incrimination. "I suppose," he said finally, in a low tone laced with regret, "I should once again offer my apologies."

Apologies again. Madeleine sighed. Was it because he thought he'd taken advantage of her? Or because he was still firmly committed to another woman? Before Madeleine could ask, he took in the shattered wine bottle at their feet and said, "I wonder if there is a broom anywhere about? I wouldn't want anyone to walk in and step on broken glass."

A quick search led to a closet with the requisite supplies. Madeleine wielded the broom, showing Lord Saunders how to hold the dustpan. He was comically inept at the business.

"This is an experience I never thought to have," he

quipped. "Helping a million-dollar heiress sweep up my kitchen."

She struggled to match his light tone, hoping he wouldn't notice that her hands and body were still trembling from their kiss. "How thoughtless of you, to state aloud the amount of my fortune."

"It is common knowledge and in all the papers."

And of no interest to you, since you have all the money you need. Madeleine found herself wishing, for an instant, that he *did* need her money. A silence fell between them as they finished sweeping up the glass and deposited it in a rubbish bin. "Should we put the food back?" Madeleine asked.

"The staff will clean it up." That same desire and yearning was once again visible in his eyes, but he turned away. "Well, then." He seemed to be about to quit the room.

"Wait. Before we go." Madeleine took a deep breath and said, "I'm not sorry we kissed. In truth, I rather liked it."

A hint of a smile. "So did I."

"So . . ."

"So?" he repeated.

Madeleine's heart pounded. "I need to know what you're thinking. If this . . . if you and I are . . ." She waited.

He paused, as if carefully considering his reply. At last he met her gaze and said softly, "I have never met anyone quite like you. You are a remarkable woman. I admire you more than I can say."

"I feel the same way about you."

"But . . ."

She knew what was coming. Still, she needed to hear him say it. "But?"

He heaved a sigh. "My fate was decided for me long ago. I gave my father my promise that Sophie and I would be officially engaged by the end of summer. I must . . . I mean to keep that promise."

Even though Madeleine had expected it, the admission hit her like a punch in the stomach. *So, he had given his promise. There was no going back.* "Of course. I see."

"I'm sorry."

"No, no. Don't be." Her cheeks felt like they were aflame. Whether or not he had any feelings for Sophie was unclear, but it didn't seem to matter. He would marry her. He would do his duty. *All a man really has in life is his honor.* She ought to admire him for that. "It's what your family has always wanted. She's a lovely girl. I'm sure you'll be very happy."

A hard look clouded his features. "And you and Oakley . . ."

"Yes, yes, Lord Oakley." Madeleine couldn't care less about Lord Oakley at the moment.

"It's just as well," she heard herself rush on, determined to rise above her hurt and embarrassment. "It's for the best. For both of us. Really. And not just because of *your* promise, or anything I might owe Lord Oakley. Because of a promise I made *myself*, years ago."

"What promise is that?"

Madeleine sank down on her stool and took a deep breath. "When I was twelve years old I had a crush on the baker's son, who used to give me a free cinnamon bun whenever I went into his father's shop. Then he started giving out free buns to my friend Ada. I cried for weeks. When I was fifteen, on summer vacation with my family, I fell hard for a farmer's son. One day, I saw him kissing Alexandra behind the barn. I never had the nerve to speak to him again."

He leaned back against the table and crossed his arms over his chest. "I am sorry that happened. But—"

Madeleine raised a hand to stop him. "When I turned eighteen, I fell in love with a young man who worked at my father's bank. I felt certain he was going to propose at my coming out ball. But that night, my best friend Pearl stole him for all the best dances." Madeleine's voice caught as she recalled the scene that had devastated her. "I saw them later on the terrace, kissing. They went together for a few months before Pearl dropped him. I never heard from Joe again."

Saunders seemed to ponder this. "So you had a crush on two boys when you were very young, and had your heart broken at eighteen."

"Three times, I lost the boy I liked to someone else—a friend I'd trusted, even my own sister! Three times, I was discarded. Betrayed. Second best. I will never forget the pain I suffered. How small and worthless it made me feel. Each time, it took my heart years to mend. I never want to make any woman suffer the way I suffered." Madeleine wasn't sure if this explanation was meant to convince him, or herself. "Which is why you are absolutely correct, my lord. I can never hurt Sophie that way. She loves you. Her future rests in your hands. And as you said, you must keep your promise."

His gaze returned to her face. "It seems we are of one mind, then."

"Yes!" If that were true, why did her heart feel so heavy? "We must rise above this . . . this . . . infatuation, or whatever it is, and agree that henceforth we will just be friends."

"Friends." He looked a bit dubious.

"Furthermore, I suggest we make a pact."

"What sort of pact?"

"To stay out of each other's way."

He frowned. "I don't know how possible that is, given that you—"

"We have to *try*. During the rest of my stay here, we can be like ships passing in the night. And we have to agree that this sort of thing can never happen again."

He hesitated, then said with obvious reluctance: "Very well."

"If we ever *should* find ourselves alone together . . ." A thought occurred to her. "We need a reminder word."

"A what?"

"When I was a girl, my mother came up with a reminder word, to keep me from doing or saying anything improper and behave."

"What was your reminder word?"

"Pineapple."

Saunders stared at her. "Pineapple."

"It's the perfect word. Pineapples are prickly and funny-looking. It's a mental image guaranteed to stop you in your tracks and make you laugh."

Saunders's eyes twinkled now and his lips twitched,

as if he were holding back a laugh. "Pineapple it is, Miss Atherton."

Madeleine slept in the next day until noon. When she finally rose and dressed, it was time for luncheon. She discovered that Dr. Hancock had come and gone, and as Madeleine had been unavailable, he had pushed Sophie around the garden in her wheelchair himself.

Madeleine was sorry to have missed seeing the doctor, as she'd hoped to talk to him again about Lord Trevelyan's state of health. Had the information she'd conveyed to him been of any value whatsoever?

Saunders, she learned, had left for London on a business matter and would be gone for a week. When Lady Trevelyan told her this, despite herself, Madeleine was keenly disappointed. Did he truly have business in London? Madeleine couldn't be certain, but she had a strong feeling he had gone deliberately, to make it easier to keep their "pact" to stay away from each other. A pact he had been obviously reluctant to make—but she knew it was for the best.

The next few days were given over to party planning. Helen and Anna were ecstatic to discover that they would be allowed to dress up and attend the festivities, although they would only be allowed to stay up until nine o'clock, and could not participate in the ballroom dancing.

Lady Trevelyan ordered invitations from a printing house in the village. When they arrived, Sophie and Madeleine joined Her Ladyship in the parlor, where they helped fill in the invitees' names on the cards and addressed the envelopes.

"Is there a theme for the fancy dress?" Madeleine asked as she dipped her pen and inscribed an envelope in her finest script.

"No," Lady Trevelyan answered. "I want everyone to dress up as anything they like. Historical figures are always popular, though. I am going as Marie Antoinette. I found the most divine gown in the attic that belonged to one of my husband's relations."

"Will we wear masks?" Sophie asked.

Lady Trevelyan shook her head. "I prefer to know the identity of the gentleman with whom I am dancing."

Madeleine laughed. "I couldn't agree more."

The following afternoon, Madeleine, Sophie, and the girls scoured the Trevelyan Manor attic for their own costumes.

"What do you think of this one?" Helen found a lady's Turkish-style costume featuring pantaloons of turquoise silk and an embroidered white bodice.

"It would suit you perfectly," Sophie said admiringly from her seat on a moth-eaten chair. Due to her ankle injury, a footman had carried Sophie up to the attic so that she could participate.

Helen tried on the outfit, which Madeleine proclaimed to be a perfect fit.

Anna pulled an old shawl of gold-colored wool from a trunk and smiled. "I know what *I* am going as. I shall be Night."

"Night?" Helen repeated. "How do you propose to do that?"

"I shall cut gold stars out of this shawl and sew them all

over my dark blue frock," Anna explained, "and wear more gold stars in my hair."

"That sounds lovely and quite creative," Madeleine said, which made Anna beam. A Regency gown of white muslin caught Madeleine's eye. The cap sleeves and Empire waist were trimmed with white ribbon, and the skirts were embroidered with cascades of tiny white flowers. "Isn't this pretty?" It looked like it had hardly ever been worn.

"It would look divine on you," Sophie commented. "You could be the Empress Josephine."

"Or Lady Hamilton." Madeleine held the gown up to herself. "But it looks too small."

"Ask Martin to alter it," Helen suggested. "I grew two inches last year and gained almost a full stone. But I had a brand-new gown I didn't want to give up, so she let it out and added a flounce to the hem."

"Okay. I'll ask her." Turning to Sophie, Madeleine added: "Now, what about you?"

"Oh, I do not think I shall wear a costume. No doubt I will still be consigned to that dreadful wheelchair."

"Dr. Hancock said there's a good chance you'll be up and dancing by August eighth," Madeleine insisted. "And in any case, you *must* go in fancy dress."

"Yes, you must," Helen agreed, pulling out a voluminous satin gown with an eight-inch stomacher. "You could go as a French king's mistress."

Sophie made a face and shook her head. "If I *could* choose a costume, there is something else I should wish to be."

"What's that?" Madeleine asked.

"A butterfly."

Anna's eyes lit up. "A butterfly! Sophie, how thrilling."

"But I do not see how that would be possible."

"We can *make* it possible." Madeleine's mind was already whirring with ideas. Flicking through the other garments on the rack, she came to a Georgian ball gown of violet satin, with a black velvet bodice and black lace trim. "This would be stunning. I've seen butterflies this exact color. We can remove the overskirt and make wings from it."

"And we can make a black hair band with antennae," Anna suggested.

Sophie laughed. "You are all quite marvelous. I do not know what I should do without you."

Madeleine was about to head downstairs the next morning to assist Sophie with her letter-writing, when Lord Trevelyan's voice boomed throughout the halls.

She heard bits and pieces: *What the devil!* and *No bread? No beer?* and *Do you mean to starve me?* He sounded as angry as a hornet.

Although curious as to what that was about, Madeleine didn't dare investigate. She ventured down to the library, where she found Sophie and Dr. Hancock seated on a sofa, involved in conversation. At Madeleine's appearance, the doctor's cheeks grew rosy and he stood.

"Miss Atherton." He cleared his throat. "I was hoping to see you. I have news about my patient's condition."

"I hope Sophie is all right?" Madeleine said, worried.

"I am not speaking of Lady Sophie, but of Lord Trevelyan."

"Oh?" Madeleine was even more worried. "What has happened?"

"It is not what has happened so much as what I have *learned*. As you seemed so interested. . . ." Dr. Hancock glanced at Sophie. "Forgive me. I do not wish to trouble you, Lady Sophie, with these particulars." Receiving a nod from Sophie, he asked Madeleine, "May we speak in the hall?"

"Of course."

Bowing to Sophie, Dr. Hancock bid her good day. Madeleine followed him out of the room.

"Miss Atherton," he said as they strode down the hall toward the front of the house, "the other day, you mentioned a Dr. 'G' at St. Bartholomew's Hospital in London. I had heard of a doctor with that name. Not a name which simply began with the letter G, but the actual surname G-E-E: Dr. Samuel Gee. So I wrote to him."

Madeleine's pulse quickened. "And?"

"Dr. Gee has an interesting theory concerning a new disease. Well, it is not actually *new*. It was discovered in the first century CE by Aretaeus of Cappadocia, a celebrated Greek physician. His theories were unfortunately lost to science for eons. Dr. Gee's fluency in ancient Greek made it possible for him to read a work by Aretaeus called *The Coeliac Affection*, which detailed the symptoms of a digestive disorder. Gee noticed that many of his patients had the same array of diverse complaints. He conducted a clinical study, and last year published the first description of a condition he calls Coeliac Disease."

Madeleine was intrigued. "Do you think His Lordship suffers from this disease?"

"I think it highly possible."

"You called it a digestive complaint?"

"Dr. Gee suspects the condition has something to do with the inability of the intestines to absorb nutrients."

"Interesting. Is there a cure?"

"Not that we know of. But happily, Dr. Gee has found a way to control it by means of changes to the diet."

"The diet?" Madeleine caught her breath. "Just as I overheard that night!"

"I met with Lord and Lady Trevelyan this morning and explained that for a trial period, His Lordship must avoid eating all foods made with wheat and barley."

"So, no bread."

"No bread, no cakes, no biscuits, no noodles. And no barley, which means no beer or malt vinegar."

Madeleine nodded solemnly. "I heard His Lordship shouting down the hallway a few minutes ago. I'm guessing breakfast had just been served?"

Dr. Hancock sighed ruefully. "He called me a quack and a charlatan, complained that I was taking away all of his favorite foods. Her Ladyship seemed more open-minded. Even so, I do not expect to be very popular with him for the next few weeks. By then, we should know if this new diet is effective or not." They had reached the front entry now, where Woodson waited at attention by the door.

"Do you think it *will* be effective?" Madeleine asked.

"Time will tell. Even if the diet does not cure Lord Trevelyan, I may have other, future patients who suffer from this ailment. I am in your debt for calling it to my attention."

"I am glad, if you think the information has been of some use. Please let me know how His Lordship does. I dearly hope he improves."

"As do we all, Miss Atherton," Dr. Hancock said with a parting bow.

Two weeks flew by. Lord Saunders was true to his word, and so excelled at staying out of Madeleine's way, that even after he returned from London, she only caught rare glimpses of him. On the few occasions when Madeleine did see him, the family was always present, and they exchanged no more than a word or two.

She wondered if Lord Saunders missed her as much as she missed him. Just thinking about him made her ache with longing. And seeing him across the room now and then, looking so impossibly handsome, only made her ache more deeply.

Madeleine had to admit, it was easier to relax when he was away, when she didn't have to worry that he might walk around a corner at any moment and send her heart racing. If she'd learned anything from their encounter in the kitchen, it was that she had to govern her feelings for him, accept the fact that he could be no more than a friend.

Dr. Hancock called daily to check on both Lord Trevelyan and Sophie. He pronounced that the latter's ankle was mending perfectly, and if healing progressed in the same vein, Sophie ought to be able to dance at the fancy dress ball.

As for the former, matters did not appear to be progressing so well. Madeleine winced at the daily barrage of curses and complaints that issued from Lord Trevelyan's bedchamber whenever his food was served. Lady Trevelyan, on the other hand, was grateful for the new regime.

"I have been saying for years that His Lordship seemed to feel worse after eating," she told Madeleine one afternoon at tea, "and I kept asking if it could be connected. The doctor would not listen to me. I pray this is the remedy, and applaud you for sharing what you heard."

Still, Madeleine didn't dare offer to read to Lord Trevelyan again. She spent her afternoons helping Sophie, Helen, and Anna work on their costumes for the ball, grateful that Martin had agreed to alter the white muslin gown for herself. When the household retired for the night, Madeleine worked on her novel, which to her satisfaction was nearing completion.

Every morning she spent assisting Sophie, who often seemed out of sorts and distracted.

"Is anything wrong?" Madeleine asked one bright day as she pushed Sophie in her wheelchair in the garden.

"Wrong? Why do you ask?" Sophie responded.

"Because you haven't spoken for twenty minutes. Nor replied to the last two questions I posed."

"Oh. Forgive me. I was miles away." Sophie paused, as if turning something over in her mind. Then making a little face, she said, "I guess I am feeling sorry for myself. It is so frustrating to be unable to walk, and to be encumbered by this cast on my hand."

"They are only temporary inconveniences," Madeleine reminded her. "With any luck, you'll be right as rain very soon."

Miss Atherton had asked him to stay away from her. Charles did his best to comply.

He took a jaunt up to London, although he had no real reason to go there, and spent the entire time thinking of her and counting the days until he could return.

When he returned to Cornwall, he didn't dine with the family, spending his time either visiting tenants, overseeing the operation of the mine, or at his workshop. Once, he wheeled Sophie around the garden himself. On the few occasions when he did see Miss Atherton at tea, he made a point of sitting across the room.

Although she had insisted on this new distance between them, and he also believed it was the right and proper thing to do, he couldn't help feeling regretful that it had become necessary.

Whenever he thought about Miss Atherton—and despite himself, Charles thought about her far too often—his blood felt as though it were on fire. It wasn't just the memory of their kisses that affected him, however incendiary those kisses might have been. It was the memory of each and every experience they had shared, in its entirety.

The day he had saved her notes in the fountain. Making wishes in the cave. Showing her his inventions at his workshop. Their late-night feast in the kitchen. Each time, they'd shared long, meaningful conversations which he had thoroughly enjoyed.

By putting an end to those wonderful discussions, Charles felt as though he'd lost something important from his life. But that was understandable, he told himself. It's what one would expect to feel, were he kept apart from someone he particularly liked and admired.

Or was infatuated with.

We must rise above this infatuation, or whatever it is, and agree that henceforth we will just be friends.

Friends. That's what Miss Atherton had deemed they should be. But what he felt for her went far beyond friendship. If only he didn't feel this intense, overwhelming . . . *attraction* to her. That's what had complicated things.

Charles was contemplating all this one morning as he left his room, when to his surprise, he encountered Miss Atherton at the head of the stairs, coming from the guest wing. He stopped, his heart leaping in his chest. It was the first time they had been alone together in weeks.

She looked inexpressibly beautiful. She was attired in a lovely blue gown that matched her eyes and showed off her perfect figure, and her hair was swept up in touchable waves.

Waves he knew he could never touch again.

In her expression, he read her silent regret at their enforced separation, a mutual feeling he did not even try to disguise.

"Good morning," he said.

Miss Atherton returned the greeting. After a pause, she glanced up at him with a half smile and a sparkle in her hooded eyes, which suggested that she was recalling some pleasant but illicit memory. Was it the same memory that had haunted his dreams for weeks, and even now danced in his head, fueling his body with desire? The memory of heated kisses and hands on naked flesh after sampling strawberries and cabernet?

Charles swallowed hard, struggling to focus on the present moment. How he longed to take her in his arms. Even if he couldn't kiss her, just to hold her, to feel her body pressed against his, would help quench some of the flames that burned within him.

He had just thought of a way to make that happen—a way that wouldn't break any code of ethics—when his father's voice bellowed out along the corridor.

"Pure nonsense! Infernal quackery! I want toast with my eggs, damn it! And cinnamon cake with my coffee!" The sound of breaking china followed, and then muffled murmurs from the nurse.

Charles glanced in that direction, and he couldn't prevent a smile. "As I understand it, *that* is all your doing?"

She stiffened slightly. "I simply shared something I once overheard."

"Overheard?"

She told him of the circumstances, how she had once escaped the tedium of a ball by hiding in the library, and overheard two gentlemen speaking about a medical condition. "I thought I should tell Dr. Hancock in case it was of significance. Now I wish I hadn't. Your father is so upset."

"Do not let Father's bluster alarm you. I am glad you said something." They started down the stairs together.

"Are you?"

"He is a man who enjoys his food—or used to. It is interesting to think that some of his favorite dishes might be the very things that have been making him so ill."

"Is he any better at all, on the new diet?"

"Mother said she has seen real improvement over the past weeks," Charles told her. "It is still early days, but some of Father's symptoms have definitely abated."

"I am so pleased to hear that." Miss Atherton looked hopeful. "Will he be able to attend the ball, do you think?"

"Father assured me that he will. Speaking of which—will you still be here, the night of the ball?"

"Yes."

"Will you promise me a dance?" *Say yes. Say yes.*

She hesitated, then shook her head. "Thank you for the offer, but I don't think that would be wise, my lord. Remember our pact."

"We agreed to stay out of each other's way. To be like 'ships passing in the night'—I believe those were your words? At which we have succeeded remarkably well of late, don't you think?"

"I do."

"What is the harm in a dance in a ballroom full of people?" *Please say yes.* He envisioned the moment: gliding together around the dance floor, holding her once again in his arms.

"Well . . ."

"I will not take no for an answer," Charles insisted. "One dance, that is all I ask. Do I have your word?"

"Well, all right then," she gave in, her tone teasing, "if my dance card is not full."

Yes yes yes. "I will look forward to it." *More than you know.* When they reached the bottom of the stairs, Charles bowed, his eyes still holding hers. "Good day, Miss Atherton."

"Are you not going in to breakfast?" she asked, apparently disappointed.

He shook his head. "I am dining elsewhere."

"Might I ask where, my lord?"

With a wink, Charles replied: "In Truro."

CHAPTER TWENTY

The morning before the ball, a small package was delivered to Madeleine's room.

"Lord Saunders told me to bring this to ye," said the maid with a curtsy before vanishing down the hall.

A note was attached:

My Dear Miss Atherton,

A little something to remind you of your stay at Trevelyan Manor.

With my best wishes for your health, happiness, and success.

Charles Grayson
The Earl of Saunders

Madeleine unwrapped the parcel to discover a copper hairpin, equally as delicate as the ones he had made for the other ladies in the household. In addition to a row of gleaming white pearls, it featured a tiny charm which looked to have been molded and sculpted by hand, and was shaped like a book.

Her heart caught. The hairpin was a thing of beauty, and clearly designed with her in mind. How kind it was of him to think of her, to make this for her. At the same time, his words made it clear that this was a parting gift, and a subtle reminder that they were just friends.

As it should be, she reminded herself. If only the reminder didn't make her feel so sad.

"Sophie: you are a vision," Madeleine said.

The fancy dress ball was due to begin in half an hour. Madeleine and Sophie stood before the looking glass in Madeleine's bedchamber, while Martin finished adjusting the glittery silk wings suspended from Sophie's arms.

"Do really you think so?" Sophie modestly studied her reflection.

"You'll turn the head of every man in the room," Madeleine assured her. Two days before, Dr. Hancock had pronounced her ankle recovered, and this morning he had removed the cast from her hand. "And how wonderful that you are able to dance."

All their hard work on Sophie's costume had paid off. In the violet-and-black gown, with her gossamer wings and a headband of delicate wire-and-velvet antenna, she looked every bit the ethereal butterfly.

Madeleine wasn't so sure about her own costume. When

she'd first tried it on after Martin had finished the alterations, it hadn't seemed *quite* so low-cut. Although the gown had been let out as far as it would go, Madeleine felt as though she'd had to pour herself into it. Her hair was done up in a nice Grecian style, though, and the old blue-ribboned Royal Navy Cross medal, which she'd found in the attic and was now pinned to her bodice, gave her *ensemble* a "Lady Emma Hamilton" flair.

Her sister had written expressing her regrets that she and Thomas could not attend. In her note to Madeleine, Alexandra had injected a hint of humor, saying:

> *Every day, I grow larger and larger, and at this point I'd look ridiculous in costume unless I appeared as a whale. In any case, I'm too close to my due date to travel. Thomas refuses to allow me to even set foot inside a carriage until after the baby comes.*

In spite of her disappointment that her sister wasn't coming, and a fatigue with regard to balls in general, having attended far too many in town, Madeleine realized she was looking forward to *this* ball. Her stay at Trevelyan Manor was almost at an end. Sophie could do her own letter-writing now. Tonight would be her one and only chance to dance with Lord Saunders, and after she left, who knew how long it would be until she saw him again?

By the end of summer, six weeks from now, he would be engaged to Sophie, and Madeleine would have to make up her mind about Lord Oakley. She was fairly certain that she would have to turn Oakley down. How could she marry a man when her mind was full of someone else—even if that man was to marry someone else?

Still, even if she couldn't have him, she could dance with him tonight. Create one last memory.

"You need a hair ornament," Sophie pronounced, breaking into Madeleine's thoughts as she studied their reflections in the mirror. "Would you like to wear the hairpin Charles gave me?"

The offer made Madeleine blush. *Was there no end to this young woman's innocent goodness?* "Actually, he gave me one of my own," Madeleine admitted. She hadn't put it on, nor mentioned it to Sophie, worried that the gift might make Sophie feel uncomfortable. But Sophie's eyes just lit up.

"Did he? How kind of him. Do let me see it."

Madeleine retrieved the hairpin from her bureau drawer and showed it to her friend.

"Oh, it is lovely. You *must* wear it. Here, let me place it for you." Sophie expertly wove the copper hairpin into Madeleine's hair. "There. Now you are perfect."

"You'll *both* be turning heads tonight, mark my words," said Martin with a smile. "No other woman in that ballroom stands a chance." With that, she quit the room.

Sophie turned to Madeleine, a worried look on her face. "Could that be true? I do not wish to draw attention away from Aunt Charlotte. It is her birthday, after all."

"I wouldn't worry. Lady Trevelyan's gown is spectacular. She is certain to be the belle of her own ball."

"I hope so. Just as I hope that . . ." Sophie's voice broke off.

"You hope what?"

Sophie's cheeks bloomed a gentle pink. "Oh, Maddie. There is something I have been meaning to speak to you about. But I felt strange somehow. Because I . . ." Sophie seemed to be groping for words. "It is just that . . ." Leaning close to Madeleine's ear, she whispered: "I am hoping for a proposal tonight."

A proposal. Madeleine's heart seized. "Are you?"

Madeleine felt as if all the air had been sapped from the room. Was it possible that Lord Saunders intended to propose to Sophie tonight? The ball, with all of the Graysons' friends in attendance, would certainly make the ideal venue to announce an engagement.

Stop being ridiculous. You knew he was going to marry Sophie. Still, *knowing* that the proposal would happen eventually and being confronted with the fact that it might take place that very evening were two different things.

"It is no doubt a vain hope," Sophie said quickly. "Please forget I mentioned it."

Before Madeleine could reply, Helen and Anna burst into the room, attired in all their finery. "Oh! You both look wonderful," Anna cried.

Anna herself looked radiant in her Night costume, her blue dress bespangled with gold stars, and Helen was pretty as a picture in her Turkish pantaloons. Several minutes were given over to inspecting and admiring each other's attire, during which time Madeleine forced herself to rally. Lord Saunders had asked to dance with her, and engagement or no engagement, he might still do so. She was determined to enjoy the ball, no matter what happened.

"Come downstairs now," Helen urged. "The guests are already arriving."

"Shall we go?" Sophie took Madeleine's arm and they followed the girls out of the room.

"Wait," Madeleine said, "I forgot my fan. You go on ahead, I'll join you downstairs."

The other three rushed off. A few minutes later, fan in hand, Madeleine stopped at the railing overlooking the grand hall and took in the scene below.

The house was decorated like a fairyland, festooned with garlands of flowers, the glimmering chandeliers supplemented by hundreds of lit candles. Newly arrived costumed guests were laughing and chattering, awaiting the procession that would lead to the ballroom.

Madeleine scanned the crowd. Many couples were dressed as pairs of historical and literary figures. She spotted Napoleon and Josephine, Queen Elizabeth and Robert Dudley, King Henry VIII and Anne Boleyn, and Romeo and Juliet. She found herself looking for Lord Saunders, but had no idea what his costume would be.

At last she spotted him at the far end of the room, wearing a dark blue, gold-trimmed Royal Navy uniform. As if he could feel her gaze upon him, Saunders glanced up in her direction. He paused in mid-conversation, his expression turning to admiration as their eyes met and held.

Madeleine's pulse skittered as she slowly descended the stairs. She saw him excuse himself from the guest to whom he was speaking and weave his way through the throng toward her, his gaze never wavering from hers. His words rang in her ears. *I have never met anyone quite like you. You are a remarkable woman. I admire you more than I can say.*

An invisible current of electricity seemed to be traveling across the space between them, connecting them. Was anyone else aware of it? To her relief, a brief, sidelong glance assured her that the general buzz of laughter and conversation continued unabated.

Her mind darted to what Sophie had whispered. Did Saunders intend to ask Sophie to marry him tonight? It pained Madeleine to think of it. So she *wouldn't* think about it. Not now. Just for the moment, to know that he could look at her this way as he crossed a room was enough.

They met at the bottom of the stairs.

In his Royal Navy uniform, embellished with epaulettes, ribbons, and medals, Saunders looked impossibly attractive. Tight-fitting white breeches accentuated the lean length of his masculine legs. A tricorne hat, which was dashingly askew, completed the outfit.

"Lady Hamilton." His expression announced his surprise and delight.

She suddenly understood his costume, and why he looked so astonished. Her cheeks went scarlet as she dipped him a curtsy. "Lord Nelson." He had come as the hero of the Battle of Trafalgar, who'd had an infamous and adulterous love affair with Lady Emma Hamilton.

"Did you know about my costume?" Madeleine asked, suddenly feeling scandalous in her filmy, low-cut gown.

"I did not." He laughed, a sound of deep, unqualified pleasure. "I found this uniform in the attic only this morning, the relic of an uncle or cousin or some such who was in the Royal Navy. Perhaps it is fate?" He caught her eye, then said with a wolfish grin, "You are not worried, are you? That someone might think we deliberately dressed as a couple?"

"A little worried," Madeleine admitted. "I would not want Sophie to think . . ."

"Do not distress yourself," Saunders interrupted with a shrug. "Tonight is all in good fun. Do you see that gentleman over there?" He gestured toward a man wearing a large, hand-made champagne label across his chest, and a cap simulating the foil-wrapped cork of a bottle. "He is a barrister, normally a very grave fellow. And the couple dressed as pirates? They are Lord and Lady Dartmoor, known and respected for their philanthropy. Yet tonight, both are carrying a knife in their boot."

Madeleine laughed, her anxiety dissolving in the face of his good humor. "Thank you for that reassurance." Then: "Didn't Nelson lose an arm?"

"He did, in later years. But it is difficult to dance with one arm. I am therefore Young Nelson, with half his medals, and as you see, no red sash." Glancing about, he added, "I do not suppose you know anyone here?"

"No one other than the family."

"Pray, allow me to remedy that." His hand at her elbow, Lord Saunders guided Madeleine around the room, introducing her to neighbors and friends disguised as Pierrot and Pierrette, Titania and Oberon, assorted Highlanders, and a monk and a nun. They had just finished making small talk with a gentleman dressed as a Bedouin sheik when Lady Trevelyan appeared, stunningly attired as Marie Antoinette.

"Charles! Madeleine! There you are."

Lady Trevelyan was beaming, clearly in her element. Her gown, fashioned of rose-and-gold satin with a blue velvet train embellished with gold fleurs-de-lis, was one of the prettiest in the room. A white wig adorned by high feathers added to the ensemble. Giving her son's hat a sharp twist to set it right atop his head, she said with an affectionate smile: "I forgot we had this old uniform. How well it fits you."

"You look absolutely magnificent, Mother. Happy birthday."

"Thank you, darling. Miss Atherton, you take my breath away."

"As do you, Your Ladyship." Madeleine curtsied.

Lady Trevelyan's notice fell on Madeleine's hair. "Charles! You made Miss Atherton a hairpin?"

"I did," Saunders admitted matter-of-factly. "It felt remiss that every other lady in the household had one."

"It is lovely." Her Ladyship cast a studied look at her son and went briefly quiet. "If I did not know better, I should think you two had come as a couple."

"A complete coincidence," Madeleine responded quickly. It was true. So why were her cheeks suddenly warm?

"Does Father plan to come down this evening?" Lord Saunders asked.

"He has assured me that he will make an appearance." Lady Trevelyan smiled at Madeleine. "That new diet may have put him in a surly mood, but I believe it is working, Miss Atherton."

"That is music to my ears," Madeleine replied with delight.

"Speaking of which." Lady Trevelyan tapped her son on the shoulder with her fan. "You and Sophie are to lead the first set. Let us go and find her."

"Forgive me, Miss Atherton." Saunders gave Madeleine an apologetic glance and moved off with his mother.

Madeleine's sense of loss was fleeting, for Helen and Anna dashed up and slipped their arms through hers.

"Miss Atherton!" Anna smiled up at her. "Mother said we could watch the dancing as long as we stay on the perimeter of the ballroom. Will you walk in with us?"

"It would be my honor." Madeleine suddenly became aware of three young men who'd been approaching from different directions, and who now paused with disappointed faces.

"You look so pretty," Helen commented as they began moving with the promenade. "I am sure you will get a great many offers to dance."

"We shall see about that," Madeleine replied.

There was only one dance that mattered to her. *If* it would even happen.

CHAPTER TWENTY-ONE

Charles whirled Sophie around the floor, his eyes searching the crowded ballroom for Miss Atherton.

At last he caught sight of her, dancing halfway across the room. She looked radiant in that white, filmy gown, free of the heavy petticoats that every other woman in the room was wearing. It made him wish that women's garments would turn back to the fashions of the Regency. The fabric of Miss Atherton's dress was so thin that when she turned at a particular angle to the light, he could see the outline of her legs beneath her skirts.

They were beautiful, shapely legs.

Her gown was cut so low that her breasts seemed to be a breath away from escaping the tight confines of her bodice. He'd heard the phrase *to take one's breath away*, but never had he experienced it as personally and literally as he had tonight, when he'd seen her coming down that staircase. His heart had nearly leapt from his chest.

Much like the first time he'd set eyes on her.

Since then, so much had changed. He had come to know her. To discover that beneath that vibrant smile and enticing body was a bright and curious mind, a warm and sensitive heart, and a passion that flamed like fire. She—

"You make a handsome Nelson," Sophie said.

Guiltily, he forced his attention back to the woman in his arms. "You make a lovely butterfly," he responded sincerely.

"Thank you. It was Maddie's idea. She is so clever."

Maddie. Did everything *always* come back to her? "Yes. She is clever."

Sophie started to say something else, but then seemed to change her mind. He sensed an odd vibration coming from her and wondered at it. Generally, Sophie was so calm and sensible. It was one of the things he liked about her. Yet for some reason, she seemed tense. He caught her darting a curious glance at him, then glancing over his shoulder distractedly.

"Are you all right?" he asked.

"Yes, thank you."

They danced on. As ever, Sophie was an accomplished dancer and did not miss a step. Which reminded him of her recent injury. And that he had forgotten to ask about it. "How is your ankle?" he inquired.

"Fine, thank you. Dr. Hancock says I am completely healed."

"I am pleased to hear it. And your hand?"

"Much better. Dr. Hancock says it will take some time to regain the strength in my grip. So it still may be difficult to write to Mother for a while."

"I am sorry." Sophie wrote more letters to her mother

than anyone Charles had ever met. They spoke no further until the waltz ended.

"Was that three dances or four?" Sophie inquired.

"Four."

"Our limit, then? I believe we are obliged to seek other partners now?"

"I believe so."

Sophie smiled. "Thank you, Charles."

He kissed her hand. "It was my pleasure." He was about to escort her to a chair, when Dr. Hancock strode up dressed as Robin Hood.

"Lord Nelson," Hancock said, "you are in fine form this evening."

"And you look quite the rogue," Charles told him with a grin.

"That was my aim." Dr. Hancock gave Sophie a graceful bow. "Lady Sophie, may I have the honor of the next dance?"

"You may." Sophie took the doctor's hand and they walked off together.

Relieved to have Sophie taken care of, Charles scanned the room for Miss Atherton, but he had lost sight of her. The musicians began to play the next song.

As the dance began, his father entered dressed as Louis XVI of France, a counterpart to his mother's Marie Antoinette, and apparently a surprise. His mother burst into tears of joy and they embraced, after which the marquess moved through the room, shaking hands.

Charles finally spotted Miss Atherton. To his disappoint-ment, she was now partnered on the dance floor with someone else. He heard his father's voice at his elbow. "Charles. Why are you not dancing with Sophie?"

"I did, sir. She is now otherwise engaged."

"Not for long, I hope." His father readjusted the gold crown atop his wig. "You know how she adores you."

"So you are always telling me. You look well, sir."

"Thank you. Feeling rather spry this evening. I do hope you will not disappear again tonight to God knows where, as you did at last year's Christmas ball."

"I would not think of it, sir. It is Mother's birthday."

"Good boy." He studied Charles a moment. "Lord Nelson, eh? Interesting choice. In light of what that Atherton woman is wearing."

His innuendo offended Charles. "Why do you call her that Atherton woman?"

"It's her name, isn't it? Watch yourself with that one, son. You almost ruined your life once with an American heiress. All the money in the world, and they think it can buy them a title. Do not make that mistake again."

Irritation speared through Charles's chest. "I have no intention of making a *mistake*. And may I remind you, Miss Atherton is here at Mother's invitation."

"She cannot leave too soon, in my opinion. Putting her nose where it does not belong, dispensing medical advice as if she were a doctor herself."

"The information she shared just might save your life."

"Nonsense. It is this diet Hancock put me on that will kill me! What, am I to never have beer again? Or bread or cake?" His father blew out a disgusted breath. "Now look here,

Charles: your mother and I have been waiting all summer for you to make your engagement official. Charlotte suspects that Sophie is expecting you to pop the question tonight."

"Is she?" Charles glanced away with a stab of guilt, struggling to keep his features calm. Sophie *had* mentioned something of the kind, the day they drove to the village. That would account for her odd demeanor.

"It is as good a time as any to follow through on your promise."

"I will ask for Sophie's hand when I am good and ready, Father, and not a moment sooner."

His father sighed again. "Well, then, at the very least, do not neglect the girl tonight. She has few acquaintances here. Dance with her, Charles, and often."

"How often is enough for you? As I recall, a gentleman is limited to four dances with a particular partner. Or has the rule changed?"

"Are you quoting ballroom etiquette at me? *You*, who look down your nose at rules? If you will not dance again with Sophie, there are other single ladies present who would be glad of your company."

"I shall keep that in mind." The music came to an end and people on the dance floor began switching partners. Charles noticed Miss Atherton across the way, unengaged for the moment. This was his chance. "If you will excuse me, Father," he began.

But he turned back to discover that the man had ushered over Miss Gordon, a spoiled, self-important woman who stood before him costumed as a shepherdess.

"Miss Gordon would be delighted to dance with you, Charles," his father ordered.

"It would indeed be my honor, my lord," said Miss Gordon with a ready smile.

Glancing back at the dance floor, Charles saw Miss Atherton moving into position with another man. *Damn it.* He gritted his teeth.

"Your wish is my command, sir," Charles said, taking the young lady's hand.

The night dragged on. Madeleine danced with a cheerful King Arthur, a sweaty King George, a bearded Merlin who kept tripping on his robe, and the man dressed as a champagne bottle. Although she attempted to make conversation, the men seemed more interested in staring at her cleavage than anything she had to say.

All the while she found herself continually scanning the ballroom for Lord Saunders, hoping he would ask her to dance. But he never did.

The first four dances he had given to Sophie. Which was only right and proper. Although Madeleine herself had been engaged for those same dances, she'd been unable to prevent herself from glancing now and again at Saunders and Sophie, whirling across the floor in each other's arms. The sight had made her ache with envy and longing—foolish feelings, she knew—but inescapable nevertheless.

After that, every time she had caught sight of Lord Saunders, he'd been dancing with someone else. Madeleine wondered if he had found a private moment and made his declaration to Sophie. When she noticed him again now, however, their behavior suggested that it must not have happened. At least not yet.

Lord Saunders was bringing Sophie a glass of punch. Although they were conversing, Madeleine detected no particular warmth in the exchange. If anything, both seemed to be working hard to smile, like people trying to act happier than they actually were. Madeleine felt bad; she knew Sophie had been hoping for a proposal tonight. At the same time, Madeleine wondered if she were being blinded by wishful thinking, and misperceiving them this way.

At half-past ten, Lord Trevelyan raised a glass of champagne in a birthday toast before the entire assembly, enumerating his wife's many good qualities, and praising her for putting on such an elegant affair. He looked to be feeling well, which Madeleine was glad to see.

When the applause ended and the music started up again, Madeleine sighed. She had no wish to dance any more. She considered retiring to her room for the night, but the birthday cake had not yet been served. It would be rude not to be present for that event. Madeleine decided instead to retreat to the library, find a book, and hide within its pages for a while.

The library was halfway across the house, a beautifully appointed room with innumerable volumes filling the shelves. Due to the warmth of the summer evening, all the windows were open, and music from the ballroom was still subtly audible as Madeleine entered.

After a brief perusal, Madeleine selected a novel and sank down onto a leather sofa positioned beside a glowing lamp. She'd been reading for a while and had lost track of time, when a masculine voice broke the stillness.

"I believe you owe me a dance."

Madeleine's heart skipped a beat. She looked up to see Lord Saunders standing not ten feet from where she sat. He was so ridiculously good-looking in his naval uniform, the amber light from the gas lamps flashing over the strong planes of his face.

"Here I thought I'd been so discreet," Madeleine said. "How did you know where to find me?"

"I recalled you saying that you sometimes got bored at a party, and retreated to the library."

"Impressive that you remembered such a tiny detail."

"It seemed to me an important detail."

The way he was looking at her made her pulse beat even faster. What did it mean that he'd sought her out this way? Shouldn't he be with Sophie? It wasn't a question she was about to ask. Instead, she held up the novel she'd been reading. "A book often proves to be an excellent companion."

"True. But tonight is meant for dancing." He moved closer and stopped immediately before her. "I have been wanting to ask you to dance all night. But every time I looked for you, you were dancing with someone else."

Had he truly been looking for her? She was almost afraid to stand, lest she give in to a trembling urge to throw herself into his arms. "Only because *you* were otherwise engaged."

"Not by choice." He removed his hat, set it on a table, and then extended a hand to her. "Will you do me the honor of dancing with me, Miss Atherton?"

"Here? In the library?"

He gestured toward the instrumental strains emanating from the ballroom. "We can still hear the music. The room is large enough. And here, there is no chance of colliding with anyone."

"We might collide with the furniture."

"We might." His hazel eyes twinkled.

Madeleine found herself rising to her feet. "What about our pact?"

"Our pact be damned." His voice was like a low growl that simmered in her belly, making her feel weak in the knees.

"Well, a lady at a ball may never refuse the invitation of a gentleman to dance, or she will be guilty of an incivility." Madeleine placed her gloved hand in his, a thrill running through her at the firm pressure of his grip.

"Is that a rule?" Lord Saunders's other hand slipped around her waist as he drew her to him in waltz position.

"It is indeed a rule." Their bodies were separated by mere inches, so close that she could feel the heat emanating from his. "One drilled into me since I was a child."

"I have never been fond of rules. But I like that one." He began to move in time with the music and she instinctively followed his lead. He spun her around the room with skill and grace. "You are an excellent dancer, Miss Atherton."

"As are you, my lord."

"Only because it has been drilled into *me* since *I* was a child," he quipped back at her. "Ballroom dancing is a vital part of a lord's training."

"So I discovered during the Season. Even if a peer had no aptitude for conversation, he could generally dance."

"Let us hope my conversation lives up to my dancing."

"Time will tell."

They smiled into each other's eyes as they moved in time to the music. With every step, Madeleine was vividly aware of his hand holding hers, the feel of his other hand at her waist, the heat of his gaze. It didn't escape her that once again, despite her best intentions, they were alone together, far from the eyes of the crowd.

"No late-night cravings lately?" he asked softly.

Madeleine wasn't about to tell him the truth, of the many nights she'd had to resist the temptation to sneak down to the kitchen, in the hopes of finding him there. "No. You?"

"I have spent most evenings at my shop this week."

"Have you made any headway?" She felt enveloped by his scent, a pleasing blend of heat and perspiration and cologne that felt as intimate as an embrace.

"A bit. How is your book coming?"

"I finished the first draft last night."

"Outstanding." The music came to an end. They stopped along with it. He didn't release her. Instead, his arms swept around her, holding her captive against his chest. "What will you do with it?" He spoke just above a whisper, his eyes smoky as they glanced at her lips and stayed there.

Madeleine's arms slid up around his shoulders. Her

blood thundered in her ears. What were they talking about? She couldn't remember. All she could think about was his nearness, and how close his mouth was to hers.

Did he mean to kiss her? They had agreed that it could never happen again. Yet Madeleine hadn't stopped dreaming that it would. He lowered his head until his lips were mere inches away and paused, as if anticipating the contact. Her senses reeled. It might be wrong to want this man. But she *did* want him. Oh, how she wanted him. Through a fog of desire, Madeleine heard a sharp intake of breath rise from his chest. A word presented itself like a warning beacon at the edges of her mind, then issued from her throat.

"Pineapple."

She realized they had both uttered it aloud at the exact same moment. For a long beat they stood there, frozen in each other's arms. He began to laugh softly, his warm breath fanning her mouth.

"You were right," he said, chuckling. "It is an excellent reminder word."

The answering laugh that rumbled up from within Madeleine's own chest was more bittersweet than mirthful. She was about to reply when another sound caught their attention. A distant voice. Someone was calling her name.

"Miss Atherton? Miss Atherton!" Footsteps approached along the hall.

Lord Saunders stepped back. "It is Woodson."

Madeleine stifled a gasp. What did Woodson want with *her*? What would he think, to find her and Lord Saunders alone together like this?

Lord Saunders grabbed his hat, then handed Madeleine the novel she'd been reading, signaling with his eyes toward the sofa. She quickly sat and opened the book. Without another word, he deliberately crossed the room, disappearing via a far door seconds before Woodson glanced in through a closer opening.

"Miss Atherton!" Woodson gave a relieved sigh and entered. "I have been searching high and low for you."

Madeleine struggled to even her respiration as she glanced up from her book. "What is it, Woodson?"

"A summons has come from Polperran House. Dr. Hancock is needed, and your presence is also requested."

Madeleine leapt to her feet. "Why? What has happened?"

"The Countess of Longford is in labor."

CHAPTER TWENTY-TWO

Madeleine grabbed a shawl in haste and departed with Dr. Hancock in his carriage. The doctor insisted that there was no time to change out of their costumes or say good-bye.

"I thought the baby wasn't due for two more weeks," Madeleine said anxiously as the coach took off at a brisk clip.

"It isn't." Hancock's lips were tight with concern. "It is not uncommon for a woman to go into labor early, but your sister's blood pressure has been high the past few weeks. There might be complications for both mother and child."

Madeleine was too alarmed to reply. Alexandra hadn't mentioned anything about her blood pressure in her recent letters, probably so as not to worry her. She wished that she hadn't been away all this time, that she had stayed at Polperran House as she had originally intended.

They rode in tense silence for most of the journey. Upon arrival, they were both immediately ushered upstairs to the master bedchamber. Alexandra was in bed, her face red and

beaded with perspiration. Several maids attended her and
Thomas was hovering anxiously.

"Doctor, thank God you've come," Thomas said.

"Lexie!" Madeleine rushed to the bedside. "I'm here."

"Maddie. Oh, Maddie. This is so much harder than I
thought it would be."

Madeleine saw fear in her sister's eyes. "You're going to be
all right, Lexie." She prayed it would be true.

Dr. Hancock quickly took charge, divesting himself of his
costume jacket and rolling up his sleeves. It was an action
Madeleine found oddly comforting. Rolling up one's sleeves
was what men did when they were about to plunge into
important work. And nothing could be more important than
helping Alexandra bring her child safely into the world.

Dr. Hancock banished Thomas from the bedchamber
and suggested that Madeleine leave as well. But Alexandra
grabbed Madeleine's hand and said, "No, Doctor. Please let
my sister stay."

He allowed it. Anxiety held Madeleine in its grip but she
ignored it, insisting: "I'm not going anywhere. You'll get through
this, Lexie. We'll get through it together."

All through the long night, Madeleine encouraged her
sister through the labor pains, and lovingly wiped her brow. It
was the first time Madeleine had ever attended a birth. There
were brief, quiet moments, when the sisters were both able to
breathe normally, and Alexandra noticed and commented on
the shocking neckline of Madeleine's Regency gown, making
them both laugh. There were moments of great anxiety as
well, when Dr. Hancock worried that Alexandra's blood

pressure was too high or things were not progressing as they should. But Madeleine bit back her fear and concentrated on presenting her sister with only the most positive energy and outlook.

Finally, just as the faint light of dawn began to streak the sky, Alexandra gave the final push that brought her baby into the world.

"It's a little boy!" Dr. Hancock smiled as he placed the newborn infant, wrapped in a blanket, into his mother's arms.

"Oh! He's beautiful." Tears of joy filled Alexandra's eyes. "Is he all right, doctor?"

"He's perfect," the doctor assured her.

"He certainly is." Madeleine sat on the bed, wrapping her arms around her sister and the baby with intense relief.

"Thank you." Alexandra breathed out a long sigh as she rested her head against Madeleine's. "I'm so grateful you were here."

"I wouldn't have wanted to be anywhere else."

Alexandra took Madeleine's hand again. In that simple, silent gesture, Madeleine felt the deep bond of love that existed between them, and the satisfaction of having come through this experience together. They sat like that for several minutes, silently gazing with adoring eyes at the new baby, who seemed like a miracle from heaven.

Thomas was soon ushered into the room. Madeleine didn't think she'd ever seen a man look more relieved or proud. Leaving the mother and father to moon over their newborn son, Madeleine fell into bed in her own room for some badly needed sleep.

When she awoke later that day, Madeleine learned that her trunks had been delivered with all the clothes she'd left behind in her haste to leave Trevelyan Manor. To her dismay, however, her manuscript wasn't included with her belongings. She realized it must still be where she'd hidden it, in the bottom drawer of the bureau in her room at Trevelyan Manor.

Madeleine considered sending a note, asking for the manuscript to be sent over. But she'd never told anyone about the book except Lord Saunders, and didn't want to call attention to it. What if someone read it? It was just a first draft. Better to leave it there for now, she decided. She'd ride over and retrieve it when she could.

The next few days were given over to the adjustments required by the addition of a newborn to a household. The baby was named Thomas after his father, with the agreement that he would go by the nickname Tommy.

The nurse brought the infant to Alexandra whenever he awoke. Julia and Lillie reveled in their roles as aunts. Alexandra, in a continual state of bliss, dictated a telegram to their mother in Paris, informing her that she was a grandmother.

One morning, Madeleine went to her sister's room and paused in the doorway. Thomas was sitting beside Alexandra on the bed, gazing down at her as she held the baby. Their eyes met with an expression so full of love that Madeleine actually felt a small pang of jealousy. That one glance made clear how deeply and dearly they adored each other.

This was the way marriage was supposed to work. Husbands

and wives were *supposed* to adore each other. Madeleine suddenly realized what she hadn't been able to fully admit to herself until that moment. *This* was how she felt about Lord Saunders.

When she was with him, she didn't want to be anywhere else. When they were apart, he was all she thought about. She and Lord Saunders met on an intellectual level that was both challenging and stimulating. He understood who she was, championed what mattered to her. Just looking at him was enough to set her blood on fire. And whenever they had touched, dear God, when they had kissed, she'd felt as if she might melt into the floor.

She loved him.

She had fallen in love with Lord Saunders. Madly, hopelessly in love with him.

And he was going to marry someone else.

Acknowledging this, along with the futility of her feelings, was like a stab through the heart. Tears studded Madeleine's eyes. It wasn't as though Saunders's intentions were a surprise. He had made his commitment to Sophie clear from the start. Oh, if only she hadn't gone back to Trevelyan Manor that second time! Now, those memories would haunt her always, lingering in her mind and heart to torment her.

"Why are you standing in the doorway?" Thomas said. "Come in."

Madeleine glanced up to discover Thomas and her sister studying her.

"What's wrong?" Alexandra asked. "Why are you crying?"

"Because you three look so beautiful," Madeleine replied,

wiped away her tears as she entered the room. "I didn't mean to interrupt."

"You haven't. I was just about to go." Thomas kissed his wife and son, then rose and kissed Madeleine on the cheek. "I will see you later." He took his leave.

Madeleine crawled up onto the bed beside Alexandra, both of them leaning against the headboard. She asked if she could hold the infant. Alexandra was happy to oblige.

"Hey, little man," Madeleine cooed, cradling Tommy in her arms and gazing down into the lovely brown eyes that matched his father's. "Did you know you're the eighth Earl of Longford? I am so happy to finally meet you."

Alexandra smiled. "You're so good with him, Maddie."

"I love babies," Madeleine admitted. "Especially this one."

"Someday, you'll have a baby of your own. Perhaps in the not-too-distant future." Alexandra gave her a meaningful look.

It was a question that, on any other day, might have made Madeleine blush. But not today. Her heart was too heavy. Fresh tears studded her eyes, unbidden. She blinked them away.

Alexandra looked at her, troubled. After a pause, in which she seemed to be carefully weighing her words, she said, "In your letters the past few weeks, you wrote mainly about the fancy dress party and about Lady Sophie. You hardly said anything about Lord Saunders."

Madeleine had anticipated this line of questioning, knew there was no way of avoiding it. "Oh, Lexie," she replied softly. "I wanted to write to you about him, but every time

I tried, it felt so wrong to put my feelings into words, I threw the letter away."

At that moment, the nurse came in to retrieve the infant. Tommy was treated to volleys of gentle kisses from his aunt and mother before being swept from the room.

Alone together now, Alexandra took Madeleine's hands in hers. "What happened, Maddie? I can tell that something has affected you deeply."

Struggling against the tears that continued to threaten, Madeleine told her sister about her discovery of Lord Saunders's workshop and the valuable work he was doing there. She told her about their late-night encounter in the kitchen. And the kiss. And the dance in the library. "I'm in love with him, Lexie. That's what you wanted me to find out, and now I have. I'm hopelessly in love with him, and there's nothing I can do about it."

"Why, Maddie? It sounds like *he's* in love with *you*."

"No, he's not." Madeleine shook her head. "He said he admires me, that he thinks me remarkable, but nothing more. He gave his father his word that he would marry Sophie. And Sophie is depending on him to keep that promise." Madeleine burst into tears.

"Oh, Maddie." Alexandra wrapped Madeleine in her arms. "Are you absolutely sure he's going to marry her?"

"Yes, I'm sure." Tears slid down her cheeks. "Sophie told me she was expecting him to propose the night of Lady Trevelyan's ball."

"Did he ask her?"

"I don't know. When he sought me out and danced with me, he certainly wasn't *acting* like a man who'd just asked someone else to marry him. But then I left to come to you. Who knows what happened after that?"

Madeleine retrieved a handkerchief from the sleeve of her dress, unfolded it, and used it to wipe her eyes and blow her nose. To her dismay, she realized it was the handkerchief Sophie had embroidered for her, which brought a fresh spate of tears. "How could I have allowed myself to grow so attached to him? He is Sophie's. He's always been Sophie's. To him, I'm probably just one more wicked American woman distracting him from his duty. He used the reminder word, after all."

"The reminder word?"

"Don't you remember? The word Mother gave us when we were little, whenever we did something out of line?"

Alexandra looked at her. "*Pineapple?* You told Lord Saunders about *pineapple?*"

Madeleine nodded, drying her eyes. "So we wouldn't do something we'd regret."

"And he said it?"

"To stop himself from kissing me."

Alexandra nodded slowly, frowning. "Well, he *is* a man of honor. After all, he stood by Elise Townsend, even when he didn't love her. But from what you just told me about the ball, I don't think he was about to propose to someone else."

"Well, one thing was clear. He knew that kissing *me* was wrong. And so did I." Madeleine leaned back against the headboard again. "It's hopeless, Lexie. Just as I feared it would be."

"I'm so sorry. This is my fault. I'm the one who insisted you should go back to Trevelyan Manor."

"Don't blame yourself." Madeleine sighed. "You may have *encouraged* me, but I chose to go. And I am responsible for everything that happened once I got there."

Silence reigned for a long moment. "What are you doing to do about Lord Oakley?" Alexandra asked finally.

Madeleine shrugged. "I have no idea. To be honest, I haven't thought about him in quite a while."

"That's understandable," Alexandra said. "You'll need time to heal from this. And you *will* heal, I promise. If you ever need to talk, I'm here for you. And when you're ready to think and talk about the future, I'm here for that as well."

Charles pulled the chariot to a stop in front of the ancient barn that served as his workshop.

"What are we doing here again, Charles?" Sophie asked from the seat beside him.

"It is a place I have been wanting to show you."

Three days had passed since Miss Atherton's departure. Three days in which Charles's mind had whirled with confusion, trying to sort through the minefield of his feelings. It was killing him to be away from her.

By day, he could not concentrate on his work. At night, he continued to dream of her.

Only last night, he had dreamt again that they were in each other's arms. She was attired, as he had seen her once before, in nothing but a thin nightdress, which he had ripped off to expose her perfect body. He had lowered her to the floor and taken her breasts in his mouth, his fingers finding and stroking the feminine heart of her between her thighs. In his dream, she had gasped and cried out as he pleasured her and then thrust inside her, completing the union of their bodies, a union he already felt between their souls. Just as he was on the verge of his own climax, he had awakened, hard as steel and filled with a wanting so deep it couldn't be assuaged, even with the work of his hand.

He knew it was wrong to dream of her this way. She was a high-born woman, not a randy actress, widow, or chambermaid. She was—he would put money on it—a virgin. He would not dream of taking advantage of her innocence.

To make love to her, he would have to marry her.

And there was no way that could happen. Not with Oakley and Sophie and the promise he had made standing between them.

Were he to break that promise, his father—God forbid—might well have another seizure, and it would be his fault. As the future Marquess of Trevelyan, he had obligations to fulfill. He had allowed his mother and Sophie to cherish certain expectations. He owed them his allegiance; he could not let them down.

No matter how much he longed to be with Miss Atherton, he could not have her. It was impossible. Which meant that all these carnal dreams and all this ridiculous longing must stop, once and for all.

Charles had finally concluded that his only course of action, the only way to make this right, was to bolster his relationship with Sophie, to include her more in his life. To try to create the kind of closeness with *her* that he had felt with Miss Atherton.

Hence today's outing.

Sophie had been more quiet than usual during the ride over, apparently lost in her own thoughts. Which was just as well, since he was so distracted himself.

Charles jumped down from the conveyance, moved to the opposite side, and helped Sophie to alight. "I have been coming here for a quite a while now."

"Coming here? To this old barn? Whatever for?"

"You shall see." Charles led the way to the door, unlocked it, and bade her wait a moment while he dashed inside and lit a few lamps. "All right. Come in." He had taken care, before bringing her here, to put away his French postcards. *That* collection was something Sophie would surely never understand.

Sophie hesitantly entered the building and stopped, wrinkling her nose. "What is that smell?"

"Machine oil, I expect. And the smell of old barn." He chuckled nervously.

She looked around, confused. "What is all this, Charles?"

"It is my shop." He gestured at his works in progress. "The place where I build and invent things."

"Invent things? But I thought you gave all that up years ago."

"As it happens, I did not give it up.'"

She looked at him. "But you gave your father your word. You never break your word."

Charles winced, feeling the weight behind that declaration, a not-so-subtle reminder of his unspoken obligation to her. "I told Father what he wished to hear, Sophie." He willed her to understand. "But don't you see? Inventing things is in my blood."

Sophie seemed to be at a loss for words.

"Those hairpins I gave you and my mother and sisters? I didn't buy them in town. I made them."

"Did you? Oh." She looked surprised, and added matter-of-factly, without a smile, "They are lovely hairpins."

"Let me show you what else I am working on."

He gave her a tour. Although Sophie tried hard to muster enthusiasm, Charles could tell she was not really interested in the things he was showing her.

"It is all very impressive," Sophie said at last.

"Do you mean that?" he replied woodenly.

She hesitated. "Well. I can see that this is important to you. But to be honest, I do not understand why. What would you do with that lamp thing, Charles, if you *did* get it to work? You could not sell it."

"No. But I could invest in a company that would manufacture it. Think what a difference it would make in the mining industry. It could save lives."

She took that in. "Still. This environment, it is so dirty and messy. Surely this kind of thing is better left to people in the trades?"

"Why? Why should *I* not pursue what interests me?"

"Because you are an earl."

"You sound just like my father." He sighed in annoyance.

Sophie's brows furrowed in distress. She seemed to go somewhere else in her mind for a moment before speaking again. "I do not wish to upset you, Charles. Perhaps it is not my place to say anything. But I have known you all my life. You must be practical. You are looked up to in your current position, and one day you will be a marquess. Surely you understand why you must give all this up?"

"Perhaps you are right. Perhaps I shall have to, one day," Charles responded grimly, before showing her to the door.

Five days after Tommy's birth, a telegram arrived at Polperran House:

TO: THE EARL AND COUNTESS OF LONGFORD POLPERRAN HOUSE, LONGFORD, CORNWALL

WELCOME BABY THOMAS. LEAVING PARIS TO-MORROW. ARRIVE BOLTON STATION AUGUST 16 ON 2 PM TRAIN. SEND CARRIAGE.
      MOTHER

Madeleine set down the telegram on the breakfast table, exchanging a sigh with her sister. The last thing she wanted right now was to see her mother, who would no doubt have only one thing on her mind: whether or not Madeleine was ready to accept Lord Oakley.

"What is that sigh for, ladies?" Thomas asked as he tucked into his scrambled eggs.

"I think you know," his wife responded, sipping her coffee.

"Because your mother is coming?"

Alexandra nodded. "Mother can be *so* difficult."

"Mother," Madeleine agreed, "can be impossible."

"Well," Thomas replied, "let us hope she will be so thrilled to see her first grandchild, she'll be on her best behavior."

When the carriage rolled up in the courtyard's gravel drive on Friday afternoon, the entire household was waiting outside to greet it.

The footman opened the coach's door and pulled down the steps. Madeleine and Alexandra's mother glanced out from the doorway with a wide, uncharacteristic smile on her face.

"Hello!" she called out.

The footman assisted Mrs. Atherton to step down. She was dressed in a meticulously fashioned suit and matching hat that could only have been made in Paris.

"What a beautiful dress," Julia commented.

"She looks so happy," Lillie noted.

"Too happy," Madeleine murmured.

"She always arrives grumpy and complaining," Alexandra whispered in agreement. "I wonder what's going on?"

A second occupant alighted: their mother's lady's maid, Fiona, with whom she always traveled. And then, to Madeleine's utter astonishment, yet another person emerged from the carriage.

Lord Oakley.

Chapter Twenty-Three

As Lord Oakley stepped down onto the gravel drive, Madeleine stared at him, stunned into silence.

What was he doing here, showing up without an invitation? The last she'd heard from Lord Oakley, he was in Italy with plans to visit France. He'd intended to be away another month at least.

He stood tall and upright, a dignified figure in his brown tweed suit and pumpkin-colored ascot, his auburn hair becomingly combed. Somehow, he managed to look fresh and immaculate, despite the fact that he must have been traveling for days.

"My lord," her mother said to Thomas, "I believe you know Lord Oakley?"

Although her sister and Thomas must have been just as surprised by this man's unexpected appearance as Madeleine was, neither showed an ounce of discomposure.

Thomas held out his hand. "Oakley! Yes, I remember you from Oxford. It has been an age."

"Nice to see you, Longford." Lord Oakley firmly returned the handshake.

"May I present my wife, Lady Longford?"

Oakley bowed to Alexandra. "Lady Longford. I believe we have met before as well, when you were first presented to English society."

"We did," Alexandra acknowledged.

Thomas introduced Oakley to his sisters Julia and Lillie, who curtsied politely.

Oakley then turned to Madeleine, his pale blue eyes imbued with warmth. "May I say, Miss Atherton, what a delight it is to see you again."

Confusion shot through her. Madeleine had forgotten how handsome he was, or the effect his smile had on her. Recovering the power of speech, she said, "And you, my lord. I hope you enjoyed your holiday abroad?"

"Very much. But after running into your mother in Paris, I was happy to cut it short."

Suddenly, Oakley's presence was beginning to make sense. Madeleine cast a dark look at her mother, but it went unnoticed.

"Imagine my surprise," her mother commented, "when I came down to the lobby of the Grand Hotel Terminus to discover that Lord Oakley was staying at the very same place!"

"It was a happy coincidence," Oakley remarked.

Coincidence my foot.

"When I told him I was coming back to Cornwall to see

my new grandson," Mrs. Atherton went on, "he wouldn't hear of me traveling on my own, absolutely *insisted* on accompanying me. But then, I already told you all this in the wire I sent." She smiled, as if daring anyone to challenge this lie.

"Yes, of course," Alexandra replied.

"Glad to have you," Thomas said.

"Glad to be here," Lord Oakley replied. "It is my first time in Cornwall." Gazing up at the massive, three-winged edifice that wrapped around the courtyard in which they stood, he added, "I say, this is a beautiful old house. The battlements and turrets are exceptional. Did there used to be a fourth wing?"

"There did—it burned down over a century ago," Thomas acknowledged.

"I thought as much. I am a bit of an architecture buff," Oakley announced proudly. "I look forward to seeing the place."

"Allow me to lead the way." Thomas gestured for Oakley and Alexandra to accompany him inside. Julia and Lillie fell in step behind them.

"So," Madeleine said under her breath, following along with her mother, "you just *happened* to run into him in Paris?"

"What do you take me for?" her mother responded in a stern whisper. "His mother gave me his itinerary."

"And he decided to return to England, just to provide you with an escort?"

"He is a gallant gentleman. What can I say? Although I'm sure the greater impetus was my insistence that a prompt visit from him was in order—and that you were quite ready to accept his offer."

"You told him that?" Madeleine was aghast. "Mother, how could you?"

"You've had plenty of time to think this over, Madeleine. Time apart does *not* make the heart grow fonder. Accept him and be done with it. You will thank me later." As they passed through the grand entry hall into the enormous drawing room where the others were chatting, Mrs. Atherton raised her voice and called out, "When do I get to meet my new grandson?"

The conversation at dinner focused on anecdotes from Lord Oakley's and Mrs. Atherton's recent travel experiences. Although the stories were interesting and often amusing, Madeleine found it impossible to attend to them.

All summer long, she'd been so distracted by her attraction to Lord Saunders, she'd given Lord Oakley very little thought—and she felt a bit guilty about that. It was hard to believe he was actually *here*, sitting beside her now. According to her mother, he'd come because he thought she was ready to accept him.

Madeleine felt as if she were on a train that was barreling down a track, destined for some inescapable end. She had fallen in love with Lord Saunders, but a relationship with him had never even been in the cards. Maybe, all along, she was supposed to marry Lord Oakley. Maybe her whole visit to Cornwall was never supposed to have happened.

Oakley's voice infiltrated her reverie. "Of all the cities I visited in Italy," he was saying as he swirled the wine in his glass, "Venice was my favorite. All those wonderful ancient buildings, particularly St. Mark's Basilica. Unforgettable."

"Thomas and I honeymooned in Italy," Alexandra nodded with enthusiasm. "I'll never forget our gondola ride in Venice. It was so romantic."

"Not quite so romantic, I am afraid, when you have no one to share it with." Oakley turned to Madeleine. "One day soon, I look forward to gliding along the canals in the moonlight with you, my dear."

Madeleine wished she could return his sentiment. She searched for a reply. "Did you visit Florence, my lord?"

"I did. A lovely city."

"I studied art in Florence," Thomas remarked as the footman served him roasted potatoes from a silver tray. "I will never forget the sense of awe that came over me the first time I saw Michelangelo's *David*."

"Incredible to think he carved that massive statue from a single piece of unwanted marble," Alexandra noted.

"An Italian Grand Duke gave Queen Victoria a replica of the *David* thirty years ago," Mrs. Atherton said with a sniff. "She was so offended by its nudity, she commissioned a plaster cast fig leaf to preserve its modesty."

Oakley nodded. "Quite the right thing to do."

Madeleine stared at him. "The right thing? How can you say so, Lord Oakley? The *David* is a masterpiece."

"It is," Oakley agreed, "but created for a different audience. The day I saw it, no fewer than three gentlewomen fainted dead away upon beholding it—one directly into my arms."

Laughter erupted along the table. Madeleine feigned a laugh she didn't feel.

After dinner, as the party arrived in the parlor for tea, Thomas and Alexandra were suddenly called away to attend to their son, and Mrs. Atherton announced that she was tired and going to bed.

"Was that a cleverly engineered subterfuge to leave us on our own?" Oakley asked Madeleine, amused, as he sat down on the sofa beside her.

Madeleine's heart quickened, but more with anxiety than anticipation. "I believe it was."

"Kind of them, though. And very much appreciated." Oakley gave her an earnest and tender smile. "Miss Atherton. I know I have only just arrived after two months apart. Perhaps it is too soon to speak, but I do not know when we shall have another opportunity like this." He took a breath. "First, I want to make sure there are no illusions between us. I fear your mother may have misled you when she explained why I have come to Cornwall."

"Oh?" She glanced at her lap.

"It is true that I did not like the idea of your mother traveling on her own, but there is a more important reason I wished to accompany her." He took one of her hands in his. His voice ringing with emotion, he said, "When I met your mother in Paris, she said that you had made a decision regarding my offer. That you have now decided to make me the happiest man on earth."

Madeleine looked up to see quiet affection in his eyes. Her heart pounded. How should she respond? She admired

Lord Oakley. He had been so patient. She'd made him wait two months already, and he'd cut short a trip to Europe just to see her. Maybe she owed it to him to say yes.

She recalled what her mother had said to her months ago, when Madeleine had professed herself to be uncertain as to whether or not she loved Lord Oakley. *Do not be so particular. You will learn to love the man you marry. As I did. As all wealthy women do.*

Maybe it was true. Maybe she could *learn* to love Lord Oakley.

Accept him and be done with it. You will thank me later.

Before Madeline could reply, however, Oakley leaned in and pressed his lips briefly and delicately against hers, then announced with a smile, "I am so glad to have the matter settled at last. We will have a perfect life together, my darling Madeleine. I love you dearly. Mother is so looking forward to discussing the wedding arrangements."

Madeleine's mind was in a whirl. What had just happened? Had she indeed accepted him? Were she and Lord Oakley now engaged? He'd kissed her and called her Madeleine, a familiarity reserved for couples who were betrothed. She felt a sense of rising panic and sinking disappointment, two disparate sensations that clanged violently within her.

"But before we get to that," Lord Oakley went on, "I feel remiss. At dinner, we talked only about me and my travels. Tell me about you. How have you occupied yourself while I was gone?"

Madeleine struggled to find her voice. "Um. Well. I have kept busy. I spent much of my time at Trevelyan Manor."

And I kissed Lord Saunders. Twice. She felt her ears grow hot. Lord Oakley's kiss just now had been so polite, so tentative. She had felt . . . nothing. The contrast between *that* kiss and the kisses she'd shared with Lord Saunders was so extreme, she could hardly countenance it.

"Trevelyan Manor?" Oakley asked. "Where is that?"

"Five miles off. It's the home of George Grayson, the Marquess of Trevelyan."

"Ah, yes. I knew Charles Grayson at school. An excellent chap! I should love to see him again. But why were you there?"

"A visiting cousin needed a companion, and I complied. I have also been writing this summer."

"Writing? Ah. Mother says that writing letters can be a pleasant pastime for a woman."

"I didn't write many letters. Actually, I wrote a play. And I finished my book."

"Your book?"

"The novel I told you about."

"A *novel?*" He pronounced the word as if he'd just taken a bite of a sour lemon.

"Yes. I did mention it. And you—"

"But you say you are all finished with that now?" he said hastily.

"Finished? Well, no. I have to revise it until it's ready for publication."

"Publication?" A short laugh escaped Oakley's lips. "My dear, you must know that as a marchioness and my future duchess, you cannot *think* of publishing a *novel*. That sort of thing simply will not do."

"Won't it?" While at Hatfield Park, he'd seemed perfectly amenable when she'd told him of her aspirations. It now occurred to Madeleine that he probably hadn't even been listening.

"Letters and journals, these are the proper and acceptable outlets for a woman's pen," Oakley insisted. "But to scribble away at novels? Mother would never hear of it. And what would other people think?"

Mother would never hear of it. It was the third time he'd mentioned his mother in as many minutes. Madeleine had never noticed before how much his mother's opinions occupied his thoughts.

As he continued talking, Madeleine's mind spun. Lord Oakley, she realized, was a genteel man with many redeeming qualities. He needed to marry a fortune, but there were plenty of other heiresses from whom to choose. He'd said that he loved her, but that couldn't possibly be true. Because he didn't really understand her, nor care what was important to *her*. More importantly, Madeleine realized, she didn't love him. And she never could. The attraction she'd felt for him when they first met had been mild at best, and fleeting. There had never been any real spark. *That*, she now comprehended, was why she hadn't been able to give him her answer two months ago.

Since then, Madeleine had discovered what true love was. She loved Lord Saunders. She might not be able to marry him, but someday, difficult as it was to imagine now, she might feel that way about someone else. Until that day came, *if* it ever came, she would settle for nothing less.

"You shan't have time for such an indulgence in any case, my dearest," Lord Oakley was saying. "You shall have a house in London and in the country to manage, children to raise, and much of your time will be devoted to charitable ventures. I trust *that* will keep any woman busy enough."

"You're right, my lord," Madeleine said, raising her eyes to his. "All that certainly *would* keep a woman busy enough. And for almost any woman in the world, it would *be* enough. But it isn't enough for me."

Lord Oakley didn't try to hide his disappointment over Madeleine's decision, but to his credit, he was a gentleman about it. He left Polperran House early the next morning, before the rest of the household had risen from bed.

When Madeleine came downstairs and learned that Oakley had gone, she sighed with relief. She hadn't realized how much this decision had been weighing her down. For the first time in months, she was filled with a sense of peace.

It was a peace, however, that she knew would be short-lived. Because any minute now, her mother was going to descend those stairs, fully anticipating that her daughter was to be a future duchess.

Madeleine couldn't face her mother's wrath. Not this morning. She needed to get away.

But where could she go? What excuse could she give for leaving the house?

An answer suddenly presented itself—an errand Madeleine

needed to run. There was no better time than the present to undertake it.

The morning breeze whipped through Madeleine's hair as she trotted along. Her mount, Black Shadow, was her favorite horse in the Polperran stables, a gentle mare she had ridden several times before.

Madeleine's visit to Trevelyan Manor, she determined, would be a brief one. She was wearing her green silk summer riding habit, after all, not dressed for a social call. Her purpose: to retrieve the manuscript she'd inadvertently left when she'd departed in such haste on the night of the ball.

It would nice to see Sophie and the family again, if only for a few minutes. Madeleine could tell them about her new nephew, promise to call again in the near future, and depart. There wouldn't be time for Lord Oakley's name to come up at all. If Lord Saunders was there . . .

Madeleine hoped that Lord Saunders *wouldn't* be there. It would be so much easier if he weren't. As she rode up to the manor house, a stable boy appeared.

"I am only staying a minute," Madeleine told the boy as she dismounted and gave him the reins. "If you could give her water and bring her straight back, I'd appreciate it."

The boy nodded and led the horse off. Madeleine looped up the long, left-hand-side drape of her riding skirt and buttoned it out of the way so she wouldn't trip on it. Before she could knock, Woodson was opening the front door.

"Miss Atherton. What a pleasure to see you." He stepped back, admitting her.

"And you, Woodson." The inner hall was quiet and still. "Are His Lordship and Her Ladyship at home?"

"I am afraid not. The family is away visiting friends at St. Austell."

"Oh." Disappointment surged through her. It felt like her first day in Cornwall all over again. "I seem to have a habit of dashing off to see people who aren't at home."

"No need to fret, miss. You can always return another day." Woodson glanced at her carefully. "Am I correct in thinking, Miss Atherton, that your reason for coming was not purely social? That you wished to retrieve something that you may have . . . inadvertently left on your previous visit?"

Madeleine smiled. "How did you know, Woodson?" Silly question. Woodson always knew everything.

"A maid found a manuscript in the bureau drawer the other day when she was cleaning. She gave it to me."

"You have it, then?"

"I am afraid not."

"Where is it?"

"His Lordship has it."

"Lord Trevelyan?" The idea that the marquess had seen and might have read her manuscript was a bit alarming.

"No, Lord Saunders."

Madeleine's heart fluttered. "Lord Saunders?"

"He took it with him two days ago when he left the house. I believe his intention was to return it to you. I deduce that he has not done so?"

"He has not." Madeleine's pulse now began to pound.

Lord Saunders had had her manuscript for two days? "Woodson. Do you know where Lord Saunders might be?"

"I do, miss." Woodson's blue eyes twinkled as he gave her a knowing smile. "He is in Truro."

D ark clouds gathered as Madeleine rode along. This was unlucky, she thought. It had been fine and warm the past two weeks. Why did the weather have to turn today, of all times, when she was so far from the house?

By the look of the sky, she figured she had just enough time to retrieve her manuscript from Lord Saunders's workshop and return to Polperran House before the promised rain began. However, she was still about a half mile away from her destination when the first drops began to fall. It was soon raining in earnest.

If only she had on her winter riding habit, which was made of wool—it would have provided far more protection than this lightweight summer habit. By the time Madeleine caught sight of the old barn, rain was dripping steadily from the brim of her hat, her face and hair were sopping, and moisture had seeped in through the layers of her clothes.

A plume of smoke rose from the chimney of the old barn, and she spied Tesla in the stables. Madeleine heaved a sigh. It was the second time this summer that she'd been caught in a storm while on horseback, the second time Lord Saunders would see her drenched to the bone. She glanced at the nearby farmhouse, but didn't want to impose on total strangers, especially in her current state. She considered giving up on her errand and returning to Polperran House, but she was so wet and cold now she was shivering.

Madeleine trotted up to the barn, dismounted, and knocked on the door. A full minute seemed to pass before it finally was yanked open.

"What is it?" Lord Saunders said testily. Upon seeing her, his irritation vanished. "Miss Atherton. Forgive me." He took in her bedraggled state, glanced at Black Shadow. "Please come in out of the rain, while I stable your horse."

Chapter Twenty-Four

It was pouring down in torrents as Charles raced from the stables back to the barn.

He had a pretty good idea what had brought her here. *Her manuscript.*

The knowledge that Miss Atherton was inside his workshop, waiting for him, alone, made his heart pound as fast as the rain.

Nothing had changed. He was still bound to Sophie. But that didn't stop him from wanting *this* woman, however wrong it might be.

Now she was here. She would have to stay here while she waited out this god-awful rain. It was going to be a test of his willpower to stay away from her. But he had to. He had already gone too far just in kissing her the way he had.

"There," he said, entering and wiping off his muddy boots on a mat inside the front door. "Your horse is fed and safely stowed in the stables."

"Thank you so much." Miss Atherton had removed her

hat and leather gauntlets and was standing in front of the
potbelly stove, as drenched as he was, holding out her hands
to the fire. Her tailored riding jacket and long skirts were
fashioned from some silky summery fabric. "I'm so sorry you
had to go out in that rain."

"I am sorry you were *caught* in it." He grabbed two small
hand towels from a nearby washstand, then crossed the room
and gave one to her. She thanked him again.

As he tousled a towel through his wet hair, she used hers
to dab her own face and hair. She was shivering. "I'm sorry to
have disturbed you."

"You didn't. It is always a pleasure to see you." Charles
began unbuttoning his wet shirt, anxious to be rid of it.

She glanced at him. Her gaze fixed on the movement of
his fingers, as if surprised by their intent. "I . . . um . . . went to
the manor house to retrieve my manuscript. Woodson said
they'd found it and that you might have it?"

"I do," he admitted a little guiltily. "I know I should have
returned it at once. But I got busy. Forgive me. I am soaked clear
through." Shrugging out of his shirt, he hung it over the line he
had strung for that purpose behind the stove, then turned back
to her. The way she was staring at him now, you would think
she had never seen a man's naked chest before. "As are you," he
added with concern. "Soaked clear through, I mean."

He noticed that her skirts were so wet they clung to her legs,
outlining their shape all the way up to the V where they met.
The sight sent blood coursing through his body. Good God, just
looking at her made him grow hard. Had she noticed?

Her gaze traveled lower now, and her eyes grew rounder

still. *Damn it.* She had noticed. His cheeks grew warm. "Allow me to get some blankets."

Grateful to escape for a moment, Charles darted upstairs to the loft, sending a silent message to his private parts. *Down, boy.* When he felt sufficiently recovered, he grabbed two quilts off the bed and brought them downstairs, where he found her taking down her hair.

He paused on the last step, drinking in the sight of her as she removed the last few pins, then gave her head a shake, letting her long hair settle around her shoulders. His breath caught. He'd only seen her hair down and long once before, when they'd shared a midnight feast in the kitchen.

The memory of the kisses they had shared came back to him again, threatening to restore the state of physical arousal he had only just banished. *Damn it to hell. This cannot go anywhere.* He cleared his throat to make his presence known and ventured in her direction.

"I hope you don't mind," she said. "I thought to dry my hair by the stove."

"Be my guest." She was still sopping wet from the neck down. "You ought to get out of those wet clothes, as well." *Did I really just say that aloud?*

Miss Atherton gave him a direct look and with a teasing smile said, "Lord Saunders, you must know I can do no such thing."

He let out a low chuckle. "You have a blouse on beneath that jacket, do you not?" Even though he knew he was tempting a fate that would send him straight to hell, he'd love to see her out of that jacket. And the blouse. And everything else.

"Of course I do."

"Surely you have entertained guests in a blouse before."

She hesitated, then shrugged. "You have a point." She turned away slightly, unbuttoned her wet riding jacket, removed it, and handed it to him.

He took it and positioned it over the line beside his shirt. When he turned back, he froze.

He hadn't counted on her white blouse being so wet as to be nearly transparent. She didn't seem to be aware of this fact and he tried not to look, but that proved to be beyond his power. Through the filmy fabric he could see her corset and chemise as plain as day, hugging the outline of her tiny waist, as well as the bare curves of her creamy breasts. Below the corset, her skirts still clung to her legs and her. . . . *Oh how I would love to see those legs.* An image came to his mind of Miss Atherton, standing entirely naked before him. *Dear God, if only.*

He swallowed hard. It wouldn't do for her to know where his thoughts had just gone. At the same time, it wasn't healthy for her to remain in such wet clothing. *That* was the reason he gave himself, in any case, for his next words. And damn it, it was a good reason. "Correct me if I am wrong, but beneath that skirt, I believe you are wearing riding trousers?"

"I am." She made a small scoffing sound. "But I can't very well walk around your workshop in trousers."

"Men do so every day," he countered.

"I am not a man."

"No. But you traipsed across the stage a few weeks ago, dressed as one."

That seemed to take her aback. "I suppose I did."

Charles stoked the fire, trying to ignore the fire that was once again smoldering in his loins. "Why is this any different?"

A myriad of expressions crossed her face. He could guess what she was thinking: *That* was a costume for the stage, in a room full of people. *This* was just the two of them. Was it decent?

She was right. It was best for her to remain as clothed as possible. "Never mind." He stood abruptly and gave her one of the blankets. "Wrap yourself in this. I hope it will help to warm you. Meanwhile, I will make tea."

"You know how to make tea?" She sounded surprised.

"A skill acquired by necessity." As Charles refilled the kettle from a pitcher on a counter, and found a box of tea and the teapot, he heard the rustling of fabric behind him. He turned in surprise to see Miss Atherton stepping out of her wet riding skirts. He nearly lost his grip on the kettle. Her riding trousers were as wet as her skirts had been, and molded to every curve of her body.

Charles watched her drape the long skirt over the drying line, nearly overcome by the desire to cross the room and take her in his arms, to once again feel the curves of that luscious, feminine body against his own.

How on earth was he going to get through the next hour or two without touching her? It might just drive him mad.

Lord Saunders was staring at her from across the room. His gaze seemed to be lingering on . . . a place a gentleman's gaze should never linger. The expression on his face was so heated, it produced an equally heated reaction within her, eliciting sparks that rose to set her cheeks aflame.

Madeleine's heart began to pound. She had decided that it would be perfectly fine for Lord Saunders to see her in trousers. After all, he'd done so before. No one had seemed much perturbed the day she'd worn masculine attire on the stage. His reaction now, though, made her question that decision.

Somehow, she had to break the unspoken tension that crackled through the air.

Madeleine shook open the blanket he'd given her and wrapped it around herself, covering her body from neck to toe. *There. That is better.* Her pants and blouse were wet, too, but she obviously couldn't take *them* off. Standing close to the stove, she drank in the heat that enveloped her, hoping he would attribute her rosy cheeks to that source.

Saunders set the kettle on to heat, then turned two chairs from the nearby table alongside each other, facing the stove.

"Thank you," Madeleine said.

He gave her an answering nod, a distracted look in his eyes.

She sat down, her heart still racing. The soft leather of her low boots was soaked through to her skin. "Do you mind if I take off my shoes?"

"If you don't think it would be too scandalous," he quipped.

She fought back a smile, took the boots off, and set them before the stove to dry, then wiggled her stocking feet before the stove.

"I hope you are more comfortable now?" he asked.

"Yes, thank you," she said again. In truth, she wasn't comfortable at all. Not just because of the damp clothes she still wore, or the fact that she was only half-dressed beneath this blanket, but because she was alone with him again, something she'd promised herself would never happen.

When he'd first removed his shirt, she'd been a bit shocked. She'd seen plenty of men naked from the waist up before—boxers and bathers and strong men in the circus—and had thought nothing of it. It was the first time she'd been *alone* with a man with a naked chest, however. And the first time she'd seen *this man's* naked chest. Which was a thing of beauty. All hard, masculine curves, which she longed to reach out and touch. A light dusting of brown hair covered his upper chest, and a narrow trail of hair led down past his trim stomach to disappear into the waist of his trousers.

His pants were damp from the rain and clung to his body, outlining every muscle and sinew and . . . everything else. Another rush of heat rose inside her, this time creating a hollow feeling of want between her legs. With his damp hair falling gently across his forehead, his striking hazel eyes in that handsome face, and his powerful, lean thighs and erect manhood showcased in those tight trousers, he was like catnip and she was the cat.

She chastised herself for these errant thoughts, struggling to direct her mind away from his looks and body. *Think about the man himself. All the reasons you love him.*

Madeleine took a deep breath and glanced around the room, searching for a topic of conversation to ease the unspoken tension in the air. "Um," she began, "how are your projects coming?"

"My battery now lasts a good five minutes longer than it did previously," he said, adding facetiously, "Hooray."

"That's a step in the right direction."

"On a very slow road." Saunders brought two cups to the table along with a teapot, to which he added fresh tea.

"And your typewriter?"

"I took your suggestion. I'm working on a new kind of type bar, hoping to make a typist's work visible with every stroke. It is rudimentary as of yet, but I remain hopeful."

"I believe you'll succeed on both counts."

"I appreciate the vote of confidence."

Madeleine suddenly noticed that the postcards of naked women she'd observed on her first visit here were nowhere in evidence on his workbenches. "What happened to your French postcards?" she asked impulsively, then wished she hadn't. The question seemed to embarrass him.

"I . . . put them away," he said, coloring. "One never knows when they are going to have a visitor."

That made her laugh. "I see." Then: "Woodson said your family went to St. Austell today."

"Did they? I have not been home in days."

"I hope this means your father is feeling better?"

"He is." Saunders opened up the second blanket and wrapped it around his own shoulders, then sat down on the other chair beside her. "He has improved vastly over the past few weeks. He does not like to admit it, but that new diet has made all the difference. My family is deeply indebted to you,

Miss Atherton. Someday, I hope my father will show proper gratitude for what you did."

"I did very little. I am just pleased it worked out so well."

"So are we."

She smiled, and after a moment said, "Again, I apologize for intruding like this. You said you have my manuscript?"

"Yes, it's upstairs. I hope you don't mind. Curiosity got the better of me. I have been reading it."

"Have you?" Madeleine felt uncomfortable again, but couldn't resist asking, "What do you think?"

"I must tell you, Miss Atherton, it is a wonderful book."

"Oh?" The single word escaped her, an exhalation of combined joy and relief. "You liked it then?"

"I liked it very much. The story grabbed me from the first page. I did not want to put it down. Yesterday, I read straight through, barely pausing to eat the meals Mrs. Smith dropped by. Today, I have been reading since I awoke. I was just finishing it when you arrived. If I seemed brusque, that's why. I was so engaged, I did not wish to be interrupted until I had taken in the last sentence."

Madeleine was so dazzled by his words, she could barely reply. "I don't know what to say. You're the first and only person besides myself who has read it."

"I am honored." The kettle was boiling now. As he filled the teapot, he continued, "You have a way with words that is . . . well, enchanting. I felt as though I was standing right there in all the places you described. I admire your characters. Every one felt like a real person to me, and I was invested in every right and wrong decision they made."

"Oh," she said again. "Thank you, Lord Saunders, for those kind words."

Leaving the brew to steep, he resumed his seat. "I am only sharing my honest opinion."

"I appreciate it more than you know. Do you think it has a chance of being accepted by a publisher?"

"I think any publisher would be lucky to have it."

A troubling thought came to her. "Are you just being kind, because you don't want to hurt my feelings?"

"Not at all. I may not be in the publishing business, but I know a good book when I read one. And I will tell you something else. I do not think a man could have written this book anywhere near as well, if at all."

"Really? *You* say that?"

He seemed a bit abashed by her innuendo, but nodded. After a moment, he said, "You were right, what you said in the coach the day you first arrived in Cornwall. You said women are equally as capable as men and just as smart, sometimes smarter. I questioned the point of women attending college. You have shown me how mistaken was my thinking. I have seen what you can do, Miss Atherton. I now understand. I believe that women absolutely *can* do anything men can do, and given the opportunity, perhaps even more."

Madeleine could feel her smile lighting up her entire face. "You have no idea how happy I am to hear you say that. If only more men felt as you do."

"You said things are changing. In time, perhaps they will."

"I hope so." Madeleine hesitated. "At the risk of sounding presumptuous, may I ask one more question?"

"Ask away."

"You implied that only a woman could have written this novel. Let us suppose that the author was a member of the nobility—maybe even a duchess—what would you think then?"

He chuckled, as if he could see where this was going. "I would think the duke in question had a very talented wife."

"You wouldn't think it scandalous that a duchess had written a novel?"

"Hardly."

Madeleine let go a long sigh. Here was further proof of the connection they shared, and why this man had become so dear to her.

Saunders sat back in his chair. "Let me guess. You ask because you are worried what Oakley might think, when he discovers what you have written?"

"Oh, my worries on that count are over. Lord Oakley knows all about it. Last night, he shared his opinion on the subject."

"Last night? But how? I thought he was out of the country."

"He returned from Europe quite unexpectedly in the company of my mother, who had apparently told him I was ready to accept his proposal."

Saunders's mouth dropped opened in surprise. He closed it again. "And . . . did you?"

"I found I could not."

He nodded slowly. Madeleine thought she detected relief in his eyes. Even though that made no sense at all. He was marrying Sophie. Why should he care who she did or didn't marry?

"May I ask why not?" he asked softly.

Madeleine stared down at her hands where they gripped the blanket. *Because I don't love him*, she wanted to say. *Because I love you*. But how could she tell him that? It would only make him feel guilty, or prompt a rash of explanations as to why it could not be. "For a variety of reasons," she said finally, "one of which was his clear declaration that he wouldn't countenance a wife who wrote novels. Such an *indulgence*, as he called it, would not do for a future duchess."

"I am sorry." Saunders turned to her as he said it.

Their chairs were so close that his thigh inadvertently bumped against hers. Despite the layers of blanket and clothing separating them, that touch sent a jolt careening through Madeleine's body. He must have felt it, too, because that distracted look returned to his face and he cautiously moved his leg aside.

Madeleine's heart began to race in tempo with the beat of the rain on the stones outside. She stared at the empty space that now existed in between where their thighs had touched, wishing she would could feel the weight of his hard limb against hers once more.

If she were honest, Madeleine wished she could feel far more than just the pressure of his thigh. She wished he would stand and pull her into his arms, that she could once again feel the length of his body pressed against hers. That he would kiss her again. Only this time, she wanted more than kissing.

She wanted him to free her from all the clothing that stood between them. She wanted to feel his hands and mouth on her breasts, on every part of her body, until this feeling of wanting inside her was sated at last.

She loved this man. She couldn't marry him, but that didn't stop her from loving him. And wanting him. She knew it was wrong to want him. But she wanted him all the same. *Just this once. No one will ever have to know.*

"Oakley is a fool," Saunders was saying.

"I don't think him a fool." Madeleine swallowed hard and raised her eyes to his. "He's just not the right man for me."

Charles caught his breath as three thoughts crossed his mind.

One: Oakley *was* a fool. He didn't know what he had with this woman. It wasn't just her beautiful face and perfect body. It was her mind and her spirit. She was, in every way, extraordinary. Oakley had lost a rare gem.

Two: She was free of obligation to Oakley.

Three: She wanted *him*.

In the blue depths of her eyes as she looked at him now, Charles read undisguised emotion. A powerful blend of affection and desire that made his heart skitter like a jackrabbit, and that part of his body which he'd been struggling so desperately to keep in check to once more rise up at attention.

He knew, from the heat of her response during kisses they'd shared in the past, that she was just as attracted to him as he was to her. She'd told him so that night in the kitchen. *I feel the same way about you.* But he had explained the way things stood. They had agreed that they should never act on those impulses again. They had made a pact.

Damn that despicable pact. He wished he had never agreed to it. With every fiber of his being, he wanted to kiss her again. More than kiss her. He wanted to carry her up to his bed and make love to her.

Don't even think about it, a voice warned. *You can't, and you know it.*

He repeated that mantra silently to himself, trying to drum up the will to stand up, cross the room, and put some distance between them.

But there was no ignoring that look in her eyes. She wanted him, too.

And before he could act, she leaned in and pressed her mouth to his.

CHAPTER TWENTY-FIVE

Charles responded with a slight intake of breath. Then, unable to help himself, his hands rose to cup her face and he was returning the kiss with feeling.

Both blankets fell to the floor. They stood in unison and Charles enveloped her in his embrace, one hand cradling her head, his other hand sweeping along the slope of her back and curves. This was wrong, so wrong, but she was luscious, he was on fire, and there was no resisting her. Her lips opened willingly, her tongue meeting and caressing his own. Dear Lord, she tasted so sweet.

Her hands were on his shoulders now and he drew her more tightly to him, pressing her softness against his hardness. She let out a small gasp—no doubt she'd felt the evidence of his arousal. But he wasn't going to hide it. How could he? He was only growing longer and harder with every kiss.

He kissed his way across her cheek, then down past her chin. The high collar of her blouse impeded further progress. He made quick work of the top few buttons of the garment, opening it to gain access to her throat. As he pressed a shower of kisses against the tender skin at the side of her neck, her body pulsed and trembled and he heard her breathing hitch. God, she was so responsive, it excited him even more.

Somewhere in the deep recesses of his mind, a voice was struggling for attention, feebly bleating out *What are you doing? Have you forgotten*—But he ignored it.

Her breasts were pressed tantalizingly against him. Charles brought up a hand between their bodies to cup one soft globe, massaging it through the layers of her clothing. She let out a small moan of pleasure against his lips as he continued the motion, his thumb finding the rise of her nipple beneath her blouse and corset. His mouth moved lower still, down from her throat to press kisses against the creamy expanse of flesh at the top of her chest. *Damn all this clothing.*

Her blouse was still damp but only semitransparent now. He wanted to see her. All of her. Charles undid a few more buttons, exposing her corset and chemise and the upper swell of her breasts, just inches from his view. He wanted those breasts in his mouth.

With the weight of his hand, he pushed one breast up until its rosy peak was visible above her corset and chemise. Her areola was pink and round and perfect, her nipple a soft temptation just waiting for his tongue. Dipping his head, he lapped at the luscious point until it hardened. She let out a gasp, arching against him, her body pressing against his erection, eliciting an answering gasp from him. His heart was hammering now and he gently rubbed himself against her, but that primal motion served to increase his arousal to such a dangerous level, he had to stop.

Forcing his lower body to remain still, Charles concentrated on the breast in his mouth, then moved to her other breast to give it the same attention, licking and suckling her and reveling in the sensations that danced inside his body, knowing from the guttural sounds that escaped her throat that she was riding a similar wave of feeling. He was breathing hard now and so was she, almost as if his touch was giving her more pleasure than she could bear.

He knew that he should stop this now, before things got entirely out of hand. That tiny voice was nagging at him now: *Are you out of your mind? This is Miss Atherton. Stop stop stop.* But he couldn't stop. Not yet. There was so much more pleasure to be had. He didn't know how far she was willing to go, was afraid to speak, afraid to break the spell.

One hand slid down the length of her torso and stopped just above the juncture of her legs, waiting to see her response. Charles felt her stiffen slightly, and he thought she was going to call things off right there. But she didn't.

Through the fabric of her trousers, he pressed his hand lower still, until it rested against the most intimate part of her, an action he had only performed with her in his dreams. With a rhythmic motion, he moved his fingers against her, feeling for that spot which he knew would give her the most pleasure. She moaned again, more deeply now as he continued his ministrations. Her head fell back and he felt her begin to sink in his arms, as if she couldn't support herself any longer.

"Wait," she said huskily.

This was the moment she would to tell him to stop. But she did no such thing. Instead, she gazed up at him with a look heavy with meaning and said, "Can we do *this* . . . *more than this* . . . without me conceiving a child?"

Charles paused, his heart pounding. The question reminded him of what he'd refused to acknowledge in the heat of the moment. *She was a virgin.* She had no idea what she was getting herself into. And he had no business doing this with her. What on earth was he thinking?

He *hadn't* been thinking, that was the problem.

He exhaled a long breath. "Yes, we could," he replied softly. "But that doesn't mean we should." With regret, he released her and stepped back.

"What if I want to?" She undid the few remaining buttons on her blouse.

"Don't."

It was too late. She slipped out of her blouse and let it drop to the floor, standing before him in her trousers, corset, and chemise. Her eyes were dusky as she wrapped her arms around him, then kissed him again.

Charles's body stiffened slightly as, all at once, he was overcome by a strange sense of déjà vu. Unaccountably, the image of another woman and another time and place infiltrated his brain: the night he had spent with Elise Townsend. *Why was he thinking about Elise Townsend?* He banished the notion, only to have it replaced by that damnable voice chanting *No no no.*

This is a bad idea, he reminded himself. *For so many reasons.*

But his thoughts began to scatter as the woman in his arms pressed her delectable breasts against his chest, and her lower body molded against that part of him that was hot, hard, and aching.

Who was he to turn down what was so willingly given? She was a grown woman. And he was no saint.

Charles melted into the kiss, overwhelmed by the need to get his hands on her naked body, to thrust into her sex, to feel her wet heat wrapping around him, until he satiated the burning desire that had been building inside him for weeks.

"Are you sure?" he asked quietly against her lips.

"I'm sure."

Without further deliberation, Charles lifted her in his arms and carried her up the stairs to the loft.

Madeleine felt like a bride being carried across the threshold. There had been no wedding. There never would be with him. But she loved him as dearly as any bride had ever loved her husband. And she wanted this, wanted to know what it felt like to make love to a man whom she loved with all her mind and heart and soul.

When they reached the loft, he set her gently on her feet and kissed her again, a long, lovely melding of lips and tongues that hinted at the union to come. He spun her slowly in his arms and began unlacing her corset, all the while pressing kisses up and down the side of her neck from behind, kisses that sent tremors up and down the length of her body and made her feel weak in the knees. She'd never realized that the skin at her throat could be so sensitive, or produce such a feeling of wanting.

When her corset was undone, he flung it aside and tugged at the hem of her thin chemise. Madeleine raised her arms above her head and allowed him to remove this last vestige of clothing from her upper body. With her breasts now free, she felt a moment of shyness and an urge to cover them with her arms, an impulse she resisted. He had just been suckling those breasts in his mouth, and oh, it had felt so wonderful, she wanted more of the same.

Turning her again to face him, he stopped to stare at her breasts. With a slow smile and glittering eyes, he said, "You are so beautiful."

The heated look in his gaze matched the glow that lit her own body like a wildfire. Her gaze drifted down, past his sculpted chest to the spot below his waist, where the evidence of his desire thrust against his trousers like a bolt of steel. The sight made her mouth go dry, as she tried to imagine that appendage fitting inside her. Yet she wanted it, yearned to experience that intimate connection with him.

His hands moved toward the waistband of Madeleine's trousers but she got there first, unbuttoned and slid them down, then stepped out of them. She wore nothing underneath, and again had to fight the urge to cover herself. Her cheeks grew hot as she removed her stockings, and then stood entirely naked to his view.

He said nothing, but the glimmer in his eyes told her that he very much liked what he saw.

He took her in his embrace again, his hands running

up and down her back and buttocks, as her own hands smoothed along the muscles of his back. Pressing her against him, he kissed her hair, her forehead, her cheeks, and then reclaimed her mouth. She gasped at the feel of his hard manhood encased between them through the fabric of his trousers, anxious now for him to remove the last barrier that stood between them.

He broke the kiss, both of them breathing hard as he drew back the covers on the bed and gently maneuvered her down to sit down beside him.

Quickly divesting himself of his boots and stockings, he stood to remove his trousers and smalls in one downward swoop. His erect manhood sprang free, and he turned to stand before her in perfect nudity. The sight made her breath catch and heart beat to a new cadence. She'd never seen a naked man before and the sight fascinated her. He was beautiful. Her fingers ached to touch him. Everywhere.

He tumbled her back onto the bed and stretched out beside her, gathering her in his arms. And then they were kissing again, their naked bodies pressed together like two pieces of a puzzle, as if they were made to fit this way, mouths and tongues entwined, hands and arms everywhere. He moved down to pay tribute to her breasts again.

"Your breasts are so perfect," he said, his voice low and deep.

She moaned in ecstasy as his mouth and tongue sent titillating electric shocks zinging through her body, resonating in her feminine core. *I love you. I love you. I love you,* she wanted to say. The admission rang in her mind and heart, even though she couldn't utter the words aloud. She knew he'd never say those words to her, but it didn't matter. The tenderness she felt in his every touch and the adoration in his gaze spoke of feelings she knew he possessed but couldn't voice. Being with him this way now, today, even knowing it could never happen again, was enough. It would have to be enough.

His hand moved lower to recapture a place he had touched before, the V of the curls between her legs. Except now there was no clothing between her body and the fingers that were working some kind of indescribable magic against her flesh, and evoking such wondrous sensations.

"My God," she heard herself murmur.

He had found a sensitive spot she didn't even know she had. She was wet there, so incredibly wet. She guessed what it must mean: that her body was readying itself for him, and for something else as well. She didn't know what.

It was as if her body were mounting toward a precipice, as if every nerve she possessed were centered at that one spot deep within her. Madeleine's mind reeled. Her breath was coming in ragged pants as the core of her femininity began to throb, and then she gasped and felt herself stiffen. A bolt of lightning shot through her body, her head tossed back and forth, and tremors pulsed through her legs as a burst of exquisite pleasure continued and continued, until she thought she might die from feeling.

"Oh," she murmured as slowly, gradually, the pulsing dissipated and her mind and body came down from heaven. "I had no idea. . . ."

She felt and heard his low chuckle vibrate against her as he kissed her mouth, then raised his head to gaze at her. "Did you like that?" His breath was warm and sweet against her lips.

"Yes." All the ecstasy she'd just experienced was encompassed in that single syllable. She felt spent, dazed, sated. At the same time, she was hazily eager, because she knew this was not yet over. His steely manhood was pressing against her thigh, reminding her that he had yet to be satisfied.

She wanted to touch him. Boldly, she took hold of his member. He inhaled sharply, then covered her hand with his own and showed her how to please him with upward and downward strokes. Soon, eyes glittering, he stopped her hand and slid on top of her, until she felt the hard length of him resting against the part of her that was hot and wet and waiting.

"Madeleine," he said huskily.

It was the first time he'd called her by her given name. She loved the way it sounded on his lips.

"Charles," she murmured in response.

With infinite slowness, he moved up and back along her feminine folds, his breath growing increasingly ragged. "I love the way you feel."

She loved the way *he* felt, and the way he was making her feel, but was too replete in sensation for words. He paused just outside her entrance. She was ready for this. She wanted him inside her, craved the completion of their union.

But suddenly his arms and shoulders tensed. Struggling to control his respiration, he rose up slightly and gazed down at her, doubt in his eyes. "Madeleine," he began again.

Madeleine raised a finger to his lips. "If you say *pineapple*, I will never forgive you."

A low chuckle escaped him. Then he said more soberly, "I don't want to take your virginity, love. I cannot. I should have stopped long before this."

"I didn't want you to stop. I don't want to stop now."

"Neither do I," he admitted tenderly, "believe me, neither do I. But—"

"Then don't." Pressing on his buttocks, she shifted her femininity against his manhood and moved beneath him, until she felt the tip of him push inside her.

That seemed to shatter his resistance. "Dear God," he said, and then he moved with her, entering her a bit more. "I will try . . . to be gentle. I do not wish to hurt you."

Madeleine was grateful for his gentleness, sensed that it was taking all his willpower not to thrust into her with force. He moved slowly, pushing into her by degrees. There was pain that made her stiffen at first, but eventually she began to feel herself relax around him.

"Are you all right?" he whispered against her ear.

"I am."

"You feel wonderful." He entered her further until he had gone as far as he could go, and that aching part of her at last was filled.

He began moving back and forth now in a rhythm that started her body tingling. The pain dissipated. But before desire could bubble up again inside her, she sensed he was reaching a crescendo.

His breath caught suddenly. With a little gasp, he pulled out of her and spent himself with a sound of pure male satisfaction. Madeleine found the act fascinating and exciting—it was so raw, so primal.

Later, after he had tenderly sponged her clean and they lay side by side in each other's arms, he pulled the covers up over them, nestling them in a warm cocoon. Madeleine felt as if she were in a drunken haze, languid from the pleasure he'd given her.

"I'm sorry," he said finally, softly, gazing at her as he brushed back a lock of hair from her face.

"Sorry for what?" Was he going to apologize for taking her virginity? For making love to her when he couldn't marry her? But no.

"For not lasting longer at the end."

So, *that* is what was uppermost on his mind. It stung a little, but Madeleine refused to let it bother her. "Don't apologize. For anything." She ran her fingers admiringly through the expanse of curly hair across his chest. "It was lovely. Indescribably lovely."

"Yes. It was." His eyes glowed as he leaned in for another kiss.

"Is it always like that?" she asked, when their lips parted.

He paused before answering, then shook his head almost as if in wonder. "No. Not always," he admitted.

They kissed sweetly for a long, tender moment. His hand reclaimed her breast. And before she knew it, they were making love once more.

Madeleine blinked open her eyes. The fading light of late afternoon bathed the room in shadows. It took her a few seconds to remember where she was.

Lord Saunders—Charles—was asleep next to her in his bed. The memory of their lovemaking flooded her mind and she blushed hotly, recalling how wanton she had been. If someone had told Madeleine this morning that she would end up here today, writhing and naked in this man's arms, she would never have believed them.

Yet it had happened. And she didn't regret a moment of it.

Madeleine studied Saunders as he slept beside her, her heart full of feeling. Oh, how she adored him. The last few hours had been among the sweetest and most thrilling of her life. She had no regrets. She'd wanted to make love with him. She knew that what she'd done was scandalous, but she didn't care.

She almost felt like a different person, as though she'd at last been made privy to a secret the entire world shared, but from which she'd previously been excluded. How wonderful lovemaking was, when shared in the right environment with the right person. It was such an intimate experience. No wonder Alexandra blushed every time the subject had been hinted at and had refused to share any details.

Madeleine wished there could be more between them than this single encounter, but she knew there could not. Her heart ached to tell him that she loved him.

But what would be the point? It would only make him feel as if he owed her something. He was already under a sense of obligation to another woman. Madeleine didn't want to add to that burden. If she admitted her feelings, it might make him feel that she expected him to choose between her and Sophie. Did she? No. No. She did not.

He had made his choice long before he met her. Sophie would always come first. Madeleine admired his sense of honor. His devotion to duty. If he were to break that vow and choose her, he might live to regret it. That was something she could never live with. Nor could she allow him to break Sophie's heart. If he did, it would weigh on his conscience, and hers, all the rest of their lives.

Outside, the sky was gray, but it had stopped raining.

Silently, Madeleine slid from the bed. She pre-laced her corset, slipped it on, and tied herself into it. As she donned her trousers, her glance fell on a bedside table, atop which lay her manuscript. His kind words came back to her. He'd read her book. He'd liked it! That meant so much to her.

Madeleine retrieved the manuscript, then crept down the stairs.

Charles awoke to the sound of movement from the workshop below. He lay still for a long moment in a sleep-induced haze, trying to process what he was hearing. Then it hit him.

Dear God. He had just made love to Miss Atherton. Twice.

A woman he did not even have the right to call by her first name.

He sat bolt upright. Her clothing was gone. She must have dressed and was downstairs at that very moment. Why? What was she doing?

He could hardly believe what had just happened. He hadn't expected her to show up at his workshop again. When she did, he could never have anticipated that things would have progressed as they did.

No, that was a lie. She had occupied his thoughts all summer, had haunted his dreams. He couldn't count how many times he had imagined making love to her. Today, in her half-dressed state, coming on to him as she had, she had been impossible to refuse.

The memory of all that had just occurred infused his mind. Their lovemaking had been thrilling, every single second of it. She'd been so passionate, so sensuous, so generous. He almost felt as though a sacred bond had been created between them.

And yet . . . he never should have done it. It was wrong, terribly wrong—he had been over and over the reasons why. Aside from his own commitments, he should never have made love to Madeleine Atherton without a promise of marriage.

An even more alarming thought followed hard and fast on the heels of that one:

It that what all this was about?

His heart began to hammer as a sudden panic set in. It explained why he'd been thinking of Elise Townsend earlier.

He had never thought the two women were alike—yet the similarities were undeniable. Both were American heiresses, in England to marry a title. Both were beautiful and eminently desirable. Both had thrown themselves into his arms, arousing him to such a fevered pitch that against his better judgment, he had taken them to bed.

Damn damn damn damn. It was the same exact scenario all over again—wasn't it? This time, a warning had flashed in his brain, but he'd ignored it.

He should have heeded it. A woman like Miss Atherton did not do what *she* just did without expecting something in return. He knew exactly what that something was. Her reason for coming to England had never been a secret, after all.

Charles's gut tensed with anger. What manner of idiot was he? How had he not seen it? How could he have put himself in this situation again?

He got up and dressed, steeling himself for the charge that was certain to follow the moment he walked down those stairs: "You have to marry me now," she would say. "You understand that, don't you?"

There was no way in hell that was going to happen this time.

The fire in the stove must have gone out because the room was freezing. Their cups of tea were still on the table, equally cold and untouched.

Shivering, Madeleine finished attiring herself in the rest of her clothing, which was thankfully dry, and put on her stockings and shoes. As she gathered up her hairpins and stowed them in her jacket pocket, she heard footsteps in the loft above. Her heart skipped a beat. She had thought it would be less awkward if she were to sneak away. But maybe it was better this way, to have a chance to say good-bye.

He descended the stairs, wearing his trousers and boots.

"Hello," Madeleine said warmly, expecting to see returned affection in his gaze.

Instead, he stopped a few yards away, a wary expression on his face. He seemed to be waiting for her to say something. What?

"It's late," she offered. "We slept for several hours, I think."

Still, he said nothing. His jaw twitched. The silence that filled the room was deafening. Madeleine's pulsed raced in confusion, unsure how to interpret his mood. Was he angry? Did he regret what had passed between them?

At last he announced, "I am waiting." His voice had an edge to it like a blade.

She paused uncertainly. "Waiting for what?"

"For the next shoe to drop." His eyes and tone were imbued with what looked like self-loathing and angry expectation. "The nice little speech you gave that night in the kitchen, about not wanting to hurt anyone, not wanting to not break a promise to yourself, it was all just talk, wasn't it?"

"I'm sorry. I—"

"What do you want?"

Madeleine struggled to make sense of his question and his unanticipated dark mood. "I don't know what you mean."

"I have been down this road before. I won't be taken in a second time." His gaze flicked up toward the loft, then back at her. "I suppose you covet the title of marchioness?"

Madeleine inhaled sharply as it suddenly became clear to her. He was talking about Elise Townsend. Comparing *her* to that woman. She was flabbergasted.

"At least this time," he went on, "I don't have to worry that you might be with child."

Shock, pain, remorse, and anger rose up inside Madeleine like a wave. He'd taken what they'd done and turned it into something sordid. Turned *her*, in his mind, into someone she was not.

It took her a moment to find her voice. When she did, she said shakily, "You seem to forget I don't need to trick anyone into marriage, Lord Saunders. I've already turned down a title higher than yours."

Trembling, Madeleine gathered her hat, her manuscript, and what was left of her dignity, and strode to the door, which she closed behind her with force. It was only when she'd left the path and reached the stables that she realized tears were streaming down her cheeks.

CHAPTER TWENTY-SIX

"Are you out of your mind?"

Her mother stared down at her, enraged, while Madeleine sat mutely on a red velvet sofa, fighting the urge to cry.

She felt as though she'd done nothing but weep for the past few hours. During her ride home from Saunders's workshop she had been nearly blinded by tears. Thank God the horse had known the way.

Even knowing Saunders's history, Madeleine had never anticipated his reaction to their lovemaking. The undisguised suspicion and disgust she'd seen in his eyes was almost impossible to bear. She supposed she ought to hate him for that. But she didn't. She couldn't. He had treated her most unjustly, but she understood his mindset. His anger, she believed, was fueled not only by anxiety from his past experience, but by shame over what *they'd* done. Which, in turn, made her feel ashamed.

In spite of everything, she still loved him. A feeling that

deep didn't disappear in an instant, no matter how much he had hurt her.

A leaden weight seemed to fill her chest and tears studded her eyes. How had she thought she could make love to a man she adored and emerge unscathed? Some people, she supposed, might be able to do so simply for physical pleasure and walk away. She knew, now, that she wasn't that kind of person. Even if he hadn't broken her heart with his accusations, it would have been broken all the same. For her, physical intimacy had only sealed their connection.

The knowledge that she would never again feel his arms around her, never again experience the kind of intimate union they'd shared, was so painful it threatened to tear her heart in two. Worse . . . far worse . . . was the knowledge that she would one day see him married to another woman.

She had put Sophie out of her mind all day. But she couldn't avoid thinking about her any longer. Fresh guilt shot through Madeleine's layers of pain. How had she repaid Sophie's regard? By coveting the man her friend was to marry. And then engaging in an afternoon of secret, carnal lovemaking with him.

She had betrayed Sophie's friendship, the very thing Madeleine had promised herself she would never do. No, she couldn't hate Lord Saunders—he had tried to stop her, after all. But she began to hate herself.

Were anyone to find out what they'd done, Madeleine knew, her reputation would be ruined. Hopefully he would never tell anyone. Why would he, since he was so appalled by his own part in what had happened? Still, someone at the farmhouse might have seen her arrive, seen her horse stabled there. She'd been inside that barn a long time. People talked. Dear Lord, what if word of this were to reach Sophie's ears? Or her mother's?

"Lord Oakley was the best prospect you'll ever get!" Her mother's voice yanked Madeleine out of her dismal reverie. They were alone in the elegant Polperran House gallery. Beyond the windows, the sun was setting in a sky as dark and gray as her mood. "The eldest son of a duke! You would have been a duchess! A position at the very highest level of English society! A position every woman would envy! Yet you turned him down?" Her mother waved her hands in frustration as she paced. "What on earth is wrong with you?"

Madeleine wiped moisture from her eyes and pocketed her handkerchief again. This onslaught was the last thing she needed right now. "I don't love him, Mother," she said wearily.

"Love!" Her mother scoffed. "You're living in a fantasy. Smart women marry for wealth and position, not love."

"Maybe I'm not as smart as some. But I want more than a grand home, a position in society, and a family to raise. I want to share my life with a man I admire and respect. A man who understands and admires *me*. A man who will encourage me in my pursuits, not look down on them."

"Pursuits? What pursuits?" Her mother stopped before her with incredulity. "Don't tell me this is about that stupid writing of yours?"

The words stung as painfully as if she'd been slapped in the face. "My writing is not stupid," Madeleine began. "It's—"

"It was a silly, childish hobby you should have given up ages ago. There is no place for it in your life now."

"I can't give it up. It's a part of me. I have written a novel, and I hope to—"

"You hope to what? Publish your little book?" Her mother seethed. "So that *is* what's going on here. You turned Oakley down because *he doesn't want you to write?*"

After all she'd been through that day, this was suddenly more than Madeleine could take. She leapt to her feet, incensed. "Mother. Do you have any idea how *difficult* it is to write? To create characters from thin air, people who want to make themselves known to you, while you struggle to make them feel like flesh and blood? To invent plots that keep you awake long into the night, trying to perfect every detail? After all that hard work, of course I hope to be published, so that people might read my words and share the stories I've invented!"

Her mother was infuriated. "You are the daughter of one of the richest men in New York. In the *world*, for that matter. You will not embarrass me with this scribbling nonsense. Are you unaware of the light in which society holds women authors? That they are looked down on, ridiculed? No, no. I will not have that for my daughter." She shook her head. "This is not over, Madeleine, not by a long shot. We might still be able to fix it. Lord Oakley left only this morning. I presume he returned home to Sussex. I have grown close to his mother. If I were to write to her immediately, let her know that you have changed your mind—"

"But I *haven't* changed my mind. I never will."

Her mother's eyes blazed. "If you let this man go, Madeleine, you will gain a reputation as being too particular. No peer will have you."

"I don't need to marry a peer to be happy, Mother. That was always your idea, not mine."

"Bite your tongue. Marriage to a peer is your destiny, young lady! Don't you want to have everything Alexandra has?"

"Everything? *No.* Just one thing."

"And what is that?"

"I already told you," Madeleine said, striving for patience. "I want to love the man I marry and be loved in return. Lord Oakley will make some woman a perfectly good husband. It's just not going to be me."

Mrs. Atherton threw her hands up in the air. "I can see I'm getting nowhere with this. You are impossible! After all I have done for you the past two years!"

Madeleine felt another twinge of guilt. Her parents *had* spent a great deal of money on her London Seasons, both this year and the previous one when she had sailed over to take her sister's place. But before she could say anything, her mother continued angrily:

"If we have to go home to New York empty-handed *again*, I will be *mortified*." Crossing her arms over her ample bosom, Mrs. Atherton frowned as she began to pace anew. "Let me think, let me think. If you are resolved not to have *him*, there is still something we can do. The Season may be over, but I recall five or six eligible young men who had their eyes on you. They only backed away when it became obvious that

Lord Oakley had attained your interest. If they discover you are free, they are sure to be interested again. We must strike while the iron is hot. I have a great many friends. I'll arrange visits to their country houses over the next few months. You will spend time with their sons. I'm sure one of them will do. You still have all your gowns at your disposal . . ."

As her mother droned on, Madeleine tuned out the words. Her mother's plans made her shudder. The London Season had been difficult enough. Now, was she really to be subjected to months on end of visits to country houses? More dinners, more parties and balls, where she'd be put on display again like a piece of meat at a market? She knew where it would lead. Her mother would hound her day and night, hoping Madeleine would finally give in and say yes to someone, just to have the ordeal over with.

Madeleine walked to a window and stared outside. In the fading evening light, she could make out a small bird flitting to and fro around a huge, leafy elm. Suddenly, the bird took off, dashing up into the sky and disappearing from view.

Oh, to be like that bird. To be able to fly away.

She'd no sooner had the thought than Madeleine realized she had the answer to her dilemma.

Charles aimed the flame of the torch at the wire, watching as the thin strip of metal liquefied, sealing the connection of the fitting. The torch wobbled in his grip and the flame singed his fingertips.

Uttering an oath, he extinguished the device and slammed it down, then moved to a basin where he submerged his stinging hand in cold water.

He glanced at the clock. It was nearly 6:00 a.m. He should have gone to bed hours ago, but he had been too agitated to sleep. All night long, his mind had kept returning to what had happened the afternoon before. Miss Atherton. *Madeleine.* Upstairs. Naked. In his bed. In his arms.

And the confrontation that had followed.

Charles dried his hand and began pacing angrily, trying to make sense of it all. The demands he had fully expected her to make had never materialized. Rather, she had seemed shocked and hurt by his reaction.

You seem to forget, I don't need to trick anyone into marriage. I've already turned down a title higher than yours.

That was true.

He'd congratulated himself on having the presence of mind to ensure that she wouldn't become pregnant. But it occurred to him now that *she* had expressly asked about such a thing, and only continued when he'd assured her that she would be safe.

Apparently he'd been wrong. Apparently she hadn't been after a marriage commitment after all.

Which meant he had behaved like an absolute bloody cad. *Damn it all to hell and back.*

Charles had made love to many women, but no experience had ever affected him this way. Their lovemaking had been wondrous, electrifying. The memory of it, he suspected, would live with him for the remainder of his days.

Yet what had he done? He'd taken her innocence and then sent her off weeping. He hated himself for that. He had never sent a woman from his bed in tears.

Guilt settled over him like a prickly blanket. How could he have intermixed in his mind what had passed between *them*, with that other affair so many years before?

With Elise, he had been drinking. He had felt nothing for Elise but lust, and could hardly even remember what they'd done. Whereas this afternoon, he'd been stone-cold sober and remembered every last detail. If he were honest with himself, his feelings for Miss Atherton went far beyond lust. Yes, he had wanted her body. But over the past couple of months, he had developed another kind of connection with her, an intellectual and emotional connection more powerful than anything he had ever felt in his life.

Charles swallowed hard, biting back his frustration. Was he never to feel that way again?

He had long known that whatever was to happen in the marriage bed between him and Sophie would be a staid, by-the-numbers experience, for the purpose of producing an heir and a spare. Until today, he had always accepted that as his fate. He hadn't allowed himself to think much about it.

But now he questioned it. Could he truly resign himself to a life without passion?

He couldn't help but recall Sophie's reaction when he'd brought her here to his workshop. How she had belittled his work. Whereas in Miss Atherton, he'd recognized a kindred creative spirit.

Simmering with fury, Charles shoved a box off a nearby

table. It crashed, spewing parts across the floor. He felt trapped. Like a tiger in a cage. Promised from childhood to a woman he did not love.

A man, he thought angrily, should not be bound by the dictates and expectations of his family. He wasn't a king, compelled to marry for the good of the country or to unite nations. He was simply a man with a title. A title he would happily walk away from this instant, if it would give him his freedom, the ability to *choose* the woman he wished to marry.

If he could choose any woman, he knew exactly who it would be.

Madeleine Atherton.

The realization hit him like a physical blow.

He wanted to marry Madeleine Atherton.

She was everything he had ever wanted in a wife. She was the most intelligent woman he'd ever met. In her arms, he had felt more passion than he had ever believed to be possible. She was highly imaginative, incredibly talented, with a sparkling personality and a generous disposition to boot. Whenever they talked, he wished it could go on forever. She understood him and what he wanted to achieve. She had ambitions of her own that went far beyond those of the members of their class, ambitions he admired.

Their class. The thought came unbidden, but he suddenly knew it was how he truly felt. When it came right down to it, they *were* in the same class. Her family was a kind of American nobility. His gut wrenched with shame as he remembered what he'd said to her—how he had accused her of title-hunting. Yes, if they married, she would gain a title, but so what? He would gain the biggest prize. He would have *her* by his side forever.

If they married, it would be a marriage of equals. And he *did* want to marry her, wanted to spend every day of the rest of his life with her.

Because I love her.

I love her with all my heart.

How was it that he hadn't seen that before?

He had not seen it, for one thing, because he'd allowed himself to be blinded by a mistrust of heiresses in general, Americans in particular. Whereas if he'd had any sense, he would have been inspired by Thomas's example, a marriage that was eminently successful—perfection itself.

But more importantly, perhaps: he had not seen it because the very idea had been forbidden to him.

Miss Atherton had felt herself to be off-limits as well, because she'd been contemplating an offer from Oakley. But that was off the table now. She was free.

Would *he* ever be free? He had promised his father that he would marry Sophie. But that promise had been made under the belief that his father was dying. The man seemed healthy as an ox now—a turn of events which, ironically, had been Madeleine's doing. Still, that marriage was what his mother wanted. What Sophie wanted. But was it fair to Sophie, to marry her when he was in love with someone else?

Had he ruined any chance he had with Madeleine, by his awful behavior?

Damn it all to bloody hell.

Charles upended another box with a thundering crash.

He didn't know what to do with all the fury inside him. Everything he wanted was forbidden to him. The woman he loved. The work he loved. He could not acknowledge any of it.

Well, *he'd had it.* He was sick and tired of sneaking out here, working in secret, keeping every thought and feeling hidden from himself and others. From now on, Charles determined, he would do things *his* way.

Although the rest of the family appeared to be still asleep, Charles had banked on the fact that his father, when he felt fit, was an early riser. He had guessed correctly. He found the man in the gun room, the disassembled pieces of his twelve-bore shotgun scattered across the table where he sat.

"Father? Might I have a word?" Charles's every muscle seethed with tension and ire, which he struggled to contain. His father didn't like displays of temper or emotion, although he didn't mind dishing it out himself.

"Certainly, my boy." The marquess looked up as Charles entered, then turned his attention back to cleaning the gun. "What a pleasure it is to have this old fellow back in my hands again. Seems like an eternity since I felt well enough to hunt."

"I am glad you are feeling better, Father."

"Timing could not be better, either." He finished swabbing out the gun's barrel. "Grouse season is just starting. I was thinking of going out tomorrow, see what I can scare up. Care to join me?"

"Thank you, no. You are well aware that I have no interest in hunting."

"Bloody shame. Nothing so satisfying as a walk in the woods, that feeling you get when you flush the bird out and *blam*! There is dinner! You are missing out on one of life's greatest pleasures, Charles."

"There are other things that give me pleasure. Which is what I have come to talk to you about." From a leather satchel, Charles removed the device he'd brought and plunked it on the table.

"What is that?" His father glanced at it briefly.

"One of my works in progress."

"What do you mean, your works in progress?" He stared at the object as if it were a piece of rubbish he had found stuck to his shoe. "Are you saying that you *made* this . . . this *thing*?"

"I did."

"Damn it, Charles! You promised me you were done with all that!"

"I lied. You gave me no choice. I built another workshop."

"Where?"

"At the Smiths' farm."

"The Smiths? They are not a tenant of ours."

"No. I made sure to go off the estate. So as not to taint your name by association, should you or anyone else find out. I knew how strongly you would disapprove."

His father's nostrils flared as he picked up an old rifle brush. "What *is* that?" he asked, gesturing with distaste toward the item on the table.

"A battery-powered head lamp."

"A what? A head lamp? Why on earth would you waste your time making something like that?"

"Because," Charles said calmly, "it will make things safer for workers in the mines."

That seemed to get his father's attention. "The mines?" For the first time, he took a real look at the lamp.

"The gas lamps now in use are a hazard, as you well know." Charles switched on the attached battery, which caused the lamp to emit a soft glow. "A battery emits no gas. A lamp like this would have saved those lives at Wheal Jenny, and it will prevent future explosions in other mines besides ours."

His father's forehead furrowed as he took that in. "Will it indeed?"

"The problem is battery power. I am hoping for three hours, if not longer. When I achieve that, it will revolutionize the way we do things in the mining industry."

His father seemed to be turning all that over in his mind. From the expression on his face, Charles sensed that, for the first time in his life, his father had heard him. And didn't *entirely* disapprove. He actually seemed intrigued by this *thing* Charles was building. Maybe even a little impressed.

Would he say so? Was it too much to ask his father to voice anything resembling interest in or praise of something Charles was doing?

Pressing his lips tightly together, his father went back to scrubbing the rifle's threads with the brush. "I suppose you intend to *sell* this thing?"

Apparently, it *was* too much to ask.

"I hope to." Charles sighed. "But do not worry. Should I be so fortunate as to perfect it and find a manufacturer willing to build this or any of my other inventions, I will keep the Grayson name out of it. It need never be known that a member of our family is involved in *trade*. But I am not giving it up, Father. Not for you, not for Mother, not for anyone."

"I see. If that is how you feel, I suppose I cannot stop you."

Well, Charles thought. At least he had laid his cards out on the table. All in all, it had gone better than he had expected. His father hadn't ranted or raved or tried to bully Charles into stopping the project. In fact, Charles had the distinct sense that his father saw merit in the enterprise, even if he couldn't bring himself to say so.

Best of all, Charles would not have to lie anymore. Which lifted an enormous weight from his mind. He felt better than he had in a long while.

But he had another declaration to make.

Stuffing the lamp and battery back inside his satchel, Charles said with fierce and unquestioning resolve: "One more thing. *I am not marrying Sophie*."

His father froze. Then he picked up a rag and kept working on the gun, his features tight with tension. "Why not?"

"Because I do not love her." Without waiting for his father's reply, Charles quit the room. As he turned sharply into the corridor, he nearly collided with his mother, who appeared to have been standing outside the door. He skidded to a surprised halt. "Mother."

"Charles." Pride warred with hesitation in her green eyes. "So, you told him at last?"

He was not sure if she was referring to his scientific work or his decision not to marry Sophie. "I did." They started down the hallway together.

"Forgive me for eavesdropping, but when I saw you march in with that satchel and that thunderous expression, something told me you were heading for a showdown. It is high time your father understood what a brilliant son he has, and what you are capable of. It has been irritating, being obliged to hide my knowledge of it all these years. But I felt it was your place to tell him, not mine."

"It is a relief to have it out in the open at last."

"And . . . Sophie?" There was disappointment in her voice.

Charles blew out a breath as they crossed the house. "I know how long you have been counting on this match, Mother, believe me I do. I realize I will be letting down Sophie as well, and I feel terrible about it." Charles's gut burned as he poured out the feelings that had been bottled up inside him for so long. "But I see no value in making good on a promise that will only make us both miserable. I don't love her. I will do my duty as the successor to this property, but I am resolved that I will be left free to choose my own wife."

Charles braced himself for the argument that was sure to follow.

Instead, his mother fell silent for a long moment. Then she said: "Charles. Will you walk with me in the garden?"

CHAPTER TWENTY-SEVEN

"Did I ever tell you about William?"

Charles glanced at his mother as she strolled beside him, the morning sun shining brightly on her pale pink gown. "William who?" he asked.

"William Edgerton." She pronounced the name with a sigh. "I met him while on holiday with my parents at Brighton when I was seventeen years old. William was studying to be a clergyman. He was a clever man with such wit and spark, such a passion for life. I had never been so drawn to another human being. We fell in love. I knew without a doubt that he was the man I wished to marry."

Charles sensed where this story was going. "But your parents . . ."

"They forbade the match. William was the third son of a gentleman. He was obliged to support himself, would inherit nothing. That was not nearly good enough for *my* family. As the daughter of an earl, I had to marry a man of noble birth."

It was an all too familiar refrain—and at the same time,

a story Charles had never once guessed at. "I am sorry. What happened to William?"

"I heard he married a curate's daughter. I never saw him again." Her expression was overcome by sadness. "I spent the next two years involved in the Season, where I met eligible young men who met my parents' notion of acceptability. But they all seemed . . . unremarkable. Interchangeable. Having experienced true love, I had no wish to attach myself for life to someone for whom I felt not an iota of passion. But I had no choice. I had to choose one of them. And so I did."

"Do you mean . . . you never loved Father?"

"Not at first. We *learned* to love each other. I know it is an old cliché, Charles, but it is true nevertheless."

Charles's stomach clenched. What was the point of this story? Did she mean to try to impress upon him that he could *learn* to love Sophie?

"However," she said. Her long skirts brushed the gravel path as they meandered past an expanse of tall hedgerows. "I never loved your father the way I loved William. William lives on in my heart and mind even now, more than forty years later."

Charles was uncertain how to reply. "I'm sorry," he said again, but his mother held up a hand and cut him off.

"Charles: when you ran off to America with Miss Townsend, was your heart really in it?"

The question took him by surprise. "No. I felt obligated to stand by her in case she was with child, and because she said I had ruined her. I am convinced that had we married, what would have actually been ruined is both our lives."

His mother nodded thoughtfully. "Sometimes, the *right thing to do* is not so clear as we think."

Charles glanced at her as they walked, wondering what she was thinking. He was resolved, no matter what, not to marry Sophie. He had no idea if Madeleine would have him. But to receive his mother's blessing on the former, at the very least, would make things so much easier. "What are you saying?"

"I am saying . . . although I have been long championing a match between you and Sophie, I have not been entirely unobservant. I have noticed that something was never quite right between you two."

"Have you?"

"Life is full of hurdles, Charles. Marriage has its ups and downs, its quarrels, its unanticipated problems. If a couple are fortunate enough to love each other at the outset, I believe it gives them a solid foundation to build on, makes it easier to weather the storms, so to speak. But without that foundation . . ." A pair of robins burst forth from a nearby hedgerow and fluttered past them. "You said you do not love Sophie. Are you in love with someone else?"

He hadn't been expecting that. Without thinking, Charles heard himself blurt: "*Yes.*"

"Miss Atherton?"

Charles caught her eye and nodded slightly. *She knows me too well.*

"Does she love you?"

"I do not know. It is possible that . . . she might have done . . . at one time. I am not certain if she does still."

"I take it she is not to marry Lord Oakley, then?"

"No."

"Do you wish to marry her?"

"*Yes!*" The admission came out more forcefully than he'd intended.

"Well, Charles. I like Miss Atherton. When she first arrived, I thought her rather too ambitious. But now I see the ways in which education can enhance a woman's life and worth. She is certainly clever. That play she wrote was marvelous. And I think she saved your father's life! She is perfectly worthy of you. I adore Sophie, of course. She is my flesh and blood, and I do not wish her to be hurt any more than you do. But she is young. She will recover." Her eyes glowed knowingly. "And something tells me she will not take the news quite as hard as you think."

Charles looked at her. "What do you mean?"

"I mean simply this: If you love Miss Atherton, then follow your heart, Charles. Marry her."

Relief flooded Charles's every vein. "It means a great deal to have your blessing. As for Father . . ."

"Do not worry about your father," she insisted. "I can manage *him*."

"I only hope it is not too late. Miss Atherton and I did not part on the best of terms."

"Then you must try to make things right." His mother's eyes were warm with nostalgia, as if she were thinking about the man she had once loved and would never see again. "But first, my boy, you must tell Sophie."

"Tell me what?"

Charles and his mother stopped in their tracks as Sophie herself appeared around the corner of a hedgerow, with Dr. Hancock beside her.

"Er . . . good morning." Charles felt his cheeks go red. How much had they overheard? "Hancock, I had no idea you were here. It is so early."

"Yes, well," Hancock replied quickly. "I came to see Lady Sophie. We have been out . . . walking."

Was it Charles's imagination, or were both of their faces a rather bright shade of pink? "It is a fine morning for it."

"Yes, it is." Hancock looked uncomfortable.

Sophie turned to Charles. "Did I hear correctly? Do you have something to tell me?"

Charles wasn't sure how to reply. He didn't want to have it out with her here and now, in front of Dr. Hancock. "I . . . *was* speaking with Mother about a matter I need to discuss with you. But I think . . ."

"We wanted to speak to you as well," Sophie interjected. She and Hancock exchanged a glance. "Since we are all here together . . . do you mind if we go first?"

"If you insist."

"Shall I leave?" Charles's mother offered magnanimously.

"No, Aunt Charlotte. This affects you as well." Lifting her gray eyes to Charles's, Sophie announced: "Charles, I hope you will forgive me, and that what I am about to say will not cause you undue distress. But I cannot marry you."

Charles was dumbfounded. "Oh?" he finally managed.

"I always believed that you and I would wed," Sophie said. "I know how long you have been anticipating our union, and

Aunt Charlotte, I know how much it meant to *you* to see us married. But lately, I have felt . . ." She glanced gently but pointedly at Charles. "I have felt that it was not meant to be. And then . . ." Sophie's gaze found Hancock's.

Hancock looked at her as if she had hung the moon, and Sophie returned the look in kind. Charles saw more genuine affection in that exchange than he had ever before witnessed in Sophie's eyes. She had certainly never looked at *him* that way.

"We have fallen in love," Dr. Hancock announced, taking Sophie's hand in his. "I just asked Sophie to be my wife, and she has accepted. We are both truly sorry for any pain that this might cause you, my lord."

"Truly sorry," Sophie repeated.

Charles was so astonished, he could barely speak. His mother, he noticed, didn't look the least bit surprised. In fact, she was hiding a little smile. At last Charles said, "When did all this happen?"

"It began, I think, when I sprained my ankle."

"*My* feelings are rather earlier in origin," Hancock admitted, "but I knew there was an understanding between Sophie and yourself, my lord, so I didn't dare to think I had a chance with her."

"It came about rather quickly the past few weeks," Sophie added. "I once mentioned that the ball might be a good time to propose. Do you remember, Charles?"

"I do," Charles replied quietly.

"Well, I soon realized your heart was not in it. Not long

after that, everything changed. And . . ." To Hancock, coloring: "I thought it might be *you* who would propose at the ball."

"I intended to, my darling," Hancock told her. "At the stroke of midnight—that was my plan. But then I was called away to attend to Lady Longford."

A rush of diverse emotions engulfed Charles, chief among which was an intense relief that he had been spared from hurting Sophie, and at the same time, that was he was free. Free!

He felt like leaping up into the air and dancing a jig. Except he had no idea how to dance a jig. Such a display would surely be inappropriate in any case. He sensed that Sophie did not expect him to feel let down by her admission. Indeed, from what he'd gleaned, she seemed to have suspected that his affections lay elsewhere—which meant she knew him better than he had known himself. Yet even so, he saw a sense of guilt reflected in both of their eyes.

"Well," Charles said, manufacturing a smile which he hoped reflected anguish and understanding, "I will not stand in the way of your happiness." Charles took Sophie's hand and kissed it. "I wish you all the best, cousin."

She thanked him. Marriage to a physician would not be regarded by *some* as the most exalted match for Sophie. But her mother's new husband was, after all, only a baron. And Hancock *was* a gentleman and highly educated. His profession was rising in people's estimation every day.

It seemed clear, at least, that his mother didn't disapprove. Holding out her hands to the happy couple, the marchioness said with a smile, "This is wonderful news, my dears. I have suspected something of this nature was brewing and I am more pleased than I can say."

"Thank you, Aunt Charlotte!" Sophie and his mother embraced.

"You will take good care of her, Dr. Hancock," his mother commanded.

"I will, my lady. You have my promise." Hancock's face was lit by a grin.

Extending his hand to the physician, Charles said, "Welcome to the family, Hancock."

The train rattled down the tracks.

The throb of the wheels hummed through Madeleine's body as she gazed out the window of the first-class car, only vaguely aware of the passing countryside.

She had no wish to leave England now. She had hoped to stay another month at least, to soak up every moment of this precious time with Alexandra and Thomas and their newborn son. To continue her long, meaningful tête-à-têtes with her sister, walk in the Polperran House gardens with Julia and Lillie, and read aloud together under the shade of a great tree.

The notion that she might not see any of them again for years—that little Tommy was going to grow up without knowing her—brought a fresh rush of tears to Madeleine's eyes.

Despite herself, her mind darted to the other person she was going to miss.

She had given her heart and soul and body to Lord Saunders, even knowing it could never go anywhere. Could it really have been only yesterday afternoon that he had held her in his arms and made passionate love to her? The harsh reckoning that had followed only served to twist the knife in a wound that was still painfully fresh and deep.

Madeleine suddenly recalled something her father had once told her when she was a girl. "There are probably a dozen men in the world with whom you could be happy," he had said, winking an eye. "It's your job to find one of them and marry him."

She *had* found one of them. But she couldn't have him.

Madeleine choked back a little sob. Maybe, someday, she'd meet another man whom she could love and envision herself marrying. How long did it take for a broken heart to heal? She had no idea, but guessed it would take years.

Wiping her eyes, Madeleine grimly returned her attention to the window. A storybook village swept by. Houses with thatched roofs. A church with a pointy spire. A long stretch of green meadow. She had come to this country with such high hopes, and hated the idea of running away. But she couldn't stay in Cornwall. She needed to put distance between herself and Lord Saunders. She couldn't stay anywhere in England, for that matter. Her mother's plans for her had made it imperative to leave.

The exercise was foolish and absurd. Alexandra's title had already opened the desired doors for their family in New York. But one titled daughter wasn't enough for Josephine Atherton. No. She wanted to achieve what no one else had done. She was bound and determined to fling *three* titled daughters in Mrs. Astor's face, to become the envy of every member of the New York elite. It was a quest from which, Madeleine knew, there would be no escape. Not so long as she remained in England.

Alexandra and Thomas had been entirely on board with Madeleine's plan and had conspired together. Madeleine had packed her trunks and Thomas had sent her off to the train station early that morning, long before her mother was up. Father might not be happy about her coming home unmarried, but hopefully he would understand. Madeleine would live quietly. She'd give time to charitable institutions. She'd read to the sick. And she would write.

She would have all the time in the world to write.

Madeleine clutched her tapestry bag to her chest, mollified by the weight of the manuscript cosseted inside. During the crossing to New York, she could begin revising her book. One day, she'd send it out to publishers with a hope and a prayer. And then she'd start writing another. Meanwhile, her timing was perfect. A ship was sailing from Liverpool harbor that very evening.

Madeleine was going to be on it.

"What do you mean, she is not here?"

Charles stared at Thomas and Alexandra, who were seated in the breakfast room, finishing their coffee.

Thomas rose and moved around the table to stand before him. In a lowered voice, he said, "Madeleine left early this morning. Lexie's mother does not know yet. She is still abed."

"Where has she gone?"

"Home," Alexandra replied softly, joining them, "to New York."

"Oh no." Charles felt all the air leave his lungs. "*Why?*" Was it because he had hurt her so badly? If so, how would he ever forgive himself?

Alexandra's face was a mask of reserve, tempered by obvious concern for her sister. "Maddie turned down Lord Oakley yesterday."

"I know," Charles admitted impatiently.

"You know?" Alexandra's blue eyes narrowed. "*How* do you know?"

"She told me, yesterday. When she—" Charles stopped himself. What had happened between them was private, something Miss Atherton had clearly not shared with her sister. He was not about to divulge it. "When she came to see me, briefly," he finished. "But why has her refusing Oakley's offer prompted her to suddenly leave the country?"

"Because Mother has become impossible. Or should I say, even more impossible than usual. She is bound and determined that Maddie will marry a title, if she has to cart my sister around the country to meet every unattached nobleman under eighty years of age."

Charles uttered a curse.

"Why are you here, Saunders?" Thomas asked.

"She knows you are to marry Sophie," Alexandra added. "It is kinder to just let her go."

"I cannot let her go." The words burst from Charles's mouth, imbued with all the pent-up passion that had been fomenting within him. "And I am not marrying Sophie. She is engaged to Dr. Hancock."

"What?" Alexandra cried.

"Since when?" Thomas said.

"They told me only an hour ago. As I was on the verge of telling *her* that I could not marry her, because I am in love with someone else." Charles took a breath, turned to Alexandra. "I am in love with your sister. I cannot marry anyone but her."

"Is that so?" Alexandra replied, with a slow smile building.

"Well," Thomas commented with a smile of his own, "it appears, my friend, that you are destined to follow in my footsteps."

"Why? Because I have fallen in love with an Atherton?" Charles heaved a desperate sigh.

"No." Thomas darted a tender look at his wife. "Because only last year, I dashed across England to go after an Atherton—the woman *I* loved. Now it is your turn."

"Maddie took the boat train," Alexandra told him. "I guess you'd better get yourself to Liverpool, Charles. The *Britannia* leaves on the evening tide."

CHAPTER TWENTY-EIGHT

There was no time to lose. Charles rode straight to Bolton, stabled his horse at the inn, and managed to get on the afternoon train.

Having only planned to ride as far as Polperran House, Charles didn't have his billfold with him. Thomas had tucked a wad of bills into his hand, far more than was required for train fare, and wished him luck.

As he sank down onto his seat in the train car, Charles's heart pounded with anxiety.

Why, oh why, hadn't he come to terms with his feelings for Miss Atherton sooner, when he'd held her in his arms the day before? Why had he not told her then and there that he loved her, and couldn't and wouldn't marry Sophie? His reckoning had taken a day too long. And now it might be too late.

He had done the mental calculations during his frantic horseback ride. He would have to change trains three times: at Exeter, Bristol, and Birmingham. If everything went like clockwork, he would reach Liverpool with an hour to spare before the *Britannia* set sail. That was enough time to reach the docks, get on board, and hopefully find Miss Atherton before the ship sailed.

If everything went like clockwork.

As the hours ticked by with excruciating slowness, Charles envisioned everything that could go wrong. The train might break down. He might miss a connection, resulting in a lengthy delay. He might not reach Liverpool before the ship left. Even if the ship was still in port when he arrived, there might not be time to board. If he *was* able to board, how would he find Miss Atherton in a sea of passengers?

Even if he *did* manage to find her, it might still be too late. He could pour out his heart to her, beg her forgiveness for what he'd said . . . and she still might say no.

Which was something he couldn't bring himself to contemplate.

As Charles feared, the train at Birmingham was delayed due to work being done on the tracks. He thought he might explode with impatience until, at last, the locomotive took off on the final leg of the trip.

Upon reaching Liverpool, Charles dashed out of the station to find the streets as dirty and busy as London's, teeming with horses, carriages, omnibuses, and pedestrians. He glanced at his pocket watch. The *Britannia* was due to set sail in forty minutes. Could he make it on board and find Miss Atherton in time?

He was going to do his damnedest to try.

The train station was five blocks away from the port. Charles hired a hack and promised the driver a hefty tip if he could make it to the berth where the *Britannia* was docked in under four minutes.

The driver wove in and out of traffic like a bat out of hell, pulling up at the designated spot in the time allotted. Charles thrust money at him and leapt from the cab. The huge transatlantic steamer lay at the wharf before him, surrounded by bustle and confusion. Crowds of passengers gazed down from the rails of the ship, waving and calling out good-byes to the throngs who waited below to see them off.

Empty wagons and carts were driving away, having finished their business. Still more wagons and carriages drew up, depositing passengers. Those traveling second or third class, some with a great many children, struggled with their luggage, while the more elegant first-class passengers ordered crewmen to unload their boxes and trunks, which were then hauled from the dockside to the deck and swung below with the rattling of machinery and chains.

The gangplank, he saw with relief, was still in place. Charles was about to make his way there when a realization struck him. Although Alexandra said her sister *intended* to sail on this ship today, Charles had no way of knowing if she had actually made it here and been able to buy a ticket. The only way to be certain was to check at the ticket office.

Charles spotted the sign for the White Star Line. He made a beeline for it, dashing past a lineup outside the telegraph office and pushing his way through the people hurrying to and fro. To his annoyance, when he reached the ticket office, the sole agent was busy with another customer. Charles's heart pounded in his chest. Would the man never finish? He considered giving up the quest, when the passenger finally moved off with hurried footsteps.

"How may I help you?" the agent asked calmly as Charles rushed up to the counter.

"Can you please verify for me that a particular passenger is on board? Her name is Madeleine Atherton."

"Are you sailing today?" A broad-shouldered, ruddy-faced man with a thick mustache and side whiskers, the agent stood with a proud air, his uniform as neat as a pin.

"No, I am just seeing her off."

"I'm sorry, sir. I can only give out passenger information to a ticket holder of the same class or higher."

"A ticket holder?" Charles repeated in frustration. "Look, my good man, I am Charles Grayson, the Earl of Saunders. Miss Atherton is a friend. It is very important that I speak to her before the ship leaves this port."

"Forgive me, my lord," the agent said, "but the ship departs in less than thirty minutes. May I point out that, in a crowd of this size, unless you have prearranged a meeting place, it seems unlikely that you will find her before the bell rings."

"I *will* find her," Charles insisted, hoping he sounded more confident than he felt. "But first I have to know if she is on that ship! If you could please check your log and tell me her cabin number, I would be most appreciative."

"My lord," the agent said again, drawing himself up imperiously, "*if* you were sailing on the *Britannia* today with a first-class ticket, I could happily give you the name of any passenger you like. Otherwise, my hands are tied. We have rules here at the White Star Line, and were you Queen Victoria herself, I should be bound to follow them."

"Fine! Fine!" Charles growled. "I will purchase a first-class ticket. How much does it cost?"

"I think we are sold out in first class," the agent said, methodically checking his log.

It was all Charles could do not to jump across the counter and grab the fellow by the neck.

The clerk twirled his mustached in his fingertips, then took a small, satisfied breath. "Ah—you're in luck. I do have one first-class cabin available. That will be sixteen pounds."

Charles pulled money from his pocket and paid the man, grateful that he had enough to cover the fee. The agent took his time processing the ticket before sliding it across the counter.

"Now will you check please, and quickly?" Charles urged. "Miss Madeleine Atherton."

"Atherton?" the agent repeated, running his finger backward up the list where he had just entered Charles's name. "Ah! Yes. I thought the name sounded familiar. Miss Atherton just bought a first-class ticket herself not two hours ago. Cabin 312."

"Thank you." Charles dashed out of the office, ticket in hand. *Twenty-five minutes to go.*

He hurried past the last-minute arriving coaches and wagons and wove his way in between the masses of people clustered at the dock who were preparing to board or had come to say good-bye.

As he approached the gangplank, he noticed a family with five children in old, faded clothing who were hauling trunks and bags. Even the youngest children, who looked to be no more than four and five years old, were struggling to pull along cases which looked as large and heavy as themselves. *No time, keep going.* But in spite of the pressure he was under, Charles couldn't bring himself to pass by without helping.

"Those bags look too big for you." Charles paused before the children with a wink and a smile. "Might I offer you some assistance?"

The boy and girl glanced up at him with surprise and gratitude on their weary faces. Charles grabbed their burdens, one in each hand. "I will just dash on ahead, shall I, and leave them for you at the top?"

"Thank you, sir," cried the woman who was undoubtedly their mother.

Charles nodded in reply and raced up the gangplank, murmuring "Forgive me" and "Beg your pardon" as he darted around the people who were ascending and descending.

Upon reaching the platform which allowed access to the ship, Charles left the bags with a steward, hastily pointing out the family to whom they belonged. Then he rushed to the stairs.

He recalled that most people preferred to stand on deck when a steamship left the dock, but you never knew. Miss Atherton might be in her cabin. It made sense to check there first. Following a brief inquiry with a passing steward, Charles found the appropriate level and raced down the long corridor to cabin 312.

Catching his breath, he knocked. There was no answer.

He called out and knocked again. "Miss Atherton? It is Charles Grayson. If you are there, please open the door."

Silence.

He turned and ran back down the corridor, then took the stairs up two at a time. She could be in the lounge. The saloon. The café. Anywhere at all. But reason told him she would be outside with the other first-class passengers.

Bursting forth from the doorway to the promenade deck, he glanced frantically in both directions. The ship was huge. The deck ran around its entire length like a racetrack, but everyone was clustered on the port side. In which direction should he head? There was no way to know.

He turned left and made his way along the open-air passageway. Excitement filled the air. There were people, people, everywhere, clustered beneath the rows of overhanging lifeboats. Crowds of passengers stood at the rail. A few last groups of visitors were saying good-bye to their departing friends, chattering and wiping away tears.

Just then the warning bell rang, a hollow, high-pitched sound that resonated above the clamor. Stewards passed by, crying: "All ashore, if you please! All ashore that's going ashore!"

Charles's heart thundered in his ears. Time was running out. All around him, people were shaking hands and exchanging final embraces. He forged on against the tide as those without tickets began to disperse. He saw a clergyman waving good-bye to his family. Women kissing each other, parting, then rushing back for one last clutch in each other's arms.

He hurried along, his pulse beating time with every step,

his eyes touching on every woman he passed. When he got to the stern of the ship, he turned around and made his way back toward the bow. But although he glimpsed several women with hair and builds similar to Miss Atherton's, when they turned and he got a look at their faces, he realized they were strangers.

"Last call!" a steward cried out as he strode by. "All ashore that's going ashore!"

With a sudden, deep rumble, like some great beast coming to life, the engine started. Overhead, smoke poured from the three huge stacks.

Dear Lord. Any minute now, they'd be removing the gangplank.

It was an impossible task. Like looking for a needle in a haystack. Passengers were gathered three and four deep at the rail, straining to look out over each other's shoulders as they waved and called out. Miss Atherton could be at the rail five feet away from him, and he would never know it—there were too many people in the way.

A sudden thought occurred to him. The passengers on this side were all saying good-bye to someone. Miss Atherton *might* still be here, hidden by the throngs, wanting to take in the exciting moment when the ship pulled away from the dock.

Or, since she had no one to see her off, she might prefer a more quiet viewing spot on the opposite side of the ship.

The wooden deck vibrated beneath his feet.

This was it. Unless he wanted to sail to New York, he had to get off the ship.

Charles made his decision. He ducked into the first doorway he came to, raced down a hall and across a vast space that appeared to be a lounge, finally emerging through a door onto the promenade deck on the opposite side of the ship. This side, as he had predicted, was far less crowded.

He ran along the deck, breathing hard, scanning every feminine face and figure.

And then he saw her. Standing at the rail about fifty feet ahead.

A vision in a white lawn frock. A despondent look on her lovely face.

He covered the space between them in seconds and stopped before her, too breathless for words, his chest feeling as though it might explode from exertion. She glanced up, her expression only vaguely curious. When she caught sight of him, her eyes widened and her lips parted in utter astonishment.

"What on earth . . . ?" she said.

He was still gasping for air. Now that they stood face-to-face, he realized that everything he'd prepared to say was useless. He had hoped to convince her to leave the ship. To stay in England. Which was pointless now.

Because as they stood staring at each other, the rumble of the engines increased in volume, and the ship began to move.

Madeleine couldn't believe her eyes. Lord Saunders was standing before her, so out of breath as to be incapable of speech. She would have been less surprised to see a kangaroo or an elephant materialize beside her on deck than she was to see him.

"You're sailing to New York?" It was a ridiculous question.

Obviously he was sailing to New York. Beneath her feet, she could feel the vibration of the huge vessel as it steamed away from the shore.

"Apparently," was all he could manage.

"Why?" She had bought passage on this ship not just to get away from her mother, but also to get away from him. Yet here he stood.

"It was not my original intention." He kept gulping for air, until he was at last able to manage a conversation. "I was hoping to stop you from leaving port. I could not let you go until you had heard my apology."

"Your apology?"

He nodded, contrition in his eyes. "Yesterday, I behaved like an ass. I shudder to think of the things I said to you. I know that I hurt you, but I was too dense and pigheaded at the time to understand the truth of my own feelings. I cannot tell you how sorry I am."

Madeleine tried to make sense of this startling declaration. "I accept your apology, Lord Saunders, and I value the great lengths which you have undergone to offer it."

Relief seemed to infuse his every feature. The look on his face promised that more was coming, along with that tantalizing phrase he had uttered . . . *the truth of my own feelings.* She had never, in her wildest dreams, expected that anything like this might happen. She waited, the first tiny flutters of hope rising in her chest.

He took a deep breath and went on. "Miss Atherton. From the first moment I saw you, descending the stairs at that party at Polperran House, I was entranced. Since I have gotten to know you this summer, my mind and heart have become entirely yours. I have tried to deny it, believing that I was duty-bound to another. But it was a commitment that should never have been asked of me. You are the woman with whom I wish to share my life."

Her heart pounded. "But . . . what about Sophie?"

"I resolved this morning that I could never marry Sophie. I informed my father and mother of such. Before I could break the news to Sophie herself, she admitted that she is in love with Dr. Hancock. They are, in fact, engaged."

"Engaged? To Dr. Hancock?" Madeleine could hardly believe it. And yet, she suddenly recalled the times she had come upon the two of them together . . . how strange and out of sorts Sophie had been acting lately . . . and what she'd said the night of the ball: *I am hoping for a proposal tonight.* Sophie hadn't been hoping for a proposal from Saunders at all, but rather from Dr. Hancock.

Saunders took both of her gloved hands in his. "Miss Atherton: You are my heart. My soul. The other half of myself. I love you. I love you more dearly than words can express. Dare I hope that you can forgive me for what I said, and for the hurt I caused you?"

Madeleine felt her mouth curving up into a smile. "You may dare, Lord Saunders."

"May I dare further, and hope that you might love me?"

"I *do* love you," Madeleine told him with feeling, "with all my heart."

His eyes brimmed with affection as he moved closer still. "Will you make me the happiest of men and agree to be my wife?"

"I will."

As the ship steamed away into the blue, he drew her into his arms and kissed her. And, her heart soaring, she kissed him right back.

T hey were married that same evening in the ship's chapel by a clergyman on board, who was only too happy to conduct the service for the Earl of Saunders and his bride. The captain himself and head steward served as witnesses, recording the event in the ship's logbook. The bride wore a white lawn frock and carried a bouquet of roses and daisies hastily thrown together by the ship's florist. The groom wore what he had arrived in.

After sending cables to their families to apprise them of the news, they returned to Madeleine's cabin, where Saunders lifted her into his arms and carried her over the threshold.

"*Now* I truly feel like a bride," Madeleine said, laughing, "although I admit, I have felt this way before."

"Do you mean to say I have committed bigamy?" Saunders quipped, setting her down gently on her feet inside the spacious cabin.

"I was thinking of yesterday. When you carried me up the stairs to your loft."

"Oh." He paused, sobering. "I deeply regret my behavior

on that occasion, my darling. I vow to spend the rest of our lives making it up to you."

"I will hold you to that."

He kissed her soundly, then took off his coat. "You know," he said, as he began undoing the buttons on her dress, "we have two first-class cabins, bought and paid for. It seems rather superfluous, does it not?"

"It does indeed. Shall we offer one to the kind clergyman who married us? I heard he's traveling second class. He might be grateful for the upgrade."

"An excellent plan." He slid her dress from her shoulders, let it drop to the floor.

She untied his cravat and slipped it from around his neck. "Am I right in supposing that you have no luggage?"

"None whatsoever. I have only the clothes on my back."

"Well, based on how much time I expect us to spend in this cabin," she said as she unbuttoned his shirt, "I'm thinking you won't need any more clothes than that."

He laughed and kissed her again. "How I love you, Lady Saunders."

"There is no need for such formality, dearest," she teased. "You have called me Madeleine before."

"So I have." He unlaced her corset and removed it. "I adore your name. But would you mind very much if I call you Maddie, as your sisters do?"

"I would love that, Charles."

"Charles," he repeated, a mere murmur. "How I love the way you say it."

They made love, rocked by the movement of the ship. It

was a tender yet passionate union, a meeting of souls made even more meaningful by the promises of love and devotion they exchanged.

Afterward, nestled in each other's arms in the quiet darkness, they talked about the future.

"I hope you do not regret being married in this fashion," Charles said, cradling her cheek in his hand as he gazed at her across the pillow.

"I don't. I know some girls, growing up, dream of a big church wedding with all the trimmings, but my sisters and I never did. That kind of affair has always seemed too stressful and extravagant to me. I loved the way we did it: a private exchange of vows, no fuss, no muss, no planning required."

"I quite agree with you. But," he added thoughtfully, "I think my mother will be disappointed. She might wish for another wedding on land. And *your* mother . . ."

"You're right. *My* mother will insist upon a lavish affair." Madeleine shrugged. "We might as well give them the pleasure."

"Where shall we have such a ceremony? In New York or England?"

"In England," Madeleine responded. "If we are to be wed a second time, I wouldn't think of holding it anywhere but on the lawn at Trevelyan Manor, overlooking the sea."

"It shall be done. Perhaps in autumn, as the leaves are turning?"

"That would be lovely." Madeleine returned his affectionate gaze. "You know, this all happened so fast, I never had time to wonder. Where will we live?"

"Where would you like to live? As long as my father remains healthy, which I hope will continue for a good many years, we aren't bound to stay in England."

"But I'd like to," Madeleine told him. "Cornwall is your home. I'd like to live near your family and near Alexandra and her family as well."

"That's easy, then. We can live at Parmoor House. It is on the edge of our estate. I believe it could be made ready and comfortable for us in a matter of months."

"I think I have seen it. Is it a redbrick house with blue shutters?"

"Yes. It is cozy compared to Trevelyan Manor, but big enough, I think, to raise a handful of children."

"A handful? Do you refer to the number of children, or to their behavior patterns?"

"Both, perhaps." He laughed and she laughed with him.

"The house looked sweet. I'm sure it will do."

"I'm glad. In the meantime, we can travel. I have always wished to see more of America. What would you say if we honeymooned there? I have heard great things about your national parks, Yellowstone and Yosemite in particular. I have always wanted to see San Francisco."

"Me, too. But we must begin in Manhattan. I'd love to share my favorite haunts with you. You might find our house on Fifth Avenue a bit ostentatious, but I know my father and Kathryn will be delighted to see you again." An idea suddenly came to her. "Charles: doesn't Nikola Tesla work in Manhattan?"

"Yes."

"Mr. Remington's typewriters are manufactured there as well?"

"I believe so."

"And Thomas Edison has a workshop in New Jersey?"

"So I have been told. Why?"

"Would you like to meet them?"

His eyes widened. "Is that even possible?"

"My father knows everyone. I can ask him to arrange an introduction. You might find an exchange of ideas with those gentlemen inspiring. And who knows? One of them might take an interest in the projects you've been working on."

"Wouldn't that be something." He shook his head in wonder. "How well you know me, darling." Smiling, he added, "This brings me to another point I wished to make. The book you wrote. I presume you have the manuscript with you?"

"I do."

"An acquaintance of mine owns a publishing house in London. They have offices in New York as well. I know you said you've only completed a first draft. But whenever you deem it ready I can contact him, see if he can do something for you."

"Charles! That would be amazing."

"*You* are amazing." He kissed her, threading his fingers through her hair. "I love you, Maddie."

"And I love you, Charles," she murmured against his lips.

The kiss became more heated. Madeleine felt a rocking sensation and was uncertain if it was the movement of the ship plowing through the open sea, or the motion of their intertwined bodies as they made love.

Either way, it was pure bliss.

ACKNOWLEDGMENTS

With deepest thanks to the team at Avon Impulse for all your hard work bringing this book to life. I am so grateful!

We hope you loved *Summer of Scandal*.
But did you by any chance miss the first in
the delightful Dare to Defy series
by Syrie James?
If so, here's a little peek at the first book,

RUNAWAY HEIRESS,

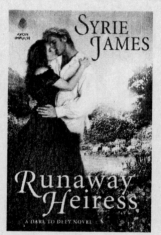

available now!
And don't miss the third book in the series,
coming in summer 2019, featuring the third
Atherton sister, Kathryn!

Chapter One

London, England
May 8, 1888

"One first-class ticket for Liverpool, please." Alexandra Atherton managed a smile for the ticket agent behind the window.

"One way or return?"

"One way." Alexandra anxiously made her way across the busy train station, hardly able to believe she was doing this: running away, dressed in her maid's old clothes, bound for Liverpool and the steamship that would take her home.

Her escape, she knew, would cause something of a scandal. Over the past few years, whenever her name or one of her sisters' names had cropped up in the press, it was always followed by "the American heiress," or "the daughter of multimillionaire banking tycoon Colis Atherton." As if they were not actual people in their own right.

Alexandra hated to feed the gossip, but after last night, what choice did she have?

She had left a note explaining where she'd gone and why, which her maid Fiona was to "accidentally discover" later that afternoon. By then, it would be too late for her mother to prevent Alexandra from sailing. She just prayed that upon her reaching Liverpool, a berth would be available aboard the *Maritime*.

The train platform was alive with the clamor of movement and conversation. Gentlemen in black frock coats and ladies in elaborate plumed hats darted to and fro, checking the printed timetables, studying the large clock hanging from the rafters, purchasing apples from a vendor and papers from the newsstand. As Alexandra wove through the crowd, she heard a high-pitched voice at her elbow:

"Got a penny for a poor orphan?"

She paused. Before her stood a raggedly dressed, dirty little girl. Alexandra's heart went out to the creature, who gazed up at her with wide eyes, her hair all in a tangle.

Alexandra wondered how a penny could possibly be of any help to a child in such need. Withdrawing her coin purse from her reticule, she offered the child a shilling. "Here you go, little one." Suddenly, more children in similarly dirty clothing appeared and crowded around her.

"Mine!" cried a boy.

"No, mine!" cried another.

A grubby fist flashed out and snatched the shilling from Alexandra's grasp. She couldn't tell if it was the first girl who took it or one of the boys; indeed, she wasn't entirely sure what happened next. All Alexandra knew was that multitudes of small, filthy hands were striking at her as young voices erupted in raucous shouts. Her coin purse was suddenly wrenched from her grasp, and a second later her handbag was gone.

"Wait! Give it back!" Alexandra cried, as the flock of children fled. "Help! Stop those children! They've stolen my bag!"

No one made any move to help her. Alexandra pushed her way through the crowd, racing after the children, but the ragamuffin band vanished as quickly as it had appeared. At the end of the platform, she stopped to catch her breath. The whole incident, she saw now, had been cleverly played, the efforts of a pack of urchins who preyed on unsuspecting travelers.

She searched for a policeman (what did they call them here? Bobbies?), but realized that even if one materialized, she couldn't report the theft. She was dressed as a servant, in the act of running away.

Alexandra stood rooted to the spot, overwhelmed by a crushing sense of horror and disappointment as the depths of her predicament became clear to her. Her handbag was gone. It had held all her money as well as her train ticket. She hadn't been able to take anything else with her, and now had nothing left except the clothes on her back. Clearly, there would be no trip to Liverpool today, and no voyage to New York.

Tears stung Alexandra's eyes as she made her way back through the train station. What should she do now?

She considered the English girls she'd met over the past five weeks of the London Season, but realized they'd be no help. Not a single one had responded to Alexandra's attempts at friendship. They'd seemed to consider Alexandra too outgoing, too outspoken, and had eyed her with reserved and stony suspicion, as if she were there to deliberately steal away all the best men. The matrons Alexandra had met had all befriended her mother. Nor could she seek refuge from Rose Parker, a debutante from Chicago who'd landed her titled man the year before and was now the most miserable human being in creation, entirely under the thumb of her husband.

As Alexandra exited through the train station's high Doric portico, she wiped tears away. It was over. It was all over. Unless she wanted to starve on the street like the poor, ragged, toothless woman selling apples at the curb, Alexandra had no alternative but to go back to Brown's Hotel with her tail between her legs.

Even though it would spell her doom.

Even though her mother would surely lock Alexandra in their suite again until she agreed to marry Lord Shrewsbury.

Well, Alexandra told herself, as she hailed one of the waiting hansom cabs and climbed aboard, her ruse had worked this time. She would just have to think of something new and try again in a few days for another ship.

"Brown's Hotel," she instructed the cabbie through the trapdoor near the rear of the roof.

"That'll be a shilling." The man's tone conveyed his distrust of such a shabby customer.

Alexandra peered up at him through the tiny window behind her. "Sir, I've been the victim of a robbery. My handbag and all my money were stolen. I'll see to it, however, that you are paid upon arrival."

"Cash in advance, Yank, or there's no ride."

"Sir, my name is Alexandra Atherton. My father is a multimillionaire. If you will please take me to Brown's Hotel, I assure you that my mother will pay my fare."

"And who's your mother? America's first lady?" A brief, contemptuous laugh escaped his mouth. "There's plenty of folk who'll be happy to pay in advance, girl. Go on, step down."

Cheeks flaming, Alexandra climbed down from the vehicle. She tried every cab in sight, but it was always the same story: no fare, no ride. Alexandra was incensed and humiliated. She was an heiress. She'd attended college! She'd been the belle of the ball at numerous events of the London Season. Yet she was being treated harshly, simply due to the clothing she wore.

Alexandra realized she'd have to walk. How many miles lay between Euston Station and Brown's Hotel? She had no idea. During the cab ride that morning, she'd been so absorbed in her thoughts, she hadn't paid attention to their route.

Pausing at a corner, Alexandra asked a shoeshine man how to get to Brown's Hotel. His instructions were long-winded and delivered in a thick cockney accent. She was able to gather, though, that it was a journey of about two miles. Following his gesticulations, she began walking south.

It was a gray, cloudy spring morning with the threat of rain. Although Alexandra had always enjoyed long walks in the countryside growing up, she'd never been enamored of strolling in a city. The sidewalks of London were jammed with men and women rushing about their business, and the streets were clogged with traffic. Horse-drawn carriages of every size and description jockeyed for position with hansom cabs, men on high-wheel bicycles, and buses topped with crowds of people. The air, heavy with soot and smoke, was further befouled by the stench of horse dung and urine that covered the street and lay piled up in heaps at the curb. A boy of twelve or thirteen dodged among the vehicles, struggling to scoop the excrement into a bucket, but it was a futile battle.

Alexandra waited for an opening in the traffic, then raised her skirts and picked her way across the street. Thank goodness she'd worn her oldest, sturdiest pair of walking boots, the only shoes she possessed that wouldn't have looked out of place with the plain black cotton dress she wore. Even so, by the time she reached the opposite curb, she'd had to scrape off the filth that clung to her soles.

She plodded on, past a street locksmith's stall, a man towing a barrel organ on wheels, and a fancy wear dealer selling porcelain ornaments from a wheelbarrow. Sandwich-board men crowded the curb, wearing signs proclaiming such slogans as TRY DR. CLARKE'S TONIC AND HAIR RESTORER and DRINK COLA: IT QUENCHES THE THIRST AS NOTHING ELSE WILL.

Twice more, she stopped to ask for directions. Eventually, a clock on a bank building told Alexandra she'd been walking for two and a half hours, and she began to wonder if she'd made a wrong turn. She should have reached Brown's Hotel by now. At the very least, she should recognize something of the neighborhood. But nothing looked familiar. Instead of elegant white houses, she saw rows of redbrick buildings and streets lined with shops and pubs.

"Fresh muffins!" shouted a woman in a cheap dress and dirty apron who was selling bread and pastries beneath a makeshift tarp.

The aroma of freshly baked goods made Alexandra's mouth water. She hadn't eaten anything since dinner the night before, having planned to purchase something at the station. Although she'd never bought food off a city street cart in her life, she would have been happy to do so now, if only she had the money.

Alexandra's feet were beginning to hurt, and she was growing tired. She was more alarmed, however, by the darkening clouds and increasing chill in the air. Shivering, she noticed a chimney sweep leaning against a wall and approached him. "Is Brown's Hotel nearby?"

"Brown's Hotel?" The sweep scratched his head beneath his cap. "Well now, miss, if you're headed for Brown's Hotel, you'd best take a cab. It's a good three or four mile from here, and looks like rain any minute."

Alexandra's spirits fell. Three or four miles! Clearly, she'd wandered very far out of her way. "I have to walk," she replied with resignation. "Can you please point me in the right direction?"

He barked out a few instructions, then indicated an alley just up the street. "You can cut through that lane beyond the Horse 'n' Hound, it'll save you ten minutes."

Alexandra thanked him, and they moved off in opposite directions.

She turned into the narrow, refuse-strewn alley, and was halfway down it when a big man in a rough coat and cap emerged from a doorway and stopped directly in front of her.

"Well, well, well, what's the hurry, lassie?" he called out in a thickly accented voice which was slurred from drink.

A foul stench emanated from his body. Alexandra wrinkled her nose, more irritated than afraid of this unexpected disturbance. "I've already been robbed once this morning," she declared flatly, as she attempted to dodge around the man. "I have nothing left to give you."

He grabbed her forcefully by the arm, grinding her to a halt. "I wouldn't say nothing, lassie." With beady eyes, he studied her slowly from head to toe, then back up again, giving her a leer that exposed a mouthful of rotten teeth.

Alexandra's pulse now quickened with apprehension. "Please, let me go."

"Not until you gives us a kiss." He pressed his free hand to her back and yanked her against his chest.

"Don't!" Panic surged through her as she turned her face away, struggling to break free.

The man persisted, pressing fleshy lips against her neck. He reeked so strongly that Alexandra felt bile rise in her throat. Her arms were trapped, so she kicked at him, landing a good one against his shin. He roared in pain and fury. Still gripping her upper arm, he raised his other hand as if to slap her, when all at once the skies opened up and unleashed a sudden, cold, and very heavy rain.

Her attacker started in surprise, the unexpected downpour causing him to loosen his grip. Alexandra took advantage of the reprieve to free herself and fled back down the alley. The pelting rain came so fast and furious that in seconds, she was wet through.

At the lane's end, Alexandra burst onto the sidewalk—and plowed directly into someone. She heard the sound of breaking glass, glimpsed a man's startled face. Spinning in a half circle, she staggered backward into the street.

What occurred next came all in a whirl: the clatter of hooves. A horse's whinny. The sight of a vehicle bearing down on her. The world tilting as she dodged sideways. A sharp pain in her head.

And then she knew no more.

"**B**loody hell!"

Thomas Carlyle stared at his recent purchase, now smashed to bits on the sidewalk, the victim of a collision with a woman who'd raced out of the alley.

As he stood there, pelted by freezing rain, he saw the woman career into the street, directly into the path of an oncoming vehicle. He gasped in horror as the woman stumbled and fell to the ground, where she lay unmoving as the horse and carriage thundered past, narrowly missing her.

Was she dead? He hoped not—the carriage didn't appear to have touched her. A few people hurried by, huddled beneath their cloaks and umbrellas, paying no attention to the prone figure lying in the muck and mud.

He ought to do the same.

This is not your affair, an inner voice warned. He was cold and wet. He had work to do. He shouldn't get involved. But another, stronger voice insisted, *This is partly your fault.* If she—whoever she was—had not run smack into him, she might not have stumbled backward into the road.

Thomas spied a carriage rapidly headed in the young woman's direction. She could be crushed in the next instant. With no time for further deliberation, he darted into the street and scooped her up. Once he regained the safety of the curb, he stared down at the limp form in his arms, rain dotting his spectacles as he noted several things in rapid succession:

She was young and slender with long limbs and a pale complexion. Her black dress and worn boots marked her as a member of the working class. The bodice of that dress pulled tight across an ample bosom—a sight mere inches from his eyes, and from which he had difficulty averting his gaze.

Those breasts, he saw now, were moving gently up and down. Thank heavens. She was breathing. She was alive. But what on earth had happened, to cause her to run full tilt like that out of the alley, without looking where she was going?

Thomas peered down the alley from which she'd emerged. No one was there. He glanced back at the street to determine if she had dropped a handbag or any other item which might help identify her, but he saw nothing other than the sodden, trampled remains of a straw hat.

The rain was coming down in buckets, rapidly washing away the street muck that had clung to the young woman's hair and clothes. What was he supposed to do now? He considered dropping her off at the Horse 'n Hound, in the hope that someone would take pity on her. But no, that wouldn't be gentlemanly. Besides, she might need medical attention. He had no idea, though, if there was a doctor's surgery in the neighborhood.

He couldn't just stand there holding her in the pouring rain. He lived a block away. It seemed best to bring her there and let Mrs. Gill take over.

When he arrived at the redbrick townhouse, unable to reach the key in his pocket, Thomas gave the dark green door a few solid kicks. "Mrs. Gill! A little help, please!"

A moment later the door was flung open. His Irish landlady, her graying hair half-hidden beneath a white cap, was all astonishment. "Mr. Carlyle! What on earth?"

"This young woman fell in the street," Thomas explained as he brushed past Mrs. Gill into the compact foyer. "She was nearly run over by a carriage and appears to be unconscious. Pray, allow me to bring her into your parlor."

"Of course," Mrs. Gill cried, skirts rustling as she bustled after him. "The poor thing! Who is she?"

"I have no idea. Forgive me," Thomas added as they entered the small, overstuffed room, where a fire was blazing in the hearth. "We are both drenched through and dripping all over your carpets."

"Just you stand by the fire and wait, Mr. Carlyle. I'll fetch towels and blankets before you set her down." Mrs. Gill disappeared into the back room.

Thomas moved to the hearth, grateful for its flickering warmth as he made a more comprehensive study of the woman in his arms. She looked to be in her early twenties, a few years younger than himself. She was pretty, her oval face and delicate features reminiscent of Romney's early paintings of Emma Hart. Her hair, too wet to determine its true shade, had come loose and hung in waves to her waist.

He guessed her to be a shop girl or seamstress, or perhaps a servant on her day off. As he gazed down at the lovely yet helpless form he was holding against his body, Thomas felt an unexpected spark of interest and compassion. He hoped she was going to be all right.

"Here we are." Mrs. Gill returned, her arms full of cottony fabric. She draped several towels over the sofa, and Thomas laid the insensible young woman down.

She was starting to shiver now, and so was he. Mrs. Gill removed the girl's gloves and dabbed at her with a towel, then tucked a blanket over her, while Thomas dried off his own face and hair and wiped his spectacles clean.

"You'd best take off that wet coat, Mr. Carlyle," Mrs. Gill advised, "lest you catch a chill."

He obliged, shrugging out of the sodden garment, which she took and hung over the fire screen. "Now what? Shall I fetch a doctor?"

"Let's give her a minute. She's young and healthy-looking, no doubt she'll wake up soon enough. A doctor would cost a pretty penny, which you and I can ill afford."

Thomas flinched at this assessment. He had never told Mrs. Gill—nor any of his clients in town, for that matter—who he really was. If anyone knew, he would be treated differently; he certainly wouldn't be able to stay here any longer, or to continue his work. But what she'd said was true. His finances were in a bad way. Ever since he was a child and aware of such things, he'd had the vague impression that money, for his family, was a problem. Now that he was twenty-eight years old and faced with all the sordid facts, his sense of mortification over the situation was acute.

A soft moan issued from the direction of the sofa, interrupting his thoughts. Glancing over, he saw that the young woman was moving restlessly beneath the blanket—hopefully, a sign that she would soon wake up.

ABOUT THE AUTHOR

SYRIE JAMES is the critically acclaimed author of historical, contemporary, and young adult fiction and romance including the international bestseller *The Lost Memoirs of Jane Austen* (Best First Novel, *Library Journal*); *Nocturne* (Best of the Year, *Suspense Magazine* and Romance Reviews); *Dracula, My Love*; *The Missing Manuscript of Jane Austen*; *Jane Austen's First Love*; *Forbidden*; *The Secret Diaries of Charlotte Bronte* (Great Group Read, Women's National Book Association; Audie Romance Award, 2011), and the *Harrison Duet* (*Songbird* and *Propositions*). Her work has been translated into 18 languages. An admitted Anglophile, Syrie loves all things 19th century. She is a member of the Writer's Guild of America and has addressed audiences across the U.S., Canada, and England.

Learn more about Syrie and her books at
www.syriejames.com.
Facebook: @AuthorSyrieJames
Twitter: @SyrieJames